AUTHOR'S NOTE

Much of the action in this book takes place on the island of Hunsey just off the Dorset coast in the south west of England. Keen observers of geography will be aware that no such place actually exists. Nonetheless, a map appears on the following page showing its rough outlines.

A powerful prescription-only painkiller named *Dramadol* also features prominently in the story, and is also fictional, though based loosely upon similarly named opiate drugs.

But apart from that, everything else is true… sort of.

I do hope you enjoy meeting Julia.

Hunsey Island

Hunsey Island sits just off the Dorset coast and is connected to the mainland via a tidal causeway. Historically home to a small fishing and farming community, its chief income is now derived from tourism as visitors come to enjoy its rugged coastline, plentiful wildlife and its – now infamous – literary connections.

Dorchester (15m)

Southampton (35m)

Hunsey Island causeway
(accesible low tide only)

Hunsey Village

Hunsey Island

Hunsey Lighthouse

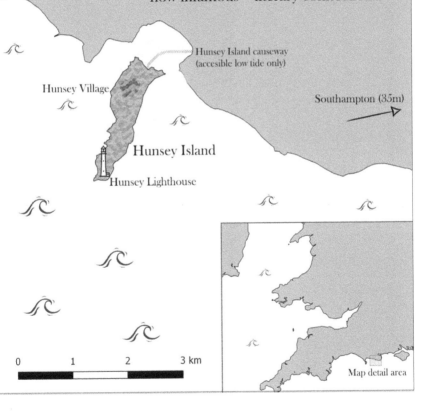

0   1   2   3 km

Map detail area

THE GLASS TOWER

GREGG DUNNETT

Old Map Books

PART ONE

ONE

IT PROMISED to be the most exciting night in Julia Ottley's life so far. And that was before the accident.

And since Julia was already well into her forties (she'd told her agent she was thirty-eight, but now she had acquired a Wikipedia page she was concerned the truth might get out) – there had been quite a few nights gone by already, rather too many of them spent on the sofa with her cats. So let's just say she hadn't lived the wildest of lives up to that point.

But lives can, and do, change.

The problem of what to wear had plagued her for days. She had gone shopping twice – Marks and Spencer on both occasions – and after much deliberation had settled on a neat and modest bottle-green skirt, a brown jacket and a cream blouse underneath. She dressed in the outfit now and inspected herself in the mirror, adjusting her hair and smoothing down the soft fabric. She noticed how her hands shook, as if the room were cold, but she knew it wasn't the temperature affecting her. But neither was it pure nerves. It was a combination, of fear and something else. Anticipation. Sheer wonder.

She allowed herself a brief moment of delicious anticipation, imagined herself walking into the room, seeing it filled with some of the most brilliant people in the country, all there for her. But then, doubts crept in. Would they really come? Was this even truly real? Her body shivered.

Her hands were on the material of the skirt. The touch of the fabric was sensual. Soft and textured. An idea sparked in Julia's mind. An idea that – for her – was quite bizarre. A *dirty* idea. In her reflection, staring back at her, she saw her own eyes widen, in surprise at even thinking about such a thing. Tonight, the self-restraint she prided herself on was strangely absent.

Turning away from the mirror, she unzipped her skirt and pushed it down, out of the way. She lay back on her bed, slipped a hand into her underwear and began to touch herself. A part of her recoiled in horror at what she was doing, but she shut it out. She began rubbing, pushing her back into the mattress. There was a noise in the cool of the room, the noise of small, urgent gasps as her fingers moved quicker and quicker.

When she had finished, which was rather sooner than these things often took, she lay still. Then she removed her hand, reached for a tissue to clean herself, and threw it in the wastepaper basket.

"Goodness!" she said as she sat up. The old Julia was back. She found her skirt and hastily stepped back into it.

A cat wandered into the room, and began scratching itself against the edge of the open bedroom door. Julia met the animal's gaze without embarrassment.

"Well, Edgar," she said after some time. "*That* hasn't happened in quite a while."

Julia saw now that her curtains were open, and had been the whole time. She was shocked that she hadn't noticed, but told herself to calm down. Her little one-bedroom cottage stood a way back from the road. The village was quiet, and she wasn't overlooked. Even so, she approached the window cautiously, and looked out, but the scene looked reassuringly normal. Her neighbours opposite were out – or at least their lights were off and she was unable to see into the rooms. Further away a tractor was doing something in a field, followed by a few gulls.

"Goodness!" she said again.

And the evening hadn't even begun yet.

TWO

JULIA CHECKED her appearance in the mirror again. She adjusted her make-up in the couple of places that had suffered over the preceding minutes, then she went downstairs.

On the wooden farmhouse table, which took up most of the little kitchen, stood two neat stacks of paper. One with the text turned face down, the other with the text facing upwards, and marked here and there by red pen. On seeing them her heartbeat pulsed again. For a moment she tried to resist touching them, but the temptation was too strong. She let a finger run down one of the pages, and as her eyes scanned the words she felt her anxiety rise. Surely this was all a mistake. They'd picked the wrong book, they didn't want *her*. But then the clarity and power of the language soothed her. It drew her in. The power of her own words. *They* wanted these words. They had bid for them. It was good. There was no mistake. She placed her hand palm down on the entirety of the manuscript, as if it were the source from which she drew all her strength.

Suddenly, her mobile rang. She looked around, unsure where she had left it. Her ears were curiously poor at locating where sound was coming from. Her eyesight wasn't great either. It had been that way since school, when she had worn glasses that were thick – but not spectacularly so.

The phrase summed up her entire experience of education. Nothing about it, or her, had been spectacular, and that theme had continued for her entire adult life. Until now.

The ringing continued, and there were only so many places in the small cottage where a phone could be. This time it was on top of the fridge. She picked it up and looked at the screen.

Geoffrey

Julia's hands moved automatically to answer, but something stopped her. Instead she stared at the name for a few moments, then moved her finger over the button to reject the call. Geoffrey could talk for hours, she told herself, and she had to be on her way. It wouldn't do to be late to one's own party.

Slipping the phone into her bag and slinging it over her shoulder, pausing only to check her reflection one more time, she opened the front door and stepped outside.

She climbed into her car – a maroon Morris Minor with biscuit interior trim – and before she could pull on her leather driving gloves the phone made another noise. Geoffrey had sent a message.

Just to wish you the best of luck tonight. We're all thinking of you.

A pang of guilt surfaced, but Julia stifled it. It wasn't *her* fault that Geoffrey wasn't coming. Nor that none of her local friends had invitations. Once the date of the party had been confirmed she had asked if she might bring along a few of those who had supported her while she was writing the book – never expecting for a moment that she might need to, after all it was supposed to be *her* party. But to her surprise, her agent had gone very quiet on the telephone. Then, clearly implying that this was a most awkward and odd request, James had replied that it *might* be possible, but would be difficult at this *late* stage. Julia had found herself waiting for nearly a week, worried that James had forgotten her request, and not wanting the further embarrassment of having to remind him. When his reply finally came it was disappointing. James told her that the publishers had already invited more people than the small hall was allowed (for insurance purposes) to hold. He went on to say that although her invitation was also valid for a partner, the caterers were assuming she would be coming alone.

She had considered inviting just Geoffrey at that point. But the thought of who else might attend stopped her. They would inevitably form the impression that she and Geoffrey were more than friends, whatever she said. It wasn't just that he was a little older than her, nor that he would talk about his own books, which might be embarrassing. It was more to do with not allowing her old life to mix with the new life that was about to begin. It was just better that way. So in the end she simply told him, the rest of her local friends, and herself, that they would have their own party, when this tiresome one was out of the way.

She slipped on the leather gloves, secured the seatbelt and started the engine. Then she carefully released the handbrake and backed out onto the road. Anyway, she thought, as she checked her mirrors, she was the one who had landed the biggest publishing deal of the decade, not them. You couldn't drag all your baggage with you.

The roads were empty and the car was behaving itself. She steered it between the hedgerows, but after a while she found herself distracted by something. In the boot she had placed a bottle of wine, and somehow it had worked its way loose. It rolled annoyingly from one side to the other as she steered around the corners. She stopped at the next lay-by, wrapped the bottle in a blanket and then firmly stuffed the package into her wicker basket. She checked the bungee cords holding the basket in place, then continued on her way.

* * *

Julia lived about an hour away from her destination, the small and curious island of Hunsey, which lay just off the coast of rural Dorset. When the tide was high, Hunsey was a true island – surrounded on all sides by water. But at low tide the half-mile of shimmering water separating it from the mainland, drained away to reveal a bank of muddy sand and shingle, neatly bisected by a concrete causeway just wide enough for cars to cross.

The location had been chosen for Julia's party – obviously – because it was where her novel was set, specifically around the beautiful but somewhat threatening lighthouse that towered over the south of the island. But again, there had been a little misunderstanding about this. Both her agent James, and as a result now the publishing house, assumed she actually *lived* on the island itself – and it would thus be a convenient venue for her. And though Julia told herself that the origins of this misunderstanding were a mystery, the truth was that she had implied as much to James when she first met him. At that point he was yet to make a firm offer to represent her, and it seemed a harmless white lie to associate herself more closely with the beautiful location that had been the inspiration for her novel. However, the result of this confusion meant the publishing house had not considered her needs when it came to the not-inconsiderable task of arranging transport to and from the party, or indeed overnight accommodation afterwards. There had been a time when Julia had considered putting the record straight, but it was now far too awkward to do that.

Once the party was confirmed, Julia had attempted to book a room on the island where she could, quietly, stay after the party had finished. But despite an increasingly desperate search it became clear there was nothing available. This should not have been a big surprise. Aside from the lighthouse itself, which was being refurbished into bed and breakfast accommodation but wasn't yet open, the village of Hunsey contained few hostelry options. Indeed, there were probably fewer than thirty buildings on the two-mile stretch of land. Whilst not a surprise, it was a problem. If Julia could find nowhere to stay – and the tide was high – she would be trapped on the island for the night. At first this caused her considerable panic but when she checked the tide tables she realised there was a simple solution. The party had in fact been planned around the tides. It began at eight, when the water would have dropped away enough to expose the road so that guests could arrive. Assuming it ended on time (indeed, the invitation stressed it would have to) there would be just time enough to depart before the rising tide cut them off. It meant she could simply drive there, and once the party was over, drive home.

The necessary subterfuge was a shame, but it couldn't be helped. Actually, while this was just the sort of thing that might have dampened the old Julia's enthusiasm, perhaps sending her into a spiral of worry and self-doubt, it seemed to have little effect on her now. Her recent extreme good fortune had enveloped her with a new-found sense of optimism that nothing was able to puncture. Even when she had to cross the main dual carriageway – which normally she dreaded, and would go miles out of her way to avoid – she did so with confidence, the car's little engine roaring proudly as she pulled across the lanes of fast-moving traffic.

But as she got closer, her nerves did begin to kick in.

Hunsey Island sits, almost like an egg nestling in the eggcup of Hunsey Bay, and both are cut off from the world by a half bowl of green hills facing out towards the sea. The bay – when approaching from the land – is completely hidden until you crest the final hill, but then it stretches out before you in a scene that has graced a million postcards. It's a view that looks almost too perfect to be real, as if sculpted by an artist and not just a happy accident of geology and coastal erosion. The island – all rocky cliffs and jewel-like bays, and topped with fresh green grass – meets the blue white ocean, and everything appears quite natural, with just the addition of the few stone houses dotted around the island – and the towering lighthouse that dominates its southern tip.

It was just getting dark as Julia climbed the hill that early spring day. Her engine whined in protest, the little car almost panting with the exertion. Julia slowed, both to let it rest a moment, and because she always lingered here to take in the sight of the island below her. That day, the sun had only just set, leaving the whole lower half of the sky a brilliant chaos of oranges and pinks, streaked here and there by wisps of cloud. The ocean itself was calm, with just a light chop to the surface. It made the sea act as a giant mirror, taking the colours of the sky and breaking them into a billion tiny parts. The island was a dark shape cut into the scene, but already punctuated with points of bright warm yellow as the island's residents turned on their lights. But Julia's eyes were drawn, as they always were, to the thin, elegant lines of the lighthouse, now silhouetted black against the reflected colours of the sea. The mysterious, beautiful tower that had inspired her novel, that had somehow led her to this wondrous moment.

Julia gripped the wheel harder through her gloves. She felt the shake of her hands again. She took two deep breaths and moved the car forwards with a jerk. Carefully, she drove down the hill and out onto the stone quay that marked where the road stopped and the causeway began. Now it was high and dry. The road across to the island was laid out before her, raised up a little from the mix of sand and patches of rough strewn rocks that made up the bay. There were no bends and it fed directly across to the island, but it dipped in the middle following the topography of the bay. In front of Julia was a sign – one of several – warning her of the danger in crossing. As always, Julia gave it due consideration and rechecked her calculations. The tide was definitely dropping – looking out she could see the water shimmering either side of the road in the middle – but soon it would pull away entirely, leaving the causeway surrounded by nearly half a mile in either direction of sand and scuttling crabs. After that the water would turn and begin to creep back, but by then the party would be over and she would be safely back on the mainland side.

It was funny though, the tide. Deceitful somehow. She had come here to write sometimes, when she needed inspiration, and tried to watch the water come in. It didn't appear to move and yet – if she were to become absorbed in her work – the next time she looked up it would have swallowed up great swathes of the beach. It was not unknown for walkers and children playing out in the bay to get cut off. It was not even unheard of for some of them to drown before reaching the safety of either the island or the mainland.

Julia calmed her nerves again and drove out onto the causeway. Her tyres splashed through the seawater puddles that reflected the dying sunset. And once on the island she drove carefully through the hamlet and on towards the tower.

It looked different now. The derelict, almost skeleton remains of the lighthouse that had first inspired her had since been the subject of a major fundraising and rebuilding programme. The tower had been shored up and made safe, and the nearby former lighthouse keepers' quarters had been extended and refashioned. Now it served as accommodation for those seeking solitude and oceanic respite, and close by a small museum had been added to host a collection of fossils found on and around the island. It wasn't normally available to hire for something so prosaic as a party. But then, this wasn't a normal party.

As Julia pulled into the gravel car park she saw it was already full of a large number of vehicles, including several minibuses. There was the faint noise of music. She felt a momentary flush of panic at the thought of going inside, then another at the thought that she might be late. For her own party. But she calmed herself. She visualised her book cover. The tower. She drew strength from its proximity. She parked at the back of the car park, intentionally hiding her car behind a camper van.

"If I'm late, I'm fashionably late," she said out loud. It was an odd comment. Julia had never been fashionable in her life.

Actually, while such a statement would definitely have been true six months previously, it was clearly no longer the case. Right now, in publishing at least, she had found herself in the peculiar position of being the very *height* of fashion. And she still had only the dimmest understanding of how this had happened.

* * *

The facts of the matter are easy to establish, so perhaps we should get them out of the way now. Julia had, some ten years previously, left her short-lived teaching career due to poor health (stress, made worse by ill-disciplined children). When sufficiently recovered she decided that rather than return to work, she would begin the novel that she had always believed herself destined to write. She put pen to paper (initially literally, only later turning to a computer for practical purposes), and relatively quickly she wrote the opening chapters. It was a strange, highly literary opening, about a woman who lived in a tower made entirely out of glass, so that everyone around her was able to see all aspects of her life. Julia then got stuck, with no idea why her heroine lived there, nor what was supposed to happen next. She soon realised the tower in her story was actually based upon the lighthouse which commanded the cliffs at the southern end of Hunsey Island, a place she enjoyed visiting. She didn't know why, or what – if anything – this meant. But she did know that there was a beauty to her words that eclipsed anything she had ever written before. She knew she had *something*. Julia spent the next two years writing and rewriting herself into various corners. But, with little else to do with her time, and supported morally by her collection of friends (who had their own creative projects they were working on), and financially by the little money left by her parents (she was an only child and rather indulged), she ground onward. Finally, five years after she began, she was in possession of a completed manuscript. And two years after that, she felt it was ready to send to publishers.

She never expected this part would be easy, and it wasn't hard at first to stay positive as the rejection letters arrived, but after nearly two more years passed, she was close to giving up. At that point she sent a letter to an agent named James McArthur, whose family just happened to own a holiday home in Dorset, not too far from Hunsey Island. He didn't tend to visit much these days, but he had fond memories of the place, which led him to give the manuscript a chance, and he saw something in its complex sentences that everyone else had missed. The book – which he suggested should be renamed *The Glass Tower* – wasn't just a strange story about a woman in a skeletal former lighthouse where nothing much happened (although that wasn't a bad summary of the plot), it was a poignant and cutting critique of the modern, social-media obsessed world, written in a thrillingly sparse, literary style. He agreed to take her on, and began shopping the manuscript to his publisher contacts. Then something quite extraordinary happened. James' summary of the work sparked the attention of two of the big publishing houses, and once their interest had been noted, other publishers wanted to take a look too. And just as these things – once every ten years or so – can explode out of all proportion, a bidding war for *The Glass Tower* began. Soon, there wasn't a single major publisher who wasn't involved in the battle to acquire the rights, pushing the price higher and higher.

For Julia, sitting in her one-bedroom cottage miles from where this was happening, it seemed both surreal and absurd. Tight finances meant that she didn't even have broadband. To check her email, to see how things had progressed, she would drive to Geoffrey's house in the next village. They would sip tea and stare wide-eyed as the bids for her worldwide publishing rights went up. Fifteen-thousand pounds. Thirty-five thousand pounds. Fifty-five thousand pounds. One-hundred thousand pounds. Julia had almost fallen from her stool at that price, and nervously read the rest of James' email, wondering whether to tell him to accept, but he merely told her to hold onto her hat. And then the numbers really started getting silly.

Two-hundred and fifty thousand pounds. *Three*-hundred and fifty thousand pounds. Five-hundred and fifty thousand pounds. *Seven-hundred and fifty thousand*. It paused at that point, and it seemed the frenzy had cooled off. But it was just the bigger guns drawing breath before they took control. The next bid was for one point three million pounds. The same day that was beaten. One point five million pounds. Then two million pounds. And finally, two point four million pounds.

It was the highest ever amount offered for a debut novelist, and the highest amount offered to *any* novelist in nearly ten years. When Julia had picked herself up off the floor, and agreed with James they should probably accept at this point, she knew her life would never be the same again.

After that, there was no way on earth she could ever criticise her agent – he had discovered a hoard of solid gold where no one else had seen anything of any value. But despite this, their relationship wasn't as she had fantasised it might be. In Julia's dreams her agent looked after her professional interests but also connected on a deeper level as well. In her mind she – it was always a she – became a friend, perhaps her closest friend, always with time for a coffee and a chat. For Julia, her agent-writer relationship was sacred. The only two people who *truly* appreciated the work.

Yet her relationship with James actually existed on a strictly professional level. During the very few times they had actually met in person (he preferred email, and often hadn't even answered the telephone when she had rung) he had done nothing to encourage any kind of friendship, and the closest she had come to sitting down to coffee with him was when she had travelled to London to review the contract in the presence of a lawyer. James had suggested they take a break, and she had wound up behind him in the queue at Starbucks. His order, she overheard in amazement, was for a tall, half-caff, soy latte served at 120 degrees. Her astonishment deepened even more when the young man serving (Julia knew the correct term was a 'barista' but she couldn't bring herself to use it) had failed to even look surprised at the request. When it came to her turn to order, she had checked if they had Earl Grey Tea, as if this might be a stretch too far.

It was moments like right now however, when she regretted how impersonal their relationship was. It would have been nice, for example, to find her agent outside the party, so that they could go in together. (There was a small covered porch area where someone could easily wait.) For about a half-second she did consider giving James a call – he had told her he would be arriving early. But she feared another one of those hesitations in his voice. Or more likely the familiar, abrupt click as he sent the call to his voicemail.

No. James had played his part in this drama, but she would make her own entrance.

* * *

Julia unwrapped the bottle of wine she had brought, considering it not for the first time. In fact she had agonised over whether it was right to bring a bottle. The very phrase stuck in her mind – *bring a bottle*. It was what people did at parties, wasn't it? Yet the invitation hadn't actually included the phrase. She had pondered the problem when buying her outfit, and finally decided it would be better to be seen as too generous, rather than too mean. It was with this in mind that she finally picked up the bottle of Marks and Spencer sparkling wine.

She crunched through the gravel and pushed open the outer door of the museum, letting the sounds of the party spill from somewhere inside. The little lobby, where people bought their tickets to see the dinosaur bones, was empty, but it was clear where she had to go. A pair of pull-up display stands stood either side of another door, and each one made her heart leap. The stands were identical, and each showed a giant mock-up of her book. In both images the tower was recreated in perfect transparent glass. It was a jaw-dropping, gorgeous cover, and she loved looking at it. She stood for a moment now, half-admiring it, half-putting off the moment when she had to enter the room.

"Excuse me." A voice interrupted her. "Are you looking for the launch party?"

Julia turned, startled, and saw a young woman, dressed in the black and white outfit of a waitress. She was a pretty girl, with a kind, open smile.

"It's just through here."

There was a gentleness to the girl's voice, a compassion that helped to calm the knot of nerves in Julia's stomach. She smiled her thanks and let the girl lead her through the doors and towards the main hall.

The second set of doors had small glass windows, giving Julia a view inside. She had visited the museum on a couple of previous occasions. Normally a fossilised skeleton of a Plesiosaurus was displayed in the centre of the room, with various other display cabinets arranged around it. But tonight these had all been moved out of the way, so that the entire space was given over to a moving sea of people.

There must have been about fifty, maybe more, standing around in small, intimate groups. Julia hesitated again, losing her nerve now. The sound of the party was louder here. A wall of conversation and underneath it the bubble of music. Julia stiffened. She noticed that all the guests were holding delicate flutes of what she suddenly realised was champagne. Champagne supplied by the company that the publisher had hired to cater for the event. Julia saw a young man moving between the groups with a bottle wrapped in a white cloth, making sure their drinks were topped up. Julia had a sudden, horrible realisation that she had miscalculated in bringing her own bottle, and she looked around for somewhere she could dump it. But there was nowhere in the little corridor that looked suitable.

At that very moment, the young waitress, who had held the first door open for her, and now hovered behind, seemed to realise the problem.

"Would you like me to take that for you?" she asked. Her face softened enough to show that she sympathised with Julia's predicament, but didn't judge her for it. Gratefully, Julia thrust the offending bottle into her hands.

"I'll pop it in the kitchen," the girl said. "It might be useful if we run out." She flashed a smile, then paused a moment, as if about to say something else, but then her eyes turned to the floor and she went back the way she had come, presumably to deposit the bottle out of sight. Julia was left at the door, with no opportunity to delay any further. So she took a deep breath and then pushed open the second door into the party.

For a moment nothing changed. No one noticed her, and the smile she had fixed on her face began to freeze in place. But then a woman from one of the nearby groups spotted her and began walking, almost running over, a beaming smile on her face.

"Julia, *darling!*" It was Julia's editor – she still couldn't quite believe she had an editor – a woman about her own age named Marion Brown. She touched Julia on her arms and then kissed both her cheeks. "You look fabulous," Marion said, winking and leading her forward. "Come over here at once. Stephen just called you *the most enigmatic and intriguing voice in literature in ten years*. So he absolutely has to meet you first." She drew Julia towards the group she had been standing with.

"That's what you called her, wasn't it, Stephen?" Marion turned to introduce them. "Julia Ottley, this is Stephen Bradley, from the *TLS*. He's been *dying* to meet you."

It was only as Stephen leaned into her and air kissed her on both cheeks that Julia registered Marion was referring to the *Times Literary Supplement*, the most influential British newspaper covering cultural affairs and literature. Stephen Bradley was, of course, its long-standing editor. Julia had been promised, or perhaps warned, that such people might be here, but even she hadn't expected to be thrown in amongst them so quickly.

"I believe I may have said something of the sort," he said. "But it's well deserved. It's an absolute honour to meet you Julia, and congratulations. I found your book both magnificent and important."

Julia couldn't think of a single suitable reply to this, so instead she buried her nose in the champagne flute that had appeared in her hand.

And from that moment onward, the party just got better and better.

Whatever fears Julia had had, about being left on her own (and she'd had plenty) proved entirely wrong. Marion barely left her side the entire evening, instead guiding her around the room, as if rationing the amount of time each of the guests was allowed to spend with her. At different points she met with journalists, authors, television presenters and publishing executives. She met the presenter of BBC Radio Four's Open Book, who spoke in glowing terms about *The Glass Tower*, and told her how her producers were working hard to get Julia onto the show. Julia wondered what could be hard about it – they only needed to ask her surely, but she didn't give away her naivety by pointing this out. She had frankly surreal conversations with not one but two Booker Prize-winning authors, one of whom assured her that *The Glass Tower* was a shoo-in for this year's prize. The other was not sure. He told her that the book *should* win, but that in his experience (he was twice shortlisted before he won) the judges might want to court controversy by *not* choosing her. Julia was so star-struck she was reduced to little more than nodding in agreement, and yet they seemed to take this as the most erudite reply imaginable.

There were other people at the party that Marion didn't deem worthy of meeting the great novelist that Julia had become. She vaguely wondered who they might be, but there was little time to find out, as she passed from one small group of influential, famous or important people to another. And though she'd begun the evening nervous and tongue-tied, expecting the guests to see through her, or to notice that she didn't have anything interesting to say, this didn't last. In fact, she found out soon enough that she *did* have things to say. Indeed, it seemed that whatever words left her mouth caused a moment of delight for whomever she was speaking to. And since all the guests were asking her similar questions, Julia was able to refine her replies, so that by the end some had genuine wit. Most guests went to great pains to praise the book. Some chose to demonstrate how they had actually read it, and understood it. Others (towards the end of the evening – the champagne was flowing freely) joked about how £2.4 million was going to change her life. She was rather pleased with the line she came up with to bat this away – she fired back with the (true) comment that she hadn't actually received any of it so far.

At one point in the evening she met, and exchanged cool air kisses with, her agent James McArthur. To Julia's surprise he had turned up with a male friend named Barney, who had clearly drunk too much and was rather good fun. For a short while Julia was hopeful that this might be the moment that James, too, would finally loosen up, but he seemed more intent than ever to maintain his professional distance, while failing to clarify exactly how Barney was connected to him. Julia supposed he must be James' partner, but the thought rather confused her. If James was actually gay – a possibility she hadn't considered before – shouldn't that make him more likely to get on well with her? That's certainly how gay men were portrayed on the television. Or maybe he (mistakenly) thought she was homophobic? On another night this confusion might have soured things. But not tonight. There simply wasn't the time to dwell on such matters.

About two hours into the proceedings – or perhaps it was three, Julia was having far too good a time to keep track – a large man in a grey suit climbed onto the stage at the far end of the room. From somewhere he was handed a microphone, and slowly the noise level in the room subsided as people turned to look.

He began by asking for people's attention, and the room quietened further.

"I just want to introduce myself, for anyone that doesn't know me." He paused to allow a ripple of laughter to roll around the room. Julia smiled but didn't laugh, since she had no idea who he was.

The man went on to introduce himself as the Managing Director of the publishing house which had bought Julia's book, and was hosting the party. Suitably impressed, Julia listened to what he had to say.

"First of all I want to thank each and every one of you for coming tonight to celebrate the upcoming launch of *The Glass Tower*."

There was a spontaneous round of applause and a small cheer. The man waited for it to subside.

" I want to tell you the story about how we came to acquire the rights for this incredible book." He went on to do just that, explaining how it had landed on his desk, how excitement had spread around the company, and about the bidding war that ensued. He then moved on to praise the team of editors, cover designers, copywriters, marketers and everyone else who had worked on the book to bring it to this point. As he name-checked them, or their departments, a small cheer would go up in different parts of the room. At first Julia looked around at each group with surprised interest. But then she understood. All the people that she hadn't been introduced to were the more junior staff who worked for her publisher. They seemed to have decamped the entire organisation for the night. As the speaker went on, seemingly determined not to leave anyone out, Julia began to find it difficult to keep the smile fixed to her face. It was her book, it was *her* party, but she didn't know these people cheering and congratulating themselves. And there was something else. The man giving the speech seemed to be winding up, but he hadn't mentioned her once. She was only the person who had actually written the bloody thing in the first place. But then, just when he appeared to have exhausted his list of people to thank, he turned on his little stage and looked squarely at her.

"And now, I want to thank the one person without whom none of this would have happened. A true literary sensation. A genius. A staggering talent. The author – the artist – Julia Ottley."

The entire room, packed with brilliant, creative people, turned to her as one and raised their glasses.

"To Julia!" the whole room roared, and they all cheered.

Julia felt her face flush red with the deepest sense of pride she had ever experienced.

THREE

At about 10.30 the party began to wind down. Julia was still with Marion Brown when there was a dip in the conversation, and a young woman came up, looking embarrassed that she might be interrupting.

"Marion, the minibuses are ready now."

"Thank you, Carla," Marion smiled. "We'll start moving people out in a little while."

"We do have to beat the tide, remember." The younger woman looked awkward at pushing the point.

Marion flashed an irritated smile and turned to Julia.

"You're so lucky, you know. Living here on this beautiful island," she said. "I meant to ask, is yours one of the lovely little thatched cottages?"

Julia felt suddenly flustered. She wasn't sure if any of the cottages on Hunsey actually had thatched roofs.

"No." She smiled a little awkwardly.

"Oh." Marion blinked. "Well never mind, I'm sure it must be lovely anyway," she went on brightly, then changed the subject. "We're all off to the Harbour Hotel. Do you know it at all?"

Julia was about to shake her head, when Marion continued.

"It's on the waterfront, over in Poole. It's a bit of a trip but obviously there isn't enough accommodation here on the island to put everyone up.

I expect I shall fall asleep on the bus!" She winked at Julia, as if she were again complementing her good judgement in being able to walk the few steps home. The younger woman, Carla, still hadn't gone away and finally Marion was forced to answer her.

"Yes, we probably should start moving people out now. We don't want to get cut off." Carla ran away to do her bidding, and Marion continued.

"It's a shame that the lighthouse itself isn't open yet. You know they're turning it into a lodge? A kind of artists' retreat I hear. I expect your book will do wonders for it. They should let you stay there for free!" Marion laughed happily at the thought.

"Yes," Julia replied, forcing herself to smile. She tried not to think about her own long drive home.

But it wasn't a truly bitter smile. Julia had always known this would happen at the end of the night. What was important was the future. The glorious future she had achieved for herself. Her glorious future.

Outside in the car park four minibuses were waiting with their engines running. They looked warm, quite cosy, and Julia felt a further pang of regret that she couldn't climb aboard with these wonderful people and let the magic of the evening continue. Furthermore, she was given a new problem. She couldn't simply get in her car and begin her drive home, since everyone would wonder why she was leaving the island. So instead she was forced to wave her goodbyes, say her thank-yous and then walk away, pretending to go on foot to whichever of the nearby cottages they believed was hers. The subterfuge sat uneasy on her, not least because it seemed impossible that one day these people wouldn't discover she didn't live on the island at all, but nearly forty miles away. But as she walked towards the row of coastguard cottages she had decided to adopt, she thought up the excuse she would use. She would claim that, though she didn't actually *live* on the island, she had a friend who did, and who had agreed to put her up for the night. They would never ask who – that would be prying. And so she left the minibuses behind and walked away into the darkness. She soon realised there was no need to cover the half mile or so to the nearest cottage; she could simply lurk in the darkness, off the road until the minibuses pulled away. So that's what she did, watching as their lights picked through the village and down onto the causeway. They were out of sight there, but she could imagine them, a procession of rear lights bumping through the puddles, with the tide creeping in unseen on either side. There was an anxious moment as she checked her watch. But there was time enough for her to cross too, if she was quick. She relaxed and walked back to the car park.

It was unfortunate, that was all, she told herself as she dug in her purse for her keys. Just one of those misunderstandings that couldn't be helped. And she had done exactly the right thing – had she come clean it would just have embarrassed everyone. It wasn't *such a* hardship to drive home. It would give her time to think. Perhaps she might even have an idea about what she would write next – a subject that was already beginning to concern her. Or perhaps it wouldn't do to worry about that now. Perhaps she could indulge herself instead by sinking into her latest fantasy, her daydream about moving house, to London. Somewhere close to where all her new friends actually lived. Maybe then she could have evenings like this all the time. She admonished herself – once again – for such grandiose thinking. The idea was preposterous, there was no way she could afford to live in London. Indeed, she only lived where she did now because it was cheap. But the thought was overtaken by her growing acceptance of reality. The simple truth was, for the first time in her life, she *could* afford it. She could afford just about anything.

The very idea of it made her stand tall. It put a spring in her step.

And thus as she approached her car, she gave little regard to the old camper van that she had parked behind, or to the fact that its bonnet was now standing open. It was only when she reached her car door that she realised a figure was standing by the wall in front of her.

"Hello again," a voice said in the darkness. Julia jumped.

"Sorry, I didn't mean to startle you!" It was a girl's voice, gentle and kind, and after a moment Julia recognised it. It belonged to the girl who had taken her wine bottle, the waitress who had helped her. There was someone else there too, leaning into the dark recess of the van's engine bay.

"It's the battery I think," Julia heard from the darkness. This was a masculine voice, sounding angry, or frustrated.

"We've got a bit of car trouble," the girl explained apologetically. "Well, van trouble. It's Rob's camper, it's always doing this."

Julia realised the man standing at the front of the van was the waiter who had served the drinks all evening. He'd been hard not to notice, tall and good-looking. Dimly, she understood he was probably the boyfriend of the girl. A flicker of irrational jealously shot through her.

She hesitated. Had she actually made it into her car by now, she might have been tempted to just drive away, but to do so with the girl standing right by her seemed impossibly rude. So instead, and knowing precisely nothing about cars or engines, she stepped forward.

"What exactly is the trouble?" she asked.

The boy didn't answer – maybe he hadn't heard. Julia saw now he was examining a part of the engine with the light from his mobile phone screen. The girl replied.

"It's the battery. Well, it is *this* time. It's always something though, with this van." She cast a look to Julia's car hopefully. "I don't suppose..." She hesitated, as if it really pained her to ask. "I don't suppose you've got any jump leads, have you?"

"Jump leads?" An image of a skipping rope formed in Julia's mind. She had no idea how it might help.

"They won't help us," the boy interrupted. He pulled his head out of the bonnet and joined the girl, wiping his hands on his jeans. "It would just drain the battery in a little car like that. We could try to bump start it, but there's a hill to get out of the car park first. I don't think we could even move it."

For a moment the three of them stood in silence. Julia hadn't fully understood what the boy had said, but the implication was clear enough. More than anything she wanted to get in her own car, fire up her (remarkably reliable) engine and get going on her drive home. But to do so would leave this young couple with a vehicle that wouldn't start, stranded in the darkness. And that seemed such an unpleasant idea, that she couldn't do it.

"Do you have far to go?" she asked, as if a broken-down van would somehow be more useful on shorter journeys than on longer ones.

"Southampton," the girl answered. "We're at uni there," she added, as if the three of them were making polite conversation. But there was hope in her voice too.

Julia felt a shaft of relief. Southampton was about thirty miles in the opposite direction from where she was going. They couldn't expect her to give them a lift that far. She exhaled theatrically, attempting to at least appear troubled by their predicament. Then an idea occurred to her.

"Are you members of the AA? Could you call them?"

At first neither of them answered. But then the girl did, though reticently, as if afraid she might upset Julia.

"I don't think so. It's quite expensive..." She sounded embarrassed. "But there's no mobile reception anyway. So I don't know how we'd call them if we were."

"Oh." Julia considered pulling out her own phone, so that perhaps they could use it and somehow get on their way. But when she'd looked earlier, she'd had no reception either.

There was an awkward moment of silence.

"Whereabouts are you headed?" the girl asked. She spoke in the same cheery voice as before. There was no suggestion that maybe she was angling for a lift. She still seemed to be just making conversation. And it worked, too. Julia replied quite enthusiastically.

"Oh, right out into the sticks. I live in a little village about ten miles past Dorchester. I'm afraid it's in quite the opposite direction to where you're headed." Julia felt herself smile in the darkness, and her hand went back to the door handle of her car.

"Dorchester?" the boy said sharply, and apparently to the girl. "That's where your folks live. If we could get there your dad could give me a lift back in his Volvo. That would get this started."

Julia's hand pulled away from her car as if she had received an electric shock. She was glad the darkness had hidden the action. Why had she said the name of a town? She could have just said she was driving out into the sticks. They wouldn't have probed as to exactly where, it would have been rude.

"Are you actually *passing* Dorchester?" the girl asked. This time the hope was clear in her voice.

Julia considered what to say. In twenty-two years of driving she had never once picked up a hitchhiker or – as far as she could remember – a stranger in any capacity. Indeed, she considered it a real risk to do so. A memory surfaced. A film she had once watched, about a woman who had hitch-hiked from a service station, and ended up buried alive. Julia didn't make a point of watching such films, but it had been a foreign language film and highly critically acclaimed. She still remembered the car – a yellow Volvo. She frowned, wondering why this had sprung to mind.

But that wasn't the same situation as this, not by a long way. This was a pleasant young couple who would be very stuck if she didn't offer to help.

Nonetheless, a variety of excuses formed in her mind. She normally used the bypass *around* Dorchester. She was low on fuel. She was late for – for what? It was eleven o'clock at night. She couldn't be late for anything. Furthermore, she realised that if she didn't give these people a lift their options were virtually nil. There was no operational phone box on the island (there was a box, but the phone had long since been removed, replaced by tubs of pretty flowers). There would certainly be no taxis passing right out here, and probably no traffic at all, apart from her. And if she didn't hurry, she too would be stuck here. She thought of the tide creeping in even now. Silently cutting off her escape. Perhaps the couple could sleep in their van? The girl had called it a camper van after all. Hope flared in Julia's mind at the thought – but then it died. It was cold. And no battery meant no lights. Their only light was the dim glow from the boy's mobile phone.

And then – beyond the scope of the couple's immediate predicament – what was she even *thinking*? She was on the verge of becoming one of the most famous, most successful, *richest* authors in the country. Was it really such a hardship to share her car for fifteen minutes to help these poor people out? Of course not! So instead of continuing to think up elaborate excuses to escape, a thought began to settle within her. A good, kind thought.

"Well, usually, yes. I go right through Dorchester. Why don't you come with me and I'll drop you off?"

There was just a second when she thought of being buried alive, but that was nonsense.

"Oh, would you?" Though she tried to disguise it, the flood of relief in the girl's voice was obvious. "Would you really? I was getting worried we were going to spend the night here."

"It would be a bit dark and scary!" Julia joked, and the girl laughed in agreement. She had a lovely laugh. It shone like a golden light in the darkness.

"Rob? What do you think? Is that a good idea?" the girl went on, and Julia found herself holding her breath while he decided their fate. Now she actually *wanted* to give the couple a lift. To spend a little more time in the company of that beautiful sound.

"That's very kind of you," he said, a little stiffly. "We hate to put you out. But that would be great."

Julia decided she liked him as well. He was polite. Perhaps a bit grumpy, but then his van had broken at a most inconvenient time, so that was only to be expected.

"Excellent," she said, getting into the spirit now. "And it's no bother at all. That's if my little car actually starts," she joked. "It's not the most reliable!"

Happily, she pulled open the door, and while the boy – Rob – put the bonnet down on the van, Julia leaned across and opened the passenger side. She helped the girl rock the front seat forward, to give her access to the back.

"I'm Becky, by the way," she said as she climbed in.

"Nice to meet you Becky," Julia replied. "My name is..."

"I know what your name is– " Becky interrupted her quickly. There was a sudden silence.

"I'm sorry. I didn't mean... It's just, I know who you are."

Julia was momentarily baffled. She remembered, of course, that they'd met earlier, but she hadn't told the girl her name.

"You're the author. You're Julia Ottley!"

Julia turned around in surprise.

"I can't wait to read your book. I've seen all the reviews. It sounds fantastic. I'm so excited," Becky said.

"Really?" Julia replied.

"Of course! I had to try so hard to stay cool when I met you earlier. But I didn't think you'd want some silly fan hassling you just when you're making your big entrance! I was okay, wasn't I?" she asked.

Suddenly she sounded worried.

"Hassling me..?"

But Julia was interrupted by Rob getting into the car. He was so tall that he had to fold himself in, and his weight made the little car sag down on the passenger side. Becky leaned forward between the two seats. It gave Julia time to recover her composure.

"I'm just a bit surprised that two young things like you would be interested."

"Oh yeah! I'm studying English Literature, you see. And creative writing. So tonight was a dream come true for me. Not just one famous writer but lots of them!"

"Oh." Julia began pulling her seatbelt across her. "That's wonderful..." She was beginning to feel invincible again. As if nothing could puncture her good spirits.

"And how about you, Rob? What are you studying?"

"Engineering."

"Oh," said Julia as she clicked the buckle home. She couldn't think of a reply to that.

But the moment of awkwardness didn't last. Julia turned the key and the engine roared into life. The headlights clicked on and lit up the darkness with a warm glow. Julia checked over her shoulder before releasing the handbrake, and saw Becky smiling at her.

"Rob doesn't read much, but I read absolutely everything I can get my hands on. So I couldn't believe it when the agency said there was this job coming up. I begged them to let me do it."

Becky was sitting forward on her seat, so that she was close enough to keep talking, but for a moment Julia ignored her. She backed carefully out of the parking space, the tyres crunching on the gravel. It then took Julia a moment or two to locate first gear and the gearbox ground in protest. But eventually it slotted in, and Julia rolled out of the car park.

"I'm actually really surprised you've heard of me," Julia said, now that she was able to concentrate on the conversation.

"Why?" Becky's sing-song voice sounded incredulous. "You're super-famous!"

"Am I?" Julia replied. She heard herself beginning to simper and pulled herself together. But with all these compliments she was almost beginning to believe it.

"Well, perhaps," she said. "But only within the very narrow world of literature."

"I'm not sure about that," said Becky. "And anyway, what's more important than literature?"

This line of reasoning delighted Julia and for a few moments she drove in silence just enjoying the strange turn that this evening had now taken. She steered the little car down off the island and out onto the causeway. The tide had risen more than she had bargained for, and already it was joining the puddles together in the middle. Another ten minutes and they would have been too late, but Julia simply splashed through as if they were no more threatening than puddles in a super-market car park.

"What was it like to write your book?" Becky asked suddenly. The question surprised Julia. Despite all the questions she had answered throughout the night, no one had asked this.

"I don't know. Hard, I suppose."

"Oh, yes. Obviously. But what I mean was, was it also thrilling? Did you know how brilliant it was?"

It was an excellent question and Julia considered for a long time before answering.

"I don't know," she said at last. "I certainly wasn't expecting it to make so much..." Julia stopped herself. Talking about the money was so vulgar, and clearly the girl was asking about something deeper.

"I just know I felt... compelled. Compelled to finish it. That it was something important, you know?" She glanced again at the girl who was smiling at her from the backseat, her big eyes wide.

"I just knew that however hard it was, I had to finish it. Whatever happened." Julia smiled back at the girl, but Becky stayed silent, as if considering what Julia had said.

"Does your mother actually live in Dorchester?" Julia asked as they moved onto a properly surfaced road and began to climb up the hill. "It's such a lovely town."

Becky seemed content to move the conversation on, too. "We've got one of those houses near the station. You know, the big ones."

"Oh, really?" Julia said, genuinely interested. "I've always wondered what those houses are like."

"Oh, they're great," Becky said. "You should come in! Have a look around."

Julia smiled but didn't reply in case it quashed the girl's delightful over-enthusiasm. It was nearing midnight. It certainly wouldn't be appropriate to accept the offer.

Yet for the next five miles the conversation continued on a similarly easy thread. It felt to Julia as if she had become firm friends with Becky, almost from the moment they began talking. Rob didn't contribute much to the conversation. In fact, later on, Julia wouldn't be able to recall a single word he'd spoken in the car beyond "engineering" – at least until the accident. But such was the wonderful flow of her and Becky's conversation that it hardly mattered.

And there were a few minutes yet before Julia's world would shatter.

FOUR

THE ROADS between Hunsey Island and Dorchester were totally empty. They weren't the type of roads that got much traffic even when they were busy, but at this time of night they were simply deserted. Julia was able to drive with her full beam headlights, although with her cautious nature she rested her hand on the steering wheel so that it was ready to flick the lights down at any moment. Becky continued to chat the whole way, and she seemed to have an inexhaustible supply of compliments and stories about how she and her friends were looking forward to Julia's book – and all the future books that Julia would, no doubt, write. In some ways it was a continuation of how well the evening had gone at the party – but in other ways it was even more gratifying. Since Becky wasn't an invited guest, with an interest in supporting Julia and the book, she was something even more wonderful – an actual fan!

As they talked Julia began to wonder if it actually might be possible – appropriate even – to stay involved, rather than simply dropping the couple off. Perhaps she *could* go into the house and accept the gratitude of Becky's parents, and reassure them that their daughter was okay, and had been safe and sensible in her decision to climb into a stranger's car? Yes, it was nearly midnight, but it was possible the parents were still up, perhaps even worrying. And if they were anything like as nice and interesting as Becky herself was – well that would be even more lovely...

"Look out!"

The voice was Rob's, but before Julia could even register this, there was the *BANG!* of an impact. Julia jerked forwards, and flinched as what looked like the wheel of a bicycle went bouncing off the bonnet of the car, then flew past the windscreen. Her foot went to the brake and pressed it hard. They hadn't been travelling that fast and the little car shuddered and slipped to a halt. They all sat in silence.

"Shit." Rob said loudly. He opened his door, then fumbled to release his seatbelt.

"What was that?" Julia asked, her voice still normal, disbelieving.

"A bike." Rob finally released himself and struggled now to get his large frame through the car door. "It was a woman on a bike. You just fucking hit her."

Julia blinked and said nothing. She gripped the steering wheel through her driving gloves, strangely aware that the elation within her was fast slipping away, as if draining out of an ever-expanding hole in the bottom of her mind. A kind of bewilderment took its place.

Then Julia realised that Becky had left the car as well. The engine was still running. It occurred to her that she could just drive off. She could leave the couple behind, and then whatever had happened – she still didn't know what that was – would be left behind too. Or perhaps wouldn't have happened at all. But the passenger door was open. She couldn't drive with the passenger door open. So instead she uncurled her fingers from their grip on the steering wheel, swung open her own door and stepped outside.

About fifty yards behind the car she saw, in the darkness, the boy bending over a shape in the road. Becky was standing next to him, her hands pressed against her cheeks. Julia found herself walking towards them. She felt like she had moved outside her own body, and was watching an actor perform her movements – badly. She could hear her own breathing, hard and fast.

The moonlight threw the slightest of shadows on the grey asphalt. Julia's eyes began to adjust to the darkness.

"Is she okay?" she heard a voice say. It was Becky. The figure in the road began to take a human shape, albeit twisted and wrong.

"Is she okay?" Becky asked again, more insistent this time.

"I didn't see her," another voice offered, tremulous and weak. Though she barely recognised it, Julia realised the voice was hers. "I didn't see her."

Then Becky began moaning. A low, consistent tone, as if she had been wounded herself.

"Rob?" Becky finally managed. She almost begged him. "Is she okay?"

"I don't think so," he replied.

None of them spoke for a long moment.

"What do you mean?" Julia said at last. She sounded more herself again. "You don't think so? What does that mean?"

"It means she's not breathing," Rob said. There was a clear undertone of anger in his voice. "What do you think it means?"

"Well, she must be. She has to be." Julia heard herself laugh at the absurdity of any alternative. "She has to be okay. Doesn't she?"

She hesitated again, and then something made her reach down, as if to check the prone figure in the road for herself. It was like pushing her hands through a portal into a horrible new universe, but still she did it. She touched the woman's coat with the tips of her gloves. But went no further.

"Can't you give the kiss of life, or..."

Becky's moaning got louder and louder.

"Shut up, Becks," Rob said. He turned back to Julia. He was breathing heavily.

"I can try," he said. Julia felt herself being pushed roughly out of the way. She didn't resist, but watched Rob as he rolled the figure onto its back. The way it moved – lifelessly – had a particularly sickening impact in the moonlight. It was hard to see for sure, but it looked as though Rob pinched the woman's nose – Julia could see she was not a young woman – and she felt a moment's disgust as Rob's lips closed over the woman's face. It wasn't clear if he knew what he was doing, or if he was simply copying the actions he had no doubt seen on countless TV shows and films.

"Oh my God," Becky said. "It's not working." Julia turned to stare at her.

"How do you know? Have you done medical training? Has he? Has Rob?"

"No! He told you. He's studying engineering."

"Did *you* see her?" Julia asked now. She remembered how she had been daydreaming about meeting Becky's parents just before the impact. Had she turned around to say that to Becky? She couldn't remember.

Then another consideration suddenly flooded Julia's brain. The concept of blame.

"Did she have lights?" Julia asked. "On her bike?"

"Yes! No. I don't know. I sort of saw her. I thought you had too. Oh my God," Becky replied.

"But did she have lights?" Julia asked again.

"Will one of you two fucking help me!" Rob interrupted them from the ground. Becky dropped at once to do what he asked, and now Julia was the only one standing back, watching with an ever-deepening sense of horror as Rob blew into the woman's face and Becky pumped her palms on her chest. After what seemed like an eternity, they stopped.

"It's no good," declared Rob. He got to his feet. The moonlight revealed the shine of sweat on his brow. Becky was moaning again.

"What do you mean no good?" Julia asked.

Rob turned to face her. "I mean she's dead."

FIVE

Rob stalked off back towards the car. The rear lights glowed in the darkness of the road ahead. A small trickle of smoke flowed out from the exhaust pipe.

"Where are you going?" Becky asked.

"To get my phone," Rob shouted back. "It must have fallen onto the seat."

Julia and Becky were left alone. Becky climbed to her feet and stared at the body, her face reflected pale in the moonlight. Neither of them spoke. Julia noticed, by the side of the road, the bicycle. She walked over towards it. When she got there she stared at the machine. It was an old-style shopper-type bicycle with a basket on the front – just the thing you would expect an old lady to ride. Just not at midnight on an unlit country road.

"There's no lights," Julia said to Becky. "She wasn't using lights."

Rob was coming back from the car now, his hand glowing where he held a mobile phone.

"No signal here, either. Can you try yours?"

Julia supposed he meant Becky and she watched while the young woman also pulled out a phone. After staring at it for a few moments, Becky shook her head.

"Nothing, not even one bar."

There was silence for a moment. Julia had absolutely no idea what to do next.

"Well?"

Julia turned. She suddenly realised that Rob was talking to her. "Do you have a signal or not?"

"My... my phone's in my handbag," Julia said.

"Well go and fucking get it!"

Without replying Julia did what he said. Actually, it was a relief to get back to the car, to get away from that horrible shape in the road.

The warm, bright icons of her mobile phone's home screen were comforting too, once she unlocked the screen. So much so that Julia thought for a moment that it was working as normal. But then she realised that for her too, the symbol indicating the signal was missing. Still she hesitated a moment before returning to where Rob and Becky were standing.

"Nothing," she said, then went on, "what do we do now?"

As if in response Becky began quietly sobbing. Rob turned and wrapped his arms around her, then said something quietly in her ear. Julia felt a sudden and utterly irrational rush of jealousy that Rob hadn't taken *her* in his arms, and it was the absurdity of this thought that shocked her into action. She looked around, trying to work out what options they had available to them. They were on a quiet and empty part of a little-used road. And it was past midnight. The moonlight was enough to make out the road stretching perhaps a quarter mile in front of them and a good two hundred yards behind to the last corner. There were no street lights. No pavements. There were no houses, or buildings of any kind in sight along the road. And looking out over the fields there were no lights from any homes either, although the glow of Dorchester was visible on one side, perhaps five or six miles away. Julia supposed there may be houses too, out in the darkness, but the occupants were surely asleep by now, which explained the lack of lights. She wished, more than anything in the world, that she were tucked up in her own bed, with Edgar curled up on the duvet beside her. She shivered. It was a cold night, too. Above them the moon and the stars twinkled.

"Are you quite sure...?" Julia began, addressing her question to Rob.

"Are you quite sure she's...?" She couldn't bring herself to say the word 'dead'. But he seemed to understand anyway.

"I think so," he replied, and his voice was steady now, as if comforting Becky had calmed him down too.

"I'm not an expert, but she definitely isn't breathing and I couldn't find a pulse." He turned to look at Julia.

"It's kind of weird to touch her. If she really is... You know."

And suddenly, despite his physical size, Julia realised just how young Rob was. He was just a boy. A scared boy.

"She looks really old," Rob went on. "Like ancient. So maybe it was a heart attack or something?"

Julia swallowed, forcing herself to focus. Was that possible? If so it seemed to offer a glimmer of hope.

"Do you mean, she might have had a heart attack that made her swerve across the road?"

"Sort of. Although she didn't really swerve. It was more like you hit her and then she had the heart attack."

Julia turned away, feeling her stomach churn. She forced herself to walk the few steps to the body. This time she didn't recoil but crouched down beside it and tried to observe. The face was of an elderly woman, perhaps older than Julia had thought before. But even so she looked fit. Her hair was short and white, and she wore a scarf that had partially come loose, perhaps from the impact, or perhaps from Rob's attempts to resuscitate her. Her eyes were open and staring, and it gave the impression of life. But no part of her was moving. Her chest was still. She was wearing a cashmere sweater under a woollen coat, which Rob had pulled open, but none of it moved with the normal roll of breath. She was quite still, like a log. She wasn't lying normally, either. Not like a person might lie in bed. Rob had rolled her onto her back, but her legs had not fallen into the normal position, although Julia couldn't see what was wrong. Perhaps a broken leg. Maybe where the bumper of the car had impacted her. Julia screwed her eyes shut at the thought, then forced herself to keep looking. The woman wore trousers, with bicycle clips around her ankles. There was no blood, thank God. That might have been too much.

There seemed no reason to touch her, to check for a non-existent pulse for example.

Julia got back to her feet, and she sensed that both Rob and Becky had moved closer to her. She felt a hand placed softly on her shoulder.

"Are you okay?" It was Becky. She seemed to have regained some of her composure too, and she didn't move her hand from Julia's shoulder. It felt nice.

"You must be in shock. This is so horrible."

Julia felt herself nodding.

"Rob says we should wait until someone comes along, and then they can go for help," Becky said.

Julia nodded again. "Okay," she said.

She looked up the road. It stretched away into the darkness. She turned around and looked the other way. Still there was nothing to see, just the line of a hedgerow, rising up behind a low ditch. The scene was partially illuminated by the moonlight, disappearing into the distance.

"I don't remember seeing a single car since we left the main road," Julia said. She wasn't deliberately trying to find fault with the idea, she was just speaking words as they appeared in her mind. But the consequence of it struck her.

"Did you? I don't think I saw a single other car."

"I don't know," Becky replied. "I wasn't... I wasn't really paying attention."

For some reason, this made Julia feel just a little better about the situation. She wasn't the only one who hadn't been paying attention. It made it less her fault.

"And she had no lights on," Julia said, returning to this theme.

"Really?" Becky said this time. "I mean that's stupid. Really bad."

"Yeah. How was I supposed to see her? How was *anyone* supposed to see her? We were just unlucky." Somewhere in Julia's mind a question formed, causing her to pause – who was more unlucky, those in the car, or the woman lying dead on the road surface? But the question didn't quite make it to her consciousness, leaving only a vague feeling of emptiness.

"Anyone that happened to drive down this road would have ended up hitting..."

"She did have lights," Rob interrupted her, his voice cool. "*I* saw them, they weren't very bright but I saw them."

For a moment Julia was silenced.

"Well, why didn't you say something?" Julia asked at last. But Rob either didn't hear her or ignored her. He walked the few steps to the bike, and this time he picked it up.

"Look, they're on a dynamo. They only work when you pedal. I guess she wasn't peddling very fast." He stopped and looked up and down the road as well. Clearly he had reached the same conclusion that Julia already had. If they were going to wait for another car to come along, they might be waiting for a very long time.

"Well, why didn't you say something?" Julia asked again. She heard the growing anger in her voice.

Rob turned to look at her. He was shaking his head.

"I dunno. I just assumed you'd seen her. I..." He shrugged and then his shoulders drooped. Again, the movement revealed him to be just a boy, and the anger within Julia dissolved at once.

"Maybe we should go and get some help?" Julia said, a few moments later. "If we struck out over the fields we might come across a house and they could phone for help."

"Which way?" It was Becky who replied. "I can't see any houses so we could be walking for ages. And it's not easy walking cross-country in the dark."

Julia looked around again. There was no obvious footpath to follow and she had to accept Becky had a point.

"Well, along the road then?"

"It might be dangerous. What if someone comes along driving too fast?"

They were all silent for a moment after that comment.

"Maybe we should drive to get help?" Rob weighed in after the silence became oppressive.

"We can't," Julia said at once. "We can't leave the scene of an accident. It's against the law."

"Well, what then? We can't just wait here all night. There might be no one along this road until the morning."

Julia sighed, a long slow exhale of breath. Then an idea occurred to her. "Maybe you could stay here while Becky and I go for help?" It wasn't until the words were out that she realised she had assumed he would be the one who stayed, alone in the darkness, with just the dead woman for company. She shuddered, and whatever Rob thought of the idea he didn't reply.

Suddenly there was a small flash. Julia turned and saw Rob was taking photographs, using his phone.

"What are you doing?" she asked.

"I'm recording the scene. That way we can all leave. And the police will be able to see how things were. You know, for evidence. Because what else can we do? They'll have to understand," Rob carried on, his flash firing again and again in the darkness. A couple of times it went off in Julia's eyes.

For a few minutes no one spoke at all. Rob moved around them, taking more pictures, and Becky stood tapping at her mobile phone, as if she might persuade it to find a signal through perseverance. When Rob finished, he moved over to the woman's bicycle and picked it up again. He wheeled it forward for a little while.

"It still works," he said. "You didn't hit her that hard."

He told Becky to hold the handlebars while he lifted the back of the bike and spun the pedals round with his hands. As the wheels spun there was the soft burring sound of the dynamo and a faint red light lit up his face. The front light came on too, but it was incredibly weak.

"How the hell could she see where she was going?" Rob asked. "And *where* was she going anyway?" He let the bicycle rest back on the ground. "I mean, what the hell was she doing cycling in the middle of nowhere this late at night?" His voice was becoming angry again. Julia felt herself nodding in agreement.

"She was asking to get herself killed. Stupid." Rob sighed. He stopped speaking.

"Maybe she lives somewhere near here?" Becky said after a while. "Actually, maybe if we drive on a bit, we can find her house. Maybe she'll have a phone, and we can call the police from there?"

Julia was about to reply that it didn't matter whose house they found, as long as there was someone there and they had a telephone. But then a second thought occurred to her. When Julia had been checking her phone, it was an ambulance that she pictured in her mind. A big, brightly-lit, comforting ambulance, full of confident, professional doctors, who were somehow going to come and fix the situation. But Becky had moved on from that. It was the *police* she wanted to phone.

"Why the police?" Julia asked.

"What?"

"Why the police?" she said again. Julia saw Becky twist to look at her.

"We need to tell them. There's a woman that's dead! We have to tell them."

For a long moment, Julia absorbed the reality of that. Of course Becky was right and she was wrong. But what would the police do? Would she, Julia, have to go with them? Would she have to sit in an interview room? Would they record the interview, like they did on the TV? *Did she need a lawyer?* Oh God! Where could she get one? She remembered how her agent had used a lawyer, to negotiate the contract she had signed. What was his name? Could she get him to come and help her? Or would he be in bed now? Would it wait until the morning…?

"How much did you drink?" Rob asked suddenly, cutting into her thoughts.

Julia started. "What?"

"Well, they're going to breathalyse you, aren't they? They always do after an accident. How much did you have?"

Julia didn't answer. Couldn't answer. It was like the question had bounced back off her. Like a stone thrown onto a thickly frozen lake.

"I know you drank quite a bit. I was serving it, remember?"

Her brain managed to absorb the question this time, and slowly it wound its way around her dulled synapses.

Julia *never* drove when she had been drinking. It wasn't a rule she had to work hard to maintain, or even needed to think about. It was just a clear, lifelong habit. It was the wrong thing to do – therefore she didn't do it. And what followed was just as clear: if she was driving she didn't drink. She'd simply tell whoever was offering her a glass of white wine that she couldn't accept it because she had to drive. It wasn't that she didn't like drinking – there was always a bottle of white wine in her fridge at home – but she would never touch it when she had to drive. Julia had never driven when she'd drunk alcohol. Never.

But tonight that had all gone out of the window. And until this awful, gut-sinking moment, *she hadn't even realised it.* It was because she'd been *hiding the fact she was driving*. Because of that, she hadn't needed to tell anyone she wasn't drinking; indeed she'd been unable to tell them. Plus, of course, she'd been so taken in with the excitement of the party, that it was simply the last thing on her mind. She had merely forgotten that she'd been drinking. Forgotten she had been driving.

How many had *she had?*

In a panic she tried to count. Three glasses at least. Maybe four. Maybe even five – her glass had just kept being topped up. She'd stopped at some point – again, not because of her need to drive, but just because that was her habit too, she wasn't a big drinker. And she certainly didn't feel drunk now – she hadn't the whole evening. Except perhaps drunk on happiness and pride.

"How many is the limit?" she asked. Now she sensed that her own voice sounded slurred.

"Uh, it's like a large glass of wine for women?" Becky said, and sighed. "How many did you have?"

Julia didn't answer.

"Weren't you counting?"

Still Julia didn't reply. She couldn't. It was as if a cloud of huge bats had invaded her brain, and they were wheeling and swirling and screeching inside her. *It was a mistake.* She didn't mean to do it. She hadn't *realised*. Would the police accept that? Surely they would? Of course they would!

But a woman was *dead*!

"You weren't drunk though!" Becky's voice sounded from a long distance away. "I wouldn't have got into the car with you if you had been."

Julia sensed that she might faint. She rocked back on her heels, looked around for something to lean against.

"It all seems so unfair," Becky went on.

"Why? What do you mean by that?" Rob asked her.

"I mean, everything that's going to happen to Julia when we tell the police. She's not really drunk but they're not going to care, are they? Just 'cos she's over their stupid limit. But it wasn't *really* her fault. You said it too. It was the stupid woman riding out here with no lights, this late at night."

"She did have lights, they were dynamo..."

"Yeah, but not proper ones. We couldn't see her, could we? And she swerved."

"What?"

"She swerved. I saw her, just before we hit. She swerved right out into the road. But that won't matter, will it? It'll still be all over the newspapers. Julia Ottley, the famous writer. How she was drunk-driving and killed some woman. It's just so unfair."

Julia didn't hear any more, because her mouth was filling with vomit.

SIX

SHE GOT NEARLY to the side of the road, and then retched, again and again, emptying the contents of her stomach onto the tarmac and the grass verge in the darkness.

When she finally finished, she knelt, panting, one hand on the rough surface of the road trying to steady herself. Her cheeks were wet with tears. Her mouth tasted bitter.

"Urgh," Rob said. "Maybe you're more drunk than we thought."

"It'll help her a bit though, won't it?" Becky asked. "Getting it out of her system?"

That thought had played no part in Julia's actions, but she listened now, suddenly almost hopeful.

"I doubt it. It's already in her bloodstream, isn't it? That's what the police test for." Rob took another step back.

"It does stink of booze, though."

To Julia, still with one hand pressed against the grit of the road, it felt as though a shift had taken place. Before they had been three people in a predicament, but now they were neatly divided. Now the young couple were mere observers, speculating on her fate. She suddenly felt more alone than she could ever remember.

"I'm gonna go check out the car," Rob said. "In case we do decide to get help. You know, see if it actually still drives?" He walked away quickly. Becky hesitated a moment, as if she was wondering whether to comfort Julia again, but then she apparently thought better of it and followed him. Julia felt a sense of horror at being left alone near the dead woman, and she quickly pushed herself up to go, too.

"It looks okay," Rob was saying when she got to the front of the car, where Rob was illuminated in the yellow glow from the headlights. "Maybe we should just go? I mean, we can't stay here all night."

"I think we should," Becky replied. It was obvious from her voice that she wanted to get away now.

Rob nodded. "Okay," he said. "What do we do with the body?"

"*What?*" Becky sounded shocked. "What do you mean by that?"

"I mean, what if someone does come along, but doesn't see it? It's right in the middle of the road. They might hit it."

"Well, the woman's already dead."

"Yeah. It still seems a bit wrong, though."

This time Becky didn't answer him.

"I guess we could move her a bit," Rob went on. "Just to the side, I mean. Just so that no one hits her."

There was another pause.

"If you're going to do that, you might as well move it a little bit further," Becky said.

There was something in the way Becky spoke that made both Julia and Rob turn around and stare at her.

"What do you mean by *that*?" Rob asked.

"I just mean, if you're going to move it a little bit, you might as well move it right the way into the ditch."

"What? *Why?*"

"Because of how *unfair* it is," Becky said. "Because of what's going to happen to Julia if someone finds it now." No one stopped her, so Becky went on.

"I mean, here she is, about to become the most famous author – in like, the whole world, or at least in the country – and now none of that's going to happen. Just because this woman wanted to go cycling at midnight without any lights..."

"She did have lights," Rob said, but it wasn't enough to interrupt Becky's flow.

"And they probably won't even publish her book now. It's like, probably the best book there's been for years, and now *none* of that's going to happen, just because this woman had no lights on."

"She did have lights," Rob said again.

"Not very good ones," Becky answered at once.

No one spoke for a long time. Julia could see Rob blinking in the moonlight, and she just watched him. It suddenly seemed incredibly important how he reacted to Becky's outburst.

"All I'm saying is, if we put the woman just a little bit in the ditch, maybe no one will find her for a while, then maybe the police don't have to know that Julia was drinking," Becky added.

"That's all."

Still Rob didn't reply.

"And then maybe Julia could go to the police tomorrow, and say that she thought she hit a deer, or something, but that she just wanted to be sure," Becky went on. "That way she wouldn't be doing anything wrong. The police would still find the lady..." Becky stopped. "I don't know..." She lapsed into silence.

"We could do that," Julia croaked. "I could do that."

She didn't know what had happened to her voice; it came out in barely a whisper. They both looked at Rob, who was now stroking his chin, as if deep in thought. Suddenly he stopped and glanced up and down the road. Nothing had changed. It was still empty and dark in both directions. A cloud passed in front of the moon, deepening the darkness. The headlights on the little Morris gave a flicker.

"What about the sick?" Rob asked.

"What?" said Becky.

"The puke all over the road?"

"What about it?"

"Well if she thought she hit a deer – but didn't stop – then how come the road is covered in sick?"

"They might not find it," Becky said.

"Did you even smell it? And what? You think, with a dead woman lying in the ditch, they won't notice something like that?" Rob turned to Julia. "Did you get any on the woman?"

"Any...?"

"Any puke? Did you hit her with it?"

Julia's first thought was to be insulted at the insolent tone he had decided was now appropriate. But she forced herself to think. To accept that he was *helping* her.

"I'm not... I don't think so. I have a bottle of water in the car. Maybe we could wash it away?"

Julia sensed a hesitation in Rob. "Maybe I could, I mean."

Both Julia and Becky turned to look at Rob again. He hesitated for a few moments but then nodded.

"Yeah. I guess it might work. If you can get it all to the verge, they probably won't see it there as easily."

But Julia didn't move. The thought of going back alone to where the woman lay dead on the ground was more than she could bear.

"Could... Could one of you come with me? Maybe you could use your phones as a torch? So I can see what I'm doing."

Neither Rob nor Becky looked keen, but after a few moments Becky muttered her agreement. Julia walked unsteadily around to the boot of her car and opened it. Inside, her wicker basket was still fixed in place with its elastic cord. She pulled out a large plastic bottle nearly full of water. She picked it up, and together with Becky she walked back to where she had been sick. The smell *was* quite strong, Julia had to agree.

Working by the light from Becky's phone, she took the lid from the bottle and poured the contents to wash the vomit from the surface of the road and onto the verge. Even with Becky holding her phone as a torch it was difficult to see clearly, but it certainly seemed as though it was less visible there. When the bottle was empty, Julia used the side of her foot to brush aside any water, or vomit, that remained.

"At least you missed her," Becky said. Julia didn't reply – she seemed to have lost the power of speech. But she nodded.

"I think we should just roll her into the ditch, and cover her up," Becky said. They were walking back to the car, where Rob was doing something with his mobile phone again. "Rob? I think we should just get rid of it. It makes sense. Otherwise Julia's whole life is going to be totally ruined, and it's not fair. When it's not her fault."

Rob didn't immediately respond. He walked a few steps away from them, as if he needed space to think.

"Rob?"

He stayed silent for a long time. Then he stepped back and looked at Julia.

"I heard someone talking about your book this evening," he began slowly. "They were saying that you're getting, like, over two million pounds for it. Is that right?"

For Julia, the question was like a reminder of a life she had lived an age ago.

"Yes," she replied.

Rob didn't say anything more for the moment. He still had his phone in his grasp and he passed it from one hand to another.

"And is that, like… dependent upon you... I don't know, not messing everything up? Like not drink-driving and killing someone?"

Julia stared at him. "I'm not sure," she replied eventually. A note of sarcasm crept into her voice. As if, despite the horrific circumstances – and how much hope she was now pinning on him – Julia was tiring of how childish they were.

"It wasn't one of the contract terms that my lawyer talked me through."

Rob didn't seem to notice the sarcasm. Instead he pressed the point.

"But it's likely? Right? I mean, if you end up going to prison, it's likely that all this success that you've been going on about – that none of that would happen?"

At his casual use of the word 'prison' Julia felt she might be sick again. The sarcasm vanished.

"I don't know," she said in the end.

There was a long silence. Eventually Becky broke it. "It's not really about the money, Rob. It's more to do with the *book*. If Julia does go to prison it will kill the book. They probably won't even publish it. Can you imagine if *Jane Eyre* had never been published? It's not just Julia who has to pay the price. The whole world would be poorer."

Rob turned away out of the light, so that Julia wasn't able to see his reaction to this. He didn't reply for a while.

"Did you get all the sick off?" Rob asked from the darkness, a moment later. "Was it on her?"

Becky shook her head. "No, and it's all gone. You'd never know it was there."

Rob moved back into the light. He was scowling now.

"I'm going to take a look." He left them, and walked back to inspect for himself. Julia and Becky waited for him in silence. Now Julia felt awkward in Becky's presence. But Rob soon returned.

"It's mostly gone," he said. "But we should still move her away. It might be more obvious in the light." He walked away again, this time over to the side of the road, still using his mobile phone as a torch. Julia watched the little cone of light move as he walked along the ditch. A little way beyond where they had stopped the car it intersected with another channel that ran perpendicular to the road and out into the field beyond.

"It's much deeper here," he called back to them. "If we do it here we could make it look like she just cycled into the ditch."

"Yeah! They'll probably never know there was a car involved anyway," Becky replied to him almost enthusiastically, leaving Julia alone and walking towards him.

"We'd have to chuck the bike in as well," Rob went on. "Who touched it?"

For a second Julia didn't know what he was talking about, then she realised he must be thinking about fingerprints. She looked down at her own hands, hidden beneath her leather driving gloves.

"Becky. Go get the bike. Pull your sleeves down to cover your fingers, then wipe it all over. Then wheel it over here. Julia, come with me and we'll move her."

Julia did what she was told, and followed Rob back to the figure lying in the road. The thought of lifting the body filled her with horror, but a sudden hope flushed it away. Might they have simply made a mistake? Might they discover that the woman was now moaning and trying to get to her feet? Was there another way out of this, even at this late stage?

But as they approached the heap in the road and Julia listened carefully, there was nothing but silence. There was no movement, either. The hope was gone.

"You take the feet end, it'll be lighter," Rob said. "And try not to drop her."

He bent down and, turning his head away so as not to look too much, he gripped the woman by her wrists. He looked to Julia, who still hadn't moved.

"Come on," he said. "I can't drag her, they'll see the scrape marks on her heels."

For a moment she was frozen in the horror of what he was asking her to do, but she was afraid too of what might happen if she didn't. In the end, she somehow parked her mind and did what she was told. She tried to hold the woman by her shoes, minimising the contact she had to have, but she realised just in time they would come off, so she braced herself and then wrapped her hands around the woman's ankles – they felt frail. Bony. At once Rob lifted his end, and, trying to keep the body level and rigid, Julia heaved the woman's legs into the air too. Julia was surprised at how light she was.

Now the emptiness of the road around them took on a different feel. Whereas before Julia had been praying to see the lights of a car, now the thought of this scared her. The idea of being caught doing what they were now doing. What would they think? She began to rush. To get the body hidden and out of the way before anyone could see what they were doing. She was almost running.

"Watch it!" Rob said. "I'm going backwards here."

"Sorry."

They drew level with the car, where Becky was busy rubbing at the frame of the bicycle with the bottom of her coat.

"Over there," Rob directed them, and they went over to the side of the road. The place where they planned to dump the body was only about forty yards from where the accident had happened, and down a ditch that was perhaps three metres across and two metres deep.

"You ready? We'll swing her in."

They lined up beside the ditch and let the body swing between them, building momentum. It felt like Julia was only half-there. Only half-doing this thing. As if in an unlikely dream.

"Now!" On Rob's command they both let go. The body flew sideways, hit the side of the ditch and tumbled the rest of the way down, splashing into the water at the bottom.

Rob had put his mobile away to free up his hands. He pulled it out again now and switched on the torch.

The woman's legs and feet had sunk out of view, and most of her stomach too, but her chest and head must have snagged on something as they stayed clear of the water. Her eyes were still open, and now her lips had pulled back too, showing her teeth. It almost looked like she had enjoyed the experience.

"Shit," Rob said.

"What?" Julia asked. "Did you think it would all go underwater?"

"No it's not that. I just thought of something."

Becky had arrived behind them now, pushing the bike before her.

"Urgh, that's freaky."

"I forgot something," said Rob. He sounded worried. "I gave her mouth-to-mouth. My DNA is gonna be all over her face."

For some reason the thought of this gave Julia a little comfort.

"You need to go down there and push her in," Rob said.

"*Me?*" Julia replied.

"Yeah, you. This is your fucking mess, isn't it?" Rob spat back. "We're just trying to help you out!"

Julia was taken aback by the sudden change in his voice. But also by the sense in his reasoning. More than that, she was terrified he might yet change his mind. So instead of arguing further she told herself this wasn't happening, and began to descend the side of the ditch. As she did so she thought how incredible it would have seemed if someone had told her an hour before that she would be doing this.

"Shit!" She swore as her foot slipped on the greasy slope.

"Here." She looked up, and saw Rob holding out his hand. She took it, and carefully climbed further down into the ditch until she was close enough to the woman's body to reach the head. Letting go of Rob now, she placed one hand into the earthy wetness, feeling the mud ooze through the fingers of her gloves, and seep inside at her wrist. With her other hand she reached out, nearly touching the woman's lips.

"What do you want me to do?" she called out.

"I don't know. Just... Splash water on it, and rub it around with your hands. Grab some leaves or something, and do it with that."

Julia hesitated a final time, then simply closed her mind and did what she was told.

"That's it. Now see if you can push her completely underwater? That way no one will find her for a while."

Again Julia did as she was being told, and she discovered that whatever the woman's body was snagged on wasn't very strong. Julia was able to push her completely underwater. The only problem was, she kept coming back to the surface.

"It's floating!" she shouted back after the third attempt.

"Wait a minute," Rob said. "I'll grab a stick, and you can pin her under the water." The light from the torch disappeared as he crossed to the other side of the road, where a couple of trees stood like silent sentinels. Slowly, Julia's eyes re-adjusted to the moonlight, and she saw the woman's eyes shining back at her. Julia looked away.

When Rob returned he handed down a forked stick, and in the light of Rob and Becky's mobile phones Julia somehow managed to pin the woman's body so that no part of her cleared the surface. When she was finished she climbed back up, her shoes now soaked through with mud, her gloves ruined.

"Well done," Becky said. She touched Julia on the shoulder.

"Now we should get the hell out of here," Rob said.

"What about the bike?" Becky reminded him. "Aren't we going to throw that in the ditch as well?"

"Shit. Yeah." Rob swung his torchlight back into the ditch. But when he went on he sounded suddenly panicked. "But there isn't any room is there? She hardly got the body in there."

"Well, what are we going to do with it?" Becky asked. "We can't just leave it here. Someone will find it." She sounded panicked too. And for a long moment no one answered.

When Rob finally did, it was like he had suddenly been taken beyond the point where he could cope with the responsibility that had been thrust upon him.

"I don't know. I don't fucking know. Maybe we should just take it?

Get it as far away from here as we can? Then it won't matter. Would it fit in the car?" Rob asked.

Together with Becky he turned to look. Julia saw them both register how small the boot on the Morris was.

"Maybe we could, like, dismantle it or something. Fit it in that way?" Becky said.

"No! There's no time," Rob replied. "Someone could come along at any moment. If they see us now, with her in the ditch, what are they going to think? We've got to get out of here!"

He stepped quickly towards the car.

"Becky, get in. Just get in."

"What are you doing?" Julia asked.

"We're gonna drive. You take the bike and ride it. When we find somewhere good we'll ditch it. But we've got to get out of here!" He was moving so quickly now that Julia didn't have time to think, much less to argue. Before she knew what was happening Becky had handed her the bike and was already in the passenger seat, putting on her seatbelt. Rob was in the driver's seat revving the engine. Each time he did so the lights brightened.

"Come on! Move. Let's go. Let's get the fuck out of here," Rob said as Becky slammed her door shut. With a lurch, the car moved forwards.

And now, feeling blind panic at the thought of being left there alone, Julia climbed astride the bicycle.

SEVEN

AT FIRST THEY DROVE FAST, the lights rapidly shrinking into the distance, and an instant panic rose up inside Julia. They were stealing her car! They were leaving her here in the middle of nowhere, with only the dead woman's bike! But then, ahead of her, the brake lights lit up on her car and it stopped. For a second Julia hesitated, but desperate to reach them she began cycling. It was a while since she had ridden a bike, and this one had a noticeable buckle to its front wheel. The dynamo lights lit up, but they were pitifully weak. Julia ignored it all, focussed only upon reaching the car. Escaping the dead and staying with the living. As she drew close, gasping with relief, she heard Rob's voice from the open window.

"Overtake us. You go in front," he said. Without questioning why, she did what she was told, wobbling past in the narrow lane. And with the lights of the car behind her it was now easier to see. She steered a straighter course as her speed increased, but felt even more unsafe. The bike was more damaged than Rob had thought. The front wheel wobbled sickeningly each time it went round. Each revolution made her veer to the right, and each time she wondered how it would feel if the car behind her were to plough into her, to knock her to the road. Just as had happened to the owner of the bicycle only a half hour before. She felt tears streaking down her face again. She wanted to wipe them away but was too scared to move her hand from the bike's handlebar.

Julia soon tired. Her legs were not used to such exercise, and she had been pedalling frantically, but Rob drove so close behind that she was terrified of slowing, in case the car ran into her. For the first time since buying the little car she didn't think of its sloping nose as something full of character and charm, but as a dangerous lump of metal, and she fought to keep away from it.

They reached a hill. It wasn't steep, but even so she had to work much harder to keep the bicycle moving at all. Behind her the car drew even closer, almost touching her, as if Rob wanted to push her to go faster. Rob revved the engine, and called out of the window for her to speed up, and between panting breaths she yelled at him she was going as fast as she could. Some of her fear became anger, and it gave her the power to keep the pedals turning. Eventually the hill levelled out, but now she faced a new danger. Now the road plunged into a valley in the landscape, and the ribbon of tarmac part-illuminated in front of her appeared to steeply and dangerously drop away. Now she didn't need to pedal at all; the bike was seemingly being sucked downward. Julia clutched at the brake levers in a new panic. It seemed that the damaged wheel was going to send her careering into the ditch. Perhaps Rob thought the same, for he had pulled back now, which further scared Julia since it meant she was more dependent on the weak dynamo light fitted to the bicycle. But the bike, now up to speed, stabilised a little, and on some level Julia – the wind sweeping her hair out behind her – felt a visceral thrill from the sensation of simply falling, momentarily letting gravity choose her fate.

Then the hill bottomed out, sapping Julia's speed. Ahead of her she saw the darkness of another incline looming ahead of her. But then she heard the honk of her car horn. Her chest still heaving, she came to a stop.

"There's a lake," Rob said from the open window. He was indicating to the left, and he papped the horn again. "Go in there."

Again, Julia did as she was told, and Rob followed her down a short dirt track that led to a parking area. When he was safely off the road, Rob turned off the engine and the lights. Julia was suddenly pitched into the dark quietness of the night.

But as her eyes adjusted she saw, through the bushes, the moon shining on the surface of water. Rob was out of the car now. Julia heard Becky getting out as well.

"It's a quarry lake. That means it'll be really deep. You just need to make sure you throw the bike a long way out."

It was a few moments before Julia was able to reply, she was panting so hard.

"No. You have to do this one. I'm not strong enough."

Rob said nothing, but Julia sensed he understood. He took the bike from her with his hands covered by the cuffs of his jacket. He wheeled it to the edge of the water, and then he lifted it and – just like they had with the woman – practised swinging it back and forth a couple of times. The only way he seemed able to do it was to swing it around, like an athletic hammer thrower, or maybe like he was dancing with it. After his practices he finally released it, right at the edge of the lake. It swung through the air, under the moonlight, but not far. Almost at once it caught the surface of the water with an ugly splash, like the black lake was some monstrous beast claiming the machine. It fell so close to the shore Julia expected a part of it to stick out, but when the water cleared, there was nothing to be seen.

"How deep do you think that is?" Becky asked.

"Deep enough," Rob said. "Now let's get out of here."

EIGHT

BANG!

Bang, BANG!

Julia woke with a start. The noise came again. She propped herself up, in her own bed. For a moment she was confused. The fragments of dreams sloughed off her like water from a surfacing submarine.

The clock on her bedside table said 11.30 a.m.

"Julia?" a voice from outside called. A jovial, genial voice. "Are you in there?"

She recognised the voice, and slowly remembered why he was here. Geoffrey said he'd pop round to see how the party had gone. His way of showing that he understood she hadn't been able to take him, and that he still supported her.

There was a moment when she felt relief. Relief that the shards of horror in her mind were about to melt away into the reality of daylight. But then came something else, the question of whether it had all been a dream or... She looked around and saw her tights, left by the bed, covered in mud.

Oh God.

She sank back onto the pillow. It was all flooding back to her now.

Her hand flew to her mouth as she remembered how she'd handled the woman's body. How she'd pushed the face under the water.

She cringed. She shuddered. She wanted to pull the covers over her head and never come out.

"Julia? Are you alright in there?" Geoffrey called again. The playful note turning to concern. She knew he was looking at her car. There was nowhere to go in Julia's village. Nowhere. If someone's car was there, they were in. Could she pretend she was sick? She had a new, fresh memory. What Rob had told her when they finally went their separate ways the night before. No, this morning.

"Whatever you do, you have to act normal."

She'd agreed, but she hadn't thought she would need to do so at once. Without even a moment to prepare.

"Julia?"

With a groan she pushed herself up off the bed, and began throwing some clothes on. Geoffrey would keep trying.

"Just coming," she called out.

Two minutes later she took the chain off the front door and pulled it open. The friendly, bearded face of Geoffrey Saunders broke into a smile.

"There you are! I was starting to get worried." From behind his back he produced a bag of *pain au chocolat*. He jiggled them about.

"Ta dah!" he said. "Pop the kettle on then. I can't wait to hear all about it."

The words, the pastries, none of it made any sense to Julia.

"Hear what?" she asked.

Geoffrey gave her a funny look and moved as if to come inside. Julia imagined herself stopping him, but reminded herself she had to act normal. It was normal for Geoffrey to invite himself inside. It was normal for her to let him in. Therefore she had to let him in. She stepped aside. But as she did so she noticed how she'd parked her little car. The front was actually in the hydrangea bush that was planted under her living room window. She remembered now that that had been a plan. An actual decision. To bury the front in there, in case anyone from the village walked past – perhaps on an early morning dog walk. She didn't want anyone noticing the front of her car, with its guilty scratches in the paintwork. But it looked strange there, almost like she'd crashed into the cottage. Had Geoffrey thought it odd how she'd parked it? She didn't know, and didn't dare ask.

"Well *you* look like you've had quite the night," Geoffrey said, once they were both in the kitchen, where Geoffrey always gravitated to. He picked up the kettle and felt its weight, to see whether it needed filling. As he did so a memory surfaced in Julia, of tearing her gloves off the night before and washing her hands in the sink. The gloves were still there, balled up in the bottom of the sink.

"No, no. Let me." Julia tried to stop him, but Geoffrey was already clicking the kettle into its base, apparently content it had enough water already.

"Don't be silly. I want you to sit down and tell me *all* about it."

Reluctantly, she did what he said. But no words came out.

"Well? Come on! I'm all ears."

Julia wondered if this was even going to be possible. The gleaming memories from the party, that had felt like they would last a lifetime, had been shredded by the horror of what came after. Now she wondered if she could even open her mouth at all. And if she could, would it be everything that had happened later that would come tumbling out? How she had run over the woman on the bicycle. How they had decided – stupidly, crazily – that they should hide her body instead of doing the sane thing of telling the police. She suddenly felt dizzy. But she couldn't hold her head. She put her elbows on the table and dropped her face into her palms.

"That good, huh? Crumbs. Well, who was there? Did anyone famous show up?"

Whatever you do, you have to act normal.

"Deborah Gooding," Julia said, lifting her head.

"No!" Geoffrey stopped what he was doing and turned around. He hadn't been watching her before, his attention taken by spooning coffee into the cafetiere. "*The* Deborah Gooding, the Booker Prize lady? You're pulling my leg!"

Julia shook her head, wondering if she were going to be sick again.

"Well, did you actually *meet* her? Or was she just there?"

Julia forced herself to concentrate. And it helped. The conversation with Deborah had been – until it was eclipsed by later events – one of the most momentous experiences of her entire life. To Julia's utter amazement, they had *chatted*. Almost like equals. Julia wondered how to express all this to Geoffrey now.

"Yeah. She was... nice," Julia managed.

"*Nice*? One of the greatest writers... No – I take that back. *Two* of the greatest writers in the country get together and that's the best you can say? Well I hope you managed to be a little more eloquent last night. Good Lord!" Geoffrey laughed at his own joke, apparently oblivious to how pale Julia had become. He continued. "I say, Julia, you're not actually hungover are you? I don't think I've ever seen you *hungover*."

Julia wondered how to respond. The idea of grasping at the excuse seemed useful, but she sensed danger too. He might go on to ask how she got home, if she had been drinking. It might make him register the badly-parked car. That might even be why he was asking. He might be putting two and two together already. He was clever. Geoffrey was clever.

"No." She willed her voice to sound as it normally did. "I just... I just haven't had my coffee yet." She forced a smile. "And it was all a bit overwhelming, I suppose." She heard in her own voice how close she was to tears.

"Oh..." Geoffrey's face crumpled with concern. "Darling! Should I ask you later? When you've had time to process it all?"

He turned around and finished making the coffee, then when he was done, placed a cup in front of her. She picked it up at once and drank as quickly as the temperature allowed her to. It helped.

"Mmmmm," Julia said. It felt like her soul was absorbing the caffeine. It helped a lot.

"Is that better?"

"I'm fine, really. I just needed that coffee. Sit down, I'll tell you all about it."

Julia forced herself to talk through exactly what happened at the party, who was there, and what she had said to them. She turned it into an exercise of discipline. She tried to remember who she had spoken to, and in what order. Whenever a moment from later tried to insert itself into the narrative she squashed it at once. All the while Geoffrey drank his coffee and ate his *pain au chocolat,* asking questions here or there, and expressing wonder at who she met, but always being clear it was nothing less than she deserved. Of course, Julia didn't mention anything about the misunderstanding over where she lived, and hence her need to drive, and obviously she didn't say anything about killing a woman on the way home.

When she had finished and their cups were empty, she began yawning, hoping he might take the hint, but instead he started talking about the latest gossip from the Rural Dorset Creative Circle, of which they were both long-standing members. It met every Friday evening, but it wasn't without its problems. A new member, Kevin, had started coming along, but he didn't seem particularly creative. He'd made little effort to contribute, and according to Marjorie who coordinated the group, so far hadn't paid his dues for the hire of the hall and the purchase of biscuits.

Julia only half-listened. It seemed incredible. Before last night, this very issue had registered quite highly on her own list of frustrations in life. The power of a little perspective.

She gave up listening altogether and wondered whether she could just tell Geoffrey. A problem shared was a problem halved and all that, and if there was anyone she could talk to it was him. He was her greatest friend. She thought for a minute. Perhaps he was her only, true friend. They always had exactly the same views when a problem – like Kevin – came along. She was tempted to confess. She imagined how he would tell her it was alright, how he would find a way to put the mess back together. But something stopped her. The sheer scale of the problem. It was more than Geoffrey could solve with his little bag of *pain au chocolat* from the shop in the village. He would insist on calling the police. And they wouldn't understand. They wouldn't accept how she had genuinely forgotten about her drinking. Nor how the woman had been so wrong to cycle with no lights, in the middle of the night. No one could. No one ever would.

"I say, I'm not boring you am I?" Geoffrey said suddenly. Julia had no idea what he might have been talking about.

"No. Of course not. I might be a bit tired still."

"Even after all that coffee? I was telling you I have a book signing in Dorchester next week. I've had two dozen copies of *The Apple Tree Killer* printed, and I was hoping you might want to come along? Obviously I know you're a superstar now, and I thought it might encourage a few other people to actually turn up."

Julia nodded. She felt too weak to protest the idea that without her no one would attend.

"You know what?" Geoffrey said a few moments later. "I'm going to love you and leave you. It looks like last night really took it out of you."

Julia gave silent thanks, and managed to raise a weak smile to her lips.

"It did a bit."

"Unless you fancy another cup of coffee first?" Geoffrey's eyes went to the kettle hopefully.

"No, really..." Julia began.

"Well, let me just wash these up then." Before Julia was able to raise a protest, he had collected the cups and plates and carried them to the sink.

"Hey, what's this?"

Julia looked up in time to see Geoffrey lifting one of her muddy driving gloves out of the sink.

"Urgh!" Geoffrey said. "What *have* you been up to?"

Julia blinked twice before an answer came to her.

"Gardening. I was... I was out in the garden yesterday. Trying to calm my nerves. They're gardening gloves."

"Really?" Geoffrey inspected the glove he was holding. "They're rather nice for gardening use." He gave her a funny look.

"Well, anyway," Geoffrey said. This time he gathered up his things and put on his jacket.

"Let me know if you need anything. I can always drop it in."

Julia smiled and walked with him to the door. As they passed through the hallway she saw the shoes she had worn the night before, covered in mud and discarded on the floor. She kicked them to one side. Geoffrey didn't seem to notice.

Outside, she watched as he climbed into his Land Rover, then waved as he drove away. Then she shut the door, put her back to it and slid down onto the floor.

* * *

It was twenty minutes before she moved. Twenty minutes while she considered the trail of evidence around the cottage. Evidence linking her directly to the killing of the night before. How had Geoffrey not seen it? How could she now cover it up? She was momentarily overwhelmed.

When she did finally get up she gathered her shoes, and tipped them into the sink with her ruined gloves. Then she turned on both taps and left them running, washing away the mud. She picked up her keys and went outside to move her car, before her neighbours saw how she'd parked. The little car looked comical buried up to the front wheels in the leaves of her hydrangea. She was amazed that Geoffrey hadn't said anything.

She climbed into the driver's seat and was hit by a wave of nausea. Just being inside the car brought everything from last night back into focus. The way the windows had steamed up with the three of them breathing so hard. The silence in the car as Rob had driven them away after dumping the bike.

She backed up a few feet and straightened the car. Then she climbed out, feeling better, but nervous too. Rob had pointed to scratches on the bonnet the previous night, but she hadn't seen them in the light. Now she crouched down to look. There were several scratches and smudges on the metal of the bumper, and when she looked closer, a significant dent in the flared wheel arch on the passenger side. All of them looked fresh. There was paint, too. Blue paint, scratched deep into the maroon of the car. An image came into her mind. Of a police team, in those funny blue suits they wear when collecting evidence, poring over her car. What would they be able to prove from those scratches and smudges? She licked a finger and tried to rub the blue paint away, but only some of it came off, transferring to her finger, and she flared in panic at the thought of that. There was more blue paint deeply embedded in the scratch. Could they link it to the bicycle? She didn't know for sure, but she'd seen enough crime dramas on the television to have a pretty good idea.

She suddenly felt exposed, standing there by the incriminating scratches, and she went inside again. The sink was now blocked with mud, and water was flowing onto the floor. She rushed to turn off the taps, and threw tea towels down to soak up the worst of the water. When that little crisis was resolved she sat at her writing desk and tried to think. But from there she could see the car again. And the dents seemed to grow with each time she glanced at them. They were like a guilty beacon, flashing for the world to see. Eventually she went outside and parked it back in the hydrangea.

She tried to pull herself together. She lit a fire in her wood burner, building it up with dry logs until it roared behind the smoked glass. Then she wrung out the gloves from the sink and fed them in, one by one. They were too wet to burn well, but after a few minutes or so of hissing steam, they dried out and finally caught. Once they did they were soon unrecognisable, just twisted black carcasses where the leather had been. The shoes were still too wet to do the same, so she hung them on the top of the iron burner to dry them first. Then she took her stockings from upstairs and burnt those. She cut her skirt and jacket into pieces with her sewing scissors, and bit by bit she fed them into the fire, too. Finally, she built the fire up again with dry wood and added the shoes. She watched as they twisted and melted behind the glass. Even with the door closed the smell was horrible.

Then she turned to her computer. She opened the internet and navigated to the website of the local newspaper. She screwed her eyes shut as the page loaded, expecting it to pop up with an image of the woman, being hoisted out of the ditch – or worse – her own face, with a policeman asking if anyone had seen *this* woman. She steadied herself with a vice-like grip on the mouse, then opened her eyes.

There was nothing. Just some scandal about primary school meals funding. She browsed around the site, as if it were possible that a woman left for dead on the road might be pushed from the front page by this story.

But it wasn't there. That meant... Julia tried to think what it meant. It meant no one had found the woman yet. That was the only thing it *could* mean. And, after all, why would they have? There was nothing to suggest that section of the road should be searched. Perhaps the woman hadn't even been reported missing yet. She might live alone. If Julia herself were to disappear it could be days before she were reported missing. Unless Geoffrey popped around sooner than that.

Two thoughts occurred to her. First, this gave her an opportunity. She could – still – do the right thing. She could hand herself into the police, and confess what had happened. Surely they would understand? She could explain it had been late, and she'd been tired – not drunk, there was no need to mention that – and perhaps use the excuse they had come up with last night. That they hadn't known what they had hit. There were a lot of deer around here. She could see them sometimes from the kitchen window, nibbling the grass around the edges of the fields.

But attractive as the idea was, there were holes. Holes that she could see straight away, so how long would it take for an experienced policeman to notice them? There was the bike to begin with. Deer might be more common these days, but they hadn't started riding bicycles yet. And the fact that *they* had moved the bike. What did that show? That they *planned* to cover it up. Was that an actual crime, even if she confessed to it now? She didn't know. She thought it probably was.

And if she confessed to the whole thing, then surely the police would also want to know where she had been coming from, that late at night? If they spoke to anyone at the party – she could barely imagine the horror of the police interviewing Deborah Gooding or Marion Brown about *her* – they would surely confirm she had been drinking.

It was all too awful.

Why had they moved the bike? Why had they been so *stupid* as to move the bike?

No. Why had *Rob* been so stupid? The original idea had been to throw it in the ditch with the dead woman. But he had panicked...

She stopped herself. What if there *was* no bike – might that actually work in her favour? After all, the scratches on her car were from the bicycle. So if the police believed the woman had been walking, they might never think to look for a bicycle. And therefore they might never think to look for a car with scratches on its bonnet filled with blue bicycle paint.

But the moment of hope died as soon as it arrived. Julia blinked as a truly horrible memory crystallised in her mind. The old woman's bony ankles. The feeling of her own hands around them, and the thin metal bands of the bicycle clips that tucked her trousers tight to them. *They could have removed them.* They could have slipped them off, then there would have been nothing to suggest she had been riding a bike. But they hadn't. It would be the first thing the police would discover.

Around the edges of Julia's vision a fierce darkness appeared, threatening to expand and take over everything. But she fought against it, gripping the sides of her chair until it receded.

She had to confess. To everything. It was the only way.

But if she confessed she would lose everything. Her book deal. Her new life. Her *old* life.

No. There must be another way. *Think. She just needed to think.* To address every issue. What else made them vulnerable? What other mistakes had they made?

Fingerprints. The police always looked for fingerprints. But Julia had worn driving gloves. So there wouldn't be any. At least, there wouldn't be any of *her* fingerprints. She remembered how Rob had instructed Becky to wipe the bicycle clean. How good a job had the girl done? There was no way to know.

And what about DNA? Julia remembered how she had vomited all over the road. Yes, she'd tried to wash it away. But wasn't DNA tiny – you couldn't get it all off, surely? Presumably – she reasoned – the longer the woman went undiscovered, the better the prospect was of her DNA (if it were there at all) being washed away by rain. Or perhaps eaten by animals. She recoiled at this thought, but swept it aside. Was there anything she could do about it? After a moment's consideration she decided there was. She could fill bottles with water mixed with bleach. She could return to the spot where it happened and do a better job of washing the road. It was a risk – she might arrive there only to find it swarming with police, who would ask her what she was doing. They could discover the bleach – the black panic began to intrude upon her vision again – but she could approach carefully, turn around if she saw any sign of police.

She envisaged how she would feel once this task was done. Comforted. For sure.

Okay. What else? Rob's DNA, on the woman's lips. Could anything be done about that? Had they done enough the night before? She cringed at the memory of her rubbing the woman's face with leaves and grass pulled from the bank of the ditch. But this time it was less from the horror of doing it, and more about the practical problems this might now present. Would it have unnaturally stained the woman's face? By now Julia's mind had the dead woman lying on stainless steel in a laboratory while a white-coated doctor calmly examined it, dictating his expert findings into a tape recorder and easily revealing everything the poor woman suffered up to and after her death. Would the police and the pathologist think this might have simply happened as she fell into the ditch? Or would this be evidence of a *crime*? Again, she had no way of knowing.

What she *did* know, however, was there was no way she was going back into that ditch. Revisiting the scene was one thing, climbing back down into the ditch quite another. If Rob's DNA was a problem it was one he would have to worry about.

That left... Oh God. Her eyes shot once again to her car sitting outside her window, as if it were patiently waiting for her thought processes to catch up with it. *The car.* The scratches on the front. How long would it take for the bike to be found? She imagined police divers already searching the lake nearby to the dead woman. It was the most obvious place to hide the damned bicycle. And once the bicycle was found, there would presumably be maroon paint scrapings on its frame. They would be a perfect match with the dents and scrapes on her car. Perhaps even with the woman's clothing. And then what? The car was registered in her name. No one else was insured to drive it. When the police found the bike it would lead them to her car, and they would have the proof. One hundred percent proof that Julia had done it.

Until that moment, Julia had loved her car. She took a certain pride in how slow it was, in how much it rattled, and even in how hard it was becoming to buy leaded petrol to keep it running. But now that pride was swept away. Now she suddenly and viscerally hated it. Feared it. It was like she could sense it sending out an invisible message to the police. It was a flashing beacon of guilt. She could imagine the police, already tuning into it. They could arrive at any moment. Drawn to her through that car.

She had to get rid of the car. Right now.

Julia's frightened mind struggled to operate. How do you get rid of a car? You sell it.

Quickly, she grabbed the mouse again and opened up her email. She began searching back through her messages. She occasionally got emails from people interested in buying her car (she had no idea how they found her email address; technology was something of a mystery to Julia). And sometimes if she parked it out in public – in the supermarket for example – she would come out to find a note stuck under its dear little wipers. She quite liked these messages; they reinforced her belief it was worth driving around in a draughty, expensive-to-run car that felt dangerously unsafe if she ever had to take the motorway.

Ah. There it was. An email from a polite gentleman in Bath. She realised she hadn't actually replied. Julia felt a stab of guilt at that. She considered it rude to not reply, even to an unsolicited approach like this one. He'd come across her ownership of the car from the *Morris Minor Owners Club* website (she dimly remembered that she had once joined). He wanted to register his interest should she ever consider selling. He'd left a telephone number as well as an email.

Julia picked up her phone, and before she could change her mind, she dialled the number.

On the third ring she slammed the phone back down.

What was she thinking?

If she simply *sold* the car, the marks on the bonnet would still be there, in all their evidential glory. And there would be a record of when she sold it. It would be the easiest piece of police work ever to connect the two. Worse, the fact she had begun selling the car the day after the accident would be concrete proof of her attempt to cover it up. It was a disastrous idea.

No. She had to *destroy* her car.

She turned back to the computer, pulled up a search window and began typing the words 'car crushing service, Dorset'. She moved her hand back to the mouse. Her finger was pressing the button to run the search, when she froze again.

She swallowed carefully. Her finger was so close to pressing the button that it felt impossible to pull away without actually doing so. But she knew that would spell disaster. Slowly – as if she were defusing a bomb – she moved her finger away. And she breathed again only when she saw the webpage didn't load. She hadn't pressed the button.

What happens *Julia*, in nearly every murder mystery you read these days? (It was a genre Julia was mildly addicted to.) The police catch the killer because of their *internet search history* (Julia wasn't quite sure on the exact term). It didn't matter if they tried to erase them on the *actual* computer. The service company, or whatever they're called, they *keep a separate record*. So how's it going to look if you're searching for a *car crushing service* the day after being accused of running someone over?

My God. She had to be more careful.

Suddenly she got up and paced the room, breathing heavily. Then her phone rang.

She didn't recognise the number at first – and then she did. It was the one she'd just dialled – the man who'd wanted to buy the car. She answered it.

"Oh, hello," a voice said. "I've just had a missed call from this number?"

"I'm sorry," Julia replied. "I dialled the wrong number."

"Oh, I see. Well, never mind."

"Goodbye," Julia blurted out, and ended the call. She set the phone down again, then stared at her reflection in the mirror on the wall. Her own, wide staring eyes looked back at her.

Everything she did right now, *everything mattered*. The police could find the body at any moment. They could be here at any moment. And the situation was far more serious now than it had been last night. Had they waited by the road, yes, it would have been disastrous, for her. She would have been breathalysed and goodness knows what would have happened then. She would have been ruined, and maybe even gone to prison. But if she was caught *now* – having conspired to cover up the crime – well that would be worse. Far, far worse. If she was caught now, prison was a *certainty*. Julia felt dizzy at the thought of that. The certain reality of it. Her skin flushed hot. She wanted to take off her clothes, take off this new, terrible reality as if it were just a set of garments, climb into the bath, and scrub it from her skin. Oh, the bliss of being able to soak and not worry about this.

And she could. She could still do that. But first she had to get rid of her car.

She went downstairs and made herself another coffee while she thought. She had already drunk three cups with Geoffrey, and normally she limited herself to just one cup a day. But she barely registered this. Besides, today wasn't normal. Today was anything but normal, and while she drank her coffee, another idea came to her.

NINE

Her first reaction was to dismiss it out of hand. But the more she thought about it, the more she was sure there was no alternative. It was an insane idea. Unthinkable. But it was the only thing she could do. And if she didn't, then it would simply mean waiting here in terror until the police came to take away her life. Not just the wonderful new life that was just coming into reach. But everything, her old life as well.

In a daze, Julia went upstairs and got changed. She put on clean underwear, and then her most chunky sweater. After a moment's thought, she pulled on jeans. It was hard to know what to wear for something like this.

Then she looked around her little cottage, wondering seriously if she would ever return to it. The idea seemed preposterous. Everything seemed preposterous. Nothing seemed real. She locked the cottage and climbed into her car. Her once-loved, now-hated car. She adjusted the seat and mirrors so that they were correctly aligned – they still didn't feel quite right where Rob had fiddled with them, him being so much bigger than she was. She checked she had her Automobile Association membership card tucked into the little pouch on the inside of the windscreen. Then she took several deep breaths, and started the engine.

Driving away from the house she felt a little better. If the police were already looking for her, then that would be the first place they would go – at least on the move she would be harder to find. But she still felt vulnerable, driving around with those scratches on full public display. Every car she passed, every pedestrian, she imagined them pointing, following her. Demanding to know who she'd hit. She checked her rear view mirror frequently for the police. But everyone ignored her. No one knew. Yet.

She thought about where to go. The nearest town was Dorchester, but she didn't want to go in that direction, because it would surely be the Dorchester police that led the investigation into the dead woman. No, better to do this somewhere else, where there was less to connect the two incidents. So instead she drove north towards Yeovil. She didn't know the town well, and she became increasingly scared as she drove, wondering if it was even suitable for what she had in mind. What if it had a pedestrianised town centre? She wouldn't be able to do it then.

That would almost be a relief.

Several times as she drove she wondered whether she was *actually* doing it at all. Could it be that she was just driving herself to the police station in Yeovil? Where she would park and calmly confess to what she had done? That seemed quite possible. And yet at the same time it felt quite possible that she was not driving at all, but imagining the entire thing. Certainly, it didn't feel as if she were in full control of her actions. She was a passenger, not in the car but in her own body. Being taken for a ride, to a destination she didn't yet know.

She shook her head to clear this thought, and then played back last night in her mind. Or rather, it began playing back, like a documentary film, projected onto the inside of her eyeballs. Rob had decided it would be safer – without discussing it with her – to not turn up at Becky's parents in the middle of the night looking as wild-eyed as they did. So he'd turned around and driven them all the way back to Southampton. To a little terraced house. They'd arrived there at about one-thirty in the morning. And then Rob had pretty much abandoned her. It meant Julia was faced with driving all the way back to her cottage – about an hour and a half drive – completely alone. She'd protested of course – if she was supposed to be over the legal alcohol driving limit, then how could Rob just send her on her way? But by then she seemed to have run out of goodwill with him or Becky. They had exchanged contact details – whose idea had that been? – and Julia had driven off.

She had tried to sleep for a while in a nearby residential street, but after a couple of uncomfortable hours she decided she was probably okay to drive. She bought coffee from a nearby petrol station and drove home. Fortunately, there had been no more incidents...

HOOOOOOOOOOOONNNNNNNNKKKKK!

In a flustered panic, Julia realised her car had drifted over onto the other side of the road. Coming straight at her – fast – was a truck. She yanked on the steering wheel and swerved back on to her own side, just in time for the truck to flash by beside her. She caught a glimpse of a driver, all stubble and greasy skin, shaking his fist at her.

"Oh my goodness," Julia said. She gripped the steering wheel tightly.

After that she forced herself to concentrate on driving until she had arrived safely in Yeovil. She followed the signs to the town centre. She wasn't sure exactly why that seemed the best place to put her plan into operation, but by that time, she was a long way past thinking straight.

When she arrived, she promptly changed her mind. The town centre was far too busy. There were parked cars, bicycles (she was giving them a very wide berth), mothers pushing prams. An elderly man struggling along the pavement on a walking frame. It was horrible, and as soon as she could she turned off the main high street and just followed where the roads took her. She didn't want witnesses, she decided. At least not too many of them. But did that even make sense? Did she need them? She wasn't sure. Didn't know. The fourth coffee was wearing off and she was beginning to feel tired. Sooooo tired.

Suddenly she just wanted to get this over and done with.

By then she had somehow arrived on a wide but not busy road, on an ugly industrial estate. Flat roofed commercial units were laid out on either side. A car garage. A little food processing plant. But no people. Yet coming towards her, still some way off, was a Post Office van, in shiny red livery. It looked quite new. New enough to have airbags, Julia thought. Or a part of her thought. The majority of her brain was no longer thinking. It was way past that. She was simply acting, driven along by a primordial sense of preservation. Fear. Desperation.

The van drew closer. Close enough that she could make out the driver, a young Asian man. He looked to be whistling. Like Postman Pat, Julia thought. The cartoon character that children watched. Although *he* wasn't Asian. At least, he hadn't been when she was little. It was possible that he *was* portrayed as Asian these days – she had no reason to watch children's television and it was quite irritating how politically correct everything had become. *Or gay.* Maybe Postman Pat was gay these days. Not that there would be anything wrong with that. Nothing wrong with her agent being gay either, come to that. Although he could have *told* her. It would just have nice if he'd *mentioned* it. Not that it was important, it was more about being civil. After all she was only his highest-earning author. By a very long way. That wouldn't hurt would it? The other one, his partner, he'd been nice. Was Postman Pat gay? A gay Asian?

Oh heavens!

Julia gripped the wheel harder again, feeling her arm muscles ache from the tension. This was really going to happen. It wasn't her doing it, but it was going to happen. It seemed quite impossible, but also quite certain. Julia had entirely ceased to be in control of her body. It was controlled by someone else.

As the van drew nearly alongside, its driver was utterly oblivious to the streams of consciousness running through the mind of the woman in the jauntily approaching Morris Minor. So he wasn't even looking when Julia swung the steering wheel violently, so that her little car lurched onto a collision course with the van. It was only the movement that caused him to look, seeing the car's thin front tyre appear almost deflated such was the additional pressure from the sudden change of direction. He stopped whistling. He tried to hit his brakes and steer out of the way at the same time. But there was no time. He began to scream but it was muffled by the explosive ballooning of his airbag as the two vehicles smashed together.

TEN

IF JULIA – or whatever part of her hyper-stressed, caffeine-soaked and sleep-deprived brain was in control at that point – had expected she would black out on impact, she was to be immediately disappointed.

The details of the actual collision were blurry. There was a screech of some sort, and then a massive, jarring *bang!*

This was immediately followed by the feeling of being pulled violently sideways, by a force of such incredible power it was almost comforting. But that was immediately followed by a sudden and shocking pain in her face as her head hit the steering wheel, then more eye-watering pain in her legs, and then in her back. She let out a horrified, shocked scream, and then found everything had stopped moving.

And though Julia had supposed she would merely wake up in hospital at this point, that didn't happen either. She found herself sitting back in her seat, the windscreen in front of her shattered. The bonnet of the car, which had stretched and dropped down to the headlights in a way she always found rather comely, was now crumpled up and short. The van she had hit was nowhere in sight, at least, until she turned her head – at the cost of a huge, shooting pain that went down her neck and towards her pelvis. But then she saw it. Somehow it had spun around so that it was facing the same direction that she was. No. She was wrong again, it was *her* car that had spun around. The greater weight of the van had meant it had barely deviated from its original path. She had hit it, and been bounced right off again, like a tennis ball hitting a wall.

Through pain that seemed to crystallise the view from her eyeballs, Julia watched as the driver of the van tried to get out. His airbag had gone off and he had to fight against the folds of material, and then bash at the door to get it to open. When he did, he staggered out. For a second he rested, with one hand on the top of the cab of his vehicle, then he made his way over to her.

"Urgh," he said. His eyes were actually spinning around, as if he might really be a cartoon character.

"You alright, lady?" He was panting as if he'd run a sprint. Then he seemed to force himself to focus.

"Oh shit," he said. It took Julia a moment to understand this was in response to the way she looked.

"Don't move, yeah? I'll call an ambulance. Just don't move anything. Okay?"

The idea that Julia might move would have been humorous in other circumstances. The pain was like nothing she had ever experienced. She felt it in her face, and sensed from the wetness that blood was leaking from her nose. She felt pain in her legs, but most of all she felt it in her back. It was like being gripped from behind by a giant, angry bear. Every breath was a new, necessary agony.

Somehow thoughts made their way into Julia's brain. Had she overdone it? Two words formed and seemed to be crawling higher in her consciousness.

Spinal injury.

She'd watched a television programme about it recently. One of those fly-on-the-wall shows following the emergency services as they deal with car accidents. RTIs they called them. Road Traffic Incidents – because apparently there was no such thing as an accident any more, there was always something that caused them. This show featured a woman in a car who had had an accident. An incident. And everyone had thought she might have a spinal injury. They'd interviewed her later from her wheelchair, because they'd been right and the woman would never walk again.

Julia moaned, out loud. What had she done? How could making herself disabled possibly make this any better? She moaned again, but it hurt too much, so she stopped and tried to sit still. Tried to understand how she could be in so much pain, and not be unconscious.

"They said they'll be here quick, just hang in there," the van driver said now. "What happened anyway? Did you have a blowout, yeah? It looked like it. Like you suddenly couldn't control the car. I saw it, yeah?"

Julia had only some idea what a blowout was, but already she was realising how this accident had to look like an accident. She tried to nod and it was agonising.

"Don't move! Yeah?" Postman Pat shouted at her. "You might have a spinal injury or something. I saw this programme on it. Just stay real still." He had his hands out to calm her down, as if she might climb from the car and start fighting.

When the pain receded enough that she could form a word, Julia replied.

"Okay," she said. And began to cry.

"They're coming lady, okay? They're on their way. Just don't move. Stay right still."

This time Julia knew not to nod.

Those ten minutes before the ambulance arrived seemed to take forever. Every breath had to be anticipated, braced for, and then taken, even though it caused a new wave of pain. Some people came up close to the car and peered in. Most moved away again, expressions of horror on their faces. Postman Pat told everyone who would listen that Julia had suffered a blowout to her tyre, that he'd actually seen it happen, and it was this that had sent her careering over to the wrong side of the road. One man took it upon himself to make sure no one tried to move, or even touch Julia. Voices told her to 'hang in there'. Julia wondered if she might not. If she was actually going to die. A part of her wished for it.

Eventually the noise of an ambulance sounded in the distance, and soon after Julia could make out the flashing blue lights with the corners of her eyes. Two green-suited figures came out. They acknowledged the driver of the van, then asked him to wait in the ambulance. Clearly, Julia was their priority.

Then they were beside her. They asked her name, and did their best to assess her injuries. They didn't look happy. Julia kept focusing on breathing in and breathing out. Bearing the impossible pain with every breath.

"We're not going to move you until the fire brigade get here, Julia," the first paramedic explained. She was a young woman, with very blonde hair.

"It's just a precaution, but we don't want to risk moving you until we've had a little look at your neck. Is that okay? We're just going to pop this neck brace on until we can get you in the ambulance." She turned away and talked to her colleague. Julia caught the word 'helicopter'. From the corner of her eye Julia saw their concerned looks.

Then the woman came back, smiling again. "We can give you a little injection for the pain? If you'd like?"

"Yes, please," Julia croaked. She felt like she were drowning and had just been offered a breath of air.

By the time the police car turned up the injection had gone in. And now the pain had receded a little, like an outgoing tide. Still there, just not so *close*.

Two officers began speaking with the paramedics, far enough away from Julia that she couldn't hear what was being said. Then they spoke to the driver of the van. Out of the corner of her eye Julia could see him gesticulating with his arms, showing how the two cars had come together. Several times the officers turned around and looked across at Julia. Finally they came over.

"Hello," one of them said. It was a woman. "My name is PC King from Yeovil police station. Try to stay calm, I'm here to help you. How are you feeling?"

Julia managed to grunt a reply.

"Felt better."

"I'm not surprised, you've had a good old shunt here. Now we're going to get you cut out of your vehicle. But while we're waiting, I need to get an account of what happened from you. Is that okay?" The police officer woman had a strong local accent and she finished the sentence with a wide smile.

Julia grunted again.

"It's Julia, isn't it? Can you state your full name?"

Julia grunted her answer. The tranquillisers were really kicking in now.

"Do you remember what happened at all, Julia?"

Julia thought. The word 'blowout' formed in her mind.

"It felt like a blowout, maybe."

PC King wrote this down.

"How did it feel exactly?"

Julia didn't know, but some of the words that Postman Pat had said repeated in her mind. She parroted them back, and they seemed to please PC King.

"That's great. Really good. Now, Julia, I have to do this I'm afraid." She cleared her throat and began what was clearly a well-practiced speech.

"As I suspect you of driving a motor vehicle on a public road which has been involved in a road traffic collision, I require you to provide me with a roadside specimen of breath for analysis. Failure to do so is an arrestable offence. Is that okay?" PC King smiled again with a little eye roll. As if to show she had to do this.

Julia was about to grunt that that was fine, when a new thought occurred to her. One she hadn't even considered. *What if she was still over the limit from the day before?* The irony of that seemed brutal.

"Grrnnngg," she said.

"That's lovely." The policewoman smiled.

There were more questions, lots of them. About what Julia had drunk and when, and whether she had used mouthwash. Julia's answers all went down on a form, and she became increasingly sure she was going to fail the test. What then? Would she be in as much trouble as she had just tried to escape from? Finally, she watched PC King unwrap a clear plastic tube and fix it to a fluorescent yellow box.

"The machine is asking your age?"

Is it? Julia thought, and told her.

"Thank you. I will hold the device. What I require from you is to take a deep breath before creating a tight seal around the end of the tube with your lips, and providing a long, continuous breath until I tell you to stop. Is that okay?"

Julia blew. It hurt like hell, even through the drugs. The policewoman didn't tell her to stop until she was nearly flat out of breath, and then she inspected her box. Eventually it beeped at her. Julia waited to hear her fate.

"Okay Julia, I'm pleased to tell you you've passed the test. You can relax now. The fire brigade has just arrived, they're going to get you out of here. Don't worry about anything. We'll get the car cleaned up. Now, is there anyone you'd like us to contact?"

Julia gave the woman Geoffrey's name, and watched as she wrote it down in a little notebook.

Then the firemen arrived. Burly men with yellow helmets and heavy-looking uniforms. They had buzzing saws and strong arms that passed things underneath different parts of her body. Julia was finally slipping out of consciousness at this point. The only part that stuck in her memory was when they moved her.

"One," the leader of the team said, as they gathered around her and the spinal board.

"Two – gently now."

"Three!"

They lifted, and the pain roared like a giant woken from his sleep. It crashed around her body and only began to back off when she'd been transferred to the ambulance and the doors were shut.

They raced through the streets. Through eye-watering pain, Julia could hear the sound of the siren.

Still she didn't pass out.

ELEVEN

In the hospital, Julia thought she was dying, and she hurt so much she thought this probably for the best. Later, she would remember a procession of doctors examining her, asking her what she could feel and where she hurt, bizarre questions about what year it was, who was President of the United States – and then backing off to have long discussions about her answers. She was x-rayed, wheeled into a huge round CAT scan machine, and then she was told they were going to operate.

Only then, some two hours after the collision, was she finally allowed to drift off to sleep and escape from the chaos that had descended upon her life.

When she awoke, it was a little like she had supposed it would be in the moments before the crash. She was in a private room, lying on her back in a bed with blue blankets, and next to her an ECG machine was beeping softly along with her heartbeat. Soothingly. Next to that stood a number of cards, and two vases of flowers. Next to them, a very crumpled, sleeping Geoffrey half-sat and half-lay across a chair.

Julia surveyed the room. Her eyes were drawn to her bed, stretched out in front of her. There was the outline of her legs beneath the blanket. Preparing herself for a jolt of pain she tried to move them, but nothing happened. She tried again, and again they wouldn't move. It felt like they were moving, but her eyes told her otherwise. She felt a physical spasm of panic. The memory of those two words.

Spinal injury.

Could she even feel them? She didn't know. What did that mean? She tried to calm herself. Was she paralysed? She thought she felt an itch in her right leg, but to her horror the sensation appeared to come from some way to the right of where the leg actually was.

"Effry," she said, desperately. She didn't understand why her voice didn't work. Had she lost the power of speech, as well as her movement? Would she spend the rest of her life in one of those wheelchairs that talks for you? The only thing that seemed to work properly was her heart, which was rapidly accelerating. The ECG's soothing beeps weren't quite so soothing any more.

"Efffrrrry!" she repeated, trying her hardest to increase the volume this time. But he didn't wake up. Julia began to cry, but now she noticed that her hand was resting close to a remote control with a red button on it. She looked at it for a long while, wondering how to make her fingers move. Aghast in horror that she needed to wonder.

It was just a few inches from her hand. She stared at it and slowly the hand began to move towards it. Almost as if it was a separate living creature, not physically connected to her at all. A five-legged crab crawling over the bed, dragging her arm behind it. Finally it arrived, her forefinger pressed the button, and a loud buzzer sounded somewhere out in the hallway. Geoffrey still didn't wake up.

About a minute later a nurse came swiftly into the room.

"Hello!" she said to Julia, in an impossibly bright voice. "Welcome back!"

Julia stared in confusion. Where had she been? Maybe they hadn't expected her to wake at all?

"You've been asleep for nearly 48 hours," the nurse told her. "That's very good." She smiled, as if to reassure Julia she hadn't been overstaying her welcome. She bustled around, doing what nurses do.

"Your poor friend here has insisted on sitting with you the whole time. I told him to go home." She looked across at Geoffrey kindly. "He looks exhausted, poor dear." For the nurse, Geoffrey's condition seemed to warrant more sympathy than Julia's. Maybe that was a good sign?

"Am I...?" Julia began, then gave up at the impossibility of pronouncing 'disabled' or even giving voice to the thought.

The nurse stopped what she was doing. "I'll call the doctor now and he can explain it to you. Don't go anywhere."

Was that a joke? Julia wondered. The sort of joke you told people who couldn't move?

But at that point Geoffrey woke up, began to stretch and then noticed that Julia was awake. He jumped up at once.

"How are you feeling?" he asked. The concern and care was heavy in his voice.

"I can't feel anything," she said, crying again.

Before Geoffrey could reply a doctor came sweeping into the room. His white coat was open and he wore a chequered golfing jumper underneath.

"That's just the drugs, you'll feel plenty when they wear off. You don't want to be in a hurry there, believe me." He raised his eyebrows and snatched up the notes from where they hung on the end of Julia's bed.

"Best thing you can do is sleep it off. So well done there. Now, has your friend here filled you in on what you've done?"

Julia glanced at Geoffrey and shook her head.

"No."

"You've suffered a rotation fracture of the upper part of the spine. That's a transverse process fracture and a fracture-dislocation." The doctor sounded impressed and Julia blinked.

"Would you like me to explain that?" The doctor's eyebrows flicked up with the question, but he didn't wait for an answer.

"Each vertebra has two transverse processes. These are extensions on either side of the bone that connect to ligaments and muscle. Like little wings, really. What's happened is you've chipped them. Several of them. It's quite rare." He nodded, as if in agreement with himself.

She blinked again and realised Geoffrey was squeezing her hand. Still, she barely felt it.

"Now, it's usually the result of an abnormal bending to one side or violent twisting, sometimes from wrestling, but more often from a car accident. I understand you managed to do a full 180-degree skid, back-wards? That would certainly do it." The doctor gave a cheery smile.

"So, what does that..." Julia wasn't even sure if she got the words out. If she did, the doctor ignored her.

"Now, you might be feeling a little bit numb. That's nothing to worry about and just the result of the drugs we're using to stabilise you. We'll try taking you off those now, unless your screams wake up all the other patients." He stopped and tipped his head to one side.

"Don't worry, I'm winding you up. There's plenty of short and long-term pain relief we can try you on. But I am afraid the recovery from this injury can be rather a painful experience. That's the bad news."

There was a silence while Julia and Geoffrey took in what the doctor had said.

"Is there any good news?" Geoffrey asked in the end.

"Oh yes. The good news is the spinal cord itself is unaffected, there's no weakness. The stability of the spine remains secure. You'll be in bed for a few weeks but it shouldn't have any effect in the longer term. Apart from the pain. That's the good news."

It took some time for the good news to sink in.

"Oh and there's one more bit of bad news."

"What's that?"

"Your car, I'm afraid. Nice little classic Morris Minor? I hear that's a total write-off."

TWELVE

WHEN GEOFFREY WAS CONVINCED that Julia was okay he agreed to go home and sleep, telling Julia she should relax and concentrate on getting better. There followed a stream of interruptions from doctors and nurses, with forms to say what she couldn't eat and others to say what she wanted to eat. But finally, Julia was left alone. Perhaps it hadn't gone exactly as she'd planned, but the car was written off. The car was dealt with. She was safe.

But even if that was true, relaxation wasn't easy to achieve. For one thing, the pain seemed to defy the drugs the doctors had prescribed. Yes, they took an edge off it, but it remained there stubbornly. It seemed to be base camped somewhere in her lower back, but would send out exploratory expeditions down her legs, or out into her arms. Raiding parties of pain. Even something so simple as finding a position to lie in – letting her body weight rest upon the mattress – hurt to the point of distraction. And her muscles ached from the effort of trying to maintain a tolerably pain-free position.

Slowly, though, Julia's more fundamental predicament ballooned to take control of her thoughts again. So the car was written off. Did that mean it would be crushed? She remembered the way the bonnet had looked, all crumpled and buckled, the paint peeling off from the twisted metal. It seemed difficult to believe there would be any evidence remaining from the impact with the bicycle. She couldn't know for sure, but she felt confident the car was dealt with. What did that leave?

The woman's body. By now, someone must have found it.

There was a TV screen on a huge articulating arm that was just in reach, and below the screen was a button labelled 'internet'. She pulled the screen towards her, and read that she needed to buy credits to use the internet and the television, but she could listen to the radio. Peeved at this, she tuned the device to a local radio station, and waited through tedious pop songs and cheap-sounding adverts (one of which asked her whether she had recently been injured in an accident) for the news to come on. When it did, she learned that, if the woman's body had been discovered, it hadn't made the local news.

When the nurse next came in to check on her, Julia asked her how she could use the internet.

"Your purse is just on the chair there," the woman replied. "Your friend Geoffrey had it recovered from the car. Shall I get it for you?"

Inside, Julia found her phone, with its battery presumably dead since it wouldn't switch on, and her purse with its credit card. She spent a frustrating half-hour using arrow keys on the TV's remote to painfully add her credit card details, but eventually she was online. She thought carefully before selecting any webpage. It wouldn't do now to give away her obsession with the woman. But Julia thought it wouldn't look suspicious to have a look at the local newspaper's site.

Again, there was nothing about a woman's body being discovered in a ditch.

It began to rain, beating against the window. The light was fading too, as a dark cloud slid over the hospital. For the first time since arriving there, Julia noticed there was still a world outside. Beyond the chaos in her mind.

THIRTEEN

It CONTINUED to rain all night.

The woman would be found eventually, Julia knew that. But for the time being there was nothing she could do. And with every passing hour, surely, her situation was getting better? The road would be being washed clean, the water in the ditch getting deeper.

Was there anything else? Any other loose ends she hadn't considered? Julia bit her lip. There was one. Well, two.

The couple who had helped her – Becky and Rob. It wasn't quite true to say that Julia hadn't considered them a threat up to this point. They were always there, in a corner of her mind. But not ready to come out. Now she had a little space to think, she could admit to herself that they were a problem. When she thought about them, the dilemma they represented came more clearly into focus.

Obviously they knew everything. Well, not *everything*. Presumably they didn't know Julia was currently sitting in hospital, having damn-near paralysed herself. But they certainly knew enough.

They knew she had been drink-driving. They knew a woman had been knocked down and killed. They knew Julia had tried to cover it up. Three crimes. Any of which could ruin her.

On the other hand, they had *assisted* in covering up the woman's death – it had been Becky's idea, for goodness sake. And Rob had taken the lead in carrying it out. So was it right to say that made them as guilty as she was? Perhaps. Would that be enough to keep them from going to the police? She didn't know.

Taking a pessimistic perspective, it certainly seemed possible they might be feeling so remorseful about what they had done that they were even now speaking to the police, confessing their part in the crime and incriminating her.

It was horribly possible. Perhaps even likely. Her fight or flight instinct surged within her. But she was unable to move; there was no one to fight against, except her own mind.

After moments – she didn't know how many – of pure panic, she forced herself to calm down. Why did they get themselves involved, Becky and Rob? Answering this question suddenly became important. It was because they were *kind*. Becky in particular. She had understood how important *The Glass Tower* was, not just to Julia, but to the wider world of literature. And she understood how unfair the situation Julia had found herself in was. Suddenly faced with losing everything for one little mistake, and all for a woman who clearly shouldn't have been out cycling late at night with no lights on.

Perhaps she could rely on Becky *not* to go to the police. Because she would continue to want to support Julia? Continue to recognise the importance of *The Glass Tower?* Because she would continue to be kind?

Maybe. But there was another side to that. Becky's kindness would apply to others, too. Becky was simply the sort of person you could rely on to do the right thing. What was the right thing in these circumstances? A woman had *died*. She would have relatives, perhaps a husband. They would be worried she was missing. And when the body was found, Becky was exactly the kind of person who would compromise herself. She would go to the police whatever the repercussions might be.

Rob was different. He *hadn't* come across as particularly nice – in fact, quite the opposite. She hadn't warmed to him at all, Julia realised now, and the thought surprised her. But actually, that made him more her ally. It wasn't hard to imagine Rob cautioning Becky against going to the police, to shield them both from danger. It was precisely the fact that Rob *wasn't* very nice that made him her best hope now.

Why had they got involved in the first place? Her mind reset to this question, and this time she nearly caught the answer that flashed quickly through her head.

Why had Rob got involved? He didn't care about Julia. He'd made that clear enough. He just wanted a lift home because his van didn't work. He didn't *read*. He had taken no interest when she and Becky had been talking about literature. In fact, he only seemed to even listen when...

Julia's mind lit up as if floodlights had been switched on inside her head.

Rob had only agreed that he and Becky should do anything to help after he remembered the money.

Rob only helped because *he planned to blackmail her*.

Julia looked around the room in sudden fear, as if Rob might leap out from behind the chair dressed as a highwayman. *My goodness*, Julia thought. How much did he want?

Then another memory crashed in. The little bursts of the LED flashing on Rob's phone as he had moved around the accident site, taking photographs. He had said he wanted to record the scene for the police, so that they would be able to drive and get help. But that was never the case. He'd wanted *evidence*. Evidence he could later use as leverage against Julia. She remembered how she'd had to shield her eyes against the brightness of the flash. He'd been trying to get her face in the pictures.

As the shock of this realisation receded, it left behind a grim positive. If Rob planned to blackmail her, then he wasn't planning to go to the police. Because if she went to prison, there would be nothing left to blackmail her with. There would be no money either. So – was this good news? Was Rob's poor character going to keep her from prison?

A new thought occurred to her. If Rob were planning on blackmailing her, might he not already have done so? They had exchanged email addresses, at the end of that terrible night – and now she thought about it, that had been his idea too. Maybe there was already a demand for cash waiting in her inbox?

She turned back to the hospital entertainment system, and struggled to enter her email username and password. She worried, as she did so, that the system the hospital used might in some way record what emails she got, but she decided that was unlikely. It wasn't something she'd ever read about in any of her murder mysteries. As a precaution, she told herself that she would just look at who the emails were from, and not open them. If there was an email from Rob she would know what it was about anyway, and could open it later, somewhere safer.

Julia had received more emails in the last three days than she normally got in a month. There were emails from Geoffrey, copying her in on how he had upgraded her to a private room. There were messages from her publisher, several from Marion, two from James McArthur, and even – gratifyingly – one from Deborah Gooding, the Booker prize-winning author she had spoken with at the party. Julia looked around when she saw that email, as if to see if there was anyone nearby who she could show it to. But there was nothing from Rob or Becky. Julia checked again, certain that she must have missed it. She checked her spam folder, in case it had inadvertently been directed there. Still nothing.

At first Julia felt confused. A little cheated almost, that she had figured Rob out but he hadn't yet proved her right. But then she decided that all it demonstrated was that he had decided to wait before issuing his demands. To let her suffer before he turned the screw. Julia felt further convinced of his general poor character the more she thought about it, but she was tiring now. It was too much thinking for her drug-addled brain.

Julia let the whirlwind of thoughts slip from her mind, and then went back to her inbox. She began reading through the messages she had received. As she was doing so – seeing all the expressions of goodwill and messages of support – she began to feel as if her accident had been just that, an accident.

The last email she read was from James McArthur. It also happened to be the most important.

In it he detailed, in a rather business-like manner, how he had now received the money from the auction of the worldwide rights to *The Glass Tower*, and would be transferring the balance to her, minus his percentage. It was a long and impersonal way of telling Julia that, for the first time in her life, she was rich.

She read on, stunned anew. She'd known, of course, that the money was coming. But it had taken so long to arrive that she'd begun to doubt she would ever actually receive it. But, according to James, the money was in her account now, or at least had left his. James had gone on to detail his own costs, most of which she hadn't known about until that point. They included a 'contract fee', expenses and something termed 'supplementary charges' – which, together with McArthur's industry-beating 17.5 percent, meant he had earned a whopping half-million pounds from the deal. Even so, at the end of the email was the figure that McArthur had transferred in Julia's bank account the previous day. Nearly £2,000,000.

It was a mind-boggling, thought-blocking, almost bed-wetting amount of money. And for a short while it succeeded where all the drugs had so far failed – it eviscerated her pain.

FOURTEEN

SHE HAD two million pounds in her account. Well, nearly.

McArthur's email went on to remind her that income tax would be due on the sum, and that it was vital she took financial advice immediately. He said he could recommend a number of financial advisers, but noted that all were based in London, and she would have to travel to meet them. He asked if she knew anyone locally who had experience in similar financial matters who might be able to assist her.

Julia thought for a moment. For some reason the only person who came to mind was Marjorie, who ran the Rural Dorset Creative Circle, for which she extracted fifty pounds a year from everyone who turned up more than three times, in order to pay for the hall and the biscuits. She blinked the idea away. Ridiculous.

Half a million pounds? she suddenly thought. Her bloody agent had taken half a million pounds of her money?

Julia puffed out her cheeks. The pain in her back returned. It had never really gone away, just hidden itself in the top of her legs for a while. She needed to wee, too. One of her earlier visits from the nurse had been to explain how the female urinal she had been issued with worked. She looked at it now. It was like some sort of watering can, made – inexplicably – from a clear plastic, so you got to show off whatever colour your wee was when you handed it to the nurse for emptying. Gritting her teeth against the onslaught of pain from moving, she slipped it into position.

Half a million bloody pounds, she thought again, once she had filled the urinal with a deep yellow, almost orange liquid.

FIFTEEN

Soon after, the body was found.

Julia learnt about it from her hospital bed. She hadn't even been watching for it at the time, and only had the local news on while waiting for a quiz programme she had grown fond of to start. But suddenly it was just as she'd imagined it. The studio presenter said something about a grim discovery near Dorchester, and then cut away to another presenter who was at the scene. And then an energetic young woman in a waterproof jacket filled the screen. She was standing on the same stretch of road where the accident had happened – it actually looked so different in the day that Julia was only able to presume it was the same stretch – and behind her two police cars stood parked so as to block the road from traffic. Behind them Julia could make out other vehicles, but not much more.

"Yes, Dominic, a farmer made a grim discovery today in a drainage ditch on this flooded stretch of the B454. This is a part of the road that is prone to flooding, and following the heavy rain of the last few nights it did indeed flood. When a local farmer tried to clear the debris that builds up in the drainage ditches to let the water flow away, that's when he made the gruesome discovery. It seems that the body of a woman was *in* the ditch, and that's what was causing the obstruction."

The presenter was having to work to tone down her excitement.

"The questions currently are – who is she? How did she get there? Dominic, at this stage both of these questions remain unanswered..."

There wasn't much more. Probably because the TV journalists didn't know anything else at this stage, but maybe also because what *was* known bordered on the too-grim-for-local-news, which usually featured snippets from the local football club, or reports into Dorchester's thriving High Street.

Julia watched the piece in a state of shock. When it finished, and the news had moved onto a report about Dorchester High Street's growing vegan movement, she turned the hospital TV/internet device (which she had now more or less mastered) onto the internet, and went at once to the local newspaper's website.

Mystery Body Found in Ditch

The headline dominated the website, but the article that followed provided Julia with little new information, other than the fact that the road was so badly flooded it had been impassable during the 24 hours preceding the discovery, and that it was this that had prompted the farmer to drive into the flood in his tractor.

But soon, more information came out.

The next day her identity was known. The dead woman was Jessica Lloyd, a seventy-five-year-old resident of a small hamlet a few miles outside Dorchester. She was well-known in her village, where most had considered her something of an eccentric. She had a reputation for striding energetically along the edges of the nearby fields, or cycling the country lanes on her bicycle. She was also quite deaf, which made it difficult to communicate with her, and quite rude, which meant that not many people tried in any case. She had been married – many years ago – to a school teacher, but after his death she had lived the life of a virtual recluse. She had no children, and no surviving close relatives.

The police were treating the death as unexplained. They made it clear in a press conference – of which only a frustratingly small snippet was shown on the TV news – that they believed Mrs Lloyd had been riding a bicycle at the time of her death, and that said bicycle had not been recovered from the scene. But it wasn't clear whether any firm conclusions had been drawn from this. Perhaps, Julia thought, they had already worked out that someone had tried to cover up the woman's death by hiding her bicycle – or perhaps they thought someone else had simply found it by the side of the road and taken it?

This second possibility was given some credence by the appeal the police went on to make. They asked for anyone who might have witnessed the accident to contact them, but were also appealing for anyone who had seen, or even taken, a bicycle from the side of the road to come forward. A photograph was shown of a bicycle very similar to the one Mrs Lloyd was believed to have been riding at the time.

However, there was a sense – evident in the amount of space devoted to the story on the local TV news and the local newspaper – that they were quickly losing interest in the story. It might have been different had the mystery woman turned out to be younger, prettier, or less widely considered to be a local loony. It seemed that the police and the journalists were somewhat going through the motions, pursuing this case only until something a bit more interesting came along.

Though Julia noted this, it did little to calm her nerves, and when, moments later, the door to her hospital room opened and a uniformed police officer walked in, she nearly leapt out of her bed in shock.

"Hello again, Julia! Ooooh, you look in a bit of a state."

It was PC King, the same female officer who had breathalysed Julia at the scene of the accident. Had Julia been able to get out of bed and run, she would have certainly done so. But that being impossible she was forced to lie still – perhaps play dead – and await her fate. They had found her. Julia didn't know how they had done it. But they had found her. She wondered if she would be handcuffed.

"Do you mind if I sit down?" PC King asked. Julia shook her head and the policewoman did so, an act complicated by the range of gadgets attached to her belt. When she'd found a comfortable position, PC King leaned forward and smiled.

"So, Julia, I'm just here to tell you we've concluded our investigation into the accident. We weren't able to get any useful evidence from your vehicle, it was too badly damaged, but a number of witnesses provided statements saying your front right tyre burst, causing the swerve across

into the opposing carriageway and into the other vehicle. A blowout."
She smiled sympathetically.

"So, I'm pleased to tell you that Yeovil police will be taking no further action on the matter."

Her job done, PC King looked awkward for a moment.

"So, err, I hope you get better soon."

She backed away out of the room.

The next day, Julia was discharged from the hospital.

SIXTEEN

TWO WEEKS later Julia had still not replaced her car, so she had to travel over to Southampton by public transport. That meant calling a taxi to take her from her cottage to Dorchester station, and then the train the rest of the way. No doubt Geoffrey would have given her a lift into Dorchester – or even all the way to Southampton if she had asked – but she didn't want him knowing where she was going.

The whole time Julia had been in hospital, Rob had failed to make contact with her. This surprised her. Julia was certain now it was just a matter of time before his grubby little blackmail demand came in. But his delay gave her time to formulate, and put into practice, a counterplan of her own. In the end, it was she who made contact first.

She made no mention of the idea in her email, but simply asked if the three of them might meet up. She'd suggested the Southampton branch of Waterstones bookstore, partly because it was much closer, and therefore more convenient for them – Julia didn't know if Rob's van had been fixed – but also because it was somewhere she felt she would be *protected*, surrounded by so many books. There was another reason, too. Geoffrey had mentioned how he had passed by the window and seen it was filled with promotional stands for *The Glass Tower*. And that was something Julia had to see for herself.

When Rob emailed back, he rather bluntly demanded to know what she wanted to talk about, without even agreeing to meet. At first this threw Julia a little. She had assumed that – since he was poised to contact her – he'd jump at the opportunity. But when she thought about it, his attitude made more sense. He was planning to blackmail her. He probably had a method worked out already, and he would be wary that this meeting might affect his plans. Actually, his was the natural response. She replied simply, saying it was very important. In his next email he agreed to meet.

On a whim, she had bought herself a first-class ticket for the train to Southampton. She couldn't recall ever travelling this way before, and it somehow seemed to suit her new status. Besides, her back was still giving her a lot of pain so she thought the more comfortable seats would help.

It was strange, adjusting to having money. When she arrived in Southampton she passed a branch of her bank, with a cash machine just inside the door. There was no one using it so she quickly pushed her way inside and slipped her card into the slot. On the options screen she pressed the button to show the balance on her account. She stared at the figure for a long time. Then she drew herself up taller, reclaimed her card, and went on her way.

The displays for *The Glass Tower* were fabulous. Almost half of the front window of the store was given over to a cardboard cut-out of the lighthouse as rendered on the book cover, half-set into the rock from which it rose up, tapered and elegant. Arranged around that, on various upturned boxes covered with matte black paper, were dozens of copies of the hardcover edition of her book. For about five minutes Julia simply stood in the street, staring at the beautiful display created entirely from her story. Then, reluctant that she had to look away, she pushed her way into the store.

She passed a table where dozens more copies of her book had been piled up, then took the stairs down to the little café in the basement. It was quiet there, not yet coffee time for the light crowd of Southampton shoppers. Julia ordered a drink and took it to the back, sitting where she could keep an eye on the stairs. Then she pulled out the paperback she was reading from her bag and settled down to wait.

Rob and Becky arrived exactly on time, but their appearance surprised Julia so much that she almost didn't recognise them – they both looked so young, almost like children. She was struck too by how handsome they looked together. She had remembered how good-looking Rob was, but Becky was pretty, too. Julia hadn't noticed that before, concentrating instead on her good character. She registered the thought that she would have actively disliked Becky when she was in her twenties. For being able to attract a boyfriend as handsome as Rob was, all because of how symmetrically her features had happened to arrange themselves before she was even born. Julia closed her book thoughtfully, as if filing that idea away for later. She watched as they came over and stood by her table.

"Hello," Julia said. She held out a £20 note to Rob. "I'm afraid there's no table service here. Would you mind getting yourselves a drink?"

Wordlessly, Rob did what she said while Becky sat down.

"I read about your accident," Becky said.

Julia smiled.

"Are you okay?"

"Well, it hurt a bit. It still does actually, but they've put me on painkillers, so I'll be okay." She smiled again.

Becky didn't reply. She seemed to be inspecting the edge of the table.

Slowly the smile faded from Julia's face, and they stayed quiet until Rob returned.

When he did, he was holding a tray with two cappuccinos.

"I didn't get you one," Rob said. "It looked like you still had some left."

Julia nodded, and she waited while Rob sat down, tore open the sachet of sugar and stirred it into his drink. He left the change on the tray, and Julia had to reach over to collect it back.

As she did so she tried to think of a way to begin. She had planned this conversation, but now they were in front of her, she felt her self-confidence cracking. She decided upon an opening and drew a breath to begin.

"Was it a real accident?" Rob asked, interrupting her thoughts. For a moment he had a milk moustache from the cappuccino, but then he brushed it away with the back of his hand.

Julia finished her breath. "I had to get rid of the car. In case there was evidence on it."

"So you crashed it on purpose?" Becky broke in. "I knew it." She turned to Rob. "I told you..." She didn't finish the sentence. Julia turned to look at him too, and his handsome face was set in a look of clear dislike.

"Why didn't you just burn it?" he asked. He sounded quite calm, genuinely interested in her answer.

"What?"

"Burn it. Take it somewhere. Chuck a bit of petrol inside and set it on fire, then report that it got stolen."

Julia opened her mouth to explain one of the many reasons why this approach wouldn't have worked, but momentarily she couldn't think of any. Her back suddenly gave a twinge of pain. The Dramadol she had taken on the train was wearing off.

She tried to ignore the pain and take control of the meeting before it got out of hand.

"Well, never mind that. I asked you here because I wanted to talk about what happened..." she began.

"Why?" said Rob at once.

"Just because... Because it's important that we all know what to say in case anybody asks."

"Who's going to ask?" Rob asked.

"Have you been following the news? About the woman?"

"I read something about her," Rob said. "But not much."

"We've been trying to forget about it," Becky explained.

Julia considered this for a moment. "Good. That's good." She fell silent again, still considering how to broach the topic she had come to discuss.

"Is that it?" Rob asked. "Is that what you brought us here to say?" He shrugged, and for a moment he looked like a sulky teenager getting a telling off. Julia found herself drawing strength from the thought.

"No," Julia said. She tried to fix her eyes on his. "I thought we should meet up. So we each know that none of us are going to do anything... silly."

"Like what? Like crash our cars into people?"

"No," Julia replied. "Like speak to the police and get us all into very serious trouble." She spoke quietly but firmly.

There was a moment of silence.

"We are just trying to forget about it," Becky said again. "We think... Well, Rob thinks..."

"It was a mistake." He finished the sentence for her. "What we did for you. I don't know *why* we did it, but we shouldn't have. We should have just waited until someone came along. It was nothing to do with us." He looked miserable now.

The thought occurred to Julia that perhaps she had misread the situation. Perhaps she could even get out of her predicament without it costing her anything – but she dismissed the idea. That wasn't why she had come. She was here to do the right thing. She was here to make *certain*.

"Well. Unfortunately, it's a little late for such thoughts now," Julia continued. "If we could turn back the clock I'd prefer to go back a little earlier and have you warn me about the woman on the poorly-lit bicycle in the middle of the road, *if* you saw her so clearly. But what's done is done. It's how we deal with it that's still to be decided." Julia took a sip of her now-rather-cold coffee and began the pre-planned part of her speech.

"My first thought, when I learnt the poor lady's name, was that I might be able to do something to help her relatives – financially I mean, perhaps with an anonymous donation. But it turns out she had no relatives. She was just a poor little old lady. It's sad really, she was probably very lonely." Julia glanced at Becky, to see how she took that.

"Once I saw that wasn't possible, I thought – what else can I do? To make this horrible situation a little better." As she'd planned to, Julia paused here.

"And?" Rob prompted her, when she hadn't resumed her speech.

But now Julia changed the subject.

"You're both studying? Isn't that right? Becky? I remember you're studying literature, aren't you? What was it you were doing, Rob? Engineering?"

"Yeah."

"I imagine that must be expensive?"

"Why would that be any of your business?" Rob asked. Becky broke in to calm him down.

"I'm sorry, Julia, but what do you actually want? Rob's missing out on a lecture to be here. And I'm supposed to be writing an essay."

In her idealised version of how this meeting would go, Becky would have told her what the essay was about. Perhaps she'd even have asked Julia's opinion. After all, a quote from a bona fide literary sensation would surely be something very special. Julia smiled just as if she had been asked.

"Look, I've just... I told you I was wondering whether there might be a way for something good to come out of this. I've heard about how young people have to spend so much on university fees these days... Your finances are your own private matters I know. But you were both working at the party the other night, so I thought you must need money...?"

Rob and Becky looked at each other. It looked like he was about to get up and walk out.

"I had this idea for a bursary," Julia said quickly.

The couple frowned.

"A bursary?" Becky asked.

"That's right. A way of helping out. We talked about it – I don't know if you remember or not – but we talked about the fact that I received a rather generous advance for my book?" Julia directed the question to Rob.

"Two million, wasn't it?" he replied. "I remember."

I knew you did. I just knew it, Julia thought to herself.

"Actually, it's a little less than that, once you factor in taxes, agent's fees – and there's all sorts of fees you have to pay, you'd be amazed." Julia gave a little laugh. "But yes, it's a substantial sum. The idea occurred to me that I could use some of that money to create a modest" she held up a hand "but nevertheless *meaningful* bursary to help a couple of local students through their studies." Julia realised that by now she was talking almost exclusively to Rob. It scared her, but she found she was enjoying the opportunity to stare into those handsome dark eyes.

"What exactly are you saying?" he asked.

Julia swallowed. This conversation, she realised, was like crossing a lake on thin ice. This part right here was the most dangerous, where the water was deepest, the ice its most fragile.

"I went to university, many years ago now." She smiled, as if she were exaggerating for effect and it wasn't *that* long ago. "But I was very lucky. I had all my fees paid and I even got a grant. From the government. It just seems so unfair that that's all changed."

Neither Rob nor Becky interrupted her.

"So the way I see it working is very simple. The money would be used to pay the students' fees. For the whole time they're in college. Just to make sure they don't need to leave with a huge, unfair debt. It would apply for as long as they study. So for example, if they – if *you*," Julia lowered her eyes, not able to keep them on Rob's face, "had already racked up debt, it would pay that off as well." She fell silent, then glanced at Becky. She was frowning in deep concentration.

"Us? Me and Becks? So it's a bribe?" Rob said, rather too loudly Julia thought – although with a glance around she was able to confirm the café was empty apart from the three of them and the girl serving, who was well out of earshot.

"You want to pay us to keep quiet?"

"*No*. Not at all. It's a *bursary*. That's what it would be legally, and... morally. But yes, I am proposing that you and Becky would be the first beneficiaries. It seems only fair. Appropriate. After you there would be others. I'm talking about putting a sum of money into a trust. Investing it so that it keeps paying out year after year. I told you, I wanted to find something good that could come out of something so horrific. And since there's no family, no one who actually misses the poor lady... Well, why shouldn't I help you both?"

Rob sat back in his chair and studied the table top. After a while he looked up at Becky, who had been waiting for his response. "I told you. Didn't I? I told you she was shitting herself we'd go to the police."

"It's not like that..." Julia began, but he interrupted her at once.

"I'm going to be fifty thousand pounds in debt when I finish this summer. *Fifty*. Are you offering to pay all that back?"

Julia drew a short breath. That was considerably more than she'd thought. "Yes," she said.

"And Becks as well? She's got money from her..." Rob stopped himself."She'd need fifty thousand too. Are you going to cover that as well?"

Julia swallowed again. "Absolutely."

Now Becky, who hadn't spoken in a while, joined in.

"Julia, this is really kind of you, but we don't need this. We weren't *expecting* this. That isn't why we..."

"I know." Julia leapt in and stopped her. "I never thought for a moment it was. This is just – like I said – a way to create something positive out of this horrible situation. I can't help that poor lady, but I can help you. And others."

Julia blinked and forced herself to look down at the table as Rob had, as if she were racked with guilt at that very moment. She was pleased with what she had said. She felt confident her theme of helping others would do the trick.

But Rob was beginning to shake his head. "I don't know. This doesn't feel right. I don't know that I want to be...*linked* to you."

Becky interrupted him, speaking earnestly. "That's not a problem if it's a bursary. I've got a friend who's on one. She doesn't have to say where the money comes from. Or why."

"It's not how it looks, Becks." Rob spoke to her quietly, as if somehow that meant Julia wouldn't be able to hear, even though she was sitting opposite. "It's how it feels. I feel bad enough already."

Julia turned to Becky.

"Did you see my book upstairs, Becky? *The Glass Tower*. It took me fifteen years to write that book. I can promise you I wouldn't have been able to do so if I'd come out of college with a huge debt hanging over my head. Who knows what the two of you might go on to achieve? Becky, you could write the next novel that changes the world. Rob could..." Julia hesitated, momentarily lost for what value engineers might bring to the world."Build a great... bridge." She glanced at him and quickly moved on. "Becky, we can't change what happened. All we can affect is what happens next." She waited, then finished.

"Please? Please will you let me help you?"

Becky's face looked drained. She turned to Rob.

"Rob? Think about it. You wouldn't have any debt. You know what a difference that would make. You could get that camera?"

Becky turned to Julia. "Rob isn't just an engineer. He wants to be a film-maker, you know, like nature documentaries."

Julia smiled but hardly cared at all, and Becky turned back to stare pleadingly at Rob's face.

"Rob, I think we should do it."

Julia sensed he was nearly there. "All I need is two things." Julia looked ahead and saw the only way forward involved the very thinnest patch of ice. She swallowed, and stepped onto it.

"What?"

"I need your bank details. And I need to see you delete all the photographs you took that night."

The mood changed at once. Rob sat back. He glanced at her, then chuckled.

"Fucking hell," he said. "So this is a bribe?" He looked across at Becky, shaking his head. "All this bullshit about helping people. It's just a straight fucking bribe."

He looked so angry that Julia thought she had misjudged the whole thing. The ice was about to give way, but then Becky made a small noise in Rob's direction. Julia had no idea what it meant – perhaps some signal they'd agreed on privately before the meeting. Whatever it was, it calmed Rob down and got him back on side. The ice held.

"Okay," Rob said. "I think it sucks. But I don't see we have a choice." Abruptly he pulled out his phone and fiddled with it for a few moments. Eventually he turned the screen so that Julia could see. It showed thumbnails of images, mostly dark, but you could make out the shape of the woman's body lying on the road. In one of them, Julia saw herself standing with her hand up to shield her eyes. The clearest part of the images was the rear number plate of her car, which had reflected the light of the flash. One by one the images disappeared as he deleted them. All except one.

"That goes when we get the money." Rob sniffed, then put away his phone.

SEVENTEEN

BEING a major financial benefactor was not something Julia had any experience in, but the research she had done in advance of the meeting proved useful. Before Rob and Becky left she promised she would confirm everything as soon as possible, then she gathered her things and caught another taxi, this time to the firm of a solicitors' office where she already had an appointment.

She was treated extremely well by the receptionist – given coffee and little pastries – and told that Mr Hedges would be right with her. And less than a minute later, the man himself appeared and ushered Julia through to his office.

"Call me Nigel," he said, as he showed her to a chair. He was a rather fat man in a creased and worn suit, but he seemed to enjoy his work, and this assignment in particular. He explained in the most jovial of manners how her money would be held in an account managed by the solicitors, and how it would be paid out to the very fortunate students on a term-by-term basis. There was a moment's awkwardness when Julia mentioned that the total amount she expected the scheme to pay to each of the first two recipients was rather more than she had outlined earlier on the telephone. The awkwardness wasn't felt by Mr Evans – who literally rubbed his hands at the thought – but by Julia when he explained that consequently she would need to load the account with a significantly larger initial sum, and larger than Julia had calculated. But they found a way forward. Rob and Becky would become the scheme's only recipients, except and unless Julia's future literary success gave her the means to extend the bursary in the future.

"Excellent," Nigel said, when the details were agreed. "I'll get started on the paperwork this week." He pushed his considerable bulk back into his reclining chair, but then leaned forward again.

"I say," he said. "I happen to know the vice chancellor of the university – we play a little golf. I could call him now if you like, I'm sure he'd like to thank you." Nigel tapped the side of his nose, ruddy from red wine.

Julia thought for a moment, and then agreed. It would be nice to be thanked. She listened in as he made the call. The university VC couldn't have been more effusive in his thanks. Julia almost felt like a genuine benefactor.

She wrote a cheque for £110,000, a little surprised that the fee was so high, but outwardly she smiled while Mr Hedges put a call into the bank to confirm her account had sufficient funds. When he was finished, he turned back to her with a beaming smile.

"All done!"

Julia treated herself to lunch before catching the train back home. When she got there she wrote a detailed explanation of everything she had been told, and sent it to Rob. Two days later he emailed back, saying they had received the money, and that he had destroyed the final photograph.

When Julia read that email, she sat back and let out a huge sigh of relief.

EIGHTEEN

THE UNFORTUNATE BUSINESS of the dead cyclist had quite interrupted Julia's plans to seriously research the London property market, but now it was settled, she could get back to it.

For as long as Julia had lived her rural existence, it had been alongside another life – an imaginary one – carried out in the beating heart of the capital. For financial reasons, this had never been anything but a fantasy – but in her head it was detailed and somewhat considered. In her mind she waltzed from intellectual bookshop to exclusive coffee house in a romanticised version of the great city. Julia's inner London was a place filled with poets, artists, and most of all *writers*. People like Marion Brown. People like Deborah Gooding.

But now she had money in the bank – more money than most people would earn in a lifetime. Now she knew that change *was* possible. A whole new life was possible. A whole new Julia. The Julia she was, perhaps, always *meant* to have been.

Shortly after concluding her affairs with Rob and Becky, Julia invited Geoffrey around to her cottage for afternoon coffee. The good thing about Geoffrey was that he wasn't actively employed, and was thus always available to come round when Julia needed company. Arguably, that was also the bad thing about Geoffrey, Julia thought as she hung up the telephone, he was always available. On the phone he said he'd be a quarter of an hour. But just ten minutes later she heard his Land Rover pulling up outside the cottage.

He came in and hung his jacket on the peg by the stairs. Julia filled the coffee pot, feeling more anxious than she expected to be. She had left her laptop open on the table, the property website she had been browsing still on the screen, and scattered across the table top were the particulars of several apartments that had taken her interest.

"What's all this, then?" Geoffrey asked, sitting down and making himself at home. He picked up one of the estate agent's particulars and scanned the front cover.

"You researching something for your next book?"

"No," Julia replied, meaningfully. Then she fell silent.

Geoffrey looked more closely at the document he was holding. It was for a two-bedroom flat overlooking the Thames. A deep frown appeared on his face.

"Julia?"

Julia didn't answer, but she watched him.

"You're not thinking of..." Geoffrey looked momentarily baffled. "Of *moving?*" Now he sounded halfway between incredulous and horrified.

"That's what I wanted to talk to you about," Julia said finally. "I am thinking about it."

"What? *Why?* Why would you want to leave?"

Julia brought the coffee to the table and sat down. "It's not that I want to leave. It's just... I've sometimes thought it would be nice to be a bit more in the centre of things. Do you know what I mean?"

His perplexed expression – a look he wore regularly – suggested not.

"But here?" He stabbed a finger at the photograph. It showed a beautiful balcony made of glass and steel. Actually, Julia had already reluctantly concluded that this one was out of her price range. By about a million pounds. But still, it was the *sort* of property she thought might suit her.

"You wouldn't be able to write *here*. Think of the noise! Twenty-four hours a day, seven days a week."

"I'm sure I'd cope."

"I'm sure you wouldn't. Believe me, you need peace and quiet to marshal your thoughts, to let the clarity percolate into your writing." He looked momentarily pleased with the expression he had come up with. Julia thought he might ask for a pen.

"You should try writing here," Julia countered. "With Mike buzzing his tractor back and forth outside the window. And that's not to mention the *smell*. When they've just put down the fertiliser."

"Well if it's clean air you're looking for, then look no further than polluted London," Geoffrey said. He sounded indignant, and Julia drew a deep breath.

"I could go to the British Museum. Use their reading room. That would be conducive to writing. Wouldn't it?" Julia asked.

He paused before answering.

"It's closed," he said. "They're refurbishing it."

Julia looked away. She was regretting asking him around. But somehow it had seemed important to get his – not exactly blessing– but agreement that it was a good idea.

"I'm not necessarily saying I would move completely. In fact, I'm not. I'd keep the cottage. But it would be handy to have a base in London. James says so. So does Marion."

She knew the effect that bringing her agent and publisher into the conversation would have. Geoffrey – in common with all her local 'creative' friends – held Julia's sudden relationship with these people in a kind of awe. The fact that she was now accepted by the very gatekeepers that had locked them out their whole lives.

"Why?"

This stopped Julia for a moment. It wasn't the answer she had expected.

"Well." She touched her hair. "There was talk about going on some radio programmes, you know, to promote *The Tower*."

Geoffrey stayed silent this time. And Julia knew she had him beaten. She was moving into a world he had no experience of.

"Then there's book launches. Award ceremonies. I suppose I'll have to attend..." She left the thought hanging.

"And it's just not practical. The other night proved that..." She stopped herself in surprised shock. She had been about to use the difficulty she'd had returning home from her own launch party to illustrate the point.

"What night?" Geoffrey asked.

"Nothing."

He turned away from her and studied some of the other properties. She had wondered about doing something to cover up the prices, but it would have been obvious that she had done so, and that would have looked even worse than leaving them on.

"Doris will miss you," he said after a while.

Doris was a watercolour painter with whom Julia had never particularly gelled, but who occasionally attended the Rural Dorset Creative Circle. Geoffrey had long pretended that she was Julia's best friend, even though it was obvious to everyone that he was really.

"Doris is busy with her..." Julia hesitated. She had no idea what Doris was busy with. "She's so busy with her art these days."

At that moment Julia's cat strode into the room and curled affectionately around Geoffrey's legs. It had always liked him.

"And Edgar Allen. How's he going to cope with the city?"

Julia sighed. "Oh, come on Geoffrey. I'm pretty sure they sell cat food in London."

"It's not the food. He's grown up in the country. He's a country cat."

"Well, you have him then." Julia suddenly found herself exasperated. She softened her voice. "I don't think he'll miss me. He likes you more than me anyway."

Geoffrey nodded thoughtfully and stroked the animal's back. "I'll miss you," he said suddenly.

Julia paused.

"Oh, Geoffrey," she said. She bit her lip, and a tear came close to escaping."I'll be here just as much as there. And you can visit me. It might even be good for your writing. You can tap into the pulse of the city!" She squeezed his shoulders.

NINETEEN

HAVING ABSORBED the news Geoffrey became, if not enthusiastic, at least active in his support.

"So where exactly were you thinking of?" he asked, a couple of days later. He'd only dropped by to ask if she wanted anything from the garden centre, given her new-found interest in horticulture. But when Julia had appeared troubled he had postponed his own visit in order to join her in a cup of tea. He dunked a digestive in it now.

"Well, actually I'm struggling a bit with that," Julia confessed. "I thought somewhere central would be nice. But none of it looks quite right."

"Let's have a look then." He pulled her laptop towards him and began typing. Moments later he had the property website on the screen.

"How many bedrooms?"

"Sorry?"

"Bedrooms. How many do you want?"

Julia tutted to show an irritation she didn't actually feel. Really she was delighted.

"Well, two I suppose. One for me and one as an office."

"So no spare room? I thought you said I'd be visiting you all the time?"

"Well I hope so!"

"You'll need a minimum of three then. Unless you're hoping to share a room." He glanced up at her and raised his eyebrows.

"No. I'm not looking to share a room."

"Okay. Three then. Now, price. What's your budget?"

Julia thought. She had never withheld anything about her earnings from the sale of *The Glass Tower* – indeed, Geoffrey had been there while the fee offered rose from crazy to spectacular to record-breaking. But he wasn't aware of her other financial affairs, like how much she might owe on the cottage. And obviously he knew nothing of the new bursary she had set up.

"Let's say a million. Maximum," Julia said. Geoffrey's eyebrows rose again, but he said nothing.

"And where are we looking? I think you should rule out anything south of the river, the transport links are terrible. Shoreditch and Hackney could work. Let's see if there's anything there..."

It was fun, sitting there with Geoffrey, looking through homes. With her generous budget, there was a host of beautiful properties to choose from, even if the true luxury homes were well beyond her reach. And when Julia's search moved beyond looking online, to actually visiting the properties they had shortlisted, Geoffrey came with her as well. Twice, estate agents mistook them for a married couple as they showed them around. Geoffrey was far more practical than her at interrogating his way past the sales speak. He asked about surveys and restrictive covenants – whereas Julia was more interested in knowing where the local coffee shops were, and whether they were frequented by creative types.

Two months later, in the darkness of a late November afternoon, Julia's offer for a luxury penthouse in a converted flower market was accepted. She was going to London.

TWENTY

THERE WAS no need to empty the Dorset cottage, as Julia had decided not to sell it, or rent it out right away. But even so Geoffrey hired a van to transport her writing desk. It was more old than antique, but it was where *The Glass Tower* had come to life and Julia couldn't imagine working anywhere else. It was however very heavy, and Geoffrey had to enlist the help of Julia's downstairs neighbour to manoeuvre it into the position Julia requested, by the window in the lounge with its views of the London rooftops. She stood back while they huffed and puffed it into position. Then Geoffrey took her in the van to IKEA to get her set up with everything else she'd need. He'd stayed that night, and much of the next two days, mostly spent screwing furniture together. But then he had to go back to make sure Edgar was settling in well at his new home. Leaving Julia to start her new life alone.

She'd never expected it to be easy. But even so, it was a shock how unfriendly people were in the city. She wasn't the most gregarious of characters, and it was quite an effort to speak to her new neighbours when she passed them in the building's lobby. And while they nodded back, they looked suspicious as they did so, and then hurried on their way. She tried drinking her morning coffee in various cafés on the commercial streets around her. But nowhere even came close to the book-lined intellectual hang-outs she had imagined. There were people frowning at their laptops, and some of them may even have been writing – it was impossible to say. She hadn't realised that everyone in London was in such a hurry all the time.

Nevertheless, Julia remained positive. Her agent had been very pleased at the move. He had suggested they now employ a PR agency in a bid to secure the media appearances that would now be possible, and this had been quite successful. Julia was booked for an appearance on a television show discussing the state of modern literature. The agency sent her for coaching – in a mocked-up studio – where she was taken through the process of what would happen in the real TV studio. She spent several hours practising what questions might be asked, and how she might answer them. They worked on her poise, her posture, the tone of her voice and gave her techniques for providing answers that would work as sound-bites. In the event, the show was cancelled, but the training had stood her in good stead and the agency was now optimistic that a similar invitation to a radio show would be forthcoming.

But now, two months after she'd moved into the penthouse, and two weeks since the PR agency's last, optimistic, but ultimately empty email, Julia unhappily admitted to herself that she could not remember when she had last actually spoken to another human being. She noticed how she wore a fixed smile as she passed the many mirrors in the apartment, and how her face dropped once she had walked past. When she spent three days without getting dressed properly she made a decision. It was time to make her own luck.

She pulled open her laptop and found the email she was looking for.

The key to her new life, Julia decided, was Marion Brown. Ever since she first began receiving emails from Marion – so enthusiastic about her writing, and the prospects for *The Glass Tower* – Julia had felt a kinship with her. They were a similar age (perhaps Marion was a little younger, but then Julia was young at heart) and clearly they shared a love of, and appreciation for, both contemporary and classic British literature. And when they had actually met in person, Julia had immediately warmed to her. She was clearly *highly* intelligent, and she spoke with a refreshing honesty about the literary scene, and the true nature of the characters who moved within it. It was through Marion, Julia felt, that she would be able to work her way into the scene.

Of course she had already, casually, let Marion know about her move to the capital. In fact, she had done so now on four separate occasions. Twice before she made the move, and now twice since. But so far these hints had not resulted in the invitation she had expected. But perhaps Marion felt she couldn't intrude upon Julia's work? Julia realised that she needed to make more of an effort to get the ball rolling.

So she spent an entire morning in her writing room, with its rooftop views and the roar of traffic which the double glazing didn't quite block out, composing an email to Marion. In it she suggested they meet up for coffee. The email, when she was finally happy with it, consisted of just forty-seven words. But forty-seven words that had taken over three hours to craft to perfection. When she finally hit send, she was so weary with the whole exercise that she was able to kid herself she didn't care if Marion responded or not.

But from the moment she sent it, her ears became alert to the *ping* sound that her mobile phone made when it received email. And whenever it did she would interrupt whatever it was she was doing and check to see if Marion had responded.

For the rest of the day, Marion did not respond. At 7 o'clock, Julia opened a bottle of white wine from the huge American fridge freezer that Geoffrey had helped her order, and grumpily pulled the cork.

By this time she had discovered that, while the pain relief she was still using was not completely effective on its own, it became considerably more effective when taken at a slightly higher dosage than it had been prescribed, and when combined with alcohol. The usage instructions were clear that it should not be used with alcohol, but Julia had come to overlook that. With her adjusted and alcohol-supplemented dosage she was able to manage the pain. It wasn't completely gone, and should she miss a dose it came flooding back, like an un-kinked hose.

And so, like she did every night at about this time, she flushed down the four tablets of Dramadol with a large glass of wine.

By 9 o'clock the bottle of South African Chardonnay was empty, and there was nothing on any of the three hundred television channels offered by her new flat screen smart TV. It was a Friday night. In her old life Friday nights meant attending the Rural Dorset Creative Circle, which, since she still got the emails, she knew was doing a Ukulele night. She began to imagine Geoffrey and all the others, playing songs and singing along, secretly seething at how Kevin was stealing all the biscuits.

Just as she was beginning to feel incredibly lonely, her phone finally *pinged* and a reply from Marion dropped in.

How lovely it was to hear from you, Marion had written. How Julia's heart leapt at this sentiment. *And yes, she was rather busy at the moment* (Julia's carefully crafted forty-seven words had anticipated she might be) but it would be *lovely* to catch up for a coffee. Could she do tomorrow at ten? Julia felt her heart flutter further – she'd anticipated having a few days to prepare herself.

After reading the email through another two times, Julia replied without further delay. She feared to do so might look overly keen – given how long it had taken Marion to reply to her, but she feared even more that not doing so might mean she missed her chance.

Julia suggested they meet in *Real Beans*, an independent café that was as close to the idealised version in her mind as she had found, but Marion replied the next morning that, while that sounded lovely, could they do the Costa by Old Street station instead, as she knew where it was, and she could use her loyalty card? Julia had of course agreed, albeit not with gushing enthusiasm.

As the clock on the wall ticked the minutes past ten o'clock, she began to panic that her message might not have been received and that, while she sat in Costa (on a carefully chosen table that was both by the window and offered a degree of privacy), Marion was roaming the streets trying to locate *Real Beans*. But then she turned up. Julia stood at once. It was awkward for a moment, with neither woman seeming quite sure how to greet the other.

In the end they kissed each other, after which Julia insisted that Marion should sit down while she queued for the coffees. Annoyingly, a small queue had formed just as Marion arrived, and the man in front of Julia seemed to be ordering for an entire football team, meaning Julia had to wait rather a long time before she was served. When she finally returned, holding her cappuccino in one hand and Marion's decaf flat white (as requested) in the other, Marion smiled at her.

"I'm trying to cut down on caffeine!" she said.

"Really?" Julia asked. Something about this troubled her.

"Yes. You wouldn't believe how much coffee I get through in a week!" Marion went on. "So many meetings."

Julia sipped her drink awkwardly.

"So – it's lovely to see you here!" Marion said. "How's your new apartment? You are right in the heart of it here, aren't you!"

"I certainly seem to be," Julia replied. "I think it's going to be very conducive to my writing."

"Well, I certainly hope so. Are you working on something new?"

Julia wasn't.

"I'm beginning to have some ideas," she said.

"How exciting!" Marion replied. "Well, do make sure you let me know as soon as you have something you are ready to show."

Julia smiled, beginning to relax.

"Actually," Marion went on, "I'm really glad you suggested we meet up. I've got some initial numbers from the launch, and I wanted to go through them with you." She leaned down to where she had placed her bag on the floor and from it she pulled out a small leather bound folder. She pushed her decaf coffee out of the way – still untouched – and opened the folder on a page marked by an elastic bookmark.

"Now, I don't want you to get worried," Marion said. "It's almost *always* the case when you have a book that receives as much promotion and – well, *hype* – as yours has, that the initial sales can appear a little disappointing. It's quite normal, and we're not worried."Marion gave her a steadying look with her soft brown eyes.

Julia leaned in to try and see what was written, but Marion's arm was preventing her. She carried on talking.

"So you've charted. That's the good news. And for a couple of weeks you were inside the top 10. It's slipped a little since then, but it may come back. It's not uncommon to see the bigger titles bounce around a little before they stabilise."

Julia felt unsettled. She had, of course, checked the ranking of her book on every bookstore that published a list, and she had experienced a degree of frustration that her novel, despite being so widely publicised, was still being beaten in the charts by so many books that she hadn't even heard of. But right now what was distressing her was how business-like Marion was being. She wanted to find a way to steer the conversation towards more personal matters.

"I haven't really been looking," Julia said. "I've been..." She thought for a moment. "Mostly I've been rummaging around the second-hand markets looking for furniture." Julia regretted the words the moment they had left her mouth. What if Marion was to come around, and notice how the flat was furnished almost entirely with Scandinavian flat pack furniture? She made a mental note that she would need to spend an afternoon or two finding some interesting older pieces to supplement it.

"Yes, well," Marion replied. "That's probably a good idea." She smiled and Julia was confused. Did Marion think it somehow useful to be buying second-hand furniture? Her hope had been that she might be interested in accompanying her.

"It can be incredibly distracting to keep an eye on the bloody charts all the time," Marion went on. "I think the less attention you pay them the better."

Julia tried again. "So what do you do when you're not keeping an eye on the charts?" she asked.

Now Marion looked confused. "How do you mean?"

Julia went on, a little unhappily. "I mean, when you're not at work?"

"Oh. Well, it hardly ever seems like I'm not at work if I'm honest," she said. "Like now!" Marion seemed relieved to have found a joke with which to answer Julia's question. "Here I am on a Saturday!"

The implication – that Marion considered the meeting work – wasn't lost on Julia, and she felt herself redden. She forced a smile onto her face.

"But as I was saying," Marion went on. "We are not worried, but we would like to ask if you might be willing to get a *little more involved* in some promotional activities we have planned. Now, James has kept me up to date on the TV and radio stuff – and that's all brilliant – but we were thinking about rolling out a bigger social media push."

She paused and took the first sip of her drink. A look of dislike flashed over her face.

"Are you on Facebook at all?"

Julia looked confused. "Facebook?"

"I get it. I do. The irony. Here I am asking the author of the novel that lays bare the horror of modern social media whether she's on Facebook. I get that. But the thing is, it's just so incredibly *powerful*. I must admit, I didn't used to be a fan, but these days almost all my social life is through Facebook, and it's the same for all my friends. I'm sure most of your friends are the same?"

Julia smiled to indicate this was probably the case.

"And that's just the point. We are increasingly seeing that Facebook is the way to reach readers. Now, we wouldn't expect you to run the whole page. But..." Marion looked hopefully at Julia. "Would you be able to give up a little of your writing time to interact with readers, maybe once or twice a week?"

Julia felt a little bit of despair. She did have a Facebook page; Geoffrey had encouraged her to set one up, a long time ago now, because he thought publishers would expect it. But she hadn't used it much. A few other teachers from the school she had worked at had tried to contact her, but Julia had little interest in keeping in touch.

"Well, I suppose..."

"It wouldn't be too onerous, I promise. We found with other authors, it can make a big difference."

"Well, okay," Julia said.

"Wonderful!" Marion said. "That's so good of you. I'll email you all the details, and if you get stuck, I can have Gavin talk you through it. He's a whizz at all that kind of stuff." Marion closed her folder.

"Well..." she began.

Julia felt a surge of panic. Marion was drawing the meeting to a close already. She launched a little desperately into one of her pre-prepared questions.

"So where, exactly, are *you* based then?"

The question came from so far out of the blue that it stopped Marion. She glanced at her coffee, still almost full, and seemed to realise she couldn't leave until she had drunk it anyway. She took a gulp, winced and sat back in her chair.

"Well, actually, we've just moved as well. Nothing so fancy as you, but we've managed to find a wonderful little house out in Ealing. It's much better for the children, they have access to parks and open spaces. It's better for my husband's work as well." She leaned in closer, as if confessing. "It is rather difficult to get over this way though, that's why I was late this morning. But then I'm not really a hip young thing anymore!"

It hadn't occurred to Julia that Marion might be married. She realised at once how stupid this was.

"What does your husband do?" she said in a monotone.

"He's a pilot," she answered. "He flies 747s." Marion smiled. She held her hands at her sides as if they were wings, then wobbled them from side to side.

"You know, the big ones," she said.

"Oh," said Julia. "How interesting."

"Well, it was when we were younger. He flew the New York route, and in those days I could get a lift in the jump seat – that's like a spare seat in the cockpit – so I used to do all my shopping over there. But these days it's not so good. He's away half the week, and it's murder with schools," Marion went on. She seemed, finally, to have slipped into exactly the casual chatty mood that Julia had hoped for, but now she felt adrift and helpless in the conversation.

"Oh," she said again, and searched for something sensible to add. "How old are the children?"

"Harry's eight now, and Geraldine is six, and then there's our little bonus, Isabel. She's three." Marion rolled her eyes. "You don't... You don't have children do you, Julia?"

"No," Julia replied.

Marion smiled, then fell silent, gulping down another mouthful of her drink.

TWENTY-ONE

LATER ON, back in the solitude of her flat, and fortified with another four Dramadol tablets, and half of another bottle of white wine, Julia finally felt able to open her laptop. It hadn't been *that* much of a disaster. They had met, they had chatted, and when Julia had glumly suggested how they must do this more often, Marion had actually sounded quite enthusiastic. She'd even suggested that, should Julia's travels around the capital's second-hand furniture auctions ever take her near her office, she should pop in and say hi. But Julia could already imagine how that might go. She shuddered at the thought.

On her laptop she found an email from Gavin. He clearly worked Saturdays as well. It included a baffling list of instructions for how she should register on the Facebook page the publisher had set up to support *The Glass Tower*. She read them through twice, and made no progress on deciphering what they wanted her to do. In the end she decided to simply follow them one by one.

1. Go to your Facebook page.

There was a link. She clicked it, and since she hadn't been on the page in quite a while, had to re-enter her password.

And when she did, she got the shock of her life.

TWENTY-TWO

SHE NEVER GOT to the second point on Gavin's list. A post on her Facebook feed took her attention instead.

At first she thought it was a joke. A strange, young person's joke that she didn't understand. But she didn't think that for long. Not even Julia was so out of touch that she could mistake the sincerity of the drama laid out in front of her.

> So I'm borrowing Rob's computer to write my essay, and I
> discover his search history is totally FULL OF PORN. #sohu-
> miliated

The post was written by Becky Lawson. Following the 'award' of funding to the two students selected for Julia's new bursary, Becky had sent Julia a Facebook 'friend request' which Julia had clicked upon, rather proud to be asked. But since then she hadn't actually logged into Facebook to do anything further.

Julia stared at the posting now, perplexed. There was a huge trail of comments below the original post, mostly (judging by their profile photographs) other young women Becky's age.

Why hon?
Ahhhhh, what's happened?
Whaaaatttttt!!!!!????
Men! Their animals. I'm on my way.

Julia winced at this last one, almost more shocked by its spelling as by the fact Becky would want to share something so very private in the first place. Or maybe it *was* a joke? Surely it couldn't really be what it looked like? Julia kept reading, fascinated, and a little further down the page was another post, this one from Becky again.

Am I not enough for him? #sohumiliated.

This had generated another slew of comments, all enthusiastically commiserating with her. But then there was another, which took the opposite view and was clearly in support of Rob. It said how lots of men looked at porn – and how some women did too – and that it was harmless. Becky had replied to this as well, saying that she knew this, but there were, 'like, hundreds of images on the computer, which made it "not okay"'.

Julia read the whole thread, which seemed to have consumed Becky and her group of friends, and split them into two polarised groups. Those who supported Becky also seemed to support her right to protest about Rob's actions on her social media page. Those who supported Rob, felt this was 'out of order' (a few requested Becky to put up some of the images that Rob had been viewing). It was astonishing to Julia that these people could talk so openly in public about such private matters.

Her confusion reminded her of some of the early literary reviews of *The Glass Tower*. She hadn't knowingly written the book as a metaphor for the modern social-media-obsessed world. She had simply gone along with James McArthur when he suggested that positioning the work as such would help sell it. But when she saw how right he was, and how this interpretation had attached rocket boosters to the book, her memory of writing it also changed. She came to believe that, though not knowingly writing the book as a social-media critique, it had nonetheless sprung from her subconscious with that theme running through it. All

James had done was help to recognise it, and even that wasn't something she wouldn't have done herself if given a little more time. Indeed, she had since come to reflect on this when asked about the book, taking talking points from the very reviews which argued the book was a critique of modern social media to explain how the book was *intended* as such.

But despite all this she had never really engaged with social media in any serious way. Now she was doing so, and suddenly she was an instant addict. She was utterly gripped by this voyeuristic window into Becky's crisis. For an hour she read through Becky's post, and the comments that followed, with both the cool, fascinated distance of a scientific observer, and a greedy desire for more and more details. And then she came to the part where Rob was sucked into the argument.

He had been entirely absent from the discussion for two whole days, Julia noticed, after she realised that every comment came with a time and date which allowed her to reconstruct the argument as it had happened. Other men – presumably Rob's friends – had posted to defend him, and one of the most frequent posters was someone named Neil Bath. However, his contributions were even more thoughtless and stupid than the average (which were quite stupid and thoughtless already). Rather than trying to calm the situation down, his intention appeared to be to further rile everyone up. He had gone from repeatedly requesting Becky share some of the 'evidence' from Rob's hard drive, to posting links to pornography sites with the suggestion they might be useful to Rob (followed by lots of, what Julia learned were called 'cry-laughing' emojis). When this failed to elicit a response, Bath had begun suggesting Becky should be careful what she said about Rob because he was a keen photographer and would therefore have lots of interesting pictures of Becky herself.

Julia was astute enough to understand he was referring to something called 'revenge porn'. She had heard about it on the radio. It was where young people took photographs of themselves naked, or having sex, or just of their genitals, and then held each other to ransom, saying they would post the pictures on the internet. It wasn't something she had ever been concerned with personally, since she was quite sure no one had ever photographed her genitals. But just the thought of such an attack was horrific enough that she understood the threat. Then Rob finally joined in the argument.

Yeah mate. I do have a couple of photos Becky wouldn't want me to release!

Under this was a fresh deluge of comments, some outraged at what Rob appeared to be implying, some enthusiastically asking to see them, some even promising to pay Rob to see them.

For a moment Julia almost chuckled at the thought of Becky being further humiliated in this way, then something else struck her. A sudden, horrible realisation, no, *certainty* that Rob wasn't talking about revenge porn at all. He was threatening Becky with releasing the final photo of the accident.

He'd never deleted it like he promised. He'd lied to her.

She knew she'd been right about him.

Julia wiped a hand across her brow, and it came away greasy with sweat. She bit her thumb anxiously. Rob was actually posting *on a public forum*, threatening to reveal Becky's involvement in the cover-up of a woman's death. How insane could you get? How *stupid*?

Julia read to the end of the thread. It petered out, finally – perhaps *The X-Factor* had come on the television, or whatever else served to distract these people. And then Julia felt starved of information. She looked back over all the comments, feeling sick but hoping she'd missed something. Some hint that she was wrong, some confession from Rob that he didn't really have the images. But all she saw was another threat from him saying that, if Becky didn't start acting reasonably, she was going to regret it even more. (He also, for what it's worth, denied ever looking at the porn, and said that his friend had put it there for a joke. But Julia paid this little attention.)

One hour, four Dramadol, and a bottle and a half of French Sauvignon Blanc later, Julia retired to her new penthouse bedroom, a very worried woman indeed.

TWENTY-THREE

THE FIRST THING she did when she awoke the next morning was log into her Facebook account to see if there was anything new. There was – the debate had rumbled on overnight – but nothing significant had changed. Julia thought about contacting Rob, somehow finding a way to imply – or even telling him outright – that if he revealed the photographs their financial arrangement was off. But even though she doubted that would have much effect – he must be aware of that – she didn't even know if it were possible. It wasn't something she had ever discussed with that nice solicitor Mr Hedges. Now that the money had been handed over, did she have any power to take it back?

Anyway, the problem wasn't what happened to Rob after he posted the photo, it was what would happen to Julia.

Someone would see them, or screenshot them – or whatever the term was – and they would be out there forever. She knew that about the internet. Once something was out there, it could never be taken down. Which meant it would only be a matter of time before someone would identify her, and work out what it meant. And then her entire life, everything she had worked for, everything she had created, would come crashing down.

The thought made her feel physically sick, and then she ran to the bathroom and *was* physically sick. Her back ached more than usual, a low rumbling ache that was constant as well as deep stabbing pains that could appear anywhere from her neck to her buttocks when she tried to move. She upped her dose of tablets and added paracetamol into the mix. Then she spent the morning alternating between refreshing her computer's Facebook page (the page actually refreshed automatically, but Julia didn't quite trust this) and biting her nails, while staring out at the rooftops of East London. She was paralysed with indecision. Worryingly, Becky changed her status from 'in a relationship' with Rob to 'single'.

By the afternoon Julia was deep in an imagined conversation with Rob, imploring and persuading him not to release the image or images (it seemed clear from Rob's comment that he had kept more than one, and Julia assumed he must have had back-ups when he pretended to delete them). But unsurprisingly this had little effect on reality, and the more she went over it in her mind, the more it was clear she would never speak to him about it. She couldn't. The problem wasn't Rob's irrationality. It was more fundamental than that. The problem was that Julia *had never been able to talk to boys like Rob.* She knew his type. There had been plenty like him at school, and in college, and in teacher-training college after that. And they were always the same. They always ignored girls like Julia. They hung about in their macho groups, talking about sports and drinking, and sometimes girls, but only *certain* girls. Girls with clear skin and glossy hair and attractive features that they'd done absolutely nothing to earn, they just happened to be born like that. Girls like *Becky*. The other girls – clever, intelligent, interesting girls – might just as well have been invisible. They weren't considered at all. It was as if they didn't exist. Yes, Julia had been able to overcome this when negotiating the bursary with Rob, but at that time she had been on a huge financial and emotional high. That advantage was now gone.

She was back to being the old Julia again, and girls like the old Julia never talked with boys like Rob. They couldn't and they never would. So if there was going to be a way out of this mess, it had to be through Becky.

TWENTY-FOUR

THERE WAS one significant change to the last time Julia had made the trip down to Southampton. By now she had replaced her car and didn't have to rely on public transport. She had considered getting another Morris Minot, or even a real classic - like a Jaguar - she imagined this would photograph well for a Sunday newspaper photo spread, should she ever be offered one. But she wasn't an expert on classic cars, and in the end decided that modern brakes and creature comforts were important too. So she had chosen one of the new editions of the VW Beetle. It had, she felt, at least some of the charm of her previous car.

It still took her hours to get there, since she had to travel out of London and then around on the M25, before heading down to the south coast. When she was off the motorway Julia stopped at a convenience store to buy some wine, and while she was there she noticed a bunch of flowers was reduced in price because they were wilting a little, so she got them for Becky too. Just after four o'clock, she rang the doorbell of Becky's small terraced house in the student district of Southampton. The last – and only – time she had been here before was on that fateful night, almost four months previously.

The girl who answered the door looked so dishevelled that Julia barely recognised her as the bright young thing who had stood up for her and helped her that night. Despite Julia's late arrival Becky was still dressed in her pyjamas. She had bare feet, and wore no bra, so when she bent over to pick up the post from the floor (it looked as though she was trying to pretend it hadn't been lying there all day) Julia couldn't help but see almost all of her breasts. Julia drew her eyes away and onto Becky's face. Her hair was tied back, her blue eyes were puffy from crying.

"How are you feeling?" Julia asked. Becky wiped awkwardly at her eye.

"I'm alright," she said. She scratched at a point on her skin below her ear that had become blotchy. "D'ya wanna to come in?"

"Yes, please. I got these for you." Julia thrust her offering of flowers towards Becky. She had the wine in her bag.

"Thanks," Becky said, trying to smile. "Tea?" she said. "Or something else? I'm on the white wine."

Julia brightened visibly. "Well, I think something else then. In the circumstances." Becky didn't smile, but shuffled out of the way to allow her inside.

The hallway of the little house was small and dark. There was a bicycle leaning against the wall, and the rubber from its handlebar grips had created a pattern of black marks on the white emulsion. Becky tramped through it and into a small kitchen. It looked like it was normally kept clean, only now there were plates piled in the sink. Becky was already halfway through a glass of wine, which was sitting on the little table next to her phone. Becky sat back down, and began stabbing at it. Julia realised she would have to get that away from her, or everything she had come to say might end up online.

"I saw what Rob said," Julia began. "What he did. Horrible."

Becky's head jerked up at the mention of his name, then dropped again.

"Bastard," she muttered.

"I'm so sorry," Julia went on. "It must have been a horrible thing to discover. Were they...?" She had been going to ask about the pornographic images that Rob had viewed, but changed her mind. Pornography wasn't really an area she had much expertise in.

"I didn't exactly examine it," Becky said. "It wasn't, like, kiddie porn or anything. But..." she began, then stopped.

"What?" Julia asked.

"It's not how bad it was that I mind. It's just, I feel like it means *I* wasn't enough for him. So what's the point? You know?"

Julia didn't really, but she nodded anyway. She glanced at Becky's glass and looked about the kitchen for the bottle it had come from, spying it next to the fridge. She pointed at it.

"I say, do you mind if I...?"

"Glasses on the shelf."

Julia had already spotted them and poured herself a large glass.

"I'm driving so I'll just have the one," she explained.

Becky waved her hand as if she didn't care either way.

"So you were passing?" she said.

"Pardon?"

"You said in your message, you had to come down here anyway?"

"Oh. Yes. I had to meet with... Actually I needed to do some research, for something I'm writing."

Becky looked up at this. She brightened slightly. "Really? What kind of research?"

Julia took a moment to sip at her wine, giving herself some time to think.

"My new book," she said at last. "I'm featuring a church here."

"Really?" Becky sounded dubious. "Why?"

"I'm thinking of doing something that speaks about the decline of organised religion in society."

"Oh," Becky said. She seemed to have lost interest.

"Well, it was just an idea," Julia went on. It had been an idea too, or the beginnings of one, but given Becky's reaction it probably wouldn't last much longer.

"Really it was an excuse to come and see if you were alright."

Becky smiled at this, and Julia sat down opposite her. She hadn't noticed Becky actually drinking, but now her glass was empty, so she leaned across and filled it up.

"Thanks," Becky said.

"So," Julia said. "Is that it with Rob then? For good?"

Becky nodded, then raised her bleary eyes and fixed them firmly on Julia's.

"Definitely. After what he's done. And what he said. There's no way I'm having him back. Ever. Even if he came begging."

"And is he?" Julia pressed. "I mean is he trying to apologise? To get back with you?"

"I don't know. I think he's staying with James. Sally saw him the other day, said he was drinking loads, and talking about going out to Starburst."

Julia had no idea who these people were, nor what Starburst might be. But she *tskked* as if this information was somehow relevant, then sipped again at her wine.

"Becky." She spoke quietly. "We need to talk. About the threat that Rob made."

For a moment the girl appeared not to have heard, but then she very slightly nodded, all without looking at Julia.

"Yeah," she said.

"I may not be quite as technologically savvy as you youngsters, but I always thought there was a possibility he hadn't deleted all the images. Clearly I was right to be concerned. But while things were... were stable between the two of you, it seemed it was all under control. Now that's not the case anymore."

"Yeah," Becky said again, then fell silent.

Julia sighed. "Becky, what I'm trying to say is this. We simply cannot allow Rob to have this power over us. Over *you*, I mean. It's not fair. It's not *right*. Do you understand?"

"Yeah," Becky said a third time. Then she looked up.

"How'd you know about 'em anyway?"

"About what?"

"About the photos."

Julia was confused. "Well, I was there..." She stopped, frowning. "What do you mean?"

"How do you know about the photos Rob took?"

"I was... What photos are you talking about, Becky?"

"You know... Those photos. The ones he took..." Becky looked away. "In bed." She studied the top of the table for a while.

"Well, not all in bed. There were some in the shower, too."

Oh God, Julia thought. She pressed a hand against her forehead.

"I don't know about those photos, Becky. Well, I didn't. But I'm not talking about them. The problem is, Rob wasn't talking about those photos either."

Becky looked back at Julia.

"What?"

"I'm talking about the ones from the accident. That's what Rob was talking about. That's what he was threatening you with."

"Was it?" Becky replied. She seemed to think for a moment. "I suppose so. It might have been."

For the briefest of moments it occurred to Julia that she might be the one who was wrong. Maybe he *hadn't* been talking about the images from the accident. Maybe he had even deleted them as he'd promised. If that was the case then she had nothing to fear. But then she remembered what kind of a boy Rob was. What boys like Rob always were. Her resolve stiffened.

"Did he delete that last image, Becky?" Julia asked, her voice urgent. "After I paid the money?"

Becky chewed on the inside of her lip. She didn't seem to want to answer.

"Did he, Becky?"

Eventually she shook her head. A tear fell from her eye.

"No. He kept it. He kept all the others too, the ones he deleted in front of you. He already had them backed up."

A spasm passed through Julia's body. Fear at the thought of the images still existing, but much more than that, it felt good to be proved right. Everything Julia had suspected had been right. She was vindicated.

"Well, we definitely need to do something about it then," she said.

The little kitchen had a small window that looked out over the back of the house – a kind of courtyard, but open to the sky, which was filled with clouds that promised rain. It looked dark and threatening. By contrast, the little kitchen felt almost cheery and light. Julia poured out the rest of Becky's wine, and wondered about pulling her own bottle from her bag.

"There's more in the fridge," Becky said, as if reading her thoughts. "I've got good girlfriends." Becky looked up at Julia, her eyes dark.

"I only sent them away because I said I had to meet someone important." She smiled weakly at Julia, then pulled the loose strands of her hair and tucked them behind her ear. She looked so sad, and so vulnerable. It made Julia forget for a moment what she had come here to say.

"I really am so sorry, Becky," she said. "I never..." Julia hesitated, then decided to share a confidence. "You know, when I was your age, I never really *knew* boys like Rob," she said. She didn't go on to say she hadn't met many since then either. "But I knew boys *like* that." She gave a little laugh.

"Oh yeah. I knew plenty like him. Only interested in one thing, and once they stop getting it..." Julia rolled her eyes. When she looked back at Becky the girl had pressed herself back in her chair, and in doing so her pyjama top was pulled tight against her breasts, clearly outlining her nipples. Julia gave a distracted laugh and ran her fingers through her hair. Reluctantly, she looked back up at Becky's face.

"I suppose what I'm trying to say is, you can't trust them. Men like that. Even when you think you can. So we have to work together now. Do you see?"

Becky blinked at her. She gave the lightest shake of her head.

"I mean he's got these images of you..." Julia's eyes were drawn back to Becky's nipples. "I don't know, naked?" For a second she hesitated, hoping Becky would confirm this, but then she rushed to continue speaking.

"Or whatever – that's not the point – and he's got those images of *me*. What I mean is it gives him power over *us*. So we need to get some power over *him*."

Julia was both relieved when Becky changed her position again, so that her pyjama top loosened and stopped defining her breasts so clearly, and somehow disappointed too. She decided she needed to get to the point quickly.

"He's directly threatening you, Becky, with those images. So we need to neutralise that. Okay?"

Becky nodded.

"So, I had an idea."

TWENTY-FIVE

"WHAT IDEA?" Becky said. She looked miserable. Julia leaned forward.

"Okay. I've given this a little bit of thought. I don't know what silly ideas Rob might have planned, but presumably he thinks he can use the images in a way that means he doesn't end up hurting himself. Do you see?"

Becky looked blank. "No."

Julia went on as if she hadn't heard. "Okay. We know that *I'm* in them – the images from the accident – and presumably you're in some of them too, but obviously *he* isn't, because he took them. So he's suggesting he could get *you* into trouble with the police, by handing them over anonymously?"

Becky didn't answer at once. But then she shrugged, and sniffed.

"Yeah."

"And in the process, he could harm me." Julia considered adding how he might damage her literary career too, but she sensed that wouldn't help her cause at the moment. No point over-egging the pudding.

"And while that's not his aim, he doesn't much worry about it either. Because that's the kind of man he is."

Becky began to cry. A few mournful sobs. Julia waited until she had finished then went on.

"So we need to work together."

Julia stopped to take a long gulp of the wine, then seeing her glass was empty she went to the fridge and found another bottle. Luckily it had a twist-off cap.

"I don't really understand," Becky said, when Julia had sat back down.

"We need to come to an agreement. That's what I'm saying. If he releases those images, as he's threatening to do, then we both need to have the same story, when the police ask us."

Becky thought for a moment.

"The police?"

"Yes. Because that's what will happen. We'll be facing very serious charges. That's why it's so important we have our stories straight. Do you understand?"

Becky shrugged, and then in response to Julia's frustrated look she nodded as well.

"Good. Now, we can't very well deny that we were there, the photographs will prove that we were. *But* if we both say that it was Rob driving, then it'll be two against one. Our word against his. And with no other witnesses, the police will believe us. Why would two people lie? And it makes more sense that Rob was driving anyway. He'd have been driving faster, plus he would have been able to force us to help him cover it up. Because of his strength." The more Julia said it, the more it made sense to her.

"Why would Rob be driving your car?"

Julia had an answer for that one.

"Because he has an interest in cars. Look at that old van he drives around in. What is it?"

"It's a mark two VW Transporter," Becky replied at once.

"Okay. Becky, would you say you're an enthusiast of classic motor cars?" Julia asked. She had slipped into the tone of a court barrister.

Becky screwed up her nose. "No."

"Yet you're able to tell me it's a mark two VW Transporter? How do you know that?"

She shrugged. "Because he's always going on about it."

"Exactly!" Julia snapped her fingers. "Which demonstrates that he has an interest in classic cars. So that's what we'll say. When I gave you a lift, we'll say that he asked if he could drive, because he'd always wanted to drive a Morris Minor. And we'll say I let him. I mean, obviously I shouldn't have, because he wouldn't have been insured, but that's not the worst crime in the world. Not as bad as running someone over and driving away. We'll say I was tired after the party, exhausted even, so we thought it would be safer that way. But then we'll say he started driving really fast. And you and I were telling him to slow down, but he wouldn't." Julia was speaking fast. She stopped and glanced at Becky.

"Becky? Are you listening? We'll say it was Rob that ran over the woman. And that *he* was the one who insisted on driving away. If we stick together then we back each other up. While he's on his own. Do you understand?"

Julia looked closely at Becky. She seemed to be crying again.

"Becky?"

"Yeah. Yeah, I get it."

"Do you want to... I don't know, have a practice or something?"

Becky shook her head. She was still sobbing. Julia wasn't the most comfortable when giving solace, but she moved her chair around the table so that it was alongside Becky's, and awkwardly she wrapped her arms around the younger woman.

"There, there." She patted her on the shoulder. She could smell shampoo on Becky's hair. "Look, I know you're a bit cut up at the moment. But this is important. In case Rob does something really stupid."

"I don't think he will," Becky managed.

"No." Julia released her grip slightly and prayed silently that this was the case. "No, you're probably right. But we still have to be protected. We'll still have awkward questions to answer. It'll still be a scandal. If we stick together it'll be him that gets into trouble. Into real trouble, I mean."

Julia squeezed again, tipping her head back and looking up at the ceiling. Within her arms, she felt Becky sobbing, and heard her cries too. She had no words, so simply kept her arms wrapped around Becky and held her tight. But it seemed to be what the girl wanted, and after a while she stopped crying. Julia noticed a box of tissues on the table, and released her grip to hand her one. Becky took it, and blew her nose.

"Thank you," she said, and Julia smiled.

Becky blew her nose a second time, louder this time, and then she folded the tissue and wiped her eyes. She smiled at Julia, a weak and fragile gesture, like a tiny flower. Julia held out her arms again, and Becky – perhaps not quite as enthusiastically this time – allowed herself to be enveloped in Julia's sympathy a third time. But this time as they came together Becky had changed position, so that when Julia leaned in her hand landed upon the side of Becky's breast. Becky, who had her head now pressed into Julia's shoulder, didn't seem to notice. After a few seconds, it felt uncomfortable to Julia to try and keep her hand from lying naturally where it had fallen, so she simply relaxed it.

Through the soft, thin material of Becky's pyjama top, Julia's fingers felt where the smoothness of Becky's skin was interrupted by the roughness around her nipple. For reasons Julia didn't fully grasp, the sensation of her fingers pressing against Becky swelled in importance. It became – over the course of mere seconds – almost the only thing Julia was aware of. She put more pressure on her hand, as if to deepen her hug – but in doing so she squeezed her hand harder over Becky's breast, and slid her hand around so that it was no longer against the side, but directly over the top of her breast. Julia heard her own breath. She began, softly, to let each of her fingers play gently over Becky's nipple.

Suddenly Julia realised Becky had stiffened, and then the girl tried to pull away. Julia let her go at once. Becky glanced up at her with eyes that were filled with confusion. Neither woman spoke. Then Julia smiled.

"It's all right," she said and she laughed to cover the fact that she was just as confused about what had just happened. But then she stopped. Becky was still staring at her, and Julia stared back. Becky's eyes were huge. Her lips were parted. They looked so soft. So inviting. For Julia it was like she was being pulled towards the younger woman by some invisible force. Invisible, yet absolutely irresistible. Julia knew they were going to kiss, and as she leaned in – her entire body crying out for the contact – she closed her eyes.

"*Julia*! What are you doing?"

Her eyes snapped open and she jerked away, as if scalded.

"Nothing," Julia said, and stood up. She walked the few steps the little kitchen allowed her. Thoughts were flying through her head. She saw the kettle in front of her, which she had shunned in place of wine.

"I think I will have a tea after all," she said, and she fumbled as she tried to turn it on.

"What were you doing? Just then?" Becky said, not willing to let it go. "Were you trying to...?"

"Nothing. *No.* Just..." Julia couldn't think of any words. Horror was rapidly filling the vacuum left in her mind, from which desire had so recently fled. "I... Nothing."

She turned and fixed a smile on her face. "I just hate to see you so upset. That's all. That bloody Rob, and... everything he's done to you." She shook her head. Wishing the black horror would dissipate.

Becky seemed confused still, but at least distracted by the explanation. And Julia, who was now wondering if a moment of utter madness might have undone all her good work, seized upon this to return to their earlier conversation.

"So do you agree? What we're going to say if Rob is ever stupid enough to use the pictures."

Becky looked away at once, but then she glanced back and, just enough for Julia to see, nodded.

"Yeah."

TWENTY-SIX

JULIA LEFT SOON AFTERWARDS. There didn't seem to be anything else to say. Instead of braving the long drive back to London she decided she would head out to the cottage for the night, and then drive back the next day.

As she drove she sat in silence, letting the countryside slip into darkness beside her as she sped along the little lanes. She realised she had missed it. The emptiness. The space.

The cottage, when she got there, felt cold and damp, but the advantage of that was the bottle of wine she had left on the microwave was as chilled as if it had been in the fridge. She put the boiler on and lit a fire in the wood burner. Then she drank all the wine on her old sofa with her favourite blanket on her knees. It hadn't made the move to London; she hadn't thought she would need blankets there. For the first time in a long time she felt at home. As she went to sleep, her Dramadol nightcap eased the shameful thought of how Becky's nipple had felt beneath her fingers.

She slept badly; her old bed felt lumpy, compared to the new mattress she was now used to. But when she got up she forced herself to feel better. The main problem, she reasoned, was solved. The threat that Rob posed may not have been entirely neutralised – that was impossible – but it was now *limited*. If he did the unthinkable, which she still thought was unlikely, she had a final line of defence. If Rob released the photographs, then the police would prosecute him for the death of the old woman. Julia wouldn't escape entirely without damage – but surely most people would see her as another victim? At least she would escape prison. And perhaps, she let herself hope, it might even help with the book sales problem that Marion had mentioned, and emailed about several times now. What was it they said about publicity? There was no bad publicity? Well, perhaps, except from it coming out that she had driven drunk and killed a poor innocent old lady.

And the thought that Rob would be bringing it upon himself – well there would be a certain poetic justice in that too.

As for whatever had happened with Becky, or nearly happened – well that was just a misunderstanding. Although that wasn't entirely true. Julia felt certain that for Becky too there were a few moments when it was anything *but* a misunderstanding. The look in her eyes had been unmistakable, especially when Julia's fingers had been oh-so-gently pressing at Becky's nipple. The thought of what might have happened next once again invaded Julia's mind. The thought of Becky pulling her pyjama top over her head. Of kissing those soft...

Stop it!

Julia slammed her palm against the kitchen worktop. It wasn't as well made as the one in her new penthouse, and the coffee pot actually bounced into the air. Still, it focused her mind. She poured herself a cup, and felt slightly better.

"Work," she said out loud. "That's what I need to do. I need to start work on a new project."

The idea, and the thought of losing herself within the hidden valleys and soaring mountains of a new book, was suddenly all-consuming. She wished she had her computer in the cottage, but of course that was back in London. She brushed away the issue. She had paper and, presumably, somewhere she would be able to dig out a pencil. And she was a *writer*. That was all she needed – that and the infinite power of her imagination.

She topped up her coffee and cleared everything from the table top in the kitchen. She placed a small pile of clean white paper in the centre, and rummaged around in a drawer for a pencil. When she found one she calmly sharpened it, thrilled at what might flow from its pointed tip. The possibilities seemed tantalisingly vast.

She sat down. She took a deep breath and gripped the pencil. She was ready to begin. Except she didn't have a single idea how to start.

Moments later she put down the pencil and drank more coffee. She drummed her fingers on the table. She picked up the pencil. Turned it in her fingers. Spun it around on the table. She placed it down again. Then quickly she picked it back up and wrote a word:

The

It wasn't right, so she crossed it out, but that left a mess on the paper, so she turned the pencil around and tried to use the eraser on the other end to rub it out. But that made a horrible grey smear across the paper, and didn't even remove the word – it was still clearly visible. It looked so horrible that she peeled away the paper and scrunched it up into a ball. With another deep breath, she tried again.

Half an hour later, the balls of scrunched-up paper had multiplied, and she still had no idea what she was going to write. She cast her mind around – flitting from items in the kitchen to what she had done yesterday. No. Not that. Anything but that.

Her restless mind settled upon the drive from Southampton the day before. What had she felt about the countryside? How she'd missed it. The fresh air. The space. A walk. *A walk in the countryside was what she needed.* Some country air would give her the inspiration she sought. After a moment's thought she had her telephone in her hand and was phoning Geoffrey to see if he wanted to accompany her. Happily, he agreed to abandon whatever other plans he had for the day and pick her up.

Twenty minutes later, his Land Rover crunched to a halt outside the cottage.

* * *

He hummed as he drove, apparently content just to be beside Julia, without expecting much in the way of conversation. It was his suggestion to head for the long curved ridge above the island of Hunsey, which offered sweeping views of the green countryside and out over the sea.

"So, how are book sales?" he asked, when they were nearly there.

Julia was shaken from her thoughts.

"Oh, you know," she said.

"No. I don't. Hence my asking," he replied. He glanced across at her, smiling through his beard.

"Well, actually I don't really know," Julia told him, coming to concentrate on what he was saying. Her frustration at her failure to write, and her lingering concern over what had happened with Becky were slowly fading. She remembered what Marion had told her, about needing to go onto Facebook.

"I don't think it's quite selling as well as everyone had hoped."

Geoffrey made a disappointed noise, and then focused on the road. It was narrow and he had to wait while a tractor came past. Bolted to the front was a vicious-looking iron contraption that looked capable of spearing the car like a marshmallow. The driver raised a hand in thanks.

"Well..." Geoffrey returned to the conversation. "You mustn't worry. With the amount of publicity it's received, you probably have to accept that the only way is down. For a little while at least."

Julia shrugged lightly. "I suppose so." She didn't sound convinced.

"How's London treating you? We haven't heard much from you here."

Julia didn't answer. With anyone else she wouldn't have hesitated to put the most positive spin on it.

"It's okay. A bit hard if I'm honest. All those people, but everyone in such a hurry."

"Are you getting any work done?"

She laughed. They pulled into the little car park, an area of rough ground where a small quarry had once been cut into the rock of the hill. Geoffrey always parked here.

"No. I can't seem to come up with any ideas that stick."

Geoffrey jerked on the handbrake.

"Well, you will," he said. They walked to the back, pulled open the double doors and sat down to pull on their walking boots.

"Second album problem. That's what it is. You've become a big star, so it puts the pressure on. Maybe you should try writing down here?"

He asked the question innocently, but Julia could hear the hope in his voice.

"Hmmmm, maybe," she said, keeping her voice non-committal.

Geoffrey laughed, as if he had expected nothing less. "Well, we could certainly do with you back at the Creative Circle. It's really gone down-hill since you left."

"Is Kevin still refusing to contribute to the biscuit fund?"

"Worse. It's turned into open warfare between him and Marjorie. He turned up last week wearing combat trousers and a camouflage jacket. I think he was trying to scare her. But you know Marjorie, he'll need to do better than that."

Julia smiled. Geoffrey struggled into the straps of his knapsack. She knew what would be in it. A flask of hot coffee, bananas and chocolate.

"You know I did a book signing the other night, at *The Three Bells*?"

"No? How did it go? Did many people turn up?"

"Three. One for every bell." He smiled at her. "So don't feel too worried if you're only selling a few thousand copies a week." He pushed the door closed and locked it.

"Shall we go?"

They set out, first skirting the edge of a field of wheat, then rising sharply until they were on top of the ridge. At the foot of the hill below them stood the channel which separated Hunsey Island from the main-land. The tide was half in, half out. In the near distance, on the tip of the island, stood the tower. Julia's tower.

They left the wheat behind them now, instead walking through pasture land, where a few sheep stood dotted around in the thick green grass. The ridge rose higher and it was hard going at first, but the air was fresh and the views spectacular. The land was clothed in colours of deep green, and the ocean glimmered in the afternoon sunlight. There was no wind, but a swell was running, so that lines were creeping into the bay, and breaking onto the rock ledges that jutted out into the ocean. They were too far away to see in detail, but tiny figures could be seen in the water, dots upon surfboards.

It felt good to be there with Geoffrey. It felt natural, and Julia began to relax. As she did so, she felt a curious desire to unburden herself. To tell him everything that had happened. The proverb came into her mind, as they hiked up the path. A problem shared is a problem halved. She pondered whether she should. Whether she could. But she knew there was nothing he could do. There was no magical solution to the problem – beyond what she had already done. And so she kept quiet.

They came to a stone bench that had been cut into the hill, and sat there, looking out over the silvery ocean below them. They took turns drinking from the single cup on Geoffrey's flask, and bit into thick chunks of chocolate. If she was going to tell him, now was the time. She gathered her composure, in readiness for the right moment.

She had met Geoffrey years before, after spotting a card in the window of a Dorchester newsagents. Someone was trying to set up a local writers' group. Julia, who at that stage had a few thousand words of *The Glass Tower* written and harboured dreams of one day being a novelist, went along to its first meeting. The group was a disaster. The woman who set it up, Marjorie, appeared to be a horrible tyrant who simply wanted an entourage to admire her own work. And after the first meeting it looked unlikely that there would ever be a second. But a slightly unkempt older man intervened. After the meeting he had a quiet word with Marjorie and then suggested to all the other attendees that they have a drink in the pub, whereupon he persuaded them to give the group another chance. That man turned out to be Geoffrey, a former insurance investigator who had taken early retirement and was trying to build a new life writing murder mystery books. He was kind, and generous with his time and praise. He became the first person to read *The Glass Tower*, in its earliest, most incomplete, roughest form, and contrary to what Julia had feared, he was immediately enthusiastic. He went on to help shape the book, and several times encouraged Julia to continue when she felt like giving up.

If anyone could understand what she had done that night – in driving away from the dead woman – it was Geoffrey. He knew the years of work and struggle that had gone into giving birth to the book. He would know that letting it die on that cold, hard night was never an option. Julia opened her mouth to speak.

"Would you like a banana?" Geoffrey beat her to it.

Julia's mouth hung open for a moment. Then, simultaneously she closed her mouth and her hopes for salvation.

"No thanks."

* * *

In the end she decided to stay nearly a week at the cottage, and the time felt like a holiday. She walked every day with Geoffrey, and she attended the Friday night session of the Rural Dorset Creative Circle, finding herself enjoying the camaraderie and catching up with the gossip. Afterwards she went on to the pub with the more sociable members of the group. She even found herself enjoying being cornered by Kevin, who was still at war with Marjorie. Over several pints of lager he explained in great detail why he had joined the group. He was writing an exposé about how Islam was secretly taking over Britain. He seemed suspicious of everyone, and was delighted when Julia mentioned how surprised she had been to see so many mosques around her in London. When Julia pulled out her painkillers to take her nightly dose, he warned her to be careful. One of the Muslims' tactics, he explained, was to infiltrate the NHS, and medicate the populace. He even offered to source her some non-Islamic painkillers if she wanted them, at very reasonable rates. Julia was quite impressed how someone so obviously insane was able to operate, more-or-less normally, in society.

But it couldn't last, and the next day she closed up the cottage and made the long drive back to the capital. She shut herself inside her lofty penthouse flat, feeling lonely but rejuvenated. Newly determined to make things work.

Then she turned on her computer and the horror returned just as if it had never gone away.

TWENTY-SEVEN

THE COMPUTER HADN'T ACTUALLY BEEN SHUT down, so when the screen lit up it did so on the same internet page she had left it on: Becky Lawson's Facebook profile. But everything about it had changed.

Becky had uploaded a new photograph – a headline image, Julia believed it was called. It was a photograph of her and Rob, kissing in silhouette against a beach sunset. A stream of small red hearts had been dotted around the couple, and her relationship status was back to 'in a relationship'. Below the image was a long trail of messages from her friends, who said as one how happy they were that she and Rob were back together.

Julia couldn't believe what she was seeing.

The implications were hard to grasp. The walks with Geoffrey – the space she had felt in the countryside – had helped to clear her mind, to shift the baggage that had been blocking her creativity. She had returned to London with the glimmer of an idea – a real idea this time. It began as *The Glass Tower* had begun, all those years before, with little more than a *sense*. She didn't have the plot, nor even the beginnings of one. But she had a glimmer. With *The Glass Tower*, it had been a sense of the tower itself. A sense of being there. Of touching the rough walls (at that stage, those walls had been made of creamy plastered brick, not the gleaming glass they would become in her novel). It was even a sense that included the taste of the salt air that flowed up from the sea and swirled around. This time the sense of place was quite different. It revolved around a near-impenetrable and dark forest. There was the smell of the undergrowth. Of wet sawn wood. She didn't know anything yet about the story it would bring with it. But she did feel there was a story there, just waiting to be discovered.

And now this. It was almost too much to take.

Julia forced herself to concentrate, feeling her *sense of forest* slip away. If Becky and Rob were back together, then what on earth did that mean for her? She had asked Becky to agree that they would lie to the police and say that Rob had been driving. In doing so, it would be Rob that was blamed for knocking down and killing the old woman, and for trying to cover it up. And that worked while Becky and Rob were finished. Over. But now they weren't over any more.

For a long time, Julia simply stared blankly at her laptop, her mind unable to penetrate the confusion of everything. But in the end she did the only thing she could do. She found Becky's number on her phone, and she called it.

Becky answered on the third ring.

"Julia!" she said. She sounded happy to hear from her. "How are you?"

How am I? Julia thought. *I'm just about losing my mind.*

"I'm wonderful, thank you. How are *you*?" Julia replied.

"Well, you know. I guess you've heard?"

"Mmmmm."

"Rob and me got back together!" Becky spoke as if this was what they had discussed the previous week. Julia resisted the temptation to sigh.

Rob and I, she thought.

"So, what happened?" she asked instead.

"Well," Becky began, as if this was quite the story. "You know how Rob said that he'd never really looked at the porn, and it was only there because he'd lent his laptop to Dave because Dave's laptop was broken, and Rob had to use the computers in uni anyway because he has to use the specialist software for engineering? Well, it turns out that Dave wasn't writing his essay like he said he was, but instead was looking at all this horrible stuff online. And I borrowed it next, not knowing that Dave had used it before me. And then when I got all upset about it he didn't know what to do because he didn't want to say anything to get Dave in trouble with Sally – that's Dave's girlfriend – because they've only just got together and everything."

Becky paused for a moment and Julia thought she had finished, but she was just drawing breath.

"Also Rob didn't know how bad it was, because he still hadn't *even seen it* so he thought I was maybe over-reacting, which I guess I do some-times, but I wasn't because it was really horrible stuff. What does that say about what Dave's into?"

There was a moment when Julia wondered if she were being invited to answer this before Becky continued.

"So anyway, it took a little time before Rob even figured out what was happening, and also that arsehole Neil was wading in trying to stir everything up which didn't help. And..." Becky stopped and gave a big happy sigh. "Well, you know how these things happen. The point is, we're back together."

Julia was silent. After a while Becky took this to mean she should go on.

"It was really sweet, actually. He came round with a bunch of flowers and wouldn't go away until I let him in. Really lovely flowers. He said that Dave had gone round to see him and admitted what he'd done and said he was actually a proper addict and he was going to get counselling, or whatever. Although Rob says he's probably just saying that so Sally won't dump him. But actually Sally was okay about it, because, well, you know what Sally's like – or you don't – but she's a bit like that and it turns out she's an addict too. So anyway, Rob said he was really sorry and I kinda realised I'd been a bit harsh on him. And, you know, he ended up staying the night."

Becky strung out the final word, and then fell silent as if to highlight its importance. Julia let her head fall back against the chair where she was sitting.

"Julia? Are you still there?"

"Yes, I'm still here. Becky I'm... I'm wondering how this leaves... us. After what we both agreed when I came to see you."

"Why?" Becky asked.

"Well..." Julia began. "We made an agreement to ensure that Rob could never... never do anything to put us at risk. And so I'm anxious that – with the situation now changed, again – that the agreement *itself* doesn't present any risk. Do you follow me?"

Becky was quiet for a moment.

"You're worried I might tell Rob we were going to tell the police that he ran the old lady over?"

"*No!*" Julia was alarmed. She hadn't thought the girl would be so stupid, but now she wasn't sure."We were never going to go to the police! We were only going to *explain it from our perspective* in the *unlikely event* that the police ever became involved. Do you remember?"

"Oh, yes," Becky replied. She spoke as if the details had just slipped her mind, and never been that important anyway. She sighed again. Another big happy sigh.

"Anyway, you don't have to worry about that. I won't tell him anything. Not about that anyway."

"You're sure Becky? You understand just how important..."

"Yes, yes. I do," Becky interrupted her. Her voice was serious for a moment. "I do, honestly. I understand."

Julia began to relax her grip on the telephone. She was unaware how tightly she had been holding it.

"Anyway, I've got something else to tell you. Something really exciting," Becky went on.

"What?" Julia asked.

"It might not happen, so don't go telling anyone yet."

Julia wondered who she might possibly tell.

"I won't."

"You know how they're rebuilding the lighthouse down on Hunsey Island? The one you used for your book?"

Stiffly, Julia allowed that she was aware of it.

"Well, they're opening it as a kind of artistic retreat. You know, for painters and writers and birdwatchers and whatever. Anyway, they were advertising for people to run it. And they said it would suit a young couple, I guess so they could keep it cheap. But anyway, me and Rob, Rob and I, I mean, we applied."

Julia hardly listened. She was still trying to process the implications of them being back together.

"And?"

"And we've got an interview! Next week. Isn't that cool?"

"Yeah."

"You have to promise not to tell anyone."

Julia sighed again. "I promise."

"Alright," Becky said. She giggled on the other end of the line. "Actually there's something else, too." She giggled again.

"What?" Julia asked.

"Well... You know how I've always looked up to you?" Becky began.

"Have you?" Julia asked. She wasn't at all sure she knew this. And she was even less sure how to answer now that she did.

"Erm..." she said.

"Oh *come on*, you know I have. I've *idolised* you. And you see, the thing is, I've always wanted to write myself, one day. I mean, it's obvious really, it's why I've been studying Creative Writing for the last three years, and why I got so excited when we got the job doing the catering for that party, where we met you."

"Yes?" Julia was beginning to get impatient now.

"Well, I've been... inspired. By *you* I mean, and everything you've achieved. And I've..." Her voice faded shyly out.

"What?" Julia asked.

When Becky went on it was nearly in a whisper.

"I've written a novel!"

Julia blinked at the telephone. She had begun the conversation thinking there was probably nothing that could be achieved to prevent her world sinking into ruin. But this? She hadn't expected this at all. A strange feeling began to climb into the hollow of her stomach.

"A novel? A whole one?" The feeling became clearer and Julia recognised it as something pleasurable. Something approaching pride.

"Well, actually no. Not quite. It isn't finished, but it's not far off. But I wanted to tell you. Because in many ways it's only happened because of you. I guess... I guess you'll see that when..." Becky stopped.

"But that's wonderful news!" Julia said at once, fully meaning it now. "What's it about?"

"Well..." Becky seemed to think for a long time. "It's a little hard to explain. But I've been thinking that..." She hesitated, and Julia could almost see her, in that little kitchen, biting her lip. "What I was thinking was – I mean if it was okay with you – because I know how busy you are. Erm."

"Go on," Julia encouraged her. She was beginning to see where this might be going.

"Well, what I was thinking was... would it be possible – maybe? For you to, I don't know, *kind of have a read through*? Because I'm a little bit stuck with how to finish it."

"Oh, Becky!"

"I'm sorry. I know that's a silly idea. You're like a national bestselling author and I'm just a nobody..."

"Becky I'd *love* to. I really would."

Julia held the phone to her chest for a moment. Then she put it back to her ear.

"Really. I'm touched that you'd ask me. And I'm so... so proud of you. I mean, you're so young!"

Julia was tempted to ask if it was any good, but she thought quickly. Probably it wouldn't be – how could it be, the girl had no life experience – and she would have to break this to her gently, that becoming a novelist was a lifelong calling. But everyone had to start somewhere, and it was wonderful that she had managed to get something down at all.

"How much do you have? How many words?"

"Seventy-five thousand words."

"Crumbs!" *The Glass Tower* was only eighty thousand.

When Julia went on, the enthusiasm in her voice was tempered.

"And how long have you been writing it?"

"Oh. I started not that long after we met," Becky replied, and Julia thought to herself, *it must be incredibly rushed. It could be truly awful.*

"But," Becky went on, interrupting her thoughts. "Like I say I am a little bit stuck with the ending."

Julia smiled indulgently.

"Well, that's okay. I mean that happens when you're learning. It's definitely a 'thing'. If you'd like to you could send it over to me now? Perhaps I can help?" Julia said. She felt more generous and more magnanimous than she had for many months. The thought occurred to her that this was happening *because of her*. Because of *her generosity* in setting up the bursary. She should mention it to James. She could almost see the headlines in the *Times Literary Supplement*. Marion would be impressed, too. Here Julia was, literally inspiring the next generation.

"Well... okay, but not just yet. I want to have another read through first. I want to make sure I've got it as good as I possibly can," Becky said. Julia could hear the gratitude running through the wires.

"Okay. Well, take care Becky. Just send it through when you're ready."

"Thanks, Julia. That means a lot. It really does."

"Of course." Julia could feel her face aching from how much she was smiling.

"Oh, and say hi to Rob for me."

Becky laughed lightly. "Yeah I will."

The line went dead. After a few moments, Julia stood up and walked over to her window, and she smiled out at the rooftops and towers of East London, and the creative crowd who lived somewhere out there.

TWENTY-EIGHT

THE NEXT DAY, at nine o'clock sharp, Julia sat in her new office and began typing her own new novel into her new laptop computer. It didn't go as badly as it had down in Dorset – there was no paper to screw up this time – and though by midday she still hadn't written a word of the actual book, she had begun to connect ideas together. There were notes, whole sentences in some cases, that suggested directions she could take. At one o'clock she stopped, and went out for lunch. After, she walked the streets, absorbing the energy and the creativity of the city. She walked until she was quite lost, and then followed the maps app on her phone to get home. By then she was tired, so she got a take-away, washed it down with four more Dramadol and a bottle of wine, and then climbed into her freestanding bath.

The next day she did the same.

And the day after that. And for all of the next ten days. Slowly, a plan began to emerge from the mists of her mind. She had her sense of place for her story – her imaginary forest – and this had developed nicely. Now she sensed how the wind rustled the leaves of the trees. How the light filtered down through the random, ever-changing patterns of the canopy. She could even hear, when she closed her eyes, how the twigs below her feet would snap as she moved around. But more importantly she was also finding the shape of the story. It was complex – like a tetrahedron (although, she realised once she decided this, that she would need to check what actual shape a tetrahedron was). The point was, everything that had come together when she finally began to make significant progress on *The Glass Tower* was happening again. And it was tremendously exciting.

It was so exciting she forgot all about Marion Brown, and her stupid kids and stupid pilot husband, and all the hopes she had harboured about the two of them browsing second-hand book shops together, or drinking coffee with the hipsters and gossiping about the publishing world. She didn't want that – she never had. What Julia wanted, what was truly exciting, was the feeling of having a live project.

So now, Julia positively bounded out of bed every day – as much as her back would allow. She'd breakfast on coffee and Dramadol, and arrive at her computer fresh and excited.

Then, just as she was really building momentum in her new project, she received an email that she'd never expected.

TWENTY-NINE

THE SUBJECT LINE SIMPLY SAID:

Hello

Julia almost didn't even look at it, since she got so much junk email these days. But something about the simplicity of the subject line drew her eye, and then she nearly fell out of her chair. The email was from Deborah Gooding. The *Booker Prize-winning* literary author Deborah Gooding. Julia held her breath as she read on.

Dear Julia,
I do hope this doesn't interrupt you at a crucial time, but I bumped into James McArthur the other night, and he mentioned you had made the move to London. That must be very exciting, and I'm sure you're very busy, but I just wondered if you fancied meeting up for coffee sometime? Please don't hesitate to say no if it's not convenient. But I understand we're actually quite close to each other.

Regards
Deborah

P.S. I've just thought you might not actually remember me but we did speak at the launch of your wonderful book in Dorset! I hope you do.

Julia read the email, then had to read it again, thinking it might be some sort of bizarre fraud. But no, it didn't seem to be. It really was from Deborah Gooding. Julia had been about to construct a sentence about how the rain funnelled down the channels of bark on the tallest tree in the forest, but all thought of that had now disappeared. *Deborah Gooding* wanted to meet her for coffee!

Julia had to resist the temptation to reply right away – that might look too keen. Instead she tried, and abjectly failed, to work for another half an hour before abandoning that for the day and starting upon a first draft of her reply. Some time later she was happy with what she'd written.

Dear Deborah

How lovely to hear from you! [It didn't take long to decide upon this opening, but she agonised over whether to include the exclamation mark. In the end she decided to use it, after all, Deborah herself had used one –quite possibly with a knowing nod as to how the English language was becoming enfeebled by modern communications such as email and texting. If that were the case, in using one herself Julia would be acknowledging Deborah's message and replying in kind. And if it wasn't a coded message, then it did add a tone of lightness to the line. It wasn't like she was using an emoji, Julia thought with a shudder.]

As it happens I am quite involved with a new project at the moment, but I'm always up for taking a break. [Technically this wasn't true; when Julia was deeply involved in a project she rather preferred to avoid all human contact, but she felt it important to stress to Deborah both that she was working at the moment, yet not scare her off by implying this was something that could not or should not be interrupted.]

A coffee and a catch-up would be terrific. [This felt a very tiny risk, as while Deborah's email had clearly stated the offer of coffee, conversation itself was only implied.]

Perhaps the most difficult part of writing the note was deciding whether to recommend a time and date. She didn't want to be presumptive and suggest somewhere, but at the same time, if she was too vague Deborah might be distracted before she replied, and then Julia would be left in the awkward position of needing to send a further email to prompt whether the meeting was going to happen at all. It was safer to suggest a date now, and hope against hope that Deborah was available on the day she picked.

It was midnight when Julia was finally happy with her email. She printed it out, and read it aloud to check for errors, and then finally she hit 'send'.

The next day, over breakfast, Deborah replied.

Great! See you there.

:–)

THIRTY

JULIA HAD two days until her meeting with Deborah, and although she had intended, and supposed, that she would simply continue on the same pattern of working in the mornings and walking in the afternoons, she found her focus was now lost. It wasn't something that concerned her at this point, but it was an irritant. She did her best, forcing herself to sit in her chair, at least typing something into her computer, even if it made little sense even to her. Perhaps, she wondered at some point, her musings on leaves, and how they cycled nutrients around the circle of the forest could be re-purposed, as a collection of poems, once the novel itself was finished. She made a mental note to ask Geoffrey what he thought of this. Whenever she next saw him.

Of the new novel itself there was still little actual sign. Her sense of place was now well-developed. She knew the setting – a forest – and she knew how that place felt. It was green. Soft and squishy underfoot. Light dappled through a canopy that was high above, and there was the noise of wind rustling leaves. However, large sections of the book were as yet undecided. She didn't know anything of the story, had no sense of the plot. And so far, there were no actual *characters*. She had made several attempts to bring into being a cabin in the woods upon which to pin the story. But whenever she did so, the cabins she pictured in her mind were simply clichés – almost as if she were merely describing the photographs of cabins in the woods that she had found when searching on the internet for inspiration. And thus she fought to push them aside.

Perhaps, she wondered, she ought to rent a cabin, somewhere? In some woods. She envisaged a clearing in the woods, in Norway, or Canada, and turned back to her computer to see if such a place existed. There were many, and many that were actively marketed towards writers in need of inspiration, quietness and solitude. But this gave her further cause for concern. Might that not indicate that it wasn't just the cabins she had so far imagined, but the entire sense that she had developed? The woods? The leaves? All of it?

Julia had her first wobble about the idea. She ran a bath and soaked in it, listening to Radio Four and drinking warm white wine (because she had forgotten to put it in the fridge). She offset this particular irritant by deciding to up her dose of Dramadol again, and this helped her go to bed reasonably happy.

But the next morning – the morning she was to meet Deborah Gooding – she put all this out of her mind. Instead, she concentrated on choosing just the right look, one that she hoped would suggest an easy style that had been achieved with minimal thought or effort.

She had wanted to arrive late, as if she had been hard at work drawing prose from the deep well of creativity inside her, but she didn't have the nerve for that. The next best thing was to arrive early and bag a decent table, and appear to be set up as if she were a regular customer – with a beautiful notebook and a trusty fountain pen (no cheap ballpoints please). So that was what she did.

Annoyingly, the *Real Beans* independent café which she had suggested for a venue, had chosen that morning to be playing music rather loudly. Although it wasn't the volume that Julia took issue with, it was the style of the music, which she assumed was probably called something like Garage Hip Hop – certainly it contained audible cursing. It was too late by then to suggest another meeting place, and Julia wasn't about to confront the barista about it, with his black apron and his goatee beard. So instead she frowned at her notepad – leather bound, and prefilled with notes that morning – the best lines she had managed from her forest project so far – written in her neatest handwriting. She hoped Deborah wouldn't notice the music.

They were to meet at ten o'clock. It was now 10.03. Julia felt alarm climbing over her body, like an army of spiders. What if she didn't turn up? Would she have to email her, asking what had gone wrong? No, she couldn't. She'd have to avoid her. Forever.

But then she saw Deborah enter the café and look around as if searching for a familiar face. The spiders fell away, replaced by a gentle nervousness. For a few seconds Julia pretended not to have noticed her, and then she dropped her head down to her notebook and wrote:

Leaves are the epitome of the trees, and yet they continue to spasm with incongruous...

"Deborah!" Julia called out. She didn't close the book, but turned it around a little to face the other seat at the table, and placed her fountain pen on top. She got to her feet.

"Julia, how nice to see you!" The two women stood close, but didn't touch. Neither seemed to know what to say next.

"I wasn't interrupting?" Deborah asked.

"Oh, no," Julia replied. "I was just...just doodling something!" She waved her hand at the notebook hopefully, but Deborah was already looking around at the café.

"Do you come to work here often?" She seemed to be appraising the location for how suitable it might be, perhaps for her own work.

"No... Well, yes," Julia swung between picking one answer or the other. "Sometimes. When the muse takes me." She cursed herself. The muse – could she have picked a more obvious cliché? She forced herself to adopt a damage limitation smile.

"I think it's lovely. I like to work in coffee shops as well. I like the energy it gives me." Deborah smiled.

Julia smiled back, her heart warming fast.

"Can I get you a coffee?" Julia asked.

Following the disaster in Costa, Julia had given a lot of thought to how to provide the drinks this time around. She could have sat at her table without ordering – but this might look awkward, and in the worst-case scenario it could lead to her being asked to vacate the table so that actual paying clients could use it. So she would need to order her drink first. But that meant that when Deborah arrived, one of them would be forced to queue for her drink. Was it appropriate for Julia to go? Having arrived first and chosen the table? Or should Deborah go, since she was the one who had suggested they meet in the first place?

A possible solution had been to ensure they met in an establishment that offered table service. But this had its own risks. Julia was consistently poor at attracting the attention of waiting staff in restaurants and cafés. It was a problem that compounded itself, in a vicious circle of poor service. Her very efforts to attract waiting staff were hampered by how tentative they were, in recognition of how little she expected them to work. As if, knowing that any attempt to signal to a waitress would be ignored, she deliberately kept them inconspicuous, so that other diners were less likely to notice her embarrassment. More importantly, she had yet to come across a suitably bohemian café that actually offered table service. She didn't want to make it look like she sat around in tea shops with old ladies.

But in the event, it was all very simple.

"Allow me," Deborah said. "Can I get you a top up?"

There was no queue, so Deborah was only gone for a moment before she returned and sat down opposite Julia. Perhaps, Julia considered, she had rather over-thought the problem.

There was no awkwardness either, and the two of them fell into easy conversation, as if this were a regular meet-up of friends and equals. Granted, they chatted almost exclusively about Deborah – Julia learnt how she had moved to London, from the Midlands, following the success of her third book, which had gone on to Booker success. And she hinted at how her life in the city wasn't the non-stop parade of parties and social events that she had dreamed of. At several points in the conversation Deborah asked Julia how she was faring, and how her work was progressing, but somehow the conversation soon switched back to Deborah. They talked about her bad knee, her frustration with the reading public and how unadventurous they were. They bemoaned the demise of good independent bookshops.

In the end, Julia was slightly relieved when it was time for them to part. Although she warmly agreed to meet up again, she made a mental note to force the conversation more onto her terms next time around. But in summary, Julia thought as she walked home along the busy streets, it had been a good meeting – exactly what she'd envisaged when moving to London.

Finally, her new life in the city as a literary figure had begun.

THIRTY-ONE

After her meeting with Deborah, Julia fell back into her writing. Except it still wasn't writing in the sense of linking words of a story together. She felt like events had knocked her backwards – so that she was back to sensing shapes and colours. That's not to say she didn't try. She tested out characters, building out both male and female personages, like empty shells. Starting sometimes from the top down, and other times from the bottom up – hair colour, shoe size. And, finally injecting a personality. But what these virtual figures would do, and how they would interact with each other, remained opaque. A mystery.

For the first time, this concerned Julia. While she did remember there had been this stage with *The Glass Tower*, it certainly hadn't lasted this long. And perhaps it hadn't happened *quite* like this. The tower in her previous book had presupposed an inhabitant, in the way a forest didn't. In her mind she had always had the story of Rapunzel (though no critics had ever made the connection, and now she wouldn't dare reveal such a prosaic origin).

On the plus side, a title had occurred to her:

The Forest

She thought it had a stark and dynamic simplicity. She thought it was very good. It was just that the story behind *The Forest* was taking a very long time to emerge.

It was against this backdrop that she received an email from her agent. The prose of it wasn't important, but the gist was clear. People – by which he appeared to mean himself and her publisher – were becoming increasingly keen to hear more about her new book. Sales of *The Glass Tower* were down even further, and there was some talk of accepting that this might not be easy to reverse. Yet with so much publicity pumped into her as an author, there would always be interest to see what she came up with next. It was all a good thing – she had a ready-made market for *The Forest*. It would surely do well, if only it existed.

What was worse, her now-regular habit of taking three times her prescribed dosage of Dramadol had resulted in a critical shortage of the soothing tablets. Her doctor had originally prescribed a two-month supply, and she had already been back once to negotiate an increased dosage, a second time for a repeat prescription, and a third time under the pretence that she'd left that second supply at the Dorset cottage. Now she had nearly run out again, which was a serious problem. The doctor had been quite clear too – he wouldn't keep writing out more prescriptions, and he knew exactly how long her supplies should last. So she was forced again to devise a plan, and as it turned out, it became a welcome break from thinking about the book.

She began by filling her least favourite handbag with a few carefully chosen items – some tissues, mascara, and dozens of empty blister packs of Dramadol recovered from around the penthouse – and throwing it behind a skip on a nearby side road. Then she took an outside table on a nearby street café and ordered a coffee. While she drank it she pretended to be utterly absorbed in a book, but actually she kept a careful eye on who was around her, and glanced around repeatedly to make sure there were no CCTV cameras covering where she was sitting. Only when she was sure about that point did she proceed.

She then got to her feet, walked inside and reported that her bag had been snatched from the table.

She wasn't quite sure what would happen next. Granted, she didn't expect a whole squad of Metropolitan Police officers to descend upon the café and declare it a major crime scene, but she did expect sympathy to extend beyond a shrug of the shoulders from the waitress (Polish, Julia suspected). In the end Julia had to visit the police station herself and queue for half an hour in order to report the crime. But once she did so she received her all-important crime number.

Armed with the number (the police never even looked for, let alone found, her handbag) she was able to go back to her doctor and claim that during the robbery her entire supply of painkilling drugs had been stolen.

"I have a crime number," Julia told the doctor – a young middle-eastern man who seemed distracted with his computer.

"I don't need that," he said, still looking at the screen instead of Julia.

"It's so silly of me to put them all in my handbag, the pills I mean, but the police said it happens all the time. It was just snatched from my table. I was there having a coffee. Reading a book. Can you believe it? Would you like a copy of the official crime report?"

"No. I don't need it. But it does say here that you've already had a repeat prescription early on one occasion already? Miss Ottley, you do have to be careful with these tablets. Very careful. You do understand that?"

Julia wasn't sure how to respond. She'd put in so much effort it would have been nice had the man at least shown an interest in her crime report. It was almost rude.

"Yes, of course I understand that."

"There can be serious side effects for taking more than the prescribed dosage. Loss of appetite. Insomnia. Audible and visual hallucination. Sometimes paranoia. Sometimes very bad paranoia. You haven't experienced anything like this?" He looked up and levelled a set of caramel brown eyes on her. Unsettled, she looked away.

"Of course not. I wouldn't take them if I had anything like that. I just need them for my back pain. Unfortunately I was involved in a rather serious accident. I'm not an..." Julia didn't complete her sentence.

"Okay." The doctor took a very deep breath. He seemed to be considering what to do. Julia glanced around his office and saw, framed upon the wall, some calligraphic writing. She looked more closely and noticed it wasn't in English but Arabic. She thought of what Kevin had told her.

"Okay," the doctor said again. He seemed to have come to a decision. "I can give you another three weeks supply, but after that you'll have to come and see me again and we'll start monitoring you a bit more carefully. And I'll have to put a note onto your record that this is the second time you've come back for more tablets. Do you understand?"

Julia was outraged. "But I explained. I have a crime number." She waved the paper at the doctor. He stared impassively back.

"Do you understand, Miss Ottley?"

Julia said she did, and she got her tablets.

While they helped with the pain, they didn't bring her any further forward with the story. The weeks rolled by.

THIRTY-TWO

IT WOULDN'T BE QUITE correct to say that Julia forgot about Becky's novel, but neither was she eagerly anticipating its arrival. She was caught up in her own work, and having started, but failed to finish, several novels of her own at a similar age, Julia assumed it was something of a fad for the girl.

Instead, she finally selected one of her potential characters as her protagonist. He was a blond-haired Norwegian man, who looked and acted rather like a Viking. He was, Julia thought, rather attractive, and she hoped her readers would think so too. She installed him in her woods, living alone in a cabin fashioned from an old railway carriage. She had no idea how the carriage came to be there – there were no railway tracks nearby in her imaginings, and she thought this rather mysterious. He was rather mysterious too – she decided upon concealing from the reader, and by extension herself, his purpose for being there, but she hinted at it in oblique ways. For example, behind the cabin she placed a well, and although she had no idea why, she was very clear that the well reached right down to the very centre of the earth.

Thus she completed chapter one. It was only two thousand words long, and she wasn't sure how it fed into chapter two. But she was very sure it was a strong two thousand words. Her second novel, the difficult second album, was finally gathering momentum.

The very next day Becky's manuscript arrived in the post.

The writing on the outside of the package was horribly childish. Like a schoolgirl's. It reminded Julia of girls from her own school – horrible girls who never spoke to her, and who huddled together in the common room whispering their secrets and shrieking their laughter. Girls who attended parties that Julia never even learnt about until after they happened. And girls who, at those parties, joined forces with boys and turned into powerful couples, with prestige and status that they flaunted and used to mock girls like her. Julia pushed the sudden flow of thought away and cut through the string that bound the package.

Becky had clearly spent some time wrapping and presenting her manuscript. It was sent in a box, and when Julia opened it, on the top page was a handwritten note. More girlish writing.

Dear Julia, thank you soooo much for agreeing to read my novel. I've not dared to show it to anyone else, and I can't tell you how nervous I am to hear what you think. As I said, it's not quite finished, and that's one of the reasons I'm asking you to help – I'm hoping you might have some ideas about how it could end. Anyway, thank you again and I'll wait to hear what you think!!!
Becky
XX

Julia frowned and turned the page. The title page bore the words:

One Shattering Secret

Julia's frown deepened, and she turned the page over again.

She read the first paragraph, and then stopped and read it again. She scanned it for errors, or words that were out of place, but she found none. The voice was fresh and engaging. There were words and phrases that set it aside from the mundane. Julia knew at once the girl could write.

"Hmmmmm," Julia said out loud.

Julia had no intention of going on to read the whole thing there and then. She wanted to get back to her own work. But something about Becky's voice kept her sitting at the table, turning one page after another. Soon she gave up thinking about her book. Instead she absently poured herself a cup of coffee, then carried it and the manuscript into the living room, where she had placed a reading chair looking out over the rooftops. But she didn't drink the coffee, letting it go cold in the cup. She read on.

Becky's story began with a couple – young lovers who needed money for their studies. Becky had used few words to describe them, and yet Julia could still picture them in her mind, and she felt emotionally connected as well. The writing was crisp and precise. The choice of words, unexpected but somehow satisfying. It felt accomplished, and there were – frequently – phrases which caused Julia to go back and read them a second time, just because they were so exquisitely *good*. How could the girl produce such flawless prose? It flowed like silk. Sentences shone like silver studded with brilliant diamonds. Her own notebook, which she had grabbed for her feedback, for jotting down the errors, was still unmarked. Julia scratched her head and read on. But this time, it wasn't just wonder she experienced as she read, it was something else. A growing sense of alarm.

In order to earn some money, the young couple in the story take a job helping with the catering at the launch party for a new literary book, also titled *One Shattering Secret*. At this launch the young couple meet the author of the book. She was depicted as a woman in her early fifties, who dressed in an eccentric fashion and had laughably poor social skills. At the end of the event, the woman – who had lied to everyone at the party as to where she lived – has to drive home, and offers to give the young couple a lift. During this journey home, the book took a sudden change in tone.

While driving along a quiet country road, the author runs down an elderly woman on her bicycle. Upon stopping, the threesome discover the woman is dead, and – at the tearful and undignified begging of the author – the three conspire to cover up the death.

Julia read on. The text was still beautifully crafted – it still *shone*, but this was now immaterial. All that Julia saw was the story unfolding in her mind. She knew every next step, and yet was surprised and horrified at its arrival.

A few weeks after the terrible accident the couple – who are wracked with guilt, and on the verge of going to the authorities – are contacted by the author, who begs them again not to reveal her dreadful secret. Then she offers them money, in the form of an academic scholarship. Begrudgingly the couple take the money. But their sense of guilt doesn't end and their relationship suffers. Meanwhile, the author herself moves to London to begin her new life as a literary sensation.

There were differences between Becky's story and what really happened, as if the girl had consciously or unconsciously tried to disguise that they were the same events. But they were small, inconsequential changes – for example in Becky's version of events the three of them conspired to dispose of the car by faking its theft, driving it to an out-of-the-way area and setting fire to it. But even such minor variations felt stolen from reality. In Becky's text the car was described as a classic VW Beetle, and the car Julia had now bought to replace her crashed Morris was exactly that – albeit the modern model.

There were other embellishments to the story that added a sense of darkness and literary beauty, but did nothing to change the structure of the story. For example, in Becky's version the woman on the bicycle had been wearing a diamond necklace, which had broken and spilled its jewels on the surface of the road, the stones glinting in the moonlight. Though the idea went nowhere – was inconsequential to the story – Julia realised Becky had used it in place of her own unfortunate moment with the vomit. Admittedly it was more elegant, but it changed nothing. The core of Becky's story, the building blocks from which it sprang, was virtually identical to what had really happened.

From which it sprang, *and to which it must return*. The thought formed in Julia's mind, but instantly its significance flew away.

Julia read on now with a cool dread, waiting to see how the story unfolded, but here – at last – the manuscript became confused. On the following pages, the fictional author's book – *One Shattering Secret* – grew and grew in popularity, and the author released a second book that was even better. But she was tortured by what she had done. And in parallel, the young couple were also unable to put the incident behind them.

There, the manuscript stopped. Unfinished. Becky had scrawled a hand-written note on the final page:

This is where I need a bit of help!!!

When she had finished, Julia sat in her chair for a very long time. As the world outside her penthouse flat darkened and a million London lights switched on beneath her, she still didn't move. Then, finally, she very carefully set the manuscript on the floor in front of her, climbed out of her chair and found her telephone. She scrolled through the few contacts slowly, until she had Becky's number on the screen. Then she pressed the button so hard the skin on her thumb turned white.

THIRTY-THREE

"Hello? Julia?" Becky's voice was breathless. As if she had been running. Grimly, Julia supposed she had been anticipating the call, anxious for her feedback.

"I received your manuscript..." Julia began, taking care to keep her voice dignified.

"Hang on a min," Becky interrupted her. "I'm just with Rob."

Her voice went away from the phone before Julia could reply, and she was left to listen to their voices in the background. It wasn't quite loud enough to understand, but Rob sounded annoyed, as if he had been doing something but was now interrupted.

"Sorry about that!" Becky's eager voice came through loud and clear again. "We were just... well, never mind – have you got it?"

"Yes."

"Well? Have you read it? I mean probably not all of it, but have you started it?"

"Yes, Becky." Suddenly even the foolish young girl's name seemed inappropriate. Why hadn't Julia taken to calling her Rebecca? "Yes, I have read it. All of it."

"Gosh! Wow."

There was a pause.

"And? What do you think? I tried really hard to keep the language as clear and sparse as I could. Like you do in *The Glass Tower*. Obviously it's nowhere near as good as that, but that's what I was going for..." She stopped, waiting.

"I think it's horrific."

"I'm sorry?"

"Horrific. Terrible. Unforgivable. Becky what on *earth* were you thinking?"

"What do you mean?" Becky replied, her voice tiny.

"What do I mean? What do you mean *what do I mean*? Becky, you've written the exact story of what happened to us. The exact same story. How could you?"

Becky gave a nervous laugh. "Oh that. I wondered if you'd notice."

"You wondered if I'd *notice*?"

"Yeah. I did base some elements on what happened between us."

"Some elements? It's the exact same story!"

"No it isn't. *One Shattering Secret* might take a little from what happened. But it's totally different really. It's a story about redemption and personal growth. At least that's what I want it to be. But I can't quite work out how it happens. That's why I wanted your help..."

"Takes a little? Becky, it's the *same bloody story! Surely you can see that?* Surely you can see you can't try and publish this as a novel."

For a moment a note of defiance sounded within Becky's voice. "Why not? It's good." But then it vanished again. "Isn't it?"

Julia put a hand to her back. She had been so distracted with reading the manuscript she had missed her dose of Dramadol. Now the pain was reminding her it was still here.

"It's not about whether it's any good or not. It's about the story. We can't talk about what happened. Ever. I thought you understood that?"

"Of course I do. I'm not an *idiot*, Julia," Becky said. Her voice had gone cold now. It unsettled Julia.

"Well... How do you expect to write it all down in a novel, and then not tell anyone?" A bizarre thought occurred to Julia. Perhaps she had misunderstood. Perhaps this was only ever intended for Julia – a way of Becky practising her prose. Finding her voice.

"Do you not intend to try and get it published?" A chink of light shone through Julia's darkness.

"Of course I want to get it published! That's my dream come true. I mean that's one of the reasons I sent it to you. You know, to help finish it, and in case you know someone you could pass it onto."

The light went out. Julia tried to back up.

"But you can't! You can't *possibly* publish it. I don't understand how you don't see this, Becky."

"It's not *real* Julia. It's *fiction*. I mean, I'm flattered in some ways if you recognised something of yourself in Joanna, but she's not *you*. She's an entirely made-up fictional character."

Julia blinked at the wall. She didn't know what to say.

"I mean, look at her," Becky went on. "She's *awful*. She'll do anything to cover up what she's done. She refuses to take responsibility for her actions. At least at the beginning. I want her to learn to do so. That's where it needs to end. With her owning her mistake..." Becky seemed to realise she had strayed from the point. "But *you're* not like that. You're not her."

Julia was silent.

"I'm just trying to say that Joanna is an entirely separate character, that just happens to have a story with some elements like yours. But no one will ever connect her to you."

Julia still didn't reply. She felt an overwhelming desire to put the phone down and erase the conversation.

"Julia?"

"What?"

"Do you think it's the sort of thing you could pass onto your agent, James McArthur? He doesn't even consider unsolicited manuscripts, but if it came from you he might be prepared to take a look. I mean, once I've finished it, obviously."

Julia considered the idea of sending what she had just read to her agent. The worst part was she could picture the response. Even in its unfinished form he would pick up his telephone and call her (which he so rarely did). He would want to know more about who wrote such crystal-clear prose, such delightful turns of phrase. Julia didn't doubt it for a second.

"Becky, I can't believe you're asking me this."

Becky stayed silent, so that Julia had to repeat her name down the telephone to check she was still on the line.

"Yes, I'm here. I just hoped that you might like it. That's all." She sounded so sad that Julia softened a little.

"I do. I do think it's quite nicely written. Very nicely written, even. It's just that you can't possibly carry on writing it. And certainly not publish it. Or even send it to anyone." Julia paused, and when Becky didn't reply she went on.

"*Ever.* You do see that, don't you?"

"Well, I know I have to finish it first," Becky replied at last.

Julia had to drag her mind away from what she wanted to hear the girl say, and back to what she was actually saying.

"What?"

"Before I send it anywhere. I know I have to finish it before I do that. That was the other thing I hoped you might be able to help me with. I mean, *The Glass Tower* was so brilliantly, yet so subtly, plotted out. I wondered if you might have some thoughts about how this story could finish. You see, I think Joanna has to redeem herself, but I don't know how she can do it."

"This story?" Julia asked. "Or our story?"

"This story," Becky replied firmly. She gave a nervous laugh. "My story, with the diamonds. They're not the same thing, Julia."

Julia slammed her fist against her head.

"Becky, the diamonds are an entirely incidental part of your story. You could take them out and they wouldn't affect the structure at all. It is *our story,* And you *can't* finish it. You simply can't."

Julia stopped and there was silence. She tried another tack.

"Why don't you start something else? Another story?"

"Start something else?"

"Yes, you can clearly write. Quite well, beautifully well even, so why not...?"

"What if someone had told you that?" Becky interrupted her. Her voice was suddenly bitter cold.

"Told me what?"

"To start something else when *The Glass Tower* was nearly finished?"

"That's different..."

"No it isn't. You said so yourself in the car, before the accident. You said you *had* to finish your book. That nothing could have stopped you. You simply wouldn't have let it. Well nothing is going to stop me either."

Julia tensed. Had she said that? She certainly recognised the feeling.

"Becky – you have to listen to me. You cannot let anyone read this, it'll destroy... It'll destroy all of us. Not just me, but you and Rob as well."

"No, it won't. It's *fiction*," Becky insisted. When she went on there was a stubborn note to her voice. "And even if it does, I don't care. I still have to finish it. I don't have a choice."

"Becky..."

"I don't want to talk about this any more," Becky interrupted her again. "I'm very disappointed Julia, I really thought you'd understand. But this is my book, you can't make me stop writing it. And if you won't help me finish it then I'll just have to finish it on my own."

"Becky!"

But the phone line had gone dead.

At once Julia threw her telephone hard against the window of her penthouse apartment. For a second she hoped it would smash and send a satisfying rain of shattered glass down onto the street below. But it was safety glass and the device simply bounced off the window and landed on the pile of papers that made up Becky's manuscript. It fell face up, showing that the only broken glass was the screen of the phone. She swore quietly under her breath, and after a very long time she pressed herself up out of the chair and went to get her tablets. Following her success in getting additional supplies she had adjusted her dose to four 200mg tablets, four times a day. It still wouldn't see her through until Dr Evil would give her some more. That was another problem that had to be solved.

Julia went to run a bath. As the tub filled she undressed, slipped into a robe, and then went to the fridge to get a bottle of wine. She poured a large glass, and then drank half of it at once. Then she pressed six tablets from the blister pack and swallowed them with the rest of the wine from the glass. She refilled it, balanced it on the side of the bath, and climbed in.

The water was hot and it stung her skin, but the sensation wasn't unpleasant. The searing feeling helped to numb the thoughts in her head. A hopeless despair. A total inability to think what to do next. She listened to the roaring sound the water made as it poured from the tap into the bath; she'd never noticed it before, how loud it was, how chaotic a sound. She watched the water fall, and her brain tried to force it to resemble a pattern. Her mind stopped the falling water, as if taking snapshots of it, but every time she tried to examine the image, it was gone, replaced by a new pattern. It was delicious, ignoring reality and concentrating on these little things. She went to sip at more of her wine, but found she had already finished her top up. Already two-thirds of the bottle had gone.

She turned off the tap and lay back in the new silence, pushing her head underwater. Slowly, the thoughts began to intrude back into her head.

Was it possible that Becky was right? Could she try and publish the book, and no one would notice that it actually told the story of what had really happened? Maybe there was no danger. Maybe no one would ever even read it. Certainly, the truth was that most books never even got close to being published. And Becky was a complete unknown. Surely the most likely outcome was that she would fail to sell the book, fail even to get an agent, and it would disappear? Julia felt hope at the thought. But then she remembered how she had felt as she was led through the clear, engaging text. The delights she encountered on nearly every page. Even if the diamonds in Becky's story were simply scattered haphazardly on the ground, in her prose they felt like an intriguing, glittering trail that led the reader onward. Julia could just imagine the excitement an agent or a publisher would feel upon following that trail. Their desperation to find out who was capable of laying such treasure. It was good. It was too damn *fucking* good.

No, if Becky sent that manuscript out – even in its unfinished form – it would spread like wildfire. Even before being published – and there is no doubt it would end up published – it would be passed around within the industry, gaining more admirers at every turn.

And then what? How long would it take before someone asked Becky whether the book was based on reality? Whether she had ever attended a launch of a novel – just as her character had? And once people made the connection between Julia and Becky, discovered about the bursary... The coincidences were too many. The consequences too awful to contemplate.

Could she persuade Becky to change the story somehow? Make it fundamentally different? Not, Julia realised, without ripping the very heart out of it.

Julia pushed her head under the water again. While there, she considered not surfacing this time. She stayed until the burn in her lungs really hurt. Then she came to the surface, spluttering for air.

She coughed and spat out bathwater. What, then? Could she somehow persuade Becky to change her mind? Surely the stupid girl would see sense in the end? It was clear to Julia that whatever damage the book would do to her, it would also harm Becky. Presumably Becky too had committed a crime in covering up the death of the woman. But then, Julia replayed scenes from Becky's novel in her mind. In every case she had subtly altered what really happened, and presented things in a way that placed more blame on the hands of the poor novelist in the story. The book, Julia realised, would act like some kind of evidential statement arguing on behalf of Becky and Rob. In Becky's story they were shown as young and naive – almost as much the victims of the situation as the old woman on the bike was. Becky's nuanced grasp of the situation in prose showed she understood perfectly what she was doing, even if she had denied it, or appeared naive to the truth on the telephone.

So what did that mean? Well, firstly that she wasn't going to be persuaded out of it, and actually Julia understood this on a more fundamental level. Becky's suggestion that Julia would never have given up on *The Glass Tower* was entirely accurate. She wouldn't have stopped that book for anything. Indeed, for ten years she had given up on everything in order to bring it into the world. Becky might be blind to the damage her book would do, but it was a willing blindness that came from love. A love for her book. And that was a love stronger than any other in the world. Stronger even than the love of a mother for her child (Julia was forced to suppose this, since she had never been a mother herself). Regardless, Julia knew that persuading Becky was impossible.

So could she be bribed? Again, a flash of hope flared within Julia's mind – was that what this was about? She quickly calculated how much money she had left. Already the windfall she had received from the record-breaking advance from *The Glass Tower*, which she had assumed would last her for the rest of her life, was rather depleted. How much could she spare? And how much would Becky need? Not enough, Julia quickly realised. Because how much might the book actually make? How much was it worth to Becky to become a name herself? To realise her ambition of being recognised as a writer on her own terms? And however much the book might make on its own would surely be dwarfed when the reality of the story behind the book came out. When people realised that it was actually based upon true events – and Julia's downfall was added to the mix – then the notoriety of the book, and how much it stood to earn, would go even higher.

There was no way Julia could buy Becky off. Even to try would be to court disaster – it would only highlight the value of what Becky had created.

Which left... what?

A happy thought occurred to Julia. It was nothing serious – just a whim of an idea – and it danced playfully into her mind. She could kill Becky. Quietly bump her off, and then all her problems would be solved. For the first time since realising what Becky's book was about, Julia smiled. She felt some of the weight of her problems lift off her mind. She could stick a knife into her back, push her in front of a train. Poison her. Choke her with a belt. She could hire a hit man to shoot her. She could beat her to death with a hammer.

Julia lay in the bath thinking about this until the water grew cold.

She finished her wine, climbed out of her bath and wrapped herself in her robe. She went to the kitchen, and at once she pulled another bottle from the wine chiller. She opened it, and as the cork popped she saw with certain clarity.

She could see the rest of Becky's story, as clearly as if Becky had typed it out in her own beautifully sparse prose.

Julia could see how their story ended.

THIRTY-FOUR

JULIA SLEPT PARTICULARLY BADLY, only falling asleep in the small hours. When she woke there were a few moments of otherworldliness and calm respite. Then, with all the subtlety of a freight train hammering past a station platform, all her problems returned, jostling and bickering for her attention.

She couldn't know how Becky's story – her story –ended. That was ridiculous. And she certainly couldn't murder the girl. That was madness. Anyway, if she did, she would obviously have to murder Rob too, because otherwise he would go to the police and tell all.

Her thoughts were preposterous, but nonetheless they lingered in her mind. In a space that would soon make way for the soaring, untethered reality that had become her new normal.

Painfully, she pulled herself upright, popped out four Dramadol, and gulped them down dry.

She made a new decision. She would visit Becky and persuade her of the craziness in continuing with the book. And if she couldn't? Well, she simply wouldn't take no for an answer.

She texted Becky at once, virtually ordering her to meet, and then she dressed carefully, ensuring there was nothing in her outfit that might fit Becky's absurd description of Joanna in her novel. She checked the train times and then decided to drive instead. By now she loathed driving in the London traffic, but what was the point of having a car if it just sat there on her allocated parking space?

The journey down was awful but uneventful, and she picked Becky up just after lunchtime. They drove out to a pizza place that Becky said was good, though Julia suspected she had only picked it because it was quite a long way from the student part of the city and Becky didn't want anyone to see who she was eating with. Well fine, thought Julia. I don't want anyone to see me either.

"So," Becky said, when they were sitting face-to-face, and their orders had been taken. "What's this about?"

Julia drew in a deep breath.

"I want to try and persuade you," she began. A glass of wine arrived by her arm and the restaurant climbed a couple of notches in her estimation. She nodded her thanks to the waitress.

"About your book. To explain why it's so impossible." She tried to smile at Becky, but the girl stared back at her tight-lipped.

"It's very beautifully written. So clear and crisp, and I understand how it's possible to be so focused on the act of creation that you simply aren't able to see the larger picture. That's what I wanted to explain."

Becky kept her eyes fixed on Julia's. She had her head bowed slightly, like a child pouting angrily. She didn't reply.

"If you send this book to anyone, you must understand what it would do." Julia glanced around. "To all of us. You would be ruining us." She dropped her voice right down. "Probably sending us all to prison. Is that what you want?"

Becky took several deep breaths. She opened her mouth to speak, then seemed to reconsider, and still sat in silence.

"Becky? Do you understand that?"

Still the girl was silent.

And you would be signing your own death warrant, a sudden voice in Julia's head announced. Julia looked around in sudden surprise. She had no idea where the voice had come from, and even feared Becky might have heard it too.

"I don't see why," Becky replied. But Julia hardly registered her. She was too shocked with what had just happened. After a moment it was clear she was the only person in the restaurant who had heard it. Cautiously, she tried to continue what she had been saying.

"You wouldn't want to hurt me? Or Rob?" Julia went on. "You're not the type to want to hurt anyone."

The look of mistrust the girl had been wearing slipped from her face. Becky glanced down at the table. The pain and confusion were obvious by her expression. Julia felt she might be winning.

"No. But..." Becky stopped again. Looked away in frustration.

"What?" Julia asked.

"But I just don't see how anyone would ever connect the book to you," Becky said.

Julia sat back for a moment. The thoughts she had had in the bath came flooding back. How the book would spread throughout the publishing world. Driven by its clarity and its sheer beauty. How it would grip the industry once people began to suspect the truth. She smiled kindly.

"It's just such a risk. When you could write something just as beautiful about something else. I really believe that, Becky. I really believe you can."

But Becky was already shaking her head. "I wish. But I've never written anything like this before. Nothing. And I don't think I'll ever write anything like it again..." She shook her head again. "It's my story." Becky fell into silence.

Julia kept her smile fixed in place, although it was harder to do so now.

"I know it might feel like that now," she began, and then had to wait as their pizzas arrived. They looked disgusting. Two huge plates of greasy melted cheese.

"But it won't always feel like that."

Becky toyed with her knife and fork. After a while she cut a chunk from her pizza and folded it neatly in half with her fork. Then she cut the parcel in two and ate the smaller piece.

"Becky?" Julia said. Suddenly she noticed that the girl was crying.

"It's my decision, isn't it?" Becky said. She closed her eyes to force the tears to stop, then dabbed at her face with her serviette. "I mean, it's my book?"

"Yes," Julia heard herself say.

"And I don't think there will ever be a problem." She spoke with a firmness that made Julia's heart sink. She re-fixed her smile in place.

"I mean, probably they'll just ignore it. It's really nice of you to say you like it, but most books just get rejected, don't they? That's the most likely outcome."

Julia didn't reply.

"Although I have thought about just publishing it anyway. You know with self-publishing? That's not what I really want, but it's an option, isn't it?"

"I suppose so," Julia said slowly. She hadn't yet considered the implications of this approach, and now tried to do so, while still smiling at Becky. It didn't seem to change anything, the book was so good it would still be found. Publishers would come to her.

"But I don't want you to worry," Becky said, and Julia snapped back to the conversation.

"Good," she began. "Why not?"

"Well, like I said. I *really* don't think anyone could ever possibly link the book to you. I think you're worrying about nothing."

"Okay," Julia said. She gripped her fork tightly, feeling for an alarming second that she needed to resist an impulse to stab it into the back of Becky's hand. She smiled.

"What about Rob?" Julia tried another approach. "What does he think? Have you told him?"

Becky shook her head. "Rob's not really a reader. I mean I've told him I'm *writing*. And he's really supportive. But he doesn't know..."

"He doesn't know what? He doesn't know what the book's about?"

"No. No one does. I wanted to show you first." She looked shyly at Julia, who was now toying with her knife, and actively suppressing the urge to plunge it into the girl's chest.

Becky misread Julia's expression for something less pathologically violent.

"I really don't think you need to worry, Julia. It's going to be fine." She smiled. "I just have to finish the book. And obviously the ending will be different to what's happened, you know, between us."

It was the first time Julia had heard her concede that the two stories were, up to this point, essentially the same. A thought struck Julia – would this meeting now find its way into the story? It was like one of those infinity mirrors you see on the silvered inside of lifts, the same image, reflecting itself, the same dilemma, endlessly replicated, one inside the other.

"So I think it's all okay," Becky was saying. "Don't you?"

Julia was silent. All the way down the motorway she had assumed the meeting would go better. That the sheer obvious logic of her argument would cut through. But the girl was stupid. A brilliant writer, yes, but also, somehow, just *incredibly* stupid. And now Julia understood that Becky would *never* see. She would never accept reality. She was too pig-headed. She was completely and totally delusional. Worse, Julia now realised that if she kept pushing, the only deviation from the current path would be that Becky would cut her – Julia – out. She would continue with the book, the threat it represented would remain, and Julia's ability to keep tabs on it would be gone.

So? You know what to do! Kill her. That's how the story ends!

The voice in her head spoke so clearly this time that Julia thought Becky must have heard it, but she hadn't. She just sat opposite her, folding up her parcels of pizza and pushing them into her pretty mouth.

Kill her right now!!!

Julia stared at her. Perhaps she could simply steal the damn manuscript? She indulged herself for a moment, imagining herself as a cat burglar, breaking into their horrible little house. Beating Becky's laptop into a smashed pile of microchips with a house brick.

She'll only write it again though, won't she?

What?

She'll only write it again. Take the brick and use it on her. Bash her brains out! Kill her!

With a huge effort, Julia silenced the voices in her head.

"Okay. Let's talk about something else, shall we?" Julia said.

Becky glanced up as if in surprise. As far as she was concerned they had been sitting in silence for nearly a minute, so perhaps the comment seemed odd.

"Okay," she said."Did I tell you we got those jobs?"

Julia made herself interested. "What jobs?"

"The ones I told you about. We're going to run the old lighthouse lodge on Hunsey Island."

Julia's face crumpled into a deep frown. "What?"

"I told you. They wanted a young couple to run it. It's a kind of cross between a B&B and an artists' retreat. Rob and I are going to manage it. It's nothing too challenging, just changing the bedding and cooking breakfasts and stuff." She smiled.

Confusion reigned in Julia's head, and apparently on her face as well. *"What?"*

"Didn't I tell you? I thought I told you."

No you didn't fucking tell me!

"No, I don't think you mentioned it."

"Oh, I thought I did. Actually, it's kind of thanks to you really," Becky said, and for the first time she offered Julia a smile that looked genuine. "I don't think they would have even considered us, but we worked that night of your party, so they remembered who we were."

"What about university?"

"Julia! We're finished!" Becky's face lit up in mirth, as if she couldn't believe how foolish Julia was being.

"And it's thanks to you that we can take such an interesting job. Thanks to your bursary, we're not stuck in debt like most of our friends."

Becky slid a glance over at Julia, like she wasn't sure this was a safe subject. But Julia's face was entirely without expression, which Becky took to be a better sign than it really was.

"And it's great because we only need to work mornings. So I'll be able to work on the book every afternoon!"

Julia's smile thinned and she saw her future again. She saw it with crystal clarity.

She was going to murder Rebecca Lawson.

THIRTY-FIVE

JULIA DROVE HOME without giving the road a moment of her conscious attention, a fresh and strong dose of Dramadol thumping through the synapses of her brain. Every single way she examined her predicament she came to the same, inevitable conclusion.

If and when Becky sent her manuscript to publishers – and Julia knew without any doubt it was a case of when, not if – it would lead, inevitably and inexorably to Julia's total ruin. A professional and personal annihilation. She would be humiliated. Arrested. Thrown in jail. Her life would be over.

But even if Becky *didn't* send her manuscript – say, for example, Julia had been able to persuade her of the folly in doing so – it would not have prevented this conclusion, only deferred it. Why? Because Becky and Rob held between them the means to destroy her. And with that in place, it was only a matter of how, and when, the knowledge they had came out. It might be that Rob would release his photographs. It might be he would get drunk and tell his story to someone in a bar. It might be Becky's damn novel, or perhaps she would become overwhelmed by guilt at her involvement – it hardly mattered. The point was it would come out. It was *inevitable*.

It might not happen right away. It might be years that they held the

threat over her before using it. They might step up their blackmail –
demanding even more money than she had already given them. Or they
might reveal her secret by accident – in a row, like the drama over Rob's
pornographic interests.

They might even, Julia realised, wait until after her death to tell their
'truth' about the *real* Julia Ottley – trashing and destroying her legacy.

The point was their story would not, and could not end until the
truth had come out. It was simply a basic fact of storytelling. And sooner
or later, Becky would see that.

Yet it wasn't the only possible ending. There was another way. With
the elimination of Rob and Becky. With their deaths.

It was brutal. It was sad. It was not a little scary to face up to what
she had to do. But it was this very inevitability that made it necessary,
and logical and therefore *reasonable*. And the more that Julia thought
about that, she began to see something else. It was all so logically, beautifully clear, that sooner or later, Becky must eventually come to the exact
same conclusion as Julia had. There simply was no other ending to their
story, and therefore no other ending to the story that Becky was writing.

Julia Ottley was going to murder Rebecca Lawson and her boyfriend
Robert Dee. The only question that remained was: How?

THIRTY-SIX

"YEAH. TYPICAL MAINLANDER ERROR THAT IS," the barman said as he pulled Rob's pint, a dark ale with a creamy head. He and Becky were in the Hunsey Inn, the tavern which stood in the centre of the village, and appeared to have done so for centuries. It had low ceilings, and its flag-stone floor was worn from the tread of generations of drinkers.

"We felt such idiots." Becky continued telling him their story. "We were so busy packing and getting ready to come here that we totally forgot you can't get across at high tide. We had to wait for the tide to fall." She smiled at her own foolishness but the man – who looked to be almost as old as the pub – simply nodded.

"That's £5.50 please," he told her, his island accent coming through strong. Becky paid with her card and the barman nodded his thanks and walked away.

Becky smiled at Rob, then raised her glass and chinked it against the rim of his pint.

"Well, here we are! The new keepers of Hunsey lighthouse! And in our new local too!" She paused, then went on. "He didn't seem all that friendly, did he?" She frowned and took a sip of her own drink.

"It'll probably take a while," Rob replied. "You know, before the locals get to recognise we're actually working here and not just tourists." He smiled reassuringly then looked around. The walls were lined with black and white photos, showing the men folk from the island holding forth large fishing catches or building stone walls. In most of the shots the lighthouse was there, an inevitable backdrop. Back in those days it warned ships of dangerous rocks and the currents that swirl to the south of Hunsey Island.

After a while the barman came back. He picked up a glass and began to dry it with a cloth.

"So you're this young couple then? Looking after the new lighthouse?"

"That's right," Rob replied. "We just arrived on the island a few days ago." He glanced at Becky. "After a bit of a delay for the tide."

Again, the barman was uninterested in this part of their story.

"I heard it was opening soon."

"Yep. That's right," Rob said again. "Actually we've got our first guests coming tomorrow." Rob tried to smile confidently, but Becky could see this still made him nervous.

"That right? I've not been up there myself, but I hear they've done a good job of it." The barman frowned, and Becky couldn't stop herself from joining in.

"You haven't been up the lighthouse? Oh, it's amazing. The view from the top is incredible. You can see the whole island, and the hills on the mainland, and for miles out to sea."

He seemed to contemplate this for a while, as if it was a shame it was something he himself would never experience.

"Well. It's good to have it back in use," he said, then added,"I suppose," as if it might have been better to let it fall further into ruin.

"So, you got many bookings have you?"

"A few. We've got a couple coming tomorrow," Rob answered him. "And then a couple more next week. You know it's owned by a charity, the Hunsey Lighthouse Trust? They reckon it'll take a while before people hear about it. You know, through word of mouth. But they're not worried. It'll give us time to get the hang of running the place."

The barman put down his glass and picked up another.

"And it's just the six rooms you've got up there?"

"That's right. They're trying to make it a kind of coastal retreat. For bird watchers, artists and so on. You know, people who want to really get away from it all," Rob continued.

"But the actual lantern room of the lighthouse is incredible," Becky interrupted. "It's like a communal area for anyone staying in the lodge. We could show you if you like?"

"No thank you, Miss," he said, then polished another glass. Becky frowned at Rob, growing frustrated. But then the barman went on.

"You do know what happened up there?" he said, and looked at them both through hooded eyes. "In the war?"

It was Rob who answered. "Yeah, we heard. The lighthouse keeper went mad and killed his wife."

"Threw her from the top is what," the barman went on, adding darkly, "right down on to the rocks below."

"But it was a long time ago," Rob argued, smiling at Becky to reassure her. The barman frowned as if he didn't agree with that.

"Anyhow," he said. "What are you doing out there? You just give 'em breakfast and that?"

"Yeah," Rob said. "And we do a packed lunch if they want it."

"But not evening meals?"

Rob shook his head. "No. We thought we'd probably be sending most of them over here."

"Not sure where else they're gonna go," the barman agreed quickly. "Nowhere else on the island, and when the tide's in they're not going nowhere else anyway."

This wasn't strictly true, Becky knew. Hunsey also had a café which stayed open to do evening meals – she and Rob had eaten there the night before – but she didn't say this now.

Suddenly the barman stretched out his hand.

"You can call me Ted," he said.

Rob smiled for real now. "I'm Rob," he said. "And this is my girl-friend, Becky."

"Nice to meet you," Becky jumped in.

"Ah well, we'll see," Ted said, as if he wasn't convinced by that last comment. "But it'll be nice to have some younger folk around," he went on. "Hunsey needs a bit of fresh blood."

They stayed for a couple of drinks before heading back – aware of needing to be up early the next day for their first guests. They had walked the half-mile from the lighthouse complex to the village and now, strolling back, the only light came from the moon and stars. The road ran down the raised spine of the island, and fell away on either side until jagged cliff met restless sea. Bats flitted around them, chasing the last of the summer bugs. They passed the small museum – where Julia's party had been held – and continued onto the next building, the newly-reconstructed lodging house which sat by the base of the lighthouse itself. In the semi-darkness it loomed above them; its sheer size still impressed Becky. A security light clicked on, throwing a pool of yellow rays over the lodge's entrance. Rob pulled out his new set of keys.

The door opened onto the lodge's small dining area, with six tables, as yet unused for real, paying guests. They had cooked a test breakfast the day before – for the builders who remained, tidying up the loose ends of the project, and the woman from the charity who had been showing them how the booking system worked. It had gone well, everyone had been fed, everyone had seemed satisfied. But the next time they had to do it would be for real. And on their own. Rob turned on the lights and stood still. Becky knew he was thinking the same as her.

"First guests tomorrow then," Rob said. He puffed out his cheeks.

"We'll be okay," Becky told him. "After a few days we'll be old hands. We can do it."

For a long time Rob didn't answer, but then he took her hand. "Yeah, I know."

She was only partly right. Their first week passed in a blur. They began working as the sun hauled itself out of the ocean to the east of the island, and were still busy long after it had set to the west. A thousand things went wrong. In truth, the rooms weren't quite ready. Rob worked into the evening with borrowed tools and other times headed to the mainland to source materials. But day-by-day, they began to make sense of it. They would finish serving breakfast at 10 a.m., with packed lunches already prepared for those that had pre-ordered them. Then, while Becky cleaned the rooms that were due to be changed, Rob would check the booking system on the computer and ensure they were stocked and ready for the next day.

Before too long, their daily routine allowed them time in the day to do what they wanted. Rob would go out in the afternoons, exploring the cliffs and rocky crevasses that led down to the water. He would take his camera to capture images of whirling sea birds, curious seals, and other wildlife. Becky, when the opportunity presented itself, preferred to collect her laptop and head up to the very top of the lighthouse – to the former lantern room.

Whilst in service, a giant lens had rotated inside there, sending a million-candle message of danger far out to sea. Two bright flashes every twenty seconds. Stay clear. The rocks of Hunsey Island are a dangerous place. The light was turned off during the Second World War, to avoid it being used by German aircraft as a means of locating themselves and lining up to attack London or the cities on the south coast. And due to the events that followed, never switched on again. Those events, the violent death of the last lighthouse keeper's wife, had never been fully explained. He claimed to have caught her up in the lantern room, sending out signals to the Nazis, but many locals believed otherwise, that he was overtaken by madness. What was known was they fought, and she was tipped to her death. These days it was just a story; a grizzly mystery to entertain visitors to the Dorchester museum, where the lighthouse's original lens and track were now on display.

Now the room had been transformed, with curved sofas and a round table in the centre, where the light had once stood. And if the 360-degree view from inside wasn't enough to thrill the guests, those with a head for heights could open a small door and walk all the way round an external balcony, forty metres above the rocks and roaring surf below.

Becky had plastered images of and from the lantern room on both her, and the lodge's Facebook page – both to try and attract more guests and just for her friends. But she wasn't too disappointed that as yet they weren't busy, because it was a truly incredible room to write in.

Or it would have been, had she been able to write. For her creativity had stalled since beginning the work running the lodge. Even though she tried to write whenever she had the opportunity – she would climb the long, twisting spiral right the way to the top of the lighthouse, push open the funny-shaped door and set herself up in front of her laptop – it wasn't happening. Even though she was inside the very tower that had inspired the great Julia Ottley, with its dizzying view of the ocean, somehow the words which had flowed so easily, suddenly wouldn't come.

THIRTY-SEVEN

JULIA WASN'T WRITING EITHER. In fact, she had temporarily stopped all work on her new novel and instead refocused her attention on one single task: working out how to murder Becky and Rob. But though she was now convinced of both the necessity and the inevitability of this outcome, the question of how to get there was proving slippery.

For nearly a week she applied herself to the task, filling notebooks with ideas and then examining them for any faults that might result in the plan failing, or her being caught. The problem was there was always a fault, usually lots of them. She realised that the task she had set herself was genuinely *difficult*. Julia was under no illusions that she was anything other than a middle-aged woman whose idea of exercise was an occasional walk in the country, usually taking in a cream tea along the way. Whereas her proposed victims were both young, and clearly fit. And there were two of them. Furthermore, it wouldn't do to only murder *one*, since whichever one survived would be certain to point to her as a possible suspect.

For six days and nights she wrestled with the problem, making little or no progress. But on the seventh day a new problem presented itself. A problem that was nearly enough to drive Julia over the edge.

It was afternoon by the time she stumbled from her bedroom and into the kitchen. She observed with blinking eyes the chaos of half-eaten take-aways, and empty wine bottles that littered the kitchen. But she barely saw them. Instead her eyes scanned the room until they found what they were looking for – a blister pack of Dramadol. She picked it up, feeling the individual pockets to count how many tablets remained. She felt a stab of alarm when she realised they were all empty. She looked again, thinking she must have picked up the wrong packet, and quickly scrabbled for the other packets on the work surface. As she did so she knocked an empty bottle onto the tiled floor where it shattered, but such was her panic that she ignored it completely. All the other blister packs were empty, too.

Fear rising fast within her, she went to her bag, where she had the remainder of her stash. And it was with intense relief that her fingers closed on a full packet. She quickly pressed out six tablets with shaking hands, and found a bottle with a little wine left in it to wash them down.

Then she turned back to her bag and searched it more carefully, pulling out all her remaining tablets. At the rate she was taking them, they would run out before the end of the day.

She stopped what she was doing and walked to her desk. Her notes from the night before, where she thought she had made some progress, didn't interest her now. The task was difficult enough if she had her medication. It was impossible without it. She pushed them away. Instead she opened her laptop, and clicked through until she reached Becky's Facebook page.

The first image she saw was the one Becky had posted of the lantern room in the old lighthouse on Hunsey Island. She had taken it at dawn, looking through the glass of the window at the sun rising from a still ocean. You could just make out the edge of the island, where patches of sheep-worn grass gave way to black rocks and then lazy water. There were others, too. Close-ups of beautiful, late summer flowers nestled between channels of weather-worn rock. Waves pushing into the tiny coves and inlets that perforated the low cliffs. Clouds of seabirds hovering over the water. There was a selfie of Becky with her arms draped lovingly around Rob's neck. Julia worked her way through them all with a feeling of empty nothingness, until she came across the final image. It was Becky, sitting in the lantern room, with a manuscript in front of her. She'd labelled the photo 'Perfect place to write'. Some of her friends had picked up on the implication.

Are you actually writing something, Becks?

A girl called Sophie had posted underneath the picture.

Sssshhhhh

Becky had replied, and added a winking emoji.

Julia looked from her screen to her own writing desk. The notes for her new novel had been pushed to the back, and some had fallen onto the floor where they had been trodden on as she had walked from the kitchen to the desk and back again in the preceding days. She had spilled red wine on the desk – not a large spill – but she hadn't bothered to clean it up and it had soaked into some papers. It smelt. So did the silver take-away tray with the scraped remains of curry in it. Somehow her fountain pen had fallen into it and become stuck to the base. She sniffed back tears.

Perfect place to write, Becky's smiling face taunted.

Julia tensed, waiting to see if the emotion kindling inside her was pity or anger. Then she sniffed again, more loudly this time as it became clear. It wasn't fair. It was *her* island. Not Becky's, *hers*. She had found that tower, before Becky had even been born. She had written the most important literary novel of the decade, about *that tower*, on that island. *Her island*. So how had it come to pass that it was Rebecca *Fucking* Lawson who was sitting in the eyrie at the top of that tower, surrounded by such peace and tranquillity? That it was she who could write and Julia who could not? How had it happened that Julia was here, surrounded by filth and squalor, with barely enough pills left to get her through the day?

She snapped the laptop closed, but the image persisted, as if it were being beamed onto the window in front of her. With a snarl, Julia bunched her hand into a fist and punched it.

Bang!

The toughened glass wobbled under her blow, but the image persisted. Julia hit it again, and again, harder each time. Until the apparition faded into a bright red smear. And through tears of anger and frustration, all she saw now were London's dirty rooftops and her own pain.

THIRTY-EIGHT

LATER, the episode of whatever it was – madness, paranoia, or a valid recognition of the horror she had descended to – cleared. Julia looked around the mess of her flat with almost-sane eyes. She even tidied, thinking again how she could solve her problems, how she could do away with Becky and Rob. But now the urgency of the problem seemed, not diminished, but certainly overtaken by the more pressing concern of how few Dramadol she had left. And a new idea formed. It wasn't clear exactly how it offered a solution, but it felt like a possibility. She had to get out. Get out of her flat. Get out of the city, with its smoke and its dirt and its plague of people crawling around like ants beneath her. She had to get back to the countryside where it was quiet and peaceful. Once there, surrounded by fresh air and space, she would find a way forward. And while Becky might have stolen her island from her – at least for now – she still had the cottage, deep in the Dorset countryside. Away from everything. So that's where she would go.

Once the decision was made Julia felt compelled to act at once. She abandoned her tidying mid-way through, and instead hurriedly packed a bag with some clothes, her computer, and what little remained of her supply of Dramadol.

Then, already sensing the fresh air that awaited her, she left her flat and walked down to her numbered parking space. Five and a half white-knuckle hours later (both for Julia, and the poor motorists whose journeys intersected with hers) she pulled up in front of the hydrangea outside her country cottage.

* * *

The little house was reassuring in its familiarity, but cold from being left empty, the heating turned off. The fridge was bare too, save from some rancid milk and a nearly-empty tin of Edgar's food with mould growing on it. The village had a shop, but she knew it would be closed already. Julia cursed that out here (in this *bastard backward backwater* – her mood hadn't improved that much) it wasn't possible to simply phone to have a takeout delivered. In the end she dined on a tin of tomatoes she found at the back of the cupboard, with stale biscuits left over from a distant Christmas. Then she took her now heavily-reduced ration of Dramadol and vowed to go to the supermarket in the morning to stock up.

A bright day woke her early, and she made coffee and drank it black. She took a single tablet but no wine, since there was none in the cottage. All of which meant that, as she pushed her trolley around the aisles of Tesco that morning, she was in a much more lucid state than had recently been the case. She was almost normal.

In fact, she was almost enjoying it. For once she wasn't plotting how to secure more drugs, her mind wasn't endlessly cycling through ways she could murder Becky and her horrible boyfriend. Julia was simply existing, in the moment. She was choosing what to have for dinner. It was like she had returned to the innocent state that she had lived in for years before she achieved her ambition of grand literary success.

This relative tranquillity meant that she didn't notice the man in front of her, with his long hair tied back in a pony-tail and his combat trousers and army boots. In fact, it was only his shopping trolley, left carelessly so that it blocked her from moving past, that made her look up at all. But when she did she saw the strangely drooping features of Kevin, the most unlikely member of the Rural Dorset Creative Circle.

There wasn't the time or space for Julia to look away.

"Alright?" Kevin said. He interrupted his frown to nearly smile, then fixed the look of confusion back again. "What you doing here?"

Julia's lips thinned as she began to force her own smile. Then she decided not to bother.

"Shopping," she said. She was about to use her trolley to barge past his own, when something stopped her. A memory she couldn't quite place.

"Rats," Kevin said, as if she had asked him what he was doing too.

"What?" Julia said.

"Rats. A plague of 'em." He held up the box he had been inspecting. From the lurid colours and artwork she identified the product as rat poison. "They're everywhere. Horrible little bastards."

Automatically Julia looked around, as if he might mean there were rats advancing upon her now, but the floor of the supermarket was free from any obvious infestation.

"Back at my trailer. Not here," Kevin went on. "Although there probably are. They just don't tell us."

"What?" Julia said again.

"Here. They probably *are* here, too. It's just they don't tell us about it. Tesco I mean."

"What?"

"Well, we don't know do we? At night they probably have all sorts of vermin crawling over the fruit and veg. Rats, mice. Cockroaches too, I shouldn't wonder. That's why I never eat anything unless it comes in a tin." Kevin snorted loudly and stared at Julia, who noticed now that his trolley contained only tins of soup, baked beans and alphabet-shaped spaghetti.

"What you doing back round here anyway?" Kevin continued. "You come to see old Geoffrey?"

Hearing Geoffrey's name surprised Julia, it almost made her smile. But at once she pulled her lips back straight.

"No, I'm just back for a few days to... Have a break from the city." Suddenly she remembered what that memory had been. Kevin's odd offer that he could *sort her out* if she ever needed... Whatever he'd said. Had he been serious? At the time she had dismissed it. But now, could it solve her problem?

She smiled at him.

"Oh. I thought you'd be here to see him," Kevin was saying now. "He never stops going on about you at the Circle," Kevin continued. "Like a lost puppy he is." Kevin seemed delighted by this observation, but it didn't interest Julia. Instead she was wondering how she might turn the conversation to her advantage. She noticed again what he was holding in his hands. Rat poison.

"So you've got a problem with rats?" she said.

"Have I?" He puffed out his cheeks. "I can't sleep for hearing them scrabbling around under the trailer. It's only a matter of time until they get inside and bite me on the nose!" He shuddered at the thought. Julia hesitated; she couldn't think of an obvious way to link this to what she wanted to say. In the resulting pause, Kevin seemed to feel the conversation had reached its conclusion.

"Well," he said, tossing the rat poison into his trolley. "I guess I'll be getting on..."

"Kevin," Julia said smartly. He stopped.

"Yeah?"

"Do you remember, when we last talked?" She smiled again, the most charming smile she could muster. "You mentioned something, when we were talking about my accident?"

Now it was Kevin's turn to look confused.

"What?"

"Well, you said you might be able to... source something, should I ever..."

"Source what?"

"Some alternative..." Julia mouthed the word instead of saying it out loud. "*Painkillers.*"

For a long moment he looked baffled. But then his face lit up in recollection. "Oh, aye. I remember. You were popping them like sweeties!"

The memory seemed to put a swagger in his stance.

"Quite. Well, is that still a possibility? Because if it is, I'd very much like to take you up on..."

"Shhhh." Kevin put his fat finger to his lips. Julia was surprised into silence.

"Look up," he said.

After a moment she did what he said.

"What do you see?"

Julia considered. There was the ceiling of the supermarket, squares of off-white ceiling tiles. "Nothing."

"See those little black things sticking out. What do you make of those?"

Julia squinted. She didn't have her glasses on. "I think they're for the sprinkler system aren't they? In case there's a fire."

"That," Kevin said meaningfully, "is what they want you to believe." He sniffed again – the man clearly had an unpleasant cold. "I think we'd better continue this conversation outside, don't you?" He gave her a knowing look, and very deliberately he returned to his trolley and moved away.

"Kevin?" Julia called out to him.

He turned at once, looking slightly irritated with her now. Then he pointed to the supermarket door and mouthed the word 'outside'.

Julia was baffled, but she had to let him go. She quickly paid for her shopping and hurried out into the car park, worried that she wouldn't find him there. But in the event it was easy. He was standing next to a red and very muddy pick-up truck that was parked in a disabled space.

She walked towards him.

"No one ever looks up do they?" Kevin asked.

Julia frowned in confusion. "I'm sorry?"

"That's how they get away with it. No one ever looks up. In a super-market. I mean, why would you?"

"I don't... I don't know."

"Exactly. So that's how they can implant listening devices in the ceiling and monitor everything that people say and do. Mostly it's to make us spend more money, but who else is bugging them, and sucking down all the data? Eh? You ever think about that?"

Julia was forced to concede she never had.

He sniffed again and leaned back on his car.

"So what exactly are you after?" he asked.

Julia considered quickly. It wasn't yet clear if he considered it safe to talk about this in the car park, or if he thought the lamp posts might possibly be listening too. She decided to risk it.

"Well, you see the problem is I've been prescribed these tablets, only the doctors have quite misunderstood the amount of pain I'm in, and so I'm getting through them a little faster than I can get hold of them."

"Uh huh." He nodded as if this were a common issue. "Muslim doc is it?"

"No… Well actually yes, but I don't think that's the issue here."

Kevin's eyebrows rose up, as if suggesting he would draw his own conclusions on that. But he let it pass. "What tablets?" he asked.

"They're called Dramadol." Julia dug in her bag for a box to show him. She handed it hopefully to Kevin but he quickly backed off.

"Whooa!" He quickly looked around. "Easy, lady." He turned half-away, but put his hand out to the side and subtly took the box from her hands. "Never know who's watching."

Then he stared at the box for a while. Julia wondered for a second if he could actually read the words.

"Well?" she asked. "Do you have any?"

Kevin hesitated, then shook his head. Julia swore under her breath.

"These are strong little buggers. I don't keep anything like this in the vehicle." He reached into his mouth and began scraping one of his teeth with his little fingernail.

"But I'll probably have something back at the trailer."

Julia's hopes dipped and rose as if on a roller coaster.

"What? Well, where's the trailer?" she asked at once.

Kevin looked at her, surprised. "It's just out in the woods. Old John from Rubblestone Farm, he lets me keep it there."

Julia had no idea who or where this was, but she didn't care either. "Well, can we go there? I can follow you?"

Kevin considered this for a moment. "You wanna come out to the trailer?"

"Yes."

"Now?"

"Yes."

"With me?"

"Yes, with you."

Kevin seemed to calculate for a while. "Okay. This isn't going to be cheap, you know." He cocked his head to one side.

"Well, how much? I can write you a cheque right now." Julia began digging in her handbag again.

"Whooaaa," he said again. "You're a funny one, aren't you?" He pointed over at the supermarket's cash machine.

"Cash only."

Kevin waited while Julia withdrew the maximum she could take on her bank card, and then all three of her credit cards. It gave her over a thousand pounds in cash. Then she hurried to where she had parked and threw her shopping in the back. She followed Kevin's truck, noting the black smoke that plumed from the exhaust pipe and the 'Baby on Board' sign attached to the rear window. They drove in the opposite direction to where Julia lived, but after a while turned off the road and onto a farm track. Kevin's truck rolled and bumped through a half-mile of pot-holed and muddy track, then he turned off again, this time leading Julia into a wood. After another half mile they came to a clearing. On one side a dishevelled static caravan appeared to have been dumped there. Next to it was a jury-rigged washing line with what looked to be dead animals, rabbits or squirrels perhaps. Kevin pulled up alongside the washing line and stopped his truck. Then he got out. Julia considered for a moment before doing the same. In the Tesco car park this had seemed a good idea, but now she was here it wasn't so clear. The woods were thick, and there was no one else in sight. In fact, as far as Julia knew, there were no other human beings within a mile of where she was. And suddenly Julia realised that Kevin was a large man. A large and obviously very unusual man. A part of her wanted to turn around and drive away as fast as she could. But a more primal part wanted the tablets. With a deep breath, she opened the door.

As she passed the line of dead rodents Julia kept her eyes fixed firmly forward, but still formed the distinct impression that the animals had been shot. She pressed the thought away and followed Kevin to the door of the caravan.

He unlocked it and held it open.

"I haven't cleaned up too much for a while," he said as she climbed the steps and went in.

There was a smell inside, the damp, rotten smell of slowly decaying furniture. The walls were stained yellow. In some places Kevin had cut out articles from newspapers. By the little bathroom, its door open, there was a pin-up of a girl in a swimsuit.

"Yeah, um…" Kevin looked around too, like he was suddenly noticing the mess of the place. "Have a seat, if you like. I'll see what I've got."

She did as he said, sitting down on a bench seat that ran around the caravan's main table. On it was a laptop and a spread of papers and other newspaper clippings.

"That's my book," Kevin said. "The one I was telling you about. How the Muslims are infiltrating society. You can have a read if you like, but it's scary stuff."

Feeling it was only polite to do so, Julia turned to look over the work, her eyes immediately spotting two instances where he had used 'their' instead of 'they're' and a misplaced apostrophe.

"It certainly is," she said. Kevin looked proud.

"Told you," he said. "Well, you keep reading, I'll see what I've got." He walked past her and into what Julia could see was the bedroom section of the caravan. She saw him kneel on the floor by the bed to pull something out from underneath. Unfortunately the act of kneeling down had opened up a gap between the top of his trousers and the bottom of his shirt, and a large slit, inviting her eyes to peer between his buttocks, opened up. Despite her hunger for the pills, Julia looked away, and tried to distract herself with the newspaper article in front of her. Its headline warned:

By 2025 four in five Britons will be MUSLIMS!

She had a glimmer of an idea. The article was illustrated with a photograph of two Islamic women in their traditional hijabs – or were they burkas? Julia was never sure of the distinction – walking down a typical British high street. Next to the newspaper was a scrapbook filled with Kevin's spidery black handwriting. From the tight, intense shapes of the letters the work radiated paranoia. The idea – if that's what it had been – passed before Julia could see what it was, and then Kevin came back and she could stop reading. He was carrying a large plastic box with him, and he dumped it down on top of the clippings. He carefully pulled off the lid and inside were scores of packets of medicine, some grouped together in their original boxes and tied with elastic bands, others just loose in their blister packs. To Julia it looked like a hoard of treasure.

"Where did you get all this?" Julia asked. She curled her hands against the table top to stop them diving into the box, rummaging for what she was looking for.

"Mate of mine works as a porter in the hospital. All these are supposed to be destroyed cos they're out of date. But he rescues them and sells them on. They still all work the same!" Kevin pulled a few of the boxes out and inspected them. Most of the names and brands meant nothing to Julia, but then she saw the familiar box of Dramadol.

"Here you go," Kevin said. He held up the box. "I knew I had some somewhere."

Julia's face lit up in delight. "How many of those do you have?" She calculated quickly. The box would last her about four days. "I need ten boxes. At least."

"That's the only one."

The disappointment was almost too much for Julia to bear.

"Well, can you get any more?"

Kevin didn't answer. Instead he spent some time looking through the plastic tub. He pulled out several other boxes and set them on the table, but they were clearly different to the familiar blue and red branding of Dramadol.

"Well, can you get some more?" Julia asked again. "This friend of yours, can you ask him to get more?" She reached for her bag, and pulled out the thousand pounds she had withdrawn. "Here. I've got the money."

Kevin's eyes seemed drawn to the cash.

"No need," he said.

"What?"

"Well, you know Dramadol is just a brand name, right? Like Heinz with ketchup. That might be the one you like best, but you can still eat a bacon sandwich with a different ketchup. It's still a bacon sandwich, isn't it?"

Julia peered at him, confused.

"I mean you can take some of these other pills and they do the same thing. Here."

Kevin rummaged in his magic box again, and this time he pulled out even more boxes of tablets with names that Julia didn't recognise. Soon he had a little tower of cardboard medicine boxes on the table in front of him. She watched the tower grow with greedy delight.

"There you go. The ten you wanted and another five on top of that!"

Julia's eyes grew wide with wonder.

When the trade was done Julia got up to leave, but Kevin stopped her.

"Say… Now that you're here Julia, I wonder if I could get you to have that look at my book?" Kevin said, as if the idea had only just occurred to him. "You know, see what you think of it?"

Julia's first response died in her throat and she hesitated. The glimmer of her idea shone again.

"Okay," she said, sitting back down.

THIRTY-NINE

ONE WEEK LATER, Rob and Becky felt like old hands running the Lighthouse Lodge. The charity's promises that word of mouth would help to fill the place and keep them busy was coming true, but it was also getting late in the season, and their guests continued to arrive in trickles rather than floods. For both of them this was just fine. Rob was happy wandering the island and photographing the wildlife, and when the waves came, surfing off the beach on the island's western side, or the rocky reefs that strung out between it and the mainland.

Becky was less happy, but that was only because her writing had now been stuck for long enough that it could no longer be described as a temporary blip. Every day that she could she still climbed into the lofty lantern room of the former lighthouse, but by now she barely noticed the breath-taking drop to the rocks below or the views that stretched out around her. Now she was fixated on the text on the screen in front of her. Text which no longer appeared like cut glass on her screen. Words that no longer fell from her mind as if tumbling down from a pure mountain stream. Now they seemed to arrive ready-highlighted with the red squiggles of her own editing pen. It wasn't that she couldn't write. With enough effort, she could turn out a decent word count each day, but she wasn't at all certain what she was writing was any good.

It wasn't that she had no vision for where her novel should go. In Becky's mind her protagonist – Joanna – was on a journey, driven by the regret over the accidental killing to change who she was. In Becky's version of reality, Joanna the author was committing more and more of her time and energy into doing more and more good deeds. In the vain hope that this would somehow settle her score with the universe. As if it only took a thousand good deeds and her one very bad deed would be wiped off the slate. Becky knew where she wanted the book to go, but it was as if the story itself was refusing to go there. As if it didn't fit.

It was Rob that highlighted that they had another, more pressing problem to address.

"Do Muslims not eat pork, or is that Hindus?" he asked. He was sitting in the reception area with the door open to the bedroom where Becky was cleaning her teeth.

"What?" she asked through the toothpaste foam. "Why?"

"That lady that arrived today. In room 3," Rob replied. "Mrs Abassi?"

Becky thought for a moment. "What about her?"

"Didn't you see her?"

"No."

"She's like..." Rob walked closer, as if not wanting to shout this across the room. "She's all dressed up in the Muslim outfit. You know, the full burka thing?"

"No, I didn't see." Becky thought for a second. "Do you mean she's got a headscarf?" One of her friends from university was a practising Muslim and Becky was familiar with the silk sashes that she wore.

"No, it's not just a headscarf, it's the full body thing. You know, you can only see her eyes," Rob went on. He laughed a little. "It's quite weird actually. She was wearing sunglasses so you couldn't even see her eyes."

Becky spat out the toothpaste and swilled some water around her mouth. Something in what Rob was saying was troubling her. Or the tone of his voice while he was saying it.

"So?" she asked. "People are free to wear whatever they like."

"I know," Rob replied, defensively. "It's just we've got to offer her breakfast tomorrow, and I don't know if it's wrong to give her bacon or not."

"Rob!" Becky said. "Don't be such a..." She didn't know what he was being so she didn't finish. "Course you can't give her bacon. And anyway, she'll probably just ask for a vegetarian breakfast. Like anyone else who doesn't like bacon. It's not that hard."

Rob continued to stand in the doorway to the bathroom. He knew how hard Becky could be pushed, and decided to keep going.

"Yeah, but how will she actually eat it?"

"What?"

"I mean, do they have a slit somewhere that they feed the food into? Like a mouth hole?" He grinned at her. "It was hard enough to hear what she said when I gave her the keys."

"*Rob!*"

"It was! It was all muffled. And she kept tripping up on her outfit. Honestly, Becks, it was pretty funny."

"Well, it shouldn't be. It's wrong to laugh at other people just because of what they believe in." Becky pulled back the cover and climbed into her side of the bed. She picked up the paperback novel she was reading, determined to send Rob a message that she was properly annoyed. She had started a book swap in the corner of the dining room, where guests were encouraged to leave any books they had finished in exchange for taking a new one. It had given her plenty of free reading material.

"I know, I'm not laughing exactly. But it's kinda funny, don't you think? A woman like that coming here, on her own? What's she going to do?"

"What do you mean?" Becky put down the book again. "Are you saying she should have come with a man? Just because she's Muslim? She's going to go bird watching and enjoy the scenery and peace like anyone else. Don't be so sexist and racist." Becky wasn't sure these were quite the right criticisms, but they were close enough.

Rob unzipped his trousers and pulled them off, then folded them and placed them on a chair. Then he pulled off his hoodie and t-shirt and threw them on top. He climbed into the bed beside her.

"I thought you liked it when I was sexy and racy," he said, putting his hand onto her belly.

"Not tonight I don't," Becky said, and she picked up the book again.

Rob waited a moment then groaned and rolled away from her. He picked up his phone to check for messages.

"Well, I think it's pretty weird," he said, but he dropped the subject after that.

They rose the next morning at six, as usual, and began preparing the breakfasts right away. The view from the kitchen window looked out over the west of the island, but from the dining room the windows were open to the east and a glorious sunrise. There was little wind, few clouds and the sea was calm. By 9.30 all the guests had ordered their food, and most were finishing or sipping coffee before heading out for the day. But still the lady from room 3 had yet to make her appearance. When she did come, moments later and tripping on her full-length dark brown burka as she stumbled to her table, Becky could see what Rob had meant the night before. Granted the room was bright, but still it seemed as though the woman was wearing sunglasses to ensure that there wasn't a single part of her body that remained uncovered, rather than to protect her eyes from the sun's rays. It *was* weird, Becky thought, before telling herself she mustn't think such things – it was just a result of a different culture. Different beliefs, equally valid.

They usually took it in turns to either cook or serve the breakfasts. It was Becky's turn that day to collect the orders.

"Hello," Becky said, taking care to approach the lady's table from the front, so that she would hopefully see her coming and not be startled (the woman somehow managed to look nervous enough already, though how Becky could tell that she wasn't sure).

"Have you decided what you want?" They had a very small menu that stood encased in plastic on every table. The woman was studying it now.

"We do have vegetarian sausages," Becky went on, but she wasn't sure whether this would be enough so she added, "and toast."

"Coffee," the woman said, in a strange robotic voice. Then she pointed at the top item on the menu. The full English option. Becky frowned.

"So, is that with or without the real bacon?" she queried.

The woman pulled the menu back in front of her. She was wearing gloves so that even her hands were hidden and Becky noticed they were shaking. The sides of her face covering were damp and stained with sweat. There was a smell too, although Becky told herself not to notice it, that she was being culturally insensitive.

The woman half-grunted and half-shrugged.

"Whatever," it sounded like.

Back in the kitchen Becky conferred with Rob. He seemed to feel that if she wasn't bothered they should just give her normal bacon, and she could always leave it if she didn't want it. But Becky overruled him, saying that she probably simply hadn't fully understood what she was being offered, and that the woman was clearly being extremely brave just to come to a place like this where people of her faith were so atypical. She determined that she – they – would do nothing further to draw attention to the fact that the woman's presence was anything unusual.

And so, as they finished with the breakfast service and began to clean up, she began chatting casually to Rob about what he was planning to do for the rest of the day. Sometimes, she had found, this was a good way to draw guests into the conversation, but on this occasion it was only the woman from room 3 left in the dining hall.

"You know those black-backed gulls in the cliffs, down by the beach," Rob told her. "I was going to try and get some photos of them." Rob knew what Becky was doing and what was expected of him.

"How about you? How's your writing going?" Rob asked. He spoke a little cautiously though, since he knew by now this was a sore topic.

"Uh…" Becky said. "I'll keep trying. I'm sure it'll come back to me soon." She smiled to dismiss that subject and return to the potential activities that were available to the Muslim woman.

"It's a lovely day," she said brightly, and loudly. "Really warm too for this late in the year." Becky wondered for a brief moment if it was insensitive to mention the temperature, on account of the woman not really being able to change her dress to take account of the weather. But she dismissed the idea. Didn't they mostly come from really hot countries anyway?

By now, though, it seemed clear the woman wasn't going to join in. Not only had she not spoken up, she had dropped her head and was clearly not looking to be approached. Becky sighed and flicked her eyebrows at Rob, signalling defeat.

"Why don't you come with me?" Rob said, a little more quietly now. "If the writing's going badly I mean? Give it a bit of a break. It might help?"

Becky was surprised by Rob's concern, and she turned her thoughts to her book. His idea was tempting. The thought of spending another whole afternoon in the lantern room failing to write wasn't that appealing, and it was a lovely day. But she felt that the only way to get through this was to keep trying.

"No. I should work."

"Okay." Rob persevered. "Well do a bit, and then come and find me? You've hardly even explored the island properly."

Becky wavered.

"*Come on*," Rob said. "Do an hour and then come and find me. Come on. I'll make some sandwiches now and you can get started, then when you've done some work you can bring them out. We'll have a picnic."

Becky smiled. It was a nice idea.

"Okay," she said. And with one last glance at the Muslim woman, still trying to drink coffee through the thick material of her face covering, she went to get her laptop.

FORTY

BUYING a full Islamic burka in rural Dorset had proved difficult. Julia's first attempts, on the high street of the market town of Dorchester, were unsuccessful. But a search online – performed at the local library, so as not to leave any trace on her internet history – revealed a shop in Bristol that specialised in such things, as well as a handy guide as to what each of the different types of face covering and gown was actually called.

Actually purchasing the item was difficult, too. While it offered, once secured, an almost perfect disguise, she still had to enter the shop, try one on (she didn't want to get the wrong size and have to come back) and buy the thing. And Julia certainly didn't want any shopkeepers remembering how a strange Western woman had recently bought a burka, just in case police later made the connection.

So before entering the shop she wrapped her hair in a headscarf and wore another around the lower part of her mouth, with some dark sunglasses between the two. The girl serving – a young Asian – had looked at her strangely, but Julia didn't think she would be able to identify her later. She paid in cash.

But it now turned out that that had been the easy part. Rob had stared at her so much when she arrived at the lodge, Julia had feared he had seen straight through her disguise. And now, as she fretted and worried in her room later that night, she realised just how hard this was going to be. The disguise would allow her to get close to Rob and Becky without them knowing, but she still had to kill them and get away without being caught. And though she thought she knew how to do it, she was reliant upon luck to give her an opportunity.

It was this that she was thinking about as she sat in the dining hall the next morning. It was almost surreal to be there, with Becky asking her what she wanted to eat, speaking slowly as if to an alien. She only wanted coffee but she pointed at the first thing on the menu, keen mostly to get Becky away from her, in case there was something recognisable of Julia that the disguise didn't cover. But then the stupid girl had started blabbering on about vegetarianism or something, and Julia had pointed desperately at the next thing on the menu instead. Then when Becky brought out the plate of food Julia realised she now had to eat it, or risk looking strange and raising their suspicions. This was the first time she had ever tried to eat in the burka. It was almost impossible to do so; she needed at least four hands. Two to cut the food as normal, and then ideally two more to lift the flap from her veil to expose her mouth and push the food in. Twice she dropped pieces of vegetarian sausage onto the floor, and her movements were so restricted she didn't feel it was safe to pick them up.

But then she got a break. The sort of break that she had been dreaming might happen, but perhaps never really believed would come along so easily.

"I'll leave the sandwiches in the fridge," Rob said while he was wiping down the other tables. Julia had just heard them arranging to eat a picnic later on. "You pick them up when you come out to find me."

Julia's mind reeled ahead of her, while she listened to the exchange.

A half hour later she listened at the door of her rented bedroom. She had just watched at the window and seen the other guests at the lodge leaving – one elderly couple in their walking boots and shorts, him with a knapsack on his back, her with a pair of hiking poles. They had stepped gingerly onto the path that led around the circumference of the island. The other couple, slightly younger, had gone off in a car. And then Rob had gone, too. Him with a larger backpack, that she supposed contained the camera equipment he had mentioned. Julia hadn't seen

Becky leave, but she understood her to be up in the top of the old lighthouse, trying to work on her novel.

She eased open the door. The corridor was empty.

Still in her cumbersome burka, Julia stepped as quietly as she could along the passageway and down the stairs which led into the dining room. At the bottom was a fire door with a small window set into it. Julia risked a look through the window before backing away. The room looked empty. Julia pushed the door half open. She listened.

All she could hear was the sound of blood pumping through her head. It was one of the problems with the damn burka – it deadened her hearing, along with completely cutting off her peripheral vision. She lifted the veil to have a better look around. The dining room was empty, the breakfast materials cleaned away. Julia passed the table she had sat at not half an hour before, while she watched Rob in the kitchen – the door left open – as he made sandwiches. Now the kitchen door was shut. If they had locked it, then her plan wouldn't work. Quickly, Julia crossed the room and put a gloved hand on the handle. The door opened.

This was the most dangerous part of her plan. While she was in the public areas of the lodge – as a paying guest – no one would question what she was doing, but if she was discovered in here, even dressed in her disguise, she would certainly be challenged. And if she was successful then it would certainly be remembered... She froze, a thought coming to her. Was there any CCTV?

It wasn't something she had considered, and she glanced quickly around the dining room. There was something fixed to the wall by the main entrance – a white plastic device with a red light – but she reassured herself it was just a sensor that turned on the light automatically. With one last check around her, Julia pulled open the kitchen door, walked inside, and then shut the door behind her.

The little kitchen area was built from the original lighthouse keeper's building, and it was cooler in here. The fridge buzzed on the far wall. The window looked out on the car park, the little courtyard of land between the lodge and the lighthouse itself. Its broad base was in clear view, and just behind it the dappled blueness of the ocean. Should either Rob or Becky come back, they would see her at once. She had to act fast.

Julia opened the fridge and quickly scanned the contents. It was less obvious than she had imagined, but after a moment she noticed a silver foil packet. She poked a gloved finger inside and lifted a corner. Inside was the tell-tale bread of a sandwich. Julia pulled the packet out and lay it on the work top. She unfolded the packet properly now, then she lifted the top layer of bread, so that the contents of the sandwiches were revealed. She took a deep breath. Then she dug under the folds of her burka until she reached her pocket. She pulled out a packet similar to the one she had seen Kevin buying in Tesco the previous week. In fact it was the exact same brand. When she had returned to buy it, she felt so nervous that somehow she was being watched, perhaps by the sprinkler system, that she hadn't stopped to choose very carefully, simply buying the first rat poison she saw. Now she nervously tried to unpick the packet, her gloves hampering her.

After a few moments she looked around, trying to find a pair of scissors or something that could pierce the packaging. She pulled open a couple of drawers at random, then finally found a knife. But when she tried to cut into the packet she nearly dropped it. A drop of sweat ran from her forehead into her eye.

She forced herself to calm down. She checked out of the window. There was no one in sight. There was no sound in the lodge. She was alone. She turned again to the packet of rat poison. Probably it was carefully sealed, she thought, to stop children from getting it. She had checked whether it was manufactured from some clever chemical that was only harmful to rodents and would leave humans untouched. But she was swiftly reassured that wasn't the case. As the warnings on the packet made clear, if even a small amount were accidentally swallowed by humans or pets immediate medical assistance should be sought, and it could prove fatal.

Finally she got the point of the knife into the plastic packaging and snagged it open. But then there was a new problem. She had assumed she was purchasing a powder, that she could then sprinkle onto the sandwiches, re-cover them, and get away from the danger. However, in her haste to buy the poison, she had accidentally bought a solid blue block – the type which fitted directly in a particular brand of rat traps.

"Shit," Julia swore as she realised her mistake. She tried to rub the corner over the first open sandwich, in the hope it would crumble into a powder, but it did nothing, except perhaps stain her glove. She made a mental note that they would have to be destroyed, and carefully so she didn't inadvertently poison herself. She looked back at the sandwiches in despair. How the hell was she going to get the poison into them? For a moment she was stumped.

"Fuck," Julia swore again at her uncooperative block of poison. But then she had an idea. To make the sandwiches – cheese and tomato – Rob had clearly used a cheese grater, since it was still sitting there, on the drying rack by the sink. Julia grabbed it and – her hands shaking quite violently now – she began trying to grate the block of poison onto the layer of cheese. A few small, blue flakes floated down like snow and settled on the cheese, but then the material from her glove caught in the blades and the poison block was knocked from her hands.

"Oh, for goodness sake!" Julia said, and she dropped to the floor to find it. But as she did so, her left walking boot made contact with the poison block, and sent it scooting across the floor and under the fridge. Julia blinked in disbelief. This couldn't be happening.

Bunching the burka around her waist she knelt down now to reclaim it, but the gap it had disappeared under was too small for her to reach with her hand. She could just wiggle a finger under it. She put her face to the cold floor for a better view and there it was, sitting just out of reach.

She stood up, searching for a stick or some kind of implement with which to fish it out. There was nothing on the worktop, so she began pulling open drawers to find cutlery. The first she tried was used to store tea towels, which she swore at, loudly. The second drawer was under the window. And as she pulled it open she saw the doorway of the light-house open too.

FORTY-ONE

Forty metres above Julia, Becky gave up for the day. As wonderful a writing retreat as the lantern room was, it didn't tell her *what* to write, and on days when the sun was bright it also quickly became both hot and rather bright to concentrate on the screen. And although she had done little but reorder parts of the story that were already just about finished, she was still able to count it as something. Making a decision, she dropped the laptop lid closed and bundled it together with her notebook. She threw both into her bag, and then opened the door and began to descend around the curving inside of the old lighthouse tower. The building was mostly hollow inside, and her footsteps echoed as she descended the stone steps, keeping a tight grip on the iron railing that protected her from the drop. But she was used to climbing up and down inside the lighthouse now and her mind was on other things. It was such a nice day. It would be lovely to see a bit more of the island. And as Rob said, she had been pushing herself hard since arriving here. Maybe it was actually a break that she needed?

She pushed open the door of the lighthouse and stepped out onto the little grassy area that connected the lodge with the great tower.

As she moved forward she stepped out of the shadow of the lighthouse and the sun hit her back, instantly warming it. She slowed, enjoying the feeling. She looked up at the lodge. In front of her was the window of the little kitchen. The sun glinted off the glass, and for a moment something caught her eye, but her mind dismissed it. It couldn't be movement because Rob was already out. She had watched him go from the top of the tower. She smiled. It seemed strange that they had been scared about running the place. In reality it was easy, and it showed just how well suited she and Rob were, that they could live together and work together so easily.

From nowhere she remembered the story of the lighthouse keeper who had gone mad those decades before, and thrown his wife from the top of the tower. She smiled at Ted's version of the story, which was different to the record in the Dorchester museum. Strange how different versions of stories could coexist, she thought. Then she smiled. Whichever was true, at least there was no chance of Rob throwing her from the tower!

Shaking her head Becky crossed the courtyard and pushed open the door to the lodge.

FORTY-TWO

THERE WAS NOWHERE in the kitchen to hide, and no time to put the kitchen back in order first, even if there had been. Julia simply dropped out of sight below the window and waited, panicking. Then her panic doubled as she heard the door to the lodge itself open, and Becky – whistling – come inside. Julia had to move then, and she half-crawled, half-shuffled until she was behind the door. From there she surveyed the mess she had made in the kitchen with a kind of disbelieving despair. In a few moments Becky was going to walk in and see it. What would she think? Julia realised she was holding a knife, a large serrated-blade kitchen knife that she had taken from the drawer to reach the poison block from under the fridge, and her hand tightened on the handle. It wasn't what she planned, but it would do. When Becky came in she would first look at the mess on the worktop, and with Julia behind the door she could then leap out on her and use the knife. She tried to visualise it. But her hand was shaking so much she wasn't sure if she would be able to do it.

Becky's footsteps came to the door of the kitchen and Julia drew herself up still and ready. But then the girl walked straight past the doorway and even out of the dining room itself. Julia didn't know where. But it didn't take her long to realise she had an opportunity. Working fast now she dropped to the floor again, ripping her veil out of the way a second time. She fished quickly under the fridge, and with the knife it was the work of seconds to lever the poison block out from underneath.

She grabbed the grater and once again began sending a blue dusting of poisoned snow on top of the sandwiches. Julia had no idea how much she needed to put on, but even though she was now desperate to get out of the kitchen she wasn't prepared to err on the side of caution. There was no question that this was a signal or a threat. Julia wanted them as dead as possible, and as quickly as possible. She continued until there wasn't enough left of the poison block to grate any more, and then she forced herself to calm down enough to rewrap the sandwiches neatly. They wouldn't need to eat them all. Just a bite should do it.

Julia put them back in the fridge and quickly surveyed the rest of the mess. She remembered the tea towel drawer and she grabbed one, and wiped the dust of grated rat poison from where it was sprinkled on the work top. She balled the tea towel up and threw it into the rubbish bin. Then she did the same with the cheese grater, but it rattled and banged as it fell to the bottom. The noise rang out around the kitchen. Julia froze again.

FORTY-THREE

As BECKY FLUSHED the toilet she heard a noise. She paused for a moment then called out.

"Rob?"

There was no answer, so she walked out of their room and back into the dining room. There she got the shock of her life. Because standing in the doorway of the kitchen, looking like some kind of evil ghost, was the lady from room 3. The lady, too, jumped in shock.

Becky put her hand to her chest, and only just managed to prevent herself from screaming out.

"Oh!" she said. "You made me jump!" She tried to smile at the lady, but wasn't sure where to look.

"I'm sorry, I didn't know anyone was here," Becky said, but the lady seemed frozen in terror.

"Are you okay?" Becky went on. In response the lady said nothing, but tried to slide past Becky in the direction of the stairs. Then she mumbled something – Becky wasn't sure what.

There was very little she could do. She watched the poor Muslim lady walk unsteadily across the room and then pull open the door to the stairs.

"Have a nice day," Becky called as the lady moved out of sight. Then she laughed quietly to herself and walked into the kitchen. She opened the fridge and pulled out the silver foil packet of sandwiches that Rob had made earlier. She slipped it into her bag and added a couple of apples. Then she closed the fridge and walked out of the kitchen. She shook her head at the thought of what a scare she had just had.

FORTY-FOUR

From her position concealed behind the curtains in her room Julia watched Becky leave, in the direction that Rob had gone earlier. Then she struggled out of her ridiculous Muslim outfit and bundled it into her backpack, leaving the walking clothes she had on underneath in place. She left on her gloves though, conscious not to leave any fingerprints at this late stage.

The room was paid for in advance. That had been difficult, since the booking had to be made on a website, but she had got round the problem by posting cash to the charity directly. Now she took her room key with her when she went downstairs. Out of her disguise she simply prayed that she wouldn't see anyone as she left, but the lodge was empty. Julia left the key on the little reception area, then, needing to be sure, she quickly stepped into the kitchen and opened the fridge. The sandwiches were gone.

Julia stared at the empty space where they had been for a long time. That empty space meant more to her than she could process at that moment.

Then she closed the fridge, took her bag and walked out of the lodge. She left on foot, in the opposite direction to the way that Becky had walked.

Julia had arrived, in her full Muslim disguise, by taxi. She was under no illusions that this would have gone unremembered by the driver, but then she clearly couldn't have taken her own car. Becky herself had seen it when Julia had visited her, and who knew what CCTV cameras would record its number plate? Walking was the next obvious option, since the island attracted a steady stream of hikers, but Julia thought that combining her ultra-devout Muslim with a long distance hiker might be a stretch too far.

It was, however, her plan for escaping. Now without her disguise, she looked entirely unremarkable as just another middle-aged outdoor enthusiast, with her hiking trousers, boots and backpack. And as she followed the coastal path north towards the causeway, she passed several women who could have been carbon copies of herself. To each of them she nodded a friendly 'hello' and kept on her way. She knew that Becky and Rob had gone up the other side of the island, and she prayed again that they hadn't decided to cross the island, in which case she would have to pass them. But she doubted it. She herself had taken the side that was out of the sun.

She was right. It took less than an hour until she reached the tidal causeway, and in a stroke of good fortune the tide was low enough for her to walk right across (had it not been the ferry would only have set her back £1.50). Another half hour later and she had reached the quarry where she and Geoffrey had parked before, and where she had left her car this time, too. She loaded her bag and drove away. A half hour after that, and twenty miles away, Julia spotted a large rubbish bin by the side of the road. She pulled up beside it, then quickly threw her burka, her gloves and the rest of her disguise inside, pushing it deep so that it wasn't even visible to anyone else that used the bin after her.

And then she drove on.

FORTY-FIVE

IT WAS mild enough that Becky had to stop and remove her hoodie, tying it around her waist before continuing. The late summer air warmed her bare legs, and the sea, rolling lazily around the rocks at the foot of the cliffs, looked inviting. She hiked a half mile along the cliff top and then took the narrow and steep path that wound down the cliff and onto the little inlet beach where Rob had said he would be.

It didn't take her long to find him, with his tripod set up at the base of the cliffs, leaning over the lens pointed at the nesting birds.

"Boo!" she said, sneaking up on him and placing both her hands on his broad shoulders. "Didn't see me, did you?"

In response he silently turned the camera around and pressed the button to make it display the last image he had taken. It was a photograph of Becky, picking her way carefully down the cliff path, her tongue poking out in concentration.

"New profile picture for you?" he asked.

"Shut up," she replied. "I'm deleting that one." Then she pressed herself up on tip-toes to land a kiss on his lips.

"What's that for?" Rob asked.

"That's for getting me out of that room. I was just getting nowhere. And what you said this morning was right. I need to give myself a break.

I need to get out and about a bit. Enjoy the island. If I can let that distract me, I'll figure out what's wrong with the book."

Rob cocked his head to one side. "Okay," he said. Then he added: "Or you could tell me what it's all about, and why it's such a big secret? I might even be able to help."

She smiled evasively.

"You *will* be able to help. With the second draft. But I need to finish it first." As if to illustrate the point she turned back to the camera and began to scroll through the other images he had taken. She knew he preferred to edit them before showing her. But he didn't stop her.

"I found some more seals," he said instead, watching her scroll through the images. "They have their pups this time of year but I'll need a boat to get out to them." She came to the images he meant and zoomed in on the pictures of their heads in the water.

"They're so cute," Becky said. "I hope you can get some pictures of the pups. That'll be amazing." When she looked up he was smiling at her.

"What?" she asked.

"Nothing."

He continued to look at her, and there was something about it that unsettled her. "Anyway, are you hungry?" she said, and picked up her bag. She drew out the sandwiches.

"Mmmm," Rob replied absently. Then he went on. "Actually I am, but I was thinking about having a swim first. You fancy it?"

"Really? Isn't it cold?"

"No, it's okay," Rob replied. "Actually, there's this other little bay just around that headland I want to check out." He pointed to the south. "You can see it on the map, but you can't get there by land, the cliff's too steep."

"And you want to swim there?" Becky immediately sounded dubious.

"It's not far. Honestly, it's just the other side of that stack of rock." He pointed less than thirty metres away. Becky was a good swimmer. It was no distance for her.

"I didn't bring my swimsuit," she said.

"I did," he replied and pointed to his camera bag where he had packed a towel and her bikini. He began pulling off his t-shirt.

A few moments later, smiling at her own daring, Becky stood with her toes in the clear, cool water. She felt both exposed and excited. She looked around and saw Rob walking down to join her in his swimming shorts. Behind him the little beach and the path back up to the cliff top were empty. Rob took her hand and together they waded deeper. There were stones under their feet, little round pebbles polished smooth by the waves, but her feet were too numb to feel them. When the water swished up her thigh and splashed onto her stomach she gasped. She looked across at Rob.

"It fucking is cold," she said.

In response he just took a deep intake of breath. "Yeah. I lied a bit," he said. "But we're in now." A moment later that was true as he pushed himself forward and dived into the water. For a second or two he was gone, and Becky watched his body swim away from her under the cold water. Then she copied him and plunged forward.

Becky had swum weekly until her early teens, even entering some competitions until she managed to convince her mother that it wasn't the future she saw for herself. The training had made her comfortable in the water, and now she opened her eyes, watching the rocks – magnified under the water – slip past her. When she broke surface it was straight into a smooth easy stroke, and she quickly overtook Rob with his weak breaststroke. When her muscles were warm she stopped and trod water to wait for him. Looking down she could still see the bottom. The sunlight played on the rocks below her.

"It's just around there," Rob breathed heavily when he caught up, and carried on swimming past her. She had forgotten where he wanted to go, but set off again, following him around the edge of the tiny bay. She felt a moment's fear as they came close to the headland, but once she saw there was another bay just around it, she relaxed. It was smaller than the main bay, but still had a place where they could come ashore. When they climbed out she felt the instant warming of the sun.

It was a beautiful spot. Here, the cliff behind them was steep, so that anyone on the path above would never see the little beach below. And above the beach, even more secluded, there was a small grassy area. Smooth weathered rocks formed an encircling wall around them, and the ground underneath was short springy grass.

"This is awesome!" Becky exclaimed. "A secret beach!" But when she swung to look at Rob his expression surprised her. He was looking at the way the water was dripping from her swimsuit. He looked around, then promptly sat down on the grass, and held out his hand for her to do the same.

When they were lying down together Rob's arm stayed on her. He began running his finger across her bare stomach, then higher to her breasts.

"Erm, Rob?" she asked. "What if someone comes along?"

"They won't." He rolled onto his side, leaned over and kissed her. Becky responded only half-heartedly, so that Rob quickly pulled back.

"Honestly, I haven't seen anyone all day, not even at that other beach where you can get to. No one's going to find us here." He moved his hand further down her belly and onto the wet fabric of her bikini bottom.

"Rob! What's got into you?" Becky asked. But she was beginning to waver now.

"You have. You always have." Rob leaned over to kiss her again.

FORTY-SIX

WHEN THEY WERE FINISHED they lay back, breathless on the grass. For a short while Becky had been able to forget how exposed they were, out in the open air, but now she felt like the very cliffs around them might have watched what they just did. She picked up her bikini, wrung out the remaining water, and quickly pulled it back on. Beside her Rob did the same with his shorts. When they were at least partially clothed, she felt better.

"I'm hungry *now*," she said, and Rob laughed.

They swam back keeping pace with each other, and this time Becky didn't feel the cold at all. Instead she felt almost overwhelmed with how lucky she was. Lucky to have met a boy like Rob. A boy who loved her so much he sometimes literally couldn't resist her. Lucky to have found a job like they had, in such an incredible location. Lucky also that they could afford to take it – Julia's bursary had relieved them of the financial worries that affected most of her friends. She almost didn't want the swim to end, but as they re-rounded the little headland and saw the first beach, Becky's sense of peace was suddenly interrupted. Pulled up on the shore, not twenty metres from where Rob had left his camera gear, was a small sailing dinghy, its sails lowered into the boat. And on the beach were an older couple, complete with old-style orange life jackets.

"No one about, huh?" She turned to Rob.

"Whoops," he said in response.

"Do you think they saw anything?" Becky said. She was a little worried now, but not very. Besides, the logic of the situation reassured her. They hadn't seen the boat from the other bay, and even if it had sailed past, they probably would have been invisible in their spot on the shore.

"I don't think so," Rob replied. "They would have come from the mainland side. Wouldn't they?"

Becky gave a theatrical shudder anyway, and an indulgent smile.

But the couple appeared to be paying them no attention at all. They were exploring the beach, and as Rob and Becky swam slowly closer to the shore, they seemed to be inspecting something in the rockpools at the north side of the inlet. And then they disappeared completely, behind a ledge of rock. It gave Rob and Becky the opportunity to come ashore and get back to where they had left their clothes. Becky felt a little exposed again, running up the beach in her bikini with the knowledge of how, moments before, she hadn't even been wearing that, but when she looked across the couple was still out of sight. Quickly, she used Rob's towel to dry herself and then as a shield to remove her wet bikini and slip into her clothes. Rob was less bashful. He simply turned his back and pulled his wet shorts off, showing his white behind. His timing couldn't have been better, since the other couple reappeared moments after he had pulled his jeans up.

Now that they were decent, it was almost impossible for the two couples not to acknowledge each other. There was no way that Rob and Becky couldn't see the sailing dinghy, and for their part, the couple sailing it must have wondered who had left expensive-looking camera equipment unattended in such an isolated spot. So when she felt the man's eyes on her, Becky raised a hand. But rather than nod, or raise his hand in return, as she expected him to do, he made a different gesture which she didn't understand. Becky watched as he walked back to his dinghy. She noticed now that the couple had a dog with them, a young Border Collie.

"Come on, let's eat," Rob said. He was sounding much more relaxed now. He pulled her bag towards her and began to dig inside it. But before he could hand her any food Becky's eye was caught by a glint of dull silver in the rocks nearby. At the same moment Becky realised the man had now left the boat and was walking towards them, a plastic shopping bag held in both hands in front of him.

"I say," he called out as he drew near. Becky and Rob both stopped what they were doing and waited.

"I'm really sorry," the man went on as he came close enough to speak normally. "But I'm afraid I have some bad news."

There was a moment when Becky was baffled. What bad news could this total stranger possibly have for her? Unless they *had* seen her and Rob in the other bay? She glanced at Rob who was frowning too.

"We didn't realise there was anyone else here when we landed," the man said. He had a brown moustache tinged with grey, and its corners jiggled up and down as he spoke. "So when we were letting the sails down we just let Jess run around. We didn't notice what she was up to until it was too late."

Rob was still frowning, but by now Becky had worked out what had happened, and she began to smile a broad smile.

"I'm afraid she found her way into your bag there," he pointed to Rob. "She had her way with your lunch. She's a terrible thief. I thought I'd better come and confess."

Now Becky could see clearly that the glint of silver was the shredded remains of the foil that had been wrapped around the sandwiches.

"Here." The man held out the bag he had been holding. "We packed far too much to eat anyway."

The dog – Jess – now came running up, and began sniffing at the empty remains of the foil, and the man shooed her away. Becky realised what was in the bag the man was offering.

"We couldn't," Becky told him. "We can't. We can't take your lunch."

"No, really. I absolutely insist," he told her, his moustache jiggling. "Jess has eaten yours and it's a long way to the shop."

Becky looked at Rob, seeing the laughter in his eyes. She took the bag. Inside was another packet of sandwiches, this time wrapped in Clingfilm.

"Tuna fish," the man said by way of explanation. "Not caught on the way unfortunately, but still fresh enough!"

FORTY-SEVEN

Neither Rob nor Becky made the connection, the following evening, as they chatted with Ted in the Hunsey Tavern. Despite their initial plans they hadn't come back as regularly to the pub – the fact that most of the guests from the Lodge headed there for their evening meal made it feel a bit too much like still being on duty. The subsistence salary for the job also meant they didn't have the budget for eating out every night. But they only had two rooms filled by then, and Becky was still keen to get out and explore the island more.

And while Ted hadn't exactly come to treat them as long-term Hunsey locals, he wasn't averse to sharing the local island gossip.

"You allow dogs over at the lodge?" he asked Rob, who frowned then shook his head.

"No, we're not allowed. Why?"

"Hmmm. Good thing probably." Ted paused for a minute, and it seemed he might be finished. But then he continued. "Couple staying with me, in the rooms upstairs, they come every year, with their little doggy." He stopped again and sucked in air through his teeth.

"It picked up some poison yesterday." Becky felt a chill, as if she knew where this might go.

"Was in a right state. Looked like it was already dead when they took it to the vets." He shook his head. "Vet managed to save it but it cost a pretty packet, and right ruined their holidays."

Becky's hand went to her mouth. "Oh, that's awful," she said.

"Reckoned it was probably something put down for rats."

While Rob was able to recover his mood fairly quickly, Becky felt a sadness that lasted for the rest of the evening. And even though they wouldn't have any dog owners staying with them at the lodge, she still shared a warning on its Facebook page.

Really sad news here on Hunsey, a visiting dog unfortunately picked up some rat poison and nearly died. Really horrible. Please be careful if ever using these products!

FORTY-EIGHT

THE RURAL DORSET Creative Circle was held in the church hall in the village of Spifton Matravers every Friday evening. The activities undertaken there ranged from poetry recitals, reviews of current and classic literature, music appreciation and discussions on any cultural affairs that might be taking place or upcoming in the area from where the group drew its members. The actual agenda for each week was emailed out in advance by Marjorie, the group's organiser and its driving force. However, the real reason that anyone actually came, although never listed on the email, was to have a good old gossip.

Almost all the members were in some way creative – or aspired to be so. There was Roger, a keen amateur local archaeologist, who had written a number of books and pamphlets on the history and pre-history of Dorset, which were available in the gift shop of the Dorchester Museum. There was Amy, a talented musician who – had she not felt an obligation to stay loyal to Dorchester District Council's planning department – might even have had a career with her folk music. There was Marjorie herself, who was a prolific, if not particularly talented, poet.

Another regular attendee of the group was one Geoffrey Saunders. Indeed, the regular Friday meeting was often the highlight of his entire week.

It hadn't always been this way for Geoffrey. In fact, it was only two cruel rolls of life's dice that had diverted Geoffrey from a very different existence where he would never even have heard of the Rural Dorset Creative Circle.

Fifteen years earlier Geoffrey had been a promising member of a team of insurance investigators – an intrepid band who visited businesses to assess whether their claims of damaging fires, high value thefts, or expensive accidents were actually made fraudulently to secure handsome insurance pay offs. The then thirty-year-old Geoffrey was a tenacious investigator whose insightful approach had cracked several high profile cases. He was regarded as someone who could 'think out of the box', too. It was Geoffrey who argued that claims should only be accepted in a handwritten form, and who brought in graphology experts to look for swirls and loops of certain letters. But it was also Geoffrey who volunteered to help organise the Christmas parties, and who engaged most on the occasional team building days. Most in the company assumed that, when his time came, Geoffrey would head up the team, and from there it was not a big stretch to assume he might even climb into the upper echelons of the company itself.

When Geoffrey came to work one morning with an ultrasound scan of his wife Anne's belly, and inside it the foetus of their baby girl, there was very real happiness for him and his new family. But rather than marking the beginning of a joyous new chapter in Geoffrey's life, it was really the beginning of the end.

The pregnancy proceeded normally at first. Anne suffered a little from morning sickness but nothing to make anybody alarmed. Yet at the twenty-week check, the midwife discovered she had unusually high blood pressure. A urine test was arranged. This revealed the presence of proteins that the doctors agreed was a possible sign of pre-eclampsia. It was a rare condition that in a very small number of cases could lead to more serious issues closer to the birth. But equally it could not. At this point the odds were very much on the side of Anne and her actuarial husband.

But as the baby grew inside her, so did the list of problems that the doctors became aware of. The sickness didn't ease up. Anne suffered from dizzy spells, and terrible headaches. And then, just before Anne began her maternity leave, and over breakfast one morning, she dropped her cereal spoon and started to jerk violently. Moments later she had slipped from the chair and continued convulsing on the floor. Geoffrey was upstairs getting dressed, but he came sprinting down, only to be confronted with his heavily pregnant wife wide-eyed on the floor and foaming at the mouth. He didn't panic, he knew what to do – they'd read all the books by then. So he also knew what it was before the doctors confirmed it – it was a seizure brought on by the now-developed condition of eclampsia. That first seizure turned out to be just a mild one.

It was the beginning of the end. Despite a cocktail of drugs the seizures kept coming, until there was no choice but to perform an emergency caesarean, under general anaesthetic. When Anne woke from that, and Geoffrey had to tell her their daughter was stillborn, he thought it was the hardest thing he would ever have to face. But just a week later he realised that was wrong. At midnight the following weekend, Anne went into cardiac arrest as a result of the trauma on her body.

She died before Geoffrey could get to the hospital.

Arguably, Geoffrey died that night too, since he would never be the same man again.

Initially he was simply stunned by how quickly life could turn. And when that wore off, Anne's death provoked a profound, and some felt ill-considered re-evaluation of what remained of his life. True, he probably had never dreamed as a boy of becoming an insurance investigator - after all, who did? But was that a good enough reason to leave his job? To leave London and hide away in the middle of nowhere? His friends thought not, but they were unable to change his mind, because hiding away was what Geoffrey wanted to do. He didn't want to recover. Not when Anne wouldn't. Not when their baby girl couldn't.

But as Geoffrey learnt from bitter experience, even the hardest pain is softened by time, and his kindly nature eventually shone through from the blackness. Geoffrey had no urgent need to work since Anne had been covered with an excellent life insurance policy (one of the perks of the job). So he volunteered for local good causes, as many as he could find. He finally admitted to himself that what he *had* dreamed about as a boy was to be a policeman – and being a bit old to start down a whole new career path, he instead tried his hand at detective fiction. Though he never thought he had much talent for it, it was these stories that led Geoffrey to respond to an advert in a Dorchester newsagents for the inaugural meeting of the Rural Dorset Creative Circle.

Yet it was also the case that, in recent months, the shine of attending the Creative Circle had worn off for Geoffrey. Though he tried to hide it, the other members were aware of this, and also aware of why. It was obvious he missed Julia now that she was too famous and too important to attend a small, provincial creative writing group. But they assumed Geoffrey would get over it. After all, life goes on. Though there would be a time when they would come to re-evaluate that.

Marjorie's email that week had promised – or threatened, depending upon your perspective – to present a PowerPoint presentation on the various Roman artefacts that had been found in the archaeological dig at the site for the new Waitrose supermarket. And rather oddly this had resulted in a packed meeting, so that the only seat available to Geoffrey when he arrived was next to Kevin. Normally he tended to avoid the man. It wasn't anything personal, but he'd once explained that he didn't have running water in his trailer, and to be honest you could tell. Still, he nodded a greeting as he sat down, and Kevin nodded back, then the presentation limited any further conversation. But, a long hour later, as they stood up to leave, Kevin turned to Geoffrey.

"Where's that Julia, then?" Kevin said to him.

"Excuse me?" Geoffrey replied.

"Your mate, Julia. I thought she might be here tonight?"

"No. She's living up in London these days." Geoffrey began explaining. "She has quite a few media commitments currently so it helps to be based–" But Kevin interrupted him.

"Nah, mate, she's back, didn't you know?" Kevin seemed both surprised and cheered by the revelation that he knew more about this than Geoffrey did.

"No, I don't think so..." Geoffrey began, but Kevin cut him off again.

"Oh she is, I've seen her. She came out to my trailer after more of those pills she's on."

Geoffrey frowned. "Pills?"

"Yeah! And then earlier this week she phoned me up for something else. You'll never guess what?"

"What?"

Kevin grinned. "A gun."

"*What?*"

"Yeah! Said she wanted it as research for a book or something."

Geoffrey stared in sheer bewilderment.

"A *gun*?"

"That's right! It was a handgun she was after specifically. Though when I told her that might be difficult she said any gun would do. Said she thought I had a shotgun at least. Since she saw my washing line with dead squirrels hung up on it. Only they weren't bleedin' squirrels were they? Them was just me kegs."

Geoffrey was struggling to follow Kevin at this point.

"What are you talking about?"

"When she came to me trailer, she saw my washing line. I'd just done my washing. Had all my pants out to dry, she thought they was dead squirrels!"

Geoffrey tried to filter this information so that it made some kind of sense. But he kept coming back to the earlier word.

"*A gun*?" Geoffrey said again. He paused for a long time. "Well, did you...?"

"Get her one? Of course I didn't! What do I look like? A bloody arms dealer? Do I have a towel on my head like some A-rab?" He shook his head and Geoffrey blinked at him.

"Yeah, she sounded pretty insistent though." Kevin kept talking. "Anyway, you on for the pub?"

Usually Geoffrey did go along for one or two, but this time the comments from Kevin had so unsettled him that he refused all offers and walked quickly back to his car. Once he was inside he pulled out his mobile phone and searched to see if he had missed any calls from Julia. He hadn't, so he phoned her. And as it usually did these days, it went directly to voicemail. Geoffrey hadn't been bothering to leave messages recently – he suspected Julia was so engrossed in her new project that she wasn't actually listening to them. Correction. He *had* suspected she was so engrossed in her new writing project. Now he didn't know what to think.

"A gun?" he said a third time, and the word sounded as ridiculous in his car as it had in his head. Julia didn't exactly write the sort of books that had guns in them. What could she possibly need to research that actually required her to *get* a gun? And why *on earth* would she decide to ask *Kevin* for one? Geoffrey considered that perhaps the man might be making it up, or maybe on some sort of pills himself – that much was almost a certainty. But he'd sounded quite sure of himself. It hardly made sense that he would decide to make up such a story – what would the purpose be?

He was troubled now, and he started the engine and drove the few miles to Julia's village, not expecting to find her in, and even less sure what to expect if she was there. But as he pulled up outside the window of her little cottage there were no signs of life. There was no car on the driveway, the lights were off, and there was no smoke coming from the chimney. He thought about asking her neighbours if they had seen her, but he knew she had got herself involved in a bit of a feud with them, and they seemed to have carried their resentment over to him as well. He sighed and decided that wouldn't be the best idea. Instead he sat outside and tried her number again. This time he left a message. Then he sent her a text message and an email asking her to contact him urgently.

Early the next morning Geoffrey came back to Julia's cottage before even having breakfast, and found the place in exactly the same state as before. This time he got out of the car and peered into the windows. Inside looked as expected, and there was nothing that really indicated whether she might be living there or not. A few empty wine glasses on the work surface, a coat dumped on the sofa – but then Julia wasn't the tidiest person. It was a product of her creative mind.

Geoffrey didn't have much on that weekend. So after checking his phone again, and finding no messages from Julia, he left a full bowl of food and water for Edgar and filled his car for a trip to London.

FORTY-NINE

JULIA EAGERLY MONITORED THE NEWS, expecting that the death of Becky and Rob would be quickly announced. But it stubbornly refused to break. At first Julia tried to convince herself that the poison might simply work slowly, but when she saw Becky's post about the poisoned dog, she had to accept that something had gone wrong. Exactly what it was she didn't know, but the coincidence seemed impossible to ignore.

And the bloody dog hadn't even died!

For a short while her disappointment prompted her to consider other, more certain methods of dispatch. She considered shooting them, and – remembering how Kevin had strung dead animals on a washing line outside his caravan – she telephoned him to ask if he could get her a gun. But that turned out to be hopeless. The stupid man denied having one, and when she insisted – pointing out the line of clearly shot animals by his trailer – he made the bizarre claim that the crumpled brown items were in fact his underpants. After he'd washed them. In the end she hung up in a mixture of disgust and despair. Then she took a deep breath and started thinking properly.

Poisoning was out. So was shooting them. What options did that leave? Perhaps she could run them down with her car? The idea was attractive, but there seemed no obvious way she could arrange to have them both in the road in front of her. Any kind of direct attack was too daunting to even think about; it would be two against one, and Rob would easily be able to overpower her. She considered burning the lodge down with them inside. But it had recently been refurbished. She had noticed the sprinkler system when she was there, mistaking it at first for security cameras.

It was a shame she couldn't get poisoning to work. It was such a nice, neat solution. She looked around her penthouse flat for inspiration.

The decoration of her new living room had begun with Geoffrey's efforts, and also ended there. He had almost single-handedly manoeuvred in the sofa, and the reading chair, and he had built the IKEA bookshelf. Then, almost as a joke, he had presented her with a signed copy of his book, *The Apple Tree Killer*. Julia's eye turned now to his sad little paperback, squashed against the end of the bookshelf by a dozen handsome hardcover editions of *The Glass Tower*. She pulled the book out now, and considered its amateurish cover. The lack of any notable review quotes. Then she remembered how they had discussed the book at a meeting of the Creative Circle. How proud he had been, and how patiently he had pushed back against Marjorie when she insisted it was unrealistic that his killer had used cyanide distilled from apple pips to carry out his dirty work.

Julia hadn't paid very much attention at the time. But Geoffrey had been adamant that it was both possible and therefore plausible. She thumbed through the book now, trying to find the section that sparked the discussion. In it Geoffrey had – rather clumsily, she thought at the time – explained the process by which the seeds of apples could be ground down and then the resulting powder mixed with simple tap water to produce concentrated hydrogen cyanide. Julia hadn't studied the sciences at school, and had offered no opinion about how effective this would be at killing a man, but she remembered now that both Geoffrey and Kevin were adamant that it would do so in just a few seconds. Marjorie had thought this ridiculous.

Julia read the controversial passage now. In Geoffrey's story, his killer dropped just a few drops into a cup of tea given to the victim, and within only a few seconds she had turned blue and was dead on the floor.

"Wouldn't she have tasted it?" Julia had asked him, in the pub afterwards. "When the killer gives her the drink? Wouldn't she have realised it was laced with such a deadly poison?" And he had smiled at her in delight.

"That's just the thing," Geoffrey had replied. "No one knows what it tastes like because no one's ever lived long enough to find out!"

Perhaps, Julia considered, she had been a little hasty in writing off poisoning as the answer. Perhaps she simply needed a *stronger* poison. And if Geoffrey were right, she could still get her poison on the shelves of the local supermarket.

Julia went to the library to check Geoffrey's claims on the internet, and she was so encouraged she went straight from there to buy twenty bags of apples.

She began by cutting each apple into quarters and carefully removing the little black seeds. It didn't matter when she inadvertently cut them in half, she was going to grind them down anyway. It took her the whole afternoon but eventually she had a small pile of apple seeds, and a huge pile of discarded apple flesh. She placed the seeds on a tray and put them in the oven at 50 degrees for an hour, and while she was waiting, she carried the remainder of the apples down to the bin and dumped them.

She had to go out again to buy a pestle and mortar, but she was confident that in isolation it couldn't be seen as suspicious, and so she used her credit card. Then she spent a tiring hour smashing and grinding the seeds to a black pulpy mess. The resulting amount of material was so pathetic she decided it would never work, so she went back to the shop, and this time bought a top of the range food processor. That did the job much better, but it reduced the already tiny pile of seeds to such a minuscule amount of black dust that she decided to buy another twenty bags of apples and repeat the whole process again.

Two full days later she very carefully poured a small amount of yellowy-clear liquid into a handy travel-sized shampoo bottle that Geoffrey had once given her from one of his holidays.

FIFTY

GEOFFREY WAS A TROUBLED MAN. Julia wasn't answering his emails. Wasn't returning his calls, and – despite what Kevin had said about seeing her in Dorset – didn't appear to be living at her cottage. And when he arrived in London, there was no answer on the buzzer for her penthouse flat either. But after driving all the way up to the capital, it didn't make much sense to just turn around and leave. Instead Geoffrey loitered outside, trying all the numbers he had for her, until one of the other residents of the building left. At that point Geoffrey ran forward to catch the door, ready to explain his reason for needing to get in. But the woman didn't even challenge him.

Geoffrey took the stairs up to the penthouse. He banged on Julia's door, and wished it had a letterbox that he could peer into. And when that didn't work, he decided to try downstairs to see if any of her neighbours knew anything.

He tried the flat directly beneath Julia's first. He remembered how the man who lived there had helped to move in Julia's desk. A nice guy, Geoffrey remembered, he had been friendly. Geoffrey pressed the doorbell.

"Yes?" The man seemed suspicious at first, and when he saw Geoffrey there was no sign he remembered him.

"Hello, I'm a friend of Julia Ottley," Geoffrey began, trying to put a reassuring smile on his face. But the man didn't respond in kind.

"Who?"

"Julia, she lives upstairs," Geoffrey went on. "But I'm struggling to reach her at the moment, and I wondered if she mentioned to you anything about–"

"Who?" The man interrupted him this time.

"Julia... The woman who lives upstairs. In the penthouse?" The smile on Geoffrey's face began to falter. Surely they couldn't have failed to see each other in the lift or the lobby downstairs?

"Oh, her." There was something pointed about the way the man spoke. "What about her?"

Geoffrey hesitated. He tried to remember what he had chatted about with this man those months before. They'd joked about the joys of DIY, that was it. About how the instructions were always inscrutable. He seemed much less friendly now.

"I, um. As I say I'm a friend of Julia's but I'm struggling to get in contact with her. I wondered if she might have mentioned to you where she was going?"

"She doesn't talk to us." The man stared at Geoffrey defiantly.

"Well, has she been around recently? Have you noticed?"

"Don't know. Like I say. Doesn't talk to us." The man held his door firmly, and Geoffrey sensed he was just waiting to shut it in his face.

"Okay. Well, could you say when you last saw her?" he asked, his own smile fading now.

"Heard her. Not saw." The man seemed to think for a moment. "Maybe last week. Last Wednesday? Sounded like she was having an argument with someone. Herself, probably." The man narrowed his eyes. "I remember you. You're the furniture man aren't you?" Geoffrey began to reply but the other man carried on without hesitation. "You should keep away from that woman. She's no good."

Geoffrey was taken aback.

"I'm sorry?" he asked. He wasn't at all sure he had heard the man right.

"She's no good. Not kind." He began to close the door.

"Now, hang on!" Geoffrey began. He almost put his foot in the door, but that would have been too strong a reaction. Instead he went on. "That's a bit strong, I know she can be..."

But there was no point finishing his sentence, since by now the door was shut.

"Extraordinary!" Geoffrey said to the closed door.

Geoffrey considered trying some of the other neighbours, and in fact did knock on one other door – there were two flats on the floor below Julia's – but whoever lived in the other flat wasn't home. Geoffrey even considered calling the police. There was the possibility that Julia was inside her flat, but for some reason unable to answer the door. But there wasn't anything to suggest that this was the case; indeed, the only evidence Geoffrey had for her whereabouts was from Kevin, who claimed she was down in Dorset. And if the police asked why he was concerned – well, he could hardly tell them it was because Kevin had told him about her requesting a gun. No. Whatever Julia had got herself mixed up in – and Geoffrey was sure it was something – calling the police was the last way to help her.

Instead, Geoffrey made his way back downstairs and returned to his car for the long drive home.

FIFTY-ONE

JULIA RESTED her elbows on the stone wall in front of her, and focused her binoculars on the former lantern room of the lighthouse. Had anyone seen her, they would have assumed she was just another visitor to Hunsey Island, a keen birdwatcher, perhaps, given her attire of dark green wax jacket, brown corduroy trousers and walking boots. Though perhaps the backpack she carried was larger than the norm.

Through the lenses she could see Becky, slightly hunched over her laptop. The light was fading now and the girl's face was illuminated by the glow from her screen – though whatever words Becky was writing were obviously too small for the binoculars to pick up. Becky had been there for nearly two hours now. Julia about the same.

Julia swivelled around to check the coastal path again. Rob had gone that way at about the same time Becky began her work for the afternoon, and Julia had noted as such in her notebook. But this time he wasn't with his camera equipment but dressed in a rubber wetsuit and carrying a surfboard. And just as she had done several times over the last week, Julia had followed him at a safe distance and watched as he picked his way down the cliff, over the rocks and into the sea.

As before she had hoped, but not expected, that he would slip when descending and tumble to his death. And just as before she had been disappointed. On some of his surfing expeditions she had also allowed herself to hope he might simply drown, or be set upon by a great white shark, launching at him from underneath, knocking and ripping the life out of him with its rows of razor-sharp teeth. But neither of those things had happened either. Instead, Julia had spied upon him for a while, from her vantage point behind a large outcrop of rock, and then gone back to spy again on Becky.

At no point had there been any opportunity to deploy her new poison. Her disguise this time around was aimed at fooling others into believing she was a normal visitor to the island, but it would not work against Rob or Becky, who would recognise her at once. Therefore she was cautious when approaching the lodge. She had been up to its windows on many occasions, and even ventured inside once, but there had been no chance to slip the poison into their food or drink. When distilling it, she had visualised dripping it stealthily into their morning coffee, but she now realised that this was so impractical as to be almost impossible. Her previous opportunity – she now realised – had been an incredible stroke of good fortune that might never be repeated.

Moreover, she had gradually lost faith in the now-colourless liquid she carried in the shampoo bottle in her jacket pocket. The rat poison had at least come with a health warning. It *looked* dangerous, yet it hadn't even proved capable of dealing with a dog! Her new poison was made from apples – how poisonous could that be? She couldn't think of a way to test it either, though she was sorely tempted to do so on one of the sheep that were dotted around the island. But every time she tried to get near they bleated and ran away.

So, as Julia hid and spied and waited, her plan evolved again. She stopped looking for an opportunity to sneak inside the lodge and slip poison into the drinks of its unsuspected inhabitants, and came again to believe that a more direct approach was the only way that would work. She found herself remembering – perhaps hallucinating is a closer description – how she had stood in the little kitchen with a knife in her hands. How, along with the fear of being discovered, she had also felt *powerful*. Had Becky entered that kitchen Julia now believed there would have been no mistakes. She would have plunged the knife into her, and after that there would be no route back.

And this now formed the core of her plan. She knew that the kitchen was unlocked, with its drawers of knives, and she knew that Becky and Rob's bedroom, just next door, was unlocked too. It wasn't a nice thought, what she would have to do. But it would get the job done.

Tonight, finally, she would do it.

It wasn't perfect. She had waited, hoping for a night when the lodge had no guests staying, but that didn't seem to happen. But tonight there was just one visitor – an elderly man, and he was frail enough that she believed she would be able to deal with him as well, if that proved necessary. But he seemed to have struck up a friendship with the island regulars in the Hunsey Tavern, and so far had spent every evening there. Becky and Rob on the other hand, seemed to believe in the old adage of early to bed, early to rise. It wasn't perfect, but she was fast running out of time. Who knew when Becky might finish her book and send it off? And just as importantly, she was fast running out of Dramadol again, or whatever it was she had got from Kevin.

For hours she had remained in her position, observing the lighthouse. Fixed in place by a complex mixture of fear and patience, and something else. Something new, a sort of excitement too. The thrill of the hunt. She stayed so long she sank into an almost Zen-like state. And when she finally moved she felt no fear. She felt nothing at all. Whatever was going to happen would happen. But it had to happen *now*.

She stood up from behind the wall, feeling her legs scream in protest at having been still so long. Automatically, she stretched them out and measured the distance between her and the public toilets outside the entrance to the small museum. Then she put her head down and walked towards it, trusting to her bird-watching disguise if anyone was watching.

Once inside she dropped to her knees to check that all the cubicles were empty, then locked herself into the one furthest from the door. She unzipped her backpack and placed it on the seat of the toilet. She removed her leather gloves, and slipped a new, silicon pair on instead, being careful not to touch anything as she did so. She pulled the leather gloves back over the top. Similarly she removed her hat, put a hairnet over her head, tucking in every loose strand of hair, then put her woolly hat back on top. Then she pulled on a pair of dark blue overalls. She had meant to buy the type you saw on the television programmes – the ones that the police forensic people wore – but she had no idea where to buy them, and these, which were meant for car mechanics, at least looked a bit less distinctive. She replaced the walking shoes she had been using. She had purposely bought them in a man's style, and two sizes too big.

She repacked her bag, unlocked the door and ventured out of the cubicle. She observed her appearance in the mirror, checking everything was in place. She didn't think how strange she looked. She didn't think how strange it was what she was preparing to do. Those thoughts were gone.

It would be harder to pass as a normal birdwatcher now, she knew. But outside it was already getting dark. The museum closed an hour ago. The few walkers who had been hiking around the island were all long gone. There was no one around to see her. No one except Becky and Rob.

Julia checked her watch. It was five minutes to six.

She left the toilets, and ran the hundred yards to the lodge.

As she did so, finally, she felt exposed and nervous, and she slammed hard against the wall of the building, grateful for the shelter it offered. Then, with her back against the stonework, Julia edged towards the corner of the building and its front facade, where the entrance was. It was a dangerous place to be. From her vantage point high up in the lighthouse Lantern Room, Becky would have a commanding view over this area, and if she happened to look down she would see Julia entering the building. And Julia was too low to be able to watch Becky's movements and find the right time to advance.

At that moment, Julia realised she was standing by a door she hadn't noticed before. It was set a little into the wall. She tried it, in case it offered an alternative way inside. But although the door opened, it disappointed her. It was a kind of outside storage area. It was almost empty, but it did contain a few pieces of gardening equipment, most of which looked brand new. Julia was about to leave when something caught her eye. Her plan up to that point – although in truth it was a stretch to call it a plan – involved finding the largest and sharpest knife she could, but suddenly here was something far better. In front of her was a shiny new gardening fork, with a long steel and wooden shaft and four shiny steel tines, each the length of a kitchen knife, and just as sharp. Julia picked it up. It had a nice weight to it. She gripped the handle tightly and considered whether this or a knife would be easier for what she intended. There was no contest. The gardening fork felt secure and powerful. At once she adjusted her plan yet again, re-visualising what she would do, now armed with the large fork. Like the poison the kitchen knife was forgotten, as if it had never existed.

She left her bag in the storage room, then carrying her fork in front of her, she took her chances and walked towards the door of the lodge.

FIFTY-TWO

Up in the lantern room, Becky's frustrations were getting the better of her. It was all very well for Rob to tell her to have a break now and then, but it had become *all* he was doing. He'd come to the island full of good intentions about how he was going to build a portfolio of wildlife photographs, and how he was going to send that to contacts he would find at the BBC and at *National Geographic,* but what he was *actually* doing more and more was going surfing and enjoying himself. A couple of times at Rob's behest, Becky had joined him, paddling out from the little beach on the west of the island when the waves were smaller, but it wasn't a very good beach for beginners and she'd been frustrated, cold and not a little scared. It wasn't much fun just sitting on the rocks and watching Rob either, so she'd returned, anxiously, to her manuscript.

She went right back to the beginning. Reading and improving the text as she went along. In part this was a profitable exercise. She fell at once back into the spell she had been in while writing the early part of the story. The words seemed perfectly chosen, the sentences clear and pure like the water around her on a still day. It lifted her heart, to read those words, and she knew once again that she really had something here. It wasn't just her hope, it really *was* good.

But as she came towards the later parts of the story, she felt herself beginning to lose it once again. Her hope was she would somehow gain momentum from starting at the beginning, so that it would carry her past the difficult part. But if that was going to happen, it hadn't yet. Still, the later direction of the book felt wrong, and when she ran out of words to revise and was confronted once again with the lack of an actual ending, she was entirely stumped as to how to finish the story off.

She tried, again and again. Taking new ideas and trying to write her way out of trouble. But each time her story felt alien. Wrong. As if she had created a beautiful painting of a giraffe but not included its neck and head, and now she was trying to graft the head of an elephant onto its body. And try as she might she simply could not picture how its head should look.

Becky stopped staring at her screen and instead looked glumly out of the window. The light was going now, which meant Rob would be back soon. She glanced around and down at the coastal path, to see if she might spot him. It was unlikely, since the little bay where he surfed was hidden from view by the overhang of the cliffs. But sure enough there he was, walking back to the lodge, the light glinting off the white of his surfboard. With a sigh she realised that whatever tiny amount of work she had done for the day, it was finished now. With a touch of irony she hit 'save' then closed the lid of her laptop. Then she yawned. An early night would be good. She would try again tomorrow when she was refreshed.

FIFTY-THREE

THE FRONT DOOR of the lodge was open – it had been left that way during Julia's stay, and she had never observed Becky or Rob locking it. Inside looked empty, and the lights were off. Julia pushed her way inside. Here she paused and listened. There was no sound apart from the soft tick of the clock on the wall.

Inside the lodge Julia felt less exposed, and with this came a strange feeling of calm. A most powerful calm, bolstered by the heavy garden fork that she carried with both hands. It was still true that Becky or Rob – or the elderly man – could walk in and discover her at any moment, but it was unlikely. Julia knew where they were. She knew their movements. So instead of moving on with her plan at once, she delayed. She slipped behind the little desk with the computer which served as the reception area, and on a whim she pushed the button to turn it on, leaning her fork against the edge of the desk. A few moments later the screen came to life, showing a dramatic picture of some seabirds taking off from a cliff edge. In the centre of the screen a box blinked at her requesting a password. The sight of that threatened to puncture her sense of calm power – she had no idea what the password could be. For a minute or so she typed possible options – Becky and Rob's names, the name of the lighthouse – but nothing worked, and soon Julia gave up. It didn't matter anyway.

She pulled open the drawer beneath the desk, trying to recapture her earlier sense of confidence and rummaged carelessly around at the few items within. A stapler and hole punch. Some tide tables. An OS map of the island. The same as the one she had in her bag, although by now she had memorised all the routes in and out.

She closed the drawer, and realised she was being complacent. Complacency was what cost her last time. She drew herself up tall and picked up the fork again. Then she left the desk and put her hand on the door to Becky and Rob's private space in the lodge. Julia hadn't been in here yet, and wasn't sure what she would find. The door was unlocked, and it opened softly under her hand.

Inside was a bedroom, smaller than the guest accommodation she had stayed in herself, but somehow more homely. A table served as a small desk, presumably either for Rob to use, or for when guests were using the lantern room and Becky had to work elsewhere. Julia looked at it carefully, but it was no good, offering little or no shelter. She looked at the bed next. She had assumed she would be able to conceal herself below it, but that was out of the question. Clearly Rob and Becky had used the space to store their bags. If Julia moved them out of the way, she would need to put them somewhere else, and storage was obviously an issue in the little room. Beginning to fret now, she poked her head into the bathroom – again, tiny. There was a shower, but rather than be concealed by a shower curtain, there was just an obscured glass shower screen. Also no good.

But then she noticed the wardrobe. It sat on the back wall of the room, facing the foot of the bed, and was a large, oak affair. It looked like it might have dated from the same era as the lighthouse itself; clearly it had been saved during the restoration. Julia opened one of the double doors and considered. Most of the hanging space had been taken by Becky, with Rob using the shelves above, but the space was deceptively large, perhaps built to fit lighthouse keepers' heavy jackets, for winter storms. Whatever, when Julia pushed the hanging clothes to one side she saw there was plenty of room behind. And so, awkwardly, she put one foot inside the wardrobe, testing the strength of the base. It creaked, but felt secure, so she pulled herself forward until she was completely inside, Becky's clothes draping themselves on her face and shoulders. She had to crouch, and the smell was overpowering and musty (despite the flowery undertones from Becky's clothes). But she fitted inside. Julia reached out and closed the door, shutting off what light there was left in the room. She rocked back on her heels. It was okay. She felt sure she could wait here, and if Becky or Rob did open the wardrobe, she felt confident she would remain hidden behind the clothes. And if not, well. What was she here for anyway? Grimly she adjusted the position of the garden fork and settled down to wait.

FIFTY-FOUR

THE DAY after his trip to London, Geoffrey was still feeling unsettled. There was no reply to any of his messages to Julia, and when he made a detour on his morning trip to the supermarket to pick up his *croissant*, there was no sign of life outside Julia's cottage. It meant he was unable to enjoy his morning coffee, but at least the caffeine helped him make a decision. Instead of worrying about it he would go and get himself some fresh air. In time Julia would reply, and no doubt there would be some crazy 'Julia' explanation for everything that had been going on. Perhaps it really was related to whatever she was writing next?

He packed his bag and loaded his walking boots into the back of the Land Rover. As he drove down to the coast he remembered how it was when Julia was writing her book, before she was famous. In a way it had been better then. Even though they had no way of knowing if it would ever be successful, or if she would even find a publisher. Back then it had just been the two of them who *really believed*. Julia writing these incredible chapters and sending them to him, and Geoffrey reading them and cheering her on.

He smiled to himself as he pulled into the quarry car park in the hill above the causeway to Hunsey, remembering how he and Julia had parked here not that long ago, to walk the ridge that curved around and above the island. And then he noticed a VW Beetle, the new style, that was exactly the same colour as Julia's new car. He stopped in the entrance to the little parking area, and then drove in and past the car. He couldn't remember the number plate on her new car – he still tended to think of her driving the old Morris – but it certainly *looked like* her car. He parked, then got out and walked back for a closer look. Now he wasn't so sure. Whoever owned this car was extremely messy. The passenger seat was wound back almost flat, and there was a sleeping bag trampled and stuffed into the foot well. The dashboard was littered with empty tins of food, and a half-eaten loaf of sliced bread. Geoffrey looked around, feeling as if he was spying on the intimate space of a stranger, who might catch him at any moment. Then he saw the notebook.

It was a dark blue, spiral-bound notebook – the sort that Julia had filled in their dozens when she was writing *The Glass Tower*. Geoffrey had seen enough of them to recognise it as Julia's. Which meant... Which meant it *must* be Julia's car. He looked around again, as if she might be lurking behind one of the other cars, or perhaps up the small craggy walls of the old quarry. But there was no one around. Geoffrey walked around the car, looking in all the windows. It seemed almost like... Geoffrey shook the thought away, it was ridiculous. But it came back, because the evidence supported it. It seemed like Julia had been *living* in the car, in the quarry.

Why was Julia camping in the old quarry above Hunsey Island? Geoffrey thought hard but could not come up with a single plausible reason for it. He tried the car's door. It was locked. He puffed out his cheeks. Now all thoughts of going for a long walk to clear his head had disappeared. Instead he returned to the Land Rover and adjusted his seat so that he could see both Julia's car, and the entrance to the quarry. He settled down to wait.

FIFTY-FIVE

BECKY OPENED the door to the lodge and flicked on the light. The tables were set for breakfast and looked neat and tidy, but she had the sudden feeling that something wasn't right. She looked around to see what it might be, but everything looked normal. She couldn't place what it was. She heard a noise coming from her room – Rob, presumably. But she was in no hurry to speak to him. Instead she decided to check whether any new guests were due to arrive in the next few days.

They were informed of new arrivals by emails on the computer kept on their little reception desk, and Becky slipped behind it now. Again, she had a strange feeling that something wasn't quite right. And when she flicked on the screen this was heightened. The password to unlock the computer had already been typed in, but instead of the five characters there should be, the box was filled with lots of stars – as if someone had tried to get in using a much longer password. Becky frowned at it for a moment, then looked up again. She got the shock of her life.

"Sorry, love! Did I make you jump?" The man had arrived so quietly he must have sneaked down the stairs. Becky put her hand to her chest to calm herself, and she smiled in relief. It was only the man from room five.

"No, it's fine. I just didn't hear you come down."

"I was just going out to the pub," the man went on. Colin was his name. He sounded jolly, but Becky wasn't entirely convinced. The man had chatted to her before about how his wife had passed away a year earlier. It wasn't a surprise, he said, they were both in their seventies, but Becky could see how difficult it was. There certainly wasn't anything scary about him.

"A quick one can't hurt." Colin smiled.

"One?"

"Pint."

"Oh, yes. Sorry," Becky smiled to show she understood now.

Colin didn't turn away. "Are you okay?" he asked. "You look a little white."

"No. I'm fine," Becky told him, then she smiled. She really was fine, she thought. What was a little struggle in finishing a book, compared to losing your partner in life?

"I just didn't hear you come in."

Colin smiled, his lined face creasing easily from a lifetime of staying cheerful.

"Well, I'm sorry I gave you a scare. Have a nice evening." He tipped an imaginary hat, and then pushed open the door.

Becky watched him go, and then turned back to the computer. She saw the password box again, still with too many asterisks in it and her unease returned. Had Rob forgotten the password? It seemed unlikely. He was the one who set it. So was it possible that one of the guests had tried to get into the computer? The island had no mobile coverage so it wasn't unknown for guests to request to use their computer, to check an email or something. They had Wi-Fi in the lodge, but it was always dropping out, and some people didn't have smartphones still. Actually maybe that was it – the Wi-Fi had dropped out, and someone had tried to reset it using the desktop computer? She didn't really like the idea of that, but she knew how annoying it was when you couldn't get a connection, so she shrugged and deleted the characters and typed the correct password. The screen came to life.

Becky made a note of the two new guests arriving the next day, then logged off. She slung her laptop bag over her shoulder and pushed her way into her and Rob's room.

"Hello?" she said, turning on the light. There was a noise she couldn't place.

"*Rob?*"

He came out of the bathroom, one towel wrapped around his waist, and drying his hair with another.

"Why are you in the dark?" she asked.

"I'm not," he said.

"You were."

"No, I wasn't. I was in the shower. With the light on." He looked at her as if she was being crazy. She shook her head.

"How was it?"

"The surf? Awesome," Rob said, and he walked past her to the little window and pulled the curtains shut. "It was really good actually. How was the writing?"

"Don't ask."

"That good?"

"No, really. I said don't ask." As Becky spoke she realised she really hoped he would. But Rob simply shrugged.

"Okay. You hungry? I can make pasta?"

"No. Not really," Becky replied. "I was thinking of an early night."

"Okay." Rob got dressed, pulling on jeans. "I'll grab something quickly for myself."

Rob left the room, and Becky heard him in the kitchen, looking in the fridge. Suddenly she didn't feel comfortable being in their room alone. It was a strange feeling – it made no sense.

"Rob?"

"Yeah?" he called back. But Becky had nothing to say, she just wanted to hear his voice. She lay back on the bed, and looked around the room. It was funny how quickly the little space had come to feel like home. And funnier still to think who else it had been home to over the years. She considered how the former lighthouse keeper and his wife must have seen the same views she had, over and over, until the fateful night when the man had killed her. What was the truth of it, that story? Had she been a spy for the Germans, or had he simply gone mad?

Her eyes fell on the wardrobe, which dominated the room, an antique almost as old as the building itself. They would have hung their clothes in that very same wardrobe that now housed hers. She smiled in spite of the unsettled feeling that seemed to have established itself upon her. She could still hear the bashing of pans in the kitchen as Rob fed himself. She closed her eyes. But then she jerked them open again.

The wardrobe had moved. Had she seen that right? Or was she now imagining things? She tried to clear her head by shaking it lightly, then she stared at the wardrobe. It certainly wasn't moving now, yet she was sure she had just seen it shift, rocking from one side to the other. Then the answer came to her. This room, and the kitchen next door, were both in the old part of the house, and the floorboards must run across both rooms. When Rob stepped on a floorboard next door, it must have lifted the wardrobe a tiny amount. There was always a rational explanation, no need to believe in silly stories.

Moments later Rob came back, carrying a bowl of pasta, reheated from the night before. He jumped on the bed next to her and began forking the contents into his mouth. It smelt quite good, and Becky realised she might be hungry after all. She rolled over and looked up into Rob's face.

"Where's mine then?"

"What? You said you weren't hungry!"

"So?" Becky took the fork from him and helped herself to some of the pasta.

"Hey!" Rob sounded outraged, but he let her have it.

"Is there any more?" Becky asked, when she'd finished the mouthful.

"No!" Rob said, but then he changed tone. "I can do you some more if you like?"

But Becky shook her head and smiled. She knew he would do, too. Because he was Rob and he would do just about anything for her. She thought again of Colin, the man in room five who had lost his partner. She thought of him, sitting alone in The Hunsey Tavern, and suddenly she felt a strong sense of obligation. They should go and talk to him. Keep him company for the evening.

"Do you fancy going out?" Becky said.

Rob looked surprised. "I thought you wanted an early night?"

"I did, but I've changed my mind," Becky said. "Let's go to the Tavern. We can get some chips."

Rob's eyebrows went up in mock delight. "Well, now you've eaten half my dinner..." He grinned and quickly finished the rest of his food, then finished getting dressed. A few moments later he led the way out of the room and into the dining area. Becky was the last to leave, and as she did so, she gave the wardrobe a last look, as if warning it to stay still while they were gone.

FIFTY-SIX

THREE HOURS later and Geoffrey was still waiting by Julia's VW. There had been a few cars entering and leaving the quarry car park, but although Geoffrey carefully inspected each one, none seemed to have any link to Julia, nor did any of the people inside give her vehicle the slightest glance. Nonetheless he took note of their registration details, if for no other reason than to pass the time.

He was grateful for his sandwiches and banana, and ate both while he waited. A couple of times he had to get out of the car to find a tree to go behind, and both times he passed close to her car when he returned, looking for some clue to explain what on earth was going on.

Now it was getting dark, and the only cars remaining were his, Julia's and one other vehicle, belonging to a couple who had turned up a couple of hours earlier, pulled on walking boots and set off towards the ridge.

Geoffrey made a decision to act. He put his fingers on the door release handle inside the Land Rover. But then he changed his mind. Instead of opening the door he softly hit the inside trim in frustration. He continued to wait.

The last car left a half hour later. The man driving gave Geoffrey a curious look as he pulled out of the car park – it was really getting dark now. Geoffrey looked at the clock, and saw it was nearly seven. But still he hesitated.

At eight o'clock Geoffrey moved the Land Rover so that he was able to flick on his headlights and illuminate Julia's car. But still he waited with the lights mostly off, worried about his car's battery. He watched as the quarry's shadows deepened and turned to proper night.

At nine he got out and had another look around Julia's car. It felt creepy now, in the quarry. The sky was clear, and the moon bright, but the walls of the quarry cut out what little light it gave. Geoffrey heard the noises of animals, snuffling around at the undergrowth. He felt relieved he had a proper torch, that he always kept in the back of the Land Rover, and charged up, too. He shone it inside Julia's car, and saw the notebook again. The writing was too small for him to make out what it said, and the book itself was obscured, partly hidden beneath a corner of the sleeping bag. He wished he could read what it said. He felt it might offer some clue as to Julia's whereabouts. He told himself that if she wasn't back by ten he would take things into his own hands.

At ten-thirty he finally did. Standing over the bonnet of the VW he dialled her number again. First her mobile, then the landline for the cottage, then for the penthouse. She didn't answer any of them. Geoffrey stroked his beard for a long time. Then he returned to the back of the Land Rover and pulled out his toolbox. He carried it around to Julia's car, then, within the flood of the Land Rover's headlights, he inspected his tools, and considered which might do least damage. He tried fitting a screwdriver into the keyhole and turning, but he was afraid he might damage the car's paintwork. He pulled the screwdriver away, then made a frustrated sound.

He tried again, this time brushing his concerns away. He put the screwdriver into place, and used a hammer to force it into the lock. When it was buried so deep that it stayed where it was when he took his hand away, he tried to turn it. First with just his hand, and then by fitting a pair of pliers around the shaft of the screwdriver. Nothing happened. He tried harder, and slowly the screwdriver turned. But it didn't open the car – all he had managed to do was lever open the keyhole so that it would never accept the real key any more. He thought for a moment, then picked up the hammer. As he felt the weight of it in his hand he decided on another course of action. He stood up and turned his face away from the car, then practised the action of swinging the hammer into the driver's window. Twice he lined up the shot, and then – with one last glance around in the hope that she might finally turn up – he swung the hammer hard.

Again, nothing happened. With the exception of the whole frame of the door bouncing outwards to absorb the impact. Geoffrey hit it harder, with the same effect. Then he stopped, and cursed himself for his stupidity. He looked again inside his toolbox until he found a counterpunch, and this time he placed it carefully at the corner of the window. Now he lined the hammer and struck it once, cleanly and hard. This time – with the hammer's blow focussed upon one tiny point – the glass instantly shattered into thousands of tiny cubes. Geoffrey removed his hands just in time.

His heart was racing, and he acted quickly now. Since he feared someone would turn up and ask what he was doing, he opened the door and reached in for the notebook. He hurriedly closed the door again, carried his tools back to the Land Rover and climbed back inside. He turned off the headlights, and from the interior light he began to read.

The first thing he noticed was a flyer from the Lighthouse Lodge B&B. It was dog-eared and had obviously been read many times. It was marking a page inside the notebook, and when Geoffrey turned his torch to read what she had written there, his sense of disquiet took a much more concrete form. In the notebook Julia appeared to have listed a variety of different ways to kill someone. Underlined twice, and then circled as well, were the words:

Kevin Rat Poison!!!

He looked closely. The word 'gun' was also on the list, but it had been crossed out so thickly Julia had nearly gone all the way through the paper. He thumbed through the notebook, at random, the hairs on his neck feeling prickly now. It seemed to be notes as if Julia had been spying on someone:

12.45: Becky in Lantern room – what is she writing??????

2.00: Becky still there. Rob surfing. Hate, hate, __hate__ Rob.
4.00: Becky stops for the day. Hear her laughing with guests. What are they laughing at? Me? Is she telling them about ME?
4.30: Rob back from surfing (not drowned, dammit!)
Only opportunity to get them together is later. Ideally when no guests!!!!!

There were pages and pages of it. Geoffrey frowned in concern. The only explanation he could come up with was that this was all some sort of bizarre research for whatever she was writing, but it didn't feel right. It didn't feel right at all. Then one of the phrases Julia had written – *lantern room* – struck him again. It was an unusual phrase, yet he'd read it just moments before. He grabbed the flyer for the Lighthouse Lodge – and there it was again. *The Lighthouse Lodge offers guests the opportunity to experience the magical old Lantern Room, now a spectacular lounge forty metres in the air.*

Was Julia spying on the old lighthouse? Clearly, she was. The real question was, why?

There was no answer to that, but Geoffrey felt a sense of profound urgency now. He started his engine, and – unsettled at leaving Julia's car unsecured – quickly pulled away. He turned left down the hill that led to the causeway and onto Hunsey Island. He was only a five-minute drive away, and he hoped he wouldn't be too late.

FIFTY-SEVEN

INSIDE THE WARDROBE, Julia was readying herself. In better times it might have occurred to her to wonder just how far a person could be driven, if subjected to the right pressure. She might even have been inspired to write about it. But right now such analysis was beyond her. She had been transformed into a much more primal entity. Living, breathing, acting, preparing, but not thinking, not in the wider sense of the word.

There was only cold planning. While she listened to Rob in the shower she ran her hand down the shaft of the garden fork and onto the steel tines. She measured their length, trying to feel how much force she would need to drive them through his body.

Then Becky came in, and Julia knew the time was almost here. The girl switched on the light, so that a tiny crack opened up onto the room. Julia saw her lie back on the bed, and very quietly she turned the garden fork around, so that her right hand was wrapped around its handle, that arm straight, and her left hand gripped the shaft, with its sharpened tines upright. It meant that she would be able to burst out of her hiding place with the weapon deployed in front of her. But not yet. She had to stay patient.

Becky had told Rob she wanted an early night, which was perfect. Julia would just wait until they were sleeping. That way they would die before they even realised what was happening. It would be quick. Maybe even silent.

But then she noticed Becky looking at the wardrobe. There was something on her face, like she suspected it in some way – but that was impossible. Even so Julia froze, riddled now with uncertainty. Eventually, Becky looked away.

Strangely, Julia felt no fear. Perhaps there was no room for it – the magnitude of what she was doing was so all-encompassing that her mind simply lacked the capacity for any kind of emotions. Or perhaps again, she was simply acting upon impulses hard wired into her by millions of years of evolution. Kill, or be killed. Fight or flight. Whatever the truth of that, the fact was she waited, tense, in the wardrobe for her moment.

And then they decided to go out to the pub.

Her first reaction was that she had to seize the moment. Right now. She gripped the fork harder, and tried to judge, through her tiny slit of light, for her opportunity. But there was none. Either only one of them was in sight, or the other was out of the room. Then, without giving her time to burst out and surprise them, the light went off and they left the room.

Her second reaction was anger. A white-hot rage descended upon her. She had waited for this opportunity. She had *worked* for it. *She deserved it.* She deserved to be free of the curse of this pair of *common thieves* who had stolen money, and still wanted more! Wanted her very life. Julia barely waited until they had left the building and then she began beating the wooden inside of the wardrobe with the heels of her hands. Some of Becky's clothes got caught up with her arm, and it only added to Julia's rage as she fought to free herself from the folds of material. But then the rage subsided, as if it were the tide surrounding the island, slowly drawing away.

Julia suddenly became aware of a desperate, overwhelming tiredness. By this time she had spent over a week stalking, spying and hiking around the island. Not wanting to take the risk of staying somewhere, she had been sleeping in her car, in the old quarry on the mainland. And that was nearly a four-mile walk each way, with early starts and late finishes to ensure she arrived at the lighthouse before the couple got up, and left after they had gone to sleep. Worse, sometimes she had got even less sleep, having to wait for the tide. Even when she did make it to the car it was hard to sleep, with its lumpy seats and her tortured visualisations of how she could reclaim her life when, and only when, Becky and Rob were dead and silent.

So now she stopped beating the wardrobe, and slumped back against its side. She could have got out of her hiding place and waited in a more comfortable place. But there was no time. Her eyes began to slide closed, and then the weight of them was such that it was impossible for her to haul them open again.

With the darkness now all around her, with no slit of light, it almost made no difference whether she fought to keep her eyes open or not. Slowly, her head slumped to one side, and Julia fell into a deep sleep.

FIFTY-EIGHT

IT WAS a lively night in the Hunsey Tavern. Becky needn't have worried about the man in room five. By the time they got there he had struck up a conversation with Ted, and two of the older local boys who seemed to spend every evening perched at the bar in their tweed jackets. Indeed it was Becky herself who felt almost isolated, since Rob bumped into a couple of friends who had also been surfing that day, and they fell into an easy conversation about how good, or bad, the waves had been – Becky didn't care to listen to which it was.

Eventually Rob noticed her sitting there and brought her into the conversation. Rob always did, and then Becky enjoyed her night, chatting with Rob's friends and letting the old boys of Hunsey Island flirt with her a little.

It was gone eleven by the time they walked back, hand-in-hand, down the spine of the island to the lighthouse complex on its southern tip. The tide was high and the water lapped calmly at the feet of the rocks below them, the only sound that broke the quiet of the night.

"I love it here," Becky said to Rob, squeezing his hand tightly. He didn't reply at once, but looked around at the moon, hanging low over the water, and the bright array of stars spread out over their heads.

"It's pretty awesome," Rob agreed.

"Should we live here forever?" she asked, but this time Rob only chuckled gently.

"What? Why not?" Becky insisted. "It's beautiful. You can surf and film seabirds. I can write. It's perfect."

"It'd be nice," Rob allowed. They walked on in silence for a few steps.

"How is the writing?" Rob went on. It wasn't a question he often asked, probably because Becky usually found a way to not answer it. But the three vodka and cokes inside her changed that. She took a deep breath of the salty air while considering how to answer.

"I'm stuck," she said at last.

"How stuck?" Rob asked. "Like you've got writers' block or something?"

Unseen by him, Becky wrinkled up her nose at the cliché. "No, I don't really believe in that. I just feel like I've taken a wrong turn somewhere, but I don't know where."

When Rob answered it was obvious he was choosing his words carefully. "I know I'm not much of a reader, but I'd like to help, Becky. I really would."

Becky stayed quiet. Tempted now to open up. Perhaps he could help? It wasn't impossible, was it?

"But you'd need to tell me what the story is about!" he added, a little playfully.

In response Becky swung her arm back and forth, her hand still embedded in Rob's strong grip. He let her do it in silence, waiting for what she would say next.

"Alright."

And she told him. Not everything about the book, but the bones of the story. How it was – loosely – inspired by what had happened to them, but how in her version of events her author, Joanna, had devoted her life to undoing the wrong she had caused.

"That sounds cool," said Rob, when Becky was finished. "So, am I in it?"

"No!" she replied. "No one's in it. None of us are anyway. It's fiction. It's not real." In the moonlight she saw a flash of his smile that showed he was teasing her.

"So what's the problem? How does it end?"

"Well, that's just the thing," she said, instantly serious again. "I've got this idea that she – Joanna I mean – works harder and harder to undo the wrong she has caused – you know, giving to charity, helping out the family of the dead woman, but whatever she does, it's never enough..."

She stopped long enough that Rob prompted her.

"So, then what? Is that the ending – she gets away with it?" There was enough in his voice to suggest it didn't impress him much.

"No," Becky replied at once. "It wouldn't really work like that. It's a *story*, so it has to be discovered. The story can't actually end until the secret is revealed."

"I don't understand."

"Well, think about it. When you read a book and..." She stopped. "Or see a film and there's a – I don't know – one of the characters discovers a gun. Does that gun ever just disappear and never get mentioned again?"

Rob shrugged. "No, it usually gets used to shoot someone."

"Not usually. *Always*. It's like a rule. You can't introduce a gun into a story and then not use it. It wouldn't feel complete as a story. It wouldn't work," Becky said. She looked over at Rob to see if he understood her.

"Yeah, I see. So is there a gun in your story?"

"No. But there is a *threat*. Everything that Joanna does is because she feels the threat hanging over her from what she's done. What will happen to her if anyone finds out how she killed the woman."

"Okay. So?"

"So the threat has to be *realised*. Until it is, the story isn't complete."

They both walked on a few more steps before Rob spoke again.

"So? What actually happens?"

When Becky spoke again she sounded unsure, having been driven to the nub of her frustration.

"Well, in my version it doesn't matter how much good she does, how many people she helps, it's never enough. So in the end she confesses to what she's done. On a talk show."

"A talk show? Like on TV?"

"Yeah. Because she's a national celebrity by then."

"And she admits that she ran someone over and hid the body?"

"Yeah. On live TV."

Rob walked a few more steps.

"Wow. Then what?"

"Then everyone forgives her, because by then everyone loves her so much. Because of all the good things she's done."

They were arriving at the lodge now, and the automatic light flicked on and cast them in a puddle of artificial yellow light.

"Okay," Rob said as he let them in. "Yeah. I can see that happening."

"It's weak though, isn't it?" Becky insisted, following him through the dining room and towards their bedroom. By putting voice to her ending, it had become clear to her just how weak it sounded.

"It's alright," Rob tried to reassure her. But then he went on. "Well, maybe something else happens instead?"

He flicked on the light in their bedroom. Neither Rob nor Becky noticed how the door of the wardrobe was now stuck just very slightly open, nor that something inside was preventing it from properly closing.

"What else could happen?" Becky asked.

"I dunno," Rob said. He went into the bathroom. Becky stood still at the end of the bed for a while, thinking. Then suddenly Rob called out.

"You know, talking about Julia, did I tell you I thought I saw her the other day?"

Becky walked to the door of the bathroom. "*No*? When?"

"Yesterday. Only I don't think it was her, just some woman who looked a bit like her. Like a scruffy version of Julia. If you could get a scruffier version. I thought she was watching me when I was in the water, surfing."

"Really? *Here*?"

"Yeah. Only no, because it wasn't her. Because she's in London, isn't she? And if it was her she'd say hello, not hide behind rocks like some kind of lunatic." Rob leaned in close to the mirror and removed his contact lenses, one after the other. He didn't bother putting on his glasses, with their thick lenses, in their place.

"Mmmmm," Becky answered him, her voice distant.

"Although it did kind of look like her," Rob went on when he'd finished. He laughed. "She had that crazy look Julia's got."

By now Becky was cleaning her teeth, and he had to wait until she removed the brush before she answered. "Rob! She hasn't got a crazy look!"

"Yeah she has!" Rob teased her. "You know what I mean. That kind of falseness she has. Like she's pretending to be nice but really she's not, and she's not even any good at hiding it."

"Rob!" said Becky again. Rob wasn't a big drinker but he'd drunk three pints that night, and when he did it often made him say things he shouldn't.

"Come on, you know what I mean. How she thinks she's some kind of legend in the book world, but actually her books aren't even that good."

"Yes they are!"

"That's not what you said. You said her *Glass House,* or whatever it's called, got some good early reviews but then people weren't buying it. And that you weren't actually surprised once you'd read it. It wasn't as good as you'd hoped?"

Becky didn't answer. She had said those things. But only because writing was hard, and sometimes it helped to look at the flaws in other's work.

"Yeah, well. It's mean to say it."

Rob squeezed past her into the bedroom.

"And she's so bloody full of herself," he went on. "I mean, I'm grateful for the bursary, but she could have just offered it to us without making out like she's some kind of god."

He jumped full length on the bed then rolled over on his back to face her.

"I know what you mean actually," Becky replied at last. A memory had come to her. Something she had kept from Rob. Something she had never imagined she would need to share. She sat down on the bed next to him and slowly removed her shoes and socks.

"Do you remember..." She began, speaking quietly this time. "When we had our *thing*?" She sensed him stiffen. It was as close to a name as they had for the weeks when they had split up over the misunderstanding about the pornography on Rob's computer, and it still wasn't something they had properly discussed.

"Yeah?" he said, guardedly.

"No, it's not that," Becky went on. "It's..." She hesitated, not sure how to tell him, nor whether she should. But she knew she wouldn't be able to just drop the topic now.

"Well, I never told you, but she came to see me. When you were living at John's."

"Julia came to see you? Why?"

Becky swallowed. "You said something online about having those photos," Becky bit her lip and hurried on. "Those ones we took, you know, in bed." Becky hurriedly went on. "I know you were just joking, but she thought you meant the ones of her the night of the accident."

Rob said nothing but when Becky looked across at him he was frowning now.

"She thought you were going to put them on Facebook, or give them to the police or something. I don't really know, she was really worried. And she thought we needed to stick together to protect ourselves."

"She thought I'd give them to the police? Why the hell would I do that?" Rob said at last.

"I dunno, I thought she was a bit crazy."

Rob thought about this.

"So what did she want from you?"

Becky hesitated now. She was thinking hard, she wasn't clear exactly what Julia had wanted. It wasn't something she had considered in detail.

"She said we should stick together. You know, against you, if you released those photographs, we should say it was you driving that night."

"*What?* Why?"

"Because then it would be two against one. The police would have to believe us, and then you'd be the one that got into trouble. Or into the most trouble."

"But that's..." Rob stopped. "So what did you tell her?"

"I didn't... I don't..." Becky was forced to swallow a lump of sudden guilt as she remembered how she had agreed with Julia's plan. She glanced at Rob, his eyebrows furrowed with a mixture of confusion and brewing anger.

"Nothing. I didn't say anything to her. I just told her not to worry. That you didn't even have those photographs anymore."

This seemed to placate him a bit, but Rob's expression was still dark.

"But did you agree to do it? To blame it on me?"

"No! Of course not." Becky held his gaze. Suddenly she laughed, a clear, beautiful, sincere sound. She had remembered something else. Something that would lighten the mood.

"Actually, something really funny happened after that." She looked at Rob, a naughty smile forming on her lips. "You know I was in a bit of a state, upset by..." She looked down, demurely, the forgiveness clear in her voice.

"Anyway, she started comforting me a bit. She was sitting next to me and..." Becky pushed off her jeans as she spoke and lay down on the bed next to Rob, in her underwear, looking him full in the face now.

"And then this really funny thing happened." She bit her lip again, waiting for him to ask her to go on.

"What funny thing?"

"I think she made a pass at me."

Rob's eyes grew wide. There seemed a moment when he was deciding whether to take a path of anger and resentment at what Julia had proposed, or a new avenue of humiliating her. He chose humiliation.

"*Julia made a pass at you?!* No way, she's like fifty years old!"

"I know!"

"Oh, man! That's *disgusting*. What did you do?"

"I didn't *do* anything. I mean, I didn't know *what* to do. I kind of pretended it wasn't happening, but she kept going..."

"Doing what?" Rob laughed loudly now. Becky almost told him to stay quiet but she remembered there was no need. The man from room five was their only guest and they had left him at the pub.

"Was she, like, trying to kiss you, or what?"

"Worse. She touched me, too."

"No!" Rob's eyes grew wide. "Where?"

"Here." Becky still had her jumper on, and through the fabric she pointed to her breast. Instantly Rob's attention changed.

"What, here?" he said. He moved his hand close to her. Not touching, but closer than he needed to indicate the area he meant. Very slowly, he then moved his hand closer and laid it on the outline of her breast.

"Right here?" he said again. He swallowed and his fingers searched for the bump of her nipple.

"Mmmmm," Becky said. She bit her lower lip. Then Rob changed his position and slipped his hand up under the front of her jumper.

"Did she touch you like this?" He rubbed at her chest and leaned in and began kissing her mouth. For a few minutes the room was almost silent, apart from the rustle of Becky's clothing. Then Rob leaned back again.

"I can't believe Julia tried it on with you!" he said, as Becky sat up and pulled her jumper off and over her head. Rob did the same with his jumper and t-shirt in one. Then he slid down his jeans.

"Can you even imagine the thought of having sex with that?" He grinned, and rolled on top of Becky so that their taut stomachs were pressed against one another.

Then, from underneath him, Becky said something strange.

"Have you noticed how the wardrobe moves when someone walks about upstairs?" She giggled the words.

"What?" Rob frowned in confusion. He stopped what he was doing, pressing himself against her and moving.

"I noticed it earlier... And then again, just now. Sorry – don't stop."

Rob started again, but he continued to look at her strangely.

"What do you mean? The wardrobe moves?"

"It moves. I don't know. I just... Forget it." Becky wrapped her hands around Rob to pull him tighter against her. But then she froze.

Scrambling now, Becky tried to push Rob off.

"Becks? Becks, what is it?"

But she was suddenly so filled with terror it was impossible for her to speak.

"Becks, what the hell is wrong?"

Becky drew herself up into a tight ball beside Rob on the bed. She fought to breathe, and she fought to speak. All the time she was staring in terror at the wardrobe. The old, antique wardrobe that must have seen so many stories over the years. Of shipwrecks and lighthouse keepers gone mad.

"*The ending to the story*. What if I got it all wrong? What if that's why I couldn't make it work." She was talking fast now, still staring at the wardrobe, just a few feet away. "You said you'd seen her, here on the island? Rob? There's another way she can end the story!"

"What are you talking about?" Rob said. He was still lying on his front, staring myopically at Becky's face, not at where she was looking.

"Another way to end it. All she has to do is silence us. Rob, what if she's in there? In there right now. What if she's here to kill us?"

Finally, Rob turned to look at the object of her terror – the door of the big, heavy wardrobe that sat at the foot of their bed. As he did so, the door creaked open.

FIFTY-NINE

IT WAS JUST a mile down to the beginning of the causeway, and Geoffrey drove faster than he normally would, working hard to steer the big Land Rover around the tight corners. But as he drew near to the road that stretched across the beach, he was forced to brake hard.

"Shit," he said.

Ahead of him the bay was filled with seawater, a billion corners of chop reflecting the light from the moon, the roadway hidden beneath six metres of salt-green water.

"Shit."

The Land Rover was an all-terrain model, capable of breaching rivers or climbing through thick mud, but there was no way it was going to get across the causeway until the tide dropped. Geoffrey stopped at the top of the ramp and pushed open the door. He swore again. There was no one about. In the summer there was a ferry service that connected Hunsey to the mainland when the tide was high, and it also ran a tractor service over the beach on low tides, but both boat and tractor were put away for the season now, hidden inside one of the dark sheds that sat by the side of the road. Geoffrey walked towards them. He found the iron clasp that held the doors closed, and rattled the padlock that held it in place. It was wrapped in plastic, and inside that coated in grease to protect it from the salt. He felt some of the grease come off on his hands but he wiped it on his trousers and looked around again.

There was nothing to see. His car stood at the head of the ramp, the door still open. Beyond it the water sparkled and, a half-mile away the dark hump of Hunsey Island rose up. Somewhere on it, presumably, was Julia.

Geoffrey looked around again. Pulled up high onto the beach, above the high tide line, there were a few private boats, mostly tenders and small fishing dinghies. In fact, the dark shapes of their hulls were dotted along the curve of the beach. Geoffrey thought for a moment and then he ran back to the Land Rover. He moved it so that it was parked by the side of the road, and then he got out and locked it. Now he began walking quickly along the head of the beach, using his flashlight to check each dinghy. It took him ten minutes to find what he was looking for, a robust dinghy secured under a tarpaulin, with a small outboard motor hidden underneath the hull. He picked it up and tried to shake it, feeling the slosh of fuel in its tank.

A thin chain secured it to a tree root higher up the beach, but the padlock looked flimsy. He ran back to the Land Rover for his tools again, and using his screwdriver and hammer he was able to smash it open relatively easily. He felt a burst of guilt at what he was doing, but he didn't stop. He flipped the dinghy and clamped the outboard to its stern. Then he dragged it down the short stretch of sand until his feet were in the water.

When the boat was fully afloat he clambered carefully inside, and at once he drifted away from the shore. He prayed the motor would start, since there were no oars or other means of propulsion. He stood to pull the starter, and on the second attempt the engine fired. The noise was like an angry rasp in the quiet night, but Geoffrey didn't think about whether it would attract attention, since there was no one about. Instead he sat in the little boat's stern and aimed its bow at the east side of the island. Then he opened the throttle fully. The little engine was just able to push the boat onto a plane, and it began sending a white wash out behind it as Geoffrey sped away from the mainland.

He ignored the landing area on the Hunsey Island side of the causeway, instead keeping close to the cliffs and turning so that the little boat travelled parallel to the steep sides of the island. It would be quicker to travel the two miles to the lighthouse in the boat.

There was little to no swell, and going down the east, protected side of the island it wouldn't have reached him even if there was. But the water was a little choppy, making the boat bounce up and down. And he had to steer well wide of the island in places, to avoid areas where he feared that rocks lurked just under the surface. Soon the tip of the lighthouse itself became visible above the curve of the cliff, and when it did he steered towards it. As he drove Geoffrey was desperately trying to remember how the landing stage looked. He knew the lighthouse had one – a tiny stone quay that was built into a natural gully in the rocks. It was a favourite spot for him to eat his sandwiches when walking around the island. He had even swum from it on one occasion, but had never approached it at night in a small boat. He slowed as he drew close. Fortunately the moonlight was sufficient that he could make out the unnatural straight edge of the quay wall, and he nosed in gently towards it. There was a crunching sound as the hull scraped over some rocks, but it was a glancing blow that served to redirect the boat in the right direction. The water in this little protected gully was perfectly calm, so that Geoffrey was able to knock the motor out of gear and glide the final few feet. He grabbed the cold stone wall hungrily, and then nearly fell into the water, such was his rush to climb from the boat and onto the quay.

He tied the boat to an iron ring cast in to the concrete, and glanced back at the dinghy, barely believing he had just stolen it. Now he was here he felt suddenly unsure why he had come, and with such urgency. There were no lights on, there was no sound, other than the lapping of water. Everything seemed quite peaceful. But having come this far he had no choice but to continue up to the lighthouse complex and check more carefully. For the first time in several hours, Geoffrey smiled at himself. He would enjoy telling Julia about this story one day. The night he completely misunderstood the situation and actually stole a boat!

He began to climb the stone steps up to where the buildings were. As he did so he heard a sudden, terrified scream.

SIXTY

WHEN JULIA AWOKE she was completely disorientated. Her arms and legs hurt from where they had been cramped up and her back was throbbing even worse than it normally did. As usual, her first conscious thoughts were for Dramadol.

Then her mind turned – almost abstractly – to *why* she had suddenly woken. There was a shaft of yellow light running up and down the border of this strange world she had awoken in. What world? Where was she? Then there was the sound of a tap running. And voices. Voices she knew. The soft, breathy sound of Becky speaking, the harsher tones of Rob.

Suddenly it all came back to her. The black, close walls were the inside of their wardrobe. The yellow slit of light was because they had returned from their night out. Why was she there? The thick, round shaft of the gardening fork explained that – she was there to kill them.

But the rage, the calculating, controlled drive which had put her there was, for the moment, gone. It was as if the Julia that had woken in that wardrobe was an entirely different person to the Julia who had climbed in a few hours earlier. She unclasped her hands in horror, then panicked as the fork banged against the inside of the wardrobe. Could she escape? Could she push her way out of this black prison and get away while they were in the bathroom? Desperately, Julia put her eye to the crack in the door. She couldn't see anyone, but she could hear them talking just a few feet away. It was too close, the room too small. If she tried to move they would see her – and what then?

And then the words they were saying registered with Julia.

"You know, talking about Julia, did I tell you I thought I saw her the other day?"

Julia froze anew. Her view of the bedroom disappeared for a moment as Becky walked right in front of the crack of light.

"She was watching me when I was in the water, surfing."

There was no opportunity now for Julia to escape, and no way she couldn't hear as Rob went on to insult her. To call her a crazy person, to tear apart her good character. To call her false. And then to be forced to listen as Becky laid into her work. To criticise her masterpiece, calling it overrated.

Quickly, Julia refilled herself with all the boiling rage, the injustice, the *furious anger* which had been momentarily absent when she woke.

Then there was something she never expected. Speaking quietly, just beyond the wooden wardrobe door, Becky began to explain how Julia had approached her with the plan to claim that Rob was driving the car on that night. As if she had been trying to frame him! She felt such outrage now that she nearly leapt out of the wardrobe screaming her innocence of such a vile accusation. Julia's suggestion had been the only reasonable thing to do in the circumstances – to paint it as anything else, to distort it as such was... was... insanity.

Julia found herself taking short, sharp intakes of breath. She found that her hands had gripped down hard on the fork. Then Becky lied again. Telling Rob that she had insisted Rob had deleted all the photographs from that night. The vixen. The deceitful, lying little vixen. Julia was baring her teeth. Grinding them together. And then came the true humiliation.

"I think she made a pass at me."

That's not true, Julia wanted to scream out. It was you. You led me on. *It was your fault, in that dirty little nothing of a pyjama top!* But Julia couldn't say a word. She was forced to keep herself still, and listen passively as they humiliated her. One thing after the other, taking it in turns to heap shame upon her.

The images began to flow through her mind now. Visualisations in her head of how it was going to happen. How she would burst out and impale them. How she would puncture and rip at their bodies until they could hurt her no more. It was almost impossible for Julia to tell what was real and what was in her mind. The images came thick and fast. She felt her arms moving, the muscles twitching as her mind tried to decipher whether they really were stabbing and tearing, or if this was just in her head.

Julia fought to hold herself together. She poised herself ready to go. And then Becky began to scream:

"Rob, what if she's in there? In there right now. What if she's here to kill us?"

And, as if answering the instructions of a higher power, she pushed open the wardrobe door.

SIXTY-ONE

FOR A MOMENT there was total silence. For Becky and Rob it was the sheer shock and surprise of seeing her there, stretching and emerging from behind the clothes, a huge gardening fork held in her gloved hands.

Then Rob screamed. Not how she had imagined it. This wasn't the scream of a capable, protecting boyfriend, but of a boy filled with terror that there really was a monster under the bed. It made Julia click into action. The last thing she wanted was someone to hear what was happening. She lifted the fork in front of her, meaning perhaps only to threaten him. To shut him up. But she tripped.

There wasn't much room between the wardrobe and the foot of the bed, so that, as Julia moved forwards, her legs struck the bed frame, and toppled forwards. She put the fork out in front of her, to break her fall. And all four of the thick steel tines planted themselves neatly into Rob's chest. In a panic Julia tried to push herself off, but all this achieved was to push the tines deeper into him, the steel slipping through the gaps between his ribs. Abruptly the scream stopped, replaced now by a sickening, gurgling sound. Becky stared and blinked in horror. Then she found her voice and screamed too, a higher-pitched, nauseating sound.

Rob's hands had gone to protect himself, and both now held onto the outer two tines of the fork, like he were a prisoner hanging from the bars of his cell. For some reason this brought to the surface an anger in Julia. It was *her* fork. He was stealing it, literally sucking it into his body in front of her. But her response was to push it still deeper into him, feeling the tines slide past his ribs, and then feeling the lessening of resistance once they were past. She pushed it deeper again, until they could sink no more.

Becky's crying grew louder, and Julia fought to her feet, using the garden fork to pull herself up, and then she was standing on the bed, her head banging into the light fitting. She put a booted foot on his chest and pulled the fork out of him, then without allowing any thought, she plunged it down again. Then again, and again and again. Blood fountained up from the holes, spraying the walls and turning the covers deep red. Julia's head kept hitting the light, sending crazy shadows rolling around the little room, and Becky's screams filled the air, ear-splitting, horrible noises. Eventually they forced Julia's broken mind to consider her too.

Julia stopped and looked across at her. Becky had crawled backward so far on the bed that she had fallen onto the floor. Now she had scrambled back to her feet, but was cowering in the corner of the room. When Julia looked at her she stopped screaming. Instead, there was only a horrified, questioning look in her eyes. For a second they stared at each other. For Becky there was no way to escape without getting past Julia, and she had no weapon or means to defend herself.

For a long, strange moment, neither of them moved. Only after a while did it dawn on Julia that Becky was trying to communicate with her. Not by speech – she didn't seem able to talk at all – but by shaking her head, as if imploring for some kind of mercy. But Julia didn't feel merciful, she felt *powerful*. For the first time in months, she felt she was taking charge of the situation. With her hand gripped tightly around the handle and shaft of her weapon she placed her boot on the head of the fork, and with her eyes on Becky she leaned all her weight onto it, driving the tines to the hilt. There was a crunch, and what movements Rob had been making stopped.

Julia glanced down at him now. The man she had hated and feared for so long, vanquished. And it was so easy. She pulled hard to release the fork, then turned back to look at Becky again. This time Julia didn't hesitate, she launched herself, steel tines first, towards the girl.

But Becky moved at exactly the same time, scrabbling frantically to her left, so that Julia's lunge didn't spear her victim as she intended. Instead the tines of the fork cut into the wall, and stuck there with the force of the blow. As fast as she could, Julia got back to her feet and pulled her weapon out, then turned, looking for Becky, this time to swipe at her head, to bash her to death. But Becky had a head start this time and was already nearly at the door – she seemed to be moving as an animal might, no longer on two legs but lurching on all fours.

Then Julia charged again. But this time Becky ran.

They ran from the bright light of the bedroom into the darkness of the dining room, the world changing from vivid horror to shadowy hell. Julia held the fork in front of herself like a spear, and had to slow down to avoid running into the furniture or walls. But Becky just ran, and from the sudden crash, had clearly not managed to avoid the tables and chairs of the dining room. In the semi-light Julia saw her sprawling on the floor, and she lunged forward again with the fork, jabbing it at where the girl was desperately trying to pick herself up. It wasn't a clean connection but she felt the fork's spikes connect with Becky's leg. She thought she saw a flash of red where her calf muscle was opened up. But it wasn't enough to stop Becky and before Julia could land another blow the girl was up and moving again, this time throwing chairs behind her to stop Julia's progress. Julia felt a sudden moment of fear. Becky was going to make it outside, and if she did that she could disappear into the darkness. There was no way Julia would be able to track her down amongst the stone walls, the rocks and gullies that surrounded the lighthouse. She would find her way to the village and raise the alarm. Julia's fear increased and she picked herself up again, but she was too late. Becky crashed into the door and disappeared through it.

Now Julia's fear hardened again into anger. How dare the girl try to escape? She had no right to threaten her. She had no right to live. Though Julia knew on some level she was beaten, she swept the chairs out of the way with the fork and followed the girl outside.

Julia expected to see nothing but night, allowing Becky to escape in almost any direction, to a dozen possible hiding places. And for a second or so she was right, but then the automatic outside lights clicked on, triggered – on a slight delay – by movement. Two wide-beamed bright spotlights suddenly threw the entire courtyard area into sharp relief. There, holding onto the outer wall for support, and making for the gate, she saw Becky.

Perhaps the girl had forgotten the light. If she had gone in the other direction she would have been out of the courtyard already and into the surrounding darkness, but she had moved in the direction of the lighthouse itself, meaning Julia was clearly able to see where she was heading. Julia didn't hesitate – she held up her garden fork again, put down her head and charged.

The sight of the bloodied and crazed Julia hurtling towards her, combined with the thought of how she had murdered Rob, must have driven Becky to new levels of terror. The wound on her leg was bad, but not enough that she couldn't move, and even now she could have run for the gate and lost herself in the unknown darkness. But that wasn't what she did. Instead, she went towards the door of the lighthouse building. Perhaps she ran there because she knew it and felt secure there, the place where she had spent so much time. Or perhaps she simply ran towards a door she thought she could lock. Whichever, it became a race, the injured Becky slowed by her leg against the raging Julia, hampered by the huge gardening fork she was holding in front of her. It was a race that Becky won, but not by quite enough. She reached the door, pulled it open, then tried and failed to slam it shut behind her, before the tip of Julia's fork crashed into it and smashed it open again. Julia went stumbling into the dark interior of the tower. Becky screamed, and retreated the only way left to her – up the tightening spiral staircase that led all the way up to the lantern room above their heads.

It wasn't quite dark. There was an emergency light that always shone, a dull red glow, just enough to illuminate the curved treads of the stairs. Without thinking, Julia began to ascend, hearing the girl's panting breaths and panicked steps directly above her.

Becky screamed now with no restraint, and the sound echoed up and down the vertical shaft of the tower. Then the sound of her footsteps stopped, and Julia sensed herself gaining on the girl, her excitement and appetite increasing as she saw how the tines would spear her. But then

Julia sensed something was wrong. With a loud metallic clang, it became clear what it was. Bouncing down and around the stairs above her was a fire extinguisher, which Becky had removed from its bracket on the wall and thrown down towards her. There was no time to do anything; the heavy container was almost upon her, and Julia threw herself back against the curved wall behind her. The fire extinguisher bounced, five steps above, and then it struck the wall just inches from where Julia stood. She felt it rush through the air in front of her, and then it was past, and continued clanging down towards the bottom of the tower. Julia paused for a second, as if fearful of another bomb raining down on her, but Becky had only had the one shot. She whimpered with despair when she saw it had missed. Julia growled in response and continued her ascent.

Becky reached the upper door that led into the lantern room just a few steps in front of Julia. Again she tried to push it shut behind her. But it was half-hearted this time, as if she knew she was beaten, and Julia burst through and up into the room at the top of the lighthouse. It seemed bright in here, with the light from the moon streaming in through the wide windows. Julia stood, panting from the effort of running up the steps. Becky was nowhere to be seen. Julia stood gripping the fork tightly and looking around, her chest heaving. Then from behind her she heard a noise, and she turned just in time to put up her fork as a defence against Becky's attack. The girl was wild, her hands formed into fists and trying to punch any part she could see, but it was easy for Julia to keep the fork between the girl and herself, so that most of Becky's blows hit the metal and wooden shaft, and she soon backed off, crying in pain. Then Becky grabbed something – a pillow from the circular sofa that curled around the perimeter of the room – and tried to swing it at Julia.

It was such a pathetic attempt that Julia grinned before she swung her weapon at Becky another time. Julia only managed a glancing blow, but it was into Becky's stomach, and she watched the girl's hands go to where the wound had landed. Becky staggered now. Julia tried again, stabbing harder, but the girl moved, this time backwards and out onto the balcony that encircled the tower. It was fitted with an iron balustrade, but beyond that there was nothing but the forty-metre drop to the rocks below. Becky moved around it, still trying to escape from Julia, but now she was slower. The combination of fear, shock and her injuries meant she was nearly beaten. Julia hesitated for only a half-second before she charged again. This time, Becky barely even tried to move. The vicious tips of the fork slammed into the soft flesh of her stomach and disappeared from view. Their eyes met for a moment, as the breath escaped from Becky for the last time. Then Julia snarled and leaned down on the fork's handle, prising Becky upwards, her back twisting on the iron railings until, for a half-second, she was balanced right upon the edge, held in place above the precipice only by Julia's goodwill. She had total control now. The power of life and death. Julia hesitated, wanting to savour the moment.

"You wanted to know how it ends?" Julia said to the girl, staring into her eyes.

"This is how it ends. This is the only way."

With a huge final effort Julia leaned down again on the handle, and Becky's body was lifted off the iron deck and tipped over the edge. Julia opened her grip, letting Becky tumble out into the night.

Becky hit the tower as she fell, leaving smears of bloody red on its new, gleaming white paintwork, and with a thud she landed on the rocks at the foot of the lighthouse.

SIXTY-TWO

JULIA LEANED out to see Becky's body lying on the ground, as if she expected the damn girl to get up and start running away – but that didn't happen. Slowly, Julia realised it was over. She was finally free. There was no jubilation, no feelings at all really; it was more as if she was descending from another plane. Becoming human again, after an episode as a monster.

She checked around – there were no lights coming towards the lighthouse complex, and it didn't seem as if the alarm had been raised. She felt for her gloves and hairnet, which had both survived the ordeal mostly intact. Then she looked around the lantern room for any incriminating evidence. There was nothing she could see.

Slowly, she descended the long spiral stair of the lighthouse, and as she did so her heightened mood seemed to sink further with her, so that every step down was taking her closer to the awfulness of what had just happened. What she had just done. By the time she reached the door that led outside, which had swung shut behind her minutes before, she almost couldn't face going through it. What had she done?

A new fear reached her, too. What if Rob wasn't dead? What if he were now crawling towards her, trying to get his revenge? Now that the mania had left her, she felt scared. As if a deeply wounded Rob would be far more than a match for poor little her. But she knew she couldn't just run away. She had to finish what she had come here to do. So she opened the door to the cool outside and looked around.

There was no one there. She looked carefully at the lodge, for any signs of Rob moving about, but it seemed still. Even so, she decided it would be less terrifying to collect the fork again before going inside, just in case. So she turned and walked unsteadily around to the other side of the lighthouse where Becky's body had fallen.

It didn't take long to find Becky; her body lay twisted and broken, a surprising distance from the base of the tower. Julia did everything she could not to look at it, but her eye was drawn to see. The girl's neck was snapped, the head broken. It was strange. This girl, now dead, had been there at the beginning of all of this, had caused it really, by distracting her on that drive home, many months before. The beginnings of a smile touched at Julia's lips, but only for a moment. Then she turned away, in search of the garden fork. It hadn't stayed in Becky's stomach, it had fallen a little further away than the body, but it wasn't hard to find. She picked it up and holding it before her again, trying to regain some of the *power* it had offered her earlier, she walked back towards the lodge.

The path she took merged with a second path – the one which led down to the small landing stage that served the lighthouse complex. As she walked she considered what she still had to do: find their laptops, and if they could be accessed to locate the photographs and the manuscript, and if not, then destroy them…

Suddenly Julia was illuminated by a shaft of yellow torchlight. There was nothing she could do. Nowhere she could hide. Whoever was holding it was only a few steps away.

"Julia?" an incredulous voice said to her. An incredulous voice she knew. An incredulous voice that swept away her mood of calm practicality at once. She put her hand up to shield her eyes.

"*Geoffrey?*"

At once Geoffrey lowered his torch so as not to shine it in her eyes. "Julia? Is that you?"

"Yes!" she replied. She was suddenly breathless. Her heart rate doubled, she could feel it hammering inside her chest.

"Geoffrey?" She heard her own disbelief. And then something else. The sound of hope. Geoffrey was here. He would make it all alright!

"What on earth are you doing here?" they both said at exactly the same time. Then they both fell silent at the same time, too.

"What's going on?" Geoffrey recovered first. For Julia it was as if she had been teleported from one world to another, completely separate one. Worlds that were never meant to meet. She couldn't line up where one world began and the other ended.

"Are you okay?" he went on, and she could hear the concern in his voice. *"I thought I heard a scream?"*

Julia opened her mouth. She closed it again.

"No. I didn't hear anything."

"I was worried about you," Geoffrey said. *"Are you sure you're okay?"*

Julia couldn't answer. She wanted to tell him that no, she was anything but okay. She wanted him to wrap his arms around her and squeeze her tight and sort out this mess in the way that only Geoffrey could.

But she couldn't say any of that. And when he went on she could hear that where he had before sounded pleased to see her, that was slipping from his voice. With every word he sounded more uncertain, more wary.

"What's going on? What is this?"

"I..." Julia hunted in her brain for an excuse to explain this. Anything.

"Kevin said you were doing some kind of research for your next book?" Geoffrey went on. "I was worried..."

It sounded impossibly feeble, but Julia grasped onto it.

"Yes," she said. But found nothing to add.

"Well..? Well, are you okay?" Geoffrey said again, and again Julia wasn't able to answer. She just nodded. She felt like she was rapidly filling up with a sadness such as she had never experienced. She didn't yet know what it signified. But she would. She soon would.

"What's that you've got there?" Geoffrey asked with a laugh.

Julia looked down at the garden fork that was still in her hands. She rested the tines on the ground in front of her, as if she might be about to turn the soil. From her perspective, with the torchlight on the ground between them, a thick veneer of black was clearly visible on the handle and the steel head. She knew it must be blood, and tried to work out if Geoffrey would be able to recognise it as such.

"Are you doing some gardening? At this time of night?"

And then Julia felt a rush of love flow into her. Dear Geoffrey. Dear, sweet Geoffrey who was so filled with goodness he couldn't even imagine how evil the world really was.

Julia opened her mouth again, meaning to find something to explain herself. But no words came out. She wanted to throw the damn fork to the side of the path. She wanted Geoffrey to come forward and hold her.

"Oh, Geoffrey," she finally managed. He moved closer. She could smell him now. The familiar aftershave he used. He really was here.

"I've been so worried about you. I've left you messages..." he said. Julia yearned for his touch.

"Why are you dressed like that?"

Julia looked down at her overalls. She thought to pull the hairnet from her head but didn't. Instead she screwed her eyes tight shut.

"It's research," she said. Her fingers curled tighter on the handle of the fork. There was no way he would believe her. She looked up, trying to judge the distance between herself and her friend. Her only true friend.

"Well, you're taking it incredibly seriously." Suddenly he cast the torch around them. "I'm sure there was a scream. Is anyone hurt?"

Julia didn't answer at once, instead watching as the beam from his torch played on the buildings of the lighthouse complex and the rocks. She almost expected it to pick out Becky's dead body, twisted and smashed, but it was lying just around the curved wall of the lighthouse.

He knows, Julia thought.

"Are you staying here? I found your car, with a leaflet advertising this place. That's why I came. I felt you might need me."

Oh, I do. I do need you, Julia wanted to say. *I need you more than anything. I've always needed you. You're the only thing that can save me, and you always were. I just didn't realise.*

But nothing came out except a garbled noise.

"Julia? Are you staying here, or what?"

She pulled herself together. She had to say something.

"Yes. I have a room. I was just..." She looked down at the fork. "I was using this earlier. I remembered I'd left it out. I couldn't sleep thinking it might be stolen."

She couldn't see his face, but at the same time she could. She could imagine perfectly the frown of confusion he wore.

"So this *is* all about a book then?" He said, a few moments later.

She understood at once. He was giving her an opportunity. The chance to explain all this away. And she wanted to take it. She even opened her mouth to do so. But Julia knew Geoffrey. She knew him too well. It *wasn't* a question. It was a test. Geoffrey might be a devoted man, but he was never a stupid man. Julia shook her head.

"No," she said. "There's something else."

He sighed, and his voice was colder when he went on. "I didn't think so. You'd better tell me what is going on then."

Julia didn't answer. She understood now the source of the sadness that weighed her down. There *was* no explanation. There was nothing she could tell Geoffrey to explain this. There was only one answer. She had to finish what she had started.

She tried to visualise herself lifting the fork and swinging it. There was a clear target, she would simply aim at the light of the torch. She already knew how much damage it would do. But this time she had no energy. The power of the fork was gone. Now it felt almost too heavy to lift.

"Okay," she said instead. And then she felt an overwhelming urge to return to a happier place, a happier time, when she and Geoffrey had spent countless hours drinking tea in her little kitchen.

"Would you like a cup of tea?"

"What?"

"There's a kitchen. Let's have a drink. I'll explain everything. And then you can call the police."

SIXTY-THREE

SHE LED him back to the lodge, keeping him away from where Becky's body lay. As they approached the door the exterior light flicked on automatically, surprising Julia again. She was still carrying her fork, and realised it would look strange to take it inside, so she left it leaning against the outside wall of the lodge.

Inside the dining room was a mess of upturned tables and chairs. She had forgotten, too, how Becky had crashed into them during her flight from the building. Geoffrey looked around in alarm, but it served to distract him from seeing into Rob and Becky's bedroom, where the door was open. Julia noticed Rob's foot was visible through the doorway, but it was part covered by the bed sheets.

"Come through," Julia said, indicating the kitchen, and using her body to shield the doorway to the bedroom. Geoffrey gave her a curious look but did what she said. Julia followed him inside, and flicked the light on the wall.

Suddenly, she was aware of how she must look. She glanced down and saw that she was splattered with blood. Yet the dark blue colour of the overalls had absorbed and hidden it better than she feared outside.

"Well?" Geoffrey asked. "What's this about the police? What's going on?"

Julia didn't answer. In response she found the kettle, and smiled at him as she filled it. There was a tiny table and two chairs up against the wall. Julia waved a hand at it.

"Sit. I'll make some tea."

He hesitated, but she turned away, taking down two mugs from the shelf. When she looked again he had taken a chair.

"Well?" Geoffrey said again. "I do hope you've got a good excuse for all this, because I actually stole a boat to get here."

Julia turned and smiled again. "A boat?" she asked, happy for any conversation to distract her from reality. She looked at his face. His lined, lived-in face with the fuzz of that beard. Why had she never felt the scratch of that beard against her face? Why had he never tried to kiss her? Why had she never invited him to do so?

"Why did you steal a boat?"

"Well, the tide was in. So I left the Land Rover on the mainland side of the causeway and just helped myself. I've moored it on the little quay down there."

Julia made herself turn away and look for tea bags. But as she moved she felt something in the pocket of her overalls. And she remembered what it was. Her plastic shampoo container of homemade cyanide. As she pulled a container marked 'tea' towards her, a new idea struck her. Not the police.

There was another way out.

"I kept calling by the cottage and even drove up to London, but I couldn't find you..." Geoffrey was saying, but now Julia wasn't listening to him at all. There was a way out.

She felt for the lump in her pocket again. Then, taking care so that the movement wasn't too awkward she slipped the plastic container from her pocket and held it, shielded from his view by her body. She thought of how she had produced it, following the directions in Geoffrey's own novel. Oh, the irony of it.

She placed a teabag in one of the mugs. Then gently, she unscrewed the lid of the poison and stared at the two mugs for a long while. She considered how she might divide the deadly liquid equally between each of them. As Geoffrey continued his explanation, talking now about things Kevin had told him, she poured it out.

When the kettle boiled she filled both mugs with hot water, and dunked the teabag in each. She looked for a bin, and dropped it in. Then she crossed and opened the fridge, taking out a bottle of milk. She remembered as she did so how she had poisoned Becky and Rob's sandwiches. The pain the dog must have gone through. Would this be the same? She closed the fridge. She poured the milk, and very carefully she turned and presented Geoffrey with his tea.

For a second it was as if they were in the kitchen of her cottage. He smiled his thanks, and he took a sip at once. Geoffrey liked his tea hot.

"Oooh," he said. He took another sip.

Julia took her own drink and sat down slowly next to him. She also took as big a sip as she could manage.

"So," Geoffrey said. "I can see you're in some sort of a pickle here. But I'm sure it's nothing that can't be sorted out. One way or another." He took another sip of his tea. "Actually, I needed this. I've been waiting by your damn car for hours." But there was a shadow of uncertainty on his face now, as if he had detected an unusual flavour in what he was drinking. He had another sip, perhaps trying to identify it. Julia matched him. She gazed levelly at his face.

No one knows what it tastes like. No one has ever lived that long.

"So, are you going to tell me?" Geoffrey asked. But at the same time he put a hand to his collar, like he was suddenly feeling hot. Julia didn't answer. She just drank her tea and watched him.

Next he began to frown, his warm, brown eyes widened in confusion. He was still holding his tea, and now he smelt it, then looked across at Julia. Still she watched him.

"Julia?" Geoffrey said. Then he began to cough, but it wasn't a proper cough, it was his body beginning to go into shock from a lack of oxygen. The cyanide was preventing its absorption into his blood stream. It was as effective as if she had placed a plastic bag over his face and pulled it tight. He put his mug down now, so that he could put both hands at his neck, as if trying to prise away whatever was tightening its grip around him. He staggered to his feet, sending the chair flying out behind him. Julia took another sip of her tea.

It wasn't quite as instant as Geoffrey had promised. Debilitating, yes. He fell to the floor, his eyes rolling back up into his head and he began to jerk violently, like a fish pulled from the water and left to die in the air. But he didn't die. He was still moving when Julia finished her tea, washed up and put away her mug, then went to find Becky's laptop.

Ten minutes later, when she had packed it into her little backpack and she leaned down to feel his pockets for his car key, she could see his chest was still moving, though he was unconscious by then. She rolled the little plastic container of cyanide, and the handle and shaft of the garden fork around his fingers and palms, she wiped some of the bed linen from Rob and Becky's room, now soaked with Rob's blood, against Geoffrey's clothes, and then she placed her gloved hands in front of his mouth and nose.

Just seconds later, Geoffrey was dead.

SIXTY-FOUR

THE LAUNCH PARTY for Julia's second novel – the hugely anticipated sequel to *The Glass Tower*, about which nothing had been revealed yet, not even the name – took place in one of London's most expensive hotels. The venue had been suggested by Julia herself, and this time around there was no question of anybody overruling her.

She was fashionably late again, but this time it was by design. Her blacked-out Range Rover, driven by her usual chauffeur, pulled up outside the hotel's entrance a full hour after she had been asked to attend, but it was James McArthur who opened the door for her. He had been waiting outside the hotel, again as instructed. The rumour going around was that she had insisted upon renegotiating his percentage even before she sent him the manuscript this time. And he'd had no choice but to accept.

He trailed behind her as she swept inside, dressed in a beautiful Givenchy woollen cape that her personal shopper had selected just for the occasion. The poor girl had been sent back three times when Julia had deemed her choice not good enough. She wore it for less than thirty seconds, striding past a small flurry of camera flashes, before shrugging it off and letting it fall into the hands of the doorman.

Julia noticed Marion as soon as she entered the ballroom, looking as fretful as ever, but she cast her eyes away and instead swept them around the room, pursing her lips as she ticked off those who had attended. Publishing industry executives. Literature prize committee judges. Politicians. This time around there were no junior employees from her publisher. Everyone in the room had been hand-selected by Julia, and it was as important who wasn't there. Deborah Gooding had not received an invite.

And yet, for all the combined power and influence of the guests that night, none knew anything about the book they were there to celebrate. Only that at some point during the evening its title and cover would be revealed to them.

The source of Julia's new-found notoriety and influence stemmed directly from the horrific events of that night on Hunsey Island. It was a crime that sent shock waves echoing around the entire world.

The elderly man from room five, when he finally left the companionship of the Hunsey Tavern, discovered the brutal scene. He went running back the way he had come, and within hours the scene was lit up and alive with police and scene-of-crime officers. But even before the dawn had arrived to reveal the full horror of the events of that night – the thick red smears down the side of the lighthouse that no tarpaulins could hide from the media helicopters and their long-lens cameras – it was a story that told itself.

Geoffrey Saunders, a failed would-be writer, had developed a deadly obsession with the novelist Julia Ottley. So much so that, when a pair of young students that Ottley had previously met and supported with a generous bursary, had begun to work at the small B&B lodge at the very lighthouse where Ottley's brilliant debut novel had been set, it had sparked a terrible jealousy in the oddball Saunders. He had spied upon them and finally hidden in the couple's bedroom. Then he had murdered Robert Dee with a garden fork, driving it repeatedly into his chest in a frenzied attack. He had then given chase to Rebecca Lawson, eventually cornering her in the lantern room at the top of the former lighthouse. From there he had thrown her to her death on the rocks below. Saunders had then calmly made himself a cup of tea laced with cyanide and drunk it. The police suspected – and eventually confirmed – that he had distilled the deadly poison from the pips of apples, just as he had once described doing in his own, unsuccessful, novel.

There were discrepancies to the picture. Little points that didn't quite fit. Why, for example, had he left his car in a quarry car park on the mainland side of the island's tidal causeway? If, as some suggested, it was simply because the tide was in when he went to cross, then how *did* he cross? But these were minor points, and it was rare for any major crime to be perfectly reconstructed, when all the witnesses were dead. What mattered was the weight of evidence against Saunders. He was well-known to Ottley – they had both been members of a local Dorset creative group – though she soon revealed she had moved to London in an attempt to escape from his increasingly threatening attentions. Members of the group confirmed that he had a particular fondness – almost obsession for – Ottley. And Ottley's London neighbours also confirmed he had harassed them, claiming that the novelist was refusing to answer his calls and emails.

The forensic irregularities were compelling, too. Saunders' fingerprints had been found on both the murder weapon and the plastic vial carrying the poison – though there were few of his fingerprints in other areas of the scene. Perhaps an insightful lawyer building a case to defend Geoffrey might have picked up on that point. But there were no insightful lawyers looking to defend him. Saunders was dead, and the whole world had no doubt this was a good thing. He was the savage killer of a beautiful young couple in horrific circumstances.

But though the case was solved quickly, its sheer brutality, and its connection to a famous author and the setting of her celebrated novel, served to reignite interest in Julia's work. First she earned out the enormous advance she had received for her debut novel, and then sales continued to grow. *The Glass Tower* became a must-read book. The crimes that lay beyond its words added an element to the book that made its rather mundane story become prophetic. Then, when rumours began to swirl that Julia was working on a follow-up that in some way touched upon the killings, the interest reached new heights. The few details of its progress that were leaked became news around the world.

When those lucky enough to read early drafts did so, they were stunned by the crystal clear quality of the language, the sparkling prose, and the gripping inevitability of the plot.

Sure, some argued that it was a risk, a jump too far for a literary novelist to change genres to what was essentially a retelling of true crime. But not Julia's publishers, nor her agent, not when they saw how well *The Glass Tower* was still selling, and not when they saw the staggering levels of anticipation for the follow up.

Some argued it was poor taste to build a fictional novel around the real-life and horrible crimes of Geoffrey Saunders, but others saw it more as a touching tribute to the young lives of Robert Dee and Rebecca Lawson.

After she had circled the room once, allowing those she deemed worthy to offer congratulations, Julia snapped her fingers at Marion Brown. At once Brown went to inform her boss that Julia was ready for the grand unveiling. The managing director of the publisher climbed onto a small stage and asked for the attention of everyone there. He gave a short speech – pre-approved by Julia, and this time largely devoted to thanking her for gracing his company with the fruits of her gifts – and then he checked that everyone had their glasses filled. Only then did he unveil the title, and the beautiful new cover for Julia's second novel:

One Shattering Secret

READ KILLING KIND FREE

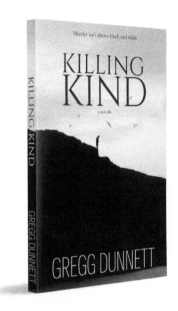

Get a free novella from Gregg Dunnett

A killer is leaving notes on London's park benches, confessing to their lifetime of crimes.

A detective has the chance to solve cases that have baffled her colleagues for decades.

But only if she can work out who he is, before he gets to her.

Because - in a story where not everything is what it seems - not even murder is black and white.

Killing Kind is a tense novella with a twist that will stay with you.

Read free by visiting this webpage:

greggdunnett.co.uk/free

THE THINGS YOU FIND IN ROCKPOOLS

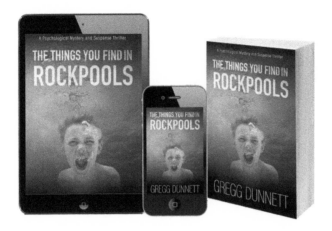

How do you catch a killer - when you're just a kid?

A teenage girl disappears from an island beach town. Two months later the police have no leads. So quirky local boy Billy Wheatley steps in to help.

At just eleven years old, he's a little young to play detective, but he's confident of success. After all, he's kind of a child prodigy - at least - he *thinks* he is. Either way, he's got one very good reason to want the police off his beach.

With an investigative style like nothing you've seen before, he follows the twists and turns of the case. But when the clues start pointing in just one direction, Billy knows he's in trouble.

Because the person who took the girl is someone close to him. Someone he thought he could trust. And when they find out what Billy is up to, they're going to have to make Billy disappear, just like that girl...

The Things you find in Rockpools is a gripping and twist-filled psychological-thriller set in a fictional island off the east coast of the United States. In 2018 it reached the top 50 in both the US and the UK Amazon charts in 2018, with over a thousand five star reviews across the two sites.

Available in print, on Amazon Kindle & KU and as an audiobook.

THE GIRL ON THE BURNING BOAT

Alice is the smart and beautiful daughter of a powerful businessman. She lives a charmed life - until her father is killed in a tragic accident.

Then she meets Jamie, a young man from a very different background, who has evidence that her father met a much darker end.

Together they embark upon a search for the truth, delving into the murky background of Alice's family fortune. What they discover leads Alice to question everything about her father - and herself. But it also turns them into targets.

Because whoever put Alice's father in his grave, meant his secrets to die with him. And now they're scrambling to bury them deep. Along with anyone who gets in their way.

Can Alice unearth the truth before it's too late? Or will her judgement be clouded by her increasingly strong attraction to Jamie?

With everyone around her lying, she must pick someone to trust. But get it wrong, and her next move will be her last.

Find out if Alice can avenge her father's death. Or if she will become his killer's next victim.

You can buy the book on Amazon, order from any good bookstore, or read free on Amazon's Kindle Unlimited.

Or listen to the story on Audiobook from Amazon, Audible or iBooks.

THE WAVE AT HANGING ROCK

Natalie, a young doctor, sees her perfect life shattered when her husband is lost at sea. Everyone believes it's a tragic accident. But a mysterious phone call prompts her to think otherwise. She sets out on a search for the truth.

Jesse, a schoolboy, is moved half way around the world when his father is blown up in a science experiment gone wrong.

Two seemingly unconnected tales. But how they come together will have you turning the pages late into the night. And the twist at the end will leave you reeling.

The Wave at Hanging Rock is Gregg's debut novel, released in 2016. With over a quarter of a million downloads it quickly became an Amazon bestseller and was shortlisted for the Chanticleer Award for Best Mystery or Suspense novel of the year.

You can buy the book on Amazon, order from any good bookstore, or read free on Amazon's Kindle Unlimited.

Or listen to the story on Audiobook from Amazon, Audible or iBooks.

THE DESERT RUN

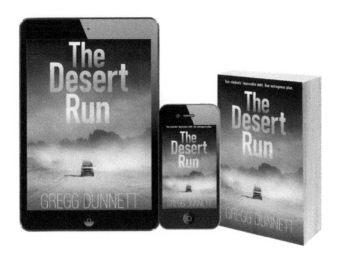

Two students' impossible debt. One outrageous plan.

Jake is just out of university and right out of cash. His former classmates are off on adventures or getting on with their lives, while he's stuck in a dead end job and can't get a break. Until his best friend comes up with a plan to reverse both their fortunes.

He's smart enough to know it's madness. But then - he's also smart enough to calculate the odds of getting caught. And just how much money they'll make if they don't. The harder Jake tries to dismiss the idea, the more the pieces fall into place.

Until one day he finds himself queuing at the border while armed customs officers search their van - packed with enough dope to put the boys away for twenty years.

Yet Jake hardly even cares. Because - by then - prison is only his second biggest problem…

You can buy the book on Amazon, order from any good bookstore, or read free on Amazon's Kindle Unlimited.

Or listen to the story on Audiobook from Amazon, Audible or iBooks.

THE HOLE IN CASEY'S GARDEN

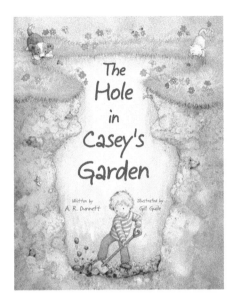

One night Casey has an *extraordinary* idea. When his parents are asleep he goes into the garden, peels back the lawn and begins to dig. . .

And what happens next will delight children and adults alike.

The Hole in Casey's Garden is the result of a collaboration between bestselling British thriller author Gregg Dunnett, and his two children Alba (6) and Rafa (4). The illustrations are painted by Gill Guile, who has written or illustrated over five hundred children's books.

Buy now in beautiful hardback edition (sorry, limited to readers in the US only)

Or in paperback and Kindle edition in most of the rest of the world.

ACKNOWLEDGMENTS

I'm very fortunate these days to have a host of people that help me in writing and producing books. These include the people around me, my family and friends who take an interest and give me valuable guidance on what might be a good idea, and what might be best left to stew a little longer (or forget altogether). For this one I'm particularly indebted to my sister in law Arancha. Without her enthusiasm this one might not have got beyond vague musings. My increasingly intrepid brother also played a big part in rescuing this story when it had taken a decidedly wrong turn. He intervened when the action had strayed five thousand miles from rural Dorset, and Hunsey Island was really born to keep him happy. He also gave up weeks of his time to give the manuscript its first proper edit, so a huge thank you for that. My mum and dad continue to give faithful and valuable feedback so thank you to both. I'm also extremely grateful to Elizabeth Ward for her professional editing.

I am also very lucky to now have a group of keen and generous readers around the world willing to give up their time and expertise in spotting typos, finding errant spaces (sorry there were so many of those) and point out the remaining holes in the plot. It's a pleasure and a honour to work with you all, and your help is very much appreciated. Thank you to all those named below, and if I've missed you out I'm very sorry. Finally my long suffering partner Maria, who gets to live out in real time the drama when I've regularly, literally, lost the plot. Thanks Maria.

Advance Readers for The Glass Tower - thank you one and all.

Alison Bryant

Anna Cole

Brian Moffett

Charlotte Swift

Claire Creaser

Cynthia Johnson

Donna Rose

Ellen Fox

Jeff Berg

Jeff Ziegler

Jenny Fisher

Jo Cruden

Sally Tovey

Sian Brewster

Jo Harper

Judi Brultz

Julie Steele

Karen Sawyer

Karen Wright

Lesley Downard

Linda Bowers

Linda Karadimitriadis

Linda Mayne

Lisa Tustin

Martin Houle

Michael W

Nancy Nairn

Pat Brooks

Patti Evans

Paul Toal

Penny Hammack

Peter Sprot

Philip Penrose
Rebecca Oberholtzer
Richard Mayes
Sharon Garde
Sian Brewster
Starla Muller
Stephen Wilson
Thom Gordon
Tina Adams
Tina Watkins
Tina Hamaker
& Jan, sorry I didn't get your surname!